Jam[illegible] Higgerson was born in the West Midlands in 1982 and [illegible]rently lives in Manchester. He has contributed to the anth[illegible]gies *Litmus: Short Stories From Modern Science* (201[illegible] [illegible]nd *Still* (2012). James was awarded second place in the 2[illegible] Luke Bitmead Bursary Award, and has previously co-r[illegible]e writing projects 'The Industry of Guilt' and 'Bad Ma[illegible]de'. Until 2011, James reviewed gigs and CDs for the [illegible] website Whisperin' and Hollerin'. He is currently fini[illegible] a PhD in European Urban Health at The University of M[illegible]ester.

You can visit James at www.jameshiggerson.com

The Almost Lizard

James Higgerson

Independent Book Publisher

Legend Press Ltd, 2 London Wall Buildings,
London EC2M 5UU
info@legend-paperbooks.co.uk
www.legendpress.co.uk

British Library Cataloguing in Publication Data available.

ISBN 978-1-9082482-8-2

Set in Times
Printed by CPI Group (UK) Ltd, Croydon, CR0 4YY

Cover design by Lupen Crook www.brokenarts.com

Independent Book Publisher

ACKNOWLEDGEMENTS

First and foremost I would like to thank Sam Mills for the enthusiasm and faith she has shown my writing over the years. I honestly believe I would not have got this far without you.

I would also like to thank my friends who have supported me, particularly Frances Turner, Rachael Pierce and Rosie Bradford for being willing readers of drafts, and for their comments and critiques. Cheers to Lupen Crook for the cover, Kate Bradbury for her proofreading eyes, and to Lucy Carroll for the author photos. Further thanks to all of those behind the Luke Bitmead Bursary Award, and especially to Elaine Hanson, for the much needed validation and that all important first step.

Finally, thanks of course to all at Legend Press for making this happen.

For Mum, Dad and Em

CONTENTS

Hello there.

My name is Danny Lizar. I'm not so strange once you scratch the surface. There are many normal things about me. I get annoyed when fat people sit next to me on a bus and take up more than half of the seat. The word 'pamphlet' makes me shudder when I hear it, and I don't know why. I think my taste in music is better than anyone else's that I have known in my lifetime. When people say I'm middle-class I assume that it's a bad thing. I don't understand the offside rule. I've been in love and I've thought I've been in love, all at the same time. I think I only found my true identity when I moved away from my hometown. I find all 'that's what she said' jokes funny, bar none. I have never had, and will never have, any interest in writing a blog. I stammer when girls that are out of my league talk to me, and I spit into the urinal before I take a leak. I kind of think I'm too old to have posters on my wall, but too young to have framed pictures. I'm twenty-one years old today, and once I've finished this little introduction I'm going to kill myself. Okay, so the last one is a little unusual.

Not many can spend their final few weeks on this earth writing their autobiography, a to-the-minute summary of all that has occurred within their lifespan. But most of us leave this world not of our own volition. Most of us make the decision to hang on in there as if life is some precious gift that we must savour every moment of. Not me. I've run my course and the day I finish writing my life story – today – is the day I have chosen to die.

If this has made it into print and been placed in the Painful Lives section of Waterstones, please pick me up and take me to the counter and inform someone – anyone – that there has been some terrible mistake. I hope in these pages you won't be seeking blame, or trying to work out who made it all go wrong for me. I blame myself on the whole; myself, circumstance, and maybe something genetic.

I just want you to know that by the time you read this, I will be dead. There isn't going to be a reprieve, or a shock twist that changes everything at the last second. I will not be spared. This isn't about whether or not I die. It's about how I've lived. I've written this primarily for the people who have known me, who have misunderstood me because I couldn't work out how to tell them the truth. Now I think I know how to do it, it's kind of too late. Hooray for irony. There are some things I want people to understand about me, but I don't mind if they still judge me after that. I just had to record my side of the story before I'm no longer able to tell it for myself.

See ya.

BEFORE ME

By no means do I wish for this to be seen as an attempt on my part to blame the parents. Before you get to me, though, I think you need to know a little about what happened before I was born. Over the years, and in particularly in recent months, I have asked around and discovered more about my family history than I could ever have believed possible. I have the sides of my mother and father and a whole stack of information from others involved. This recounting is to the best of my knowledge. That's all it can be.

An Unlikely Pair

1.

Jacqueline Anne Hepworth was born in Lancaster Royal Infirmary at 11.54pm on August 31st 1958, to her proud parents Cyril and Hilary. They had been trying for some time to conceive a child and were thrilled to have finally succeeded. Hilary's pregnancy had represented a triumph over failure and they had made plans to make their only-born the rightful centre of their world. They looked forward to spoiling the child over the years and growing themselves a fine, upstanding citizen. She was their little miracle, and they loved her instantly.

Using this logic, the surprise arrival of a second child only nine minutes later should have made them feel truly blessed. But when Hilary continued with her contractions the moment after her daughter had been born, it was with a sense of being cheated. There had been no talk of twins throughout the pregnancy, and neither Cyril nor Hilary was particularly happy with the surprise.

In his confusion, Cyril blamed Hilary. He couldn't help but think that she must have somehow known, and that he had been tricked into having two children, instead of the one that he had craved. He gave the impression outwardly that he was thrilled to have been gifted a second child so unexpectedly, but he also worried about the financial aspect of having twins, which made him an agitated and quite often angry new father.

Hilary resented Cyril's resentment. She would be in charge of the raising of the girls, and her workload had effectively been doubled with no notice. She didn't like being thought of as deceitful, and she could tell from the way Cyril regarded her suspiciously that this was precisely his interpretation.

Wordlessly they had made a distinction between the two children. As Jacqueline had been born first, she was the expected child. The second daughter, only by nine minutes, was the unplanned for spanner in the works.

They named their second-born Anne Hepworth. They had decided on only one boy's name and one girl's name, so they gave Anne her slightly older sister's middle name rather than think up a whole new one.

That was the first thing that Anne grew to resent about her childhood.

Jacqueline didn't detect any favouritism going on in her formative years, but of course that may be because she benefited from it. She remembers their being treated like twins. They were dressed the same, given similar presents on birthdays and at Christmas, and they went to the same school.

On the contrary, Anne felt that her parents had a different way of looking at her. There was a certain kindness that Anne saw in them, but it was only ever directed towards her sister. Anne recalls always feeling like she had done something wrong, but never having explained to her what.

It really is hard to tell whether adults can remember their early years with any accuracy. As with all personal history, it is replayed and twisted with rehearsal. If it were all about glances and tones, then it would be easy to say that Anne was taking the easy route by blaming her childhood for the way she turned out. But from the age of five, society conspired to place the Hepworth twins in chronological order.

Many people had commented on how unusual it was for a couple to have twins with different birthdays, and it was only lack of foresight on Cyril and Hilary's part that prevented them from seeing it as anything but a neat little quirk. Shortly after the girls turned four, their parents started to look at the local schools. They went to an open evening at nearby Appleby Road Primary School with both of their daughters.

Upon seeing nearly identical twins, one of the teachers from the school approached the family and enquired about them. "Twins, hey? They'll be the stars of any class they join. Fascinating isn't it? Who is the eldest?"

"Jacqueline here," Cyril answered, with what Anne perceived to be a disproportionate amount of pride. "By nine minutes. She was born on the last day of August, whilst this one here came along on the first day of September. Just."

"Oh, that is unfortunate," the teacher said to Anne. "You won't be joining us for another year."

It wasn't something that either Hilary or Cyril had considered. Anne couldn't blame them for that. She would instead blame them for not trying to do anything about it. They accepted that this was the way the system worked, and that it was a little bit unfortunate, but by no means disastrous.

Anne couldn't understand why her sister got to go and discover this whole new world whilst she had to stay behind at home. Each day Jacqueline came home from school with new stories about friends she was making and things that she was doing. Hilary was at home with Anne and therefore knew everything that she had been doing. There was no need to show any interest in her life. This was the beginning of a year long advantage that Anne felt her slightly older sister held over her.

Cyril would read through books with Jacqueline and test her on the things that she had learned, something which he purposely excluded Anne from. "You should wait until it's your turn to start. You don't want the other kids thinking you're cleverer than you are."

By the time it came for Anne to start school, she felt it had been done to death. "Oh yes, Jacqueline did that last year," became a sentence that Anne grew to despise. They knew who her teacher was because she had been Jacqueline's teacher the year before. They knew which books she would be reading and how educated she should expect to be by the end of the year. Hers seemed to be a life of no surprises.

It isn't uncommon for younger siblings to feel like they are doing nothing but following in the footsteps of their older brothers or sisters, but not many would have to carry this weight with the sense of injustice that Anne did. She had been nine minutes off having the same chances as her sister, but instead she was always one year behind. Explaining that life is sometimes unfair to a five year old is not easy, if at all possible.

Anyone who remembers Anne from when she started at Appleby Road Primary School will recall a surly young girl. School turned out to be a disappointment to her in almost every way. A pecking order amongst children soon develops, and even at such a young age, the stigma of which year you're in is a salient enough boundary. Jacqueline couldn't hang out with her slightly younger sister because she was in the year below, and thus Anne was something of a subordinate to her.

Being rejected by her slightly older sister upset Anne a lot, and she cried many times during her first weeks at primary school. All of the other children in the reception class were making new friends and playing games whilst Anne sat miserable. Her classmates gave her a wide berth; the sad looking girl didn't figure in their plans to have fun and play as much as possible.

Even though teachers knew that they were twins, they were prone to referring to Anne as Jacqueline Hepworth's younger sister. Anne couldn't help but feel inferior. When she reached the heady heights of the last year of infants, Jacqueline was off experiencing the first year of juniors. For her last year Anne was officially the oldest girl in the school, but this was tempered by the knowledge that her sister had moved on to an infinitesimal amount of new experiences at high school.

Anne arrived at Hill Crest Comprehensive School already a victim of the rumour-mill. Word had been spread that Jacqueline Hepworth had a slow twin sister, who had been held back in primary school until she had learned how to hold a pen properly. Jacqueline had heard this a few times and made attempts to deny the rumours, but as a rule, the school children were more inclined to believe the tittle-tattle. "We admire your loyalty," they said to her before walking away giggling and imitating someone struggling to hold a pen properly.

Even when the rumour faded and Anne tried to establish herself in her own right, people were always a little suspicious of the girl in the year below her twin sister.

There was no way for Jacqueline and Anne to be friends at high school, either. By the time Anne arrived at Hill Crest, her slightly older sister was already popular and fully involved. She had taken on a minor role in the school play in the first year, and as such was a recognisable face around the school.

Anne, then, was the identical face of the recognisable face around school. Along with the rumours of her apparent 'slowness,' she also had to put up with people saying hello to her when they really thought it was her sister. On the first couple of occasions this happened, her hopes had raised and she believed that people might just want to know her, but this was quickly dispelled. Soon, Anne moved around the school hoping that people didn't try and say hello, just to save her any further embarrassment.

Jacqueline's peers were a year older than Anne's, and feigned indifference when Jacqueline attempted brief introductions. There was nothing Jacqueline could do beyond that, for she was concerned that people may turn against her.

First boyfriend, first kiss, first cigarette, first school award;

there was nothing new to explore for the slightly younger sister. It didn't help that Jacqueline was scoring top grades in most of her subjects, so when Anne appeared in the same classes the next year, her less than brilliant progress could only result in disappointment. Anne's attitude was lethargic at best, but it's hard to say which came first. Some teachers felt that she was fazed by her slightly older sister's successes, whereas others said that she just wasn't as naturally brilliant. Whichever way they looked at it, they couldn't help but compare the sisters.

Jacqueline was showing great promise in drama as well as general academia. It happens with most siblings in one way or another, but with twins – and identical twins at that – people are more alarmed if the similarities aren't there. It was hard for most people to imagine that they could have different personalities, and so when people first met her, their first impression was that Anne was simply unpleasant compared to her slightly older sister.

By the time puberty kicked in, Anne felt the urge to rebel quite severely. Everyone, herself included, considered her to be a second-rate version of Jacqueline. It dawned on her that if she were to be anything but Jacqueline Hepworth's disappointing shadow, then she would have to make some fundamental differences appear between them.

Every decision Anne made from the age of thirteen was deliberately executed to make her the exact opposite of her slightly older sister.

2.

Resolved, Anne sought ways to be different to Jacqueline. She soon found that there were not very many ways for the academically challenged to achieve at school. She hadn't tried with her work at all, and by this stage teachers knew which ones to keep an eye on when it came to promising outcomes.

Besides, some of them did wonder whether there was any truth in the rumours about her being held back at primary school. An honest school report for Anne would have described her as 'mediocre at best', or more unkindly, 'she is clearly the stupid twin'. Academia aside, she knew that she could no more draw a decent picture than hold a tune together, so she decided instead to make her mark on the school netball team.

Around this time, Hilary had started to worry about their slightly younger daughter. It was clear to both her and Cyril that Jacqui (as she was almost exclusively known by this age) seemed to be doing better than Anne. It was Hilary's view that Anne was being deprived of the positive influence that Jacqui could have on her, and it was with that in mind she suggested that Jacqui try out for the netball team as well.

Anne was enraged by the intervention; she didn't want her sister gate crashing 'her thing'. The idea of spending any time with Jacqui repulsed her – her slightly older sister had stolen her thunder every step of the way. Anne was even more crushed when Jacqui was the only one of the two to make it onto the team.

Rejection ebbed away any sense of ambition in Anne. If it was the path of her slightly older sister to succeed, then she would just have to do the opposite.

Jacqui was a teenager who always seemed to have plans. Anne, on the other hand, spent every night in her room listening to loud and objectionable music. She would lie on her bed and stare at the ceiling, or sometimes she would read a book. She made great efforts to do very little, in order to establish herself as a completely different entity to her sister.

Jacqui would have been highly self-involved not to notice the hostility she faced from her twin sister on a daily basis, an aggression that she knew was beyond the usual realms of sibling rivalry. She tried to talk to Anne about her future, and she tried to motivate her towards doing something more than just lying around listlessly, but any form of interest from Jacqui was received as condescension and routinely resulted in an argument.

Whilst Jacqui kept her hair long, Anne cropped hers to what her father called a 'boyish length'. Jacqui appeared in the local paper with her successes in drama and netball, whilst Anne ensured that she did nothing remotely notable. Jacqui did well in her exams, so Anne worked extra hard to fail. That is, she didn't prepare at all, and was silently pleased to let the family down when it came to results day. Jacqui headed to college, and Anne saw her chance to break free and move into the world of work. The day she left school, she took a job in a bakery on the Morecambe sea-front, and in doing so entered a world where no-one asked her about her sister.

For Jacqui to succeed at college, she needed to keep her head down and work as hard as she could. Anne disentangled herself from education and instead associated herself with men who could offer her very little in life aside from a few joints and a place to crash when she didn't wish to go home. Jacqui had one steady boyfriend throughout college, so Anne drifted towards a series of ill-founded one night stands with the most undesirable looking types in the room. She went for the stoners, or the bikers or the bedroom revolutionaries – people who were disillusioned with the world but too apathetic to do anything about it. She became quite adept at spotting a no-hoper at ten paces, the people who were destined to reflect on their lives as a series of wasted opportunities. She liked the instant gratification and the delayed self-loathing that these encounters afforded her. It was the opposite of succeeding, and to Anne, that was success in itself.

This made it so much easier for Cyril and Hilary to love Jacqui more. In Jacqui they saw a studious, friendly and talented girl. In their other daughter they saw trouble, rebellion and unhappiness. It was obvious who was the more likeable of the two, and it would have been a challenge for even the most impartial parents not to have a preference. Being disliked was the opposite of being liked, so it stuck with Anne's theme.

Jacqui valued beauty sleep and occasional bouts of fun. Anne used her wages to become something of a party girl. She didn't tell her family where she was going and couldn't have been surprised when her constant detachment eventually resulted in their disinterest. Jacqui was showing real dramatic ambition, she had won lead roles in local theatre group productions, and was developing into a well rounded and valued member of the community. People would stop Hilary on the streets and tell her how proud she must be of her slightly older daughter. These people usually chose not to mention Anne lest they cause offence.

There was no relationship between the two sisters as their eighteenth birthdays approached. Jacqui had spent years trying to humour Anne through her rebellions, but eventually she had given up. It wasn't for Jacqui to consider how deeply unhappy Anne must have been to have actively carved out the non-future that she was heading towards. Jacqui just saw a bitter, unpleasant version of herself, and was by this point as keen to dissociate from Anne as Anne was from her. It felt to both of them that they had been pulling away from each other for most of their lives. I wasn't there, so it's hard to know who was more to blame.

3.

Jacqui was admitted to the Central School of Speech and Drama in London, a huge achievement for which she was celebrated by her family, her school and by the community in general. She left for London shortly after her eighteenth birthday.

Anne had expected this to be the beginning of something special in her life. For years she had wanted her sister out of the way, and was initially thrilled to be the only Hepworth twin left in Morecambe. She soon realised, however, that she had spent so much time trying to be the opposite of her sister that she hadn't considered what she could be. She had left school with barely a qualification to her name, and there was no progression to be had at the bakery at that time.

She had devoted her youth to not being her sister, and now on her own, she didn't have a clue who she was. Her reference point had upped and moved to London. Despite all of the pent up hatred and resentment, Anne felt like a part of her had been taken away – that twin bond shining through even the most turbulent of circumstances. Now she didn't have to be the second best twin, Anne struggled to think what it was that she could be.

Her parents shared her fears privately, or so they thought. Anne couldn't sleep one night and accidentally heard Cyril and Hilary talking about her. "The only hope is that she finds herself a good man," Hilary was saying.

"That's right, there is that. But she's going to have to learn to smile," Cyril agreed. "I think any man would think twice about approaching her when she glowers the way she does."

"I do worry about her. I can just see her ending up alone, and I'm not sure she'd make it by herself."

"Well a baker's wage is not enough to sustain a woman, that's for sure. She needs a strong husband."

Those words hurt Anne because she knew that they were true. With no other options presenting themselves, Anne Hepworth was happy to write off her life and turned her attentions on finding the man who could offer her a future.

The way Jacqui saw it, Anne got an extra year off from the world than she did. Jacqui had to trail-blaze through their childhood, and had to be good to set the standard. Jacqui took the brunt of Cyril and Hilary's expectations and knew that she couldn't fail. There was no opportunity for her to rebel, as people just wouldn't have tolerated it from her. She grew up in fear of generating the same disappointment that Anne did.

University was always going to happen for her, even if she hadn't wanted to go. Teachers had been making recommendations for her to pursue drama from when she was twelve, so she had studied drama at college, and then, in turn, at university.

She was forced into being the sensible one, and it was only when she had left Morecambe and her family that she was able to see this. She discovered a sudden rush of freedom upon arrival at university and she made the most of the opportunity to do just as she pleased. There was a fun side to Jacqui that she had kept largely to herself in favour of the pursuit of academic success. There was no need to hide this anymore. She loved the anonymity of living in the capital, and surely would have devastated her parents if they had learned of half of the things she did as a drama student.

It was at university that Jacqui really discovered drama and the exhilaration of method acting. The friends she made there were the types who would happily refer to themselves as bohemian, and wished for their lives to be as dramatic and exciting as they were in the pieces they performed. This meant plenty of experimentation and exploration of the self through various drug trips and bed-hopping adventures. Two months after arriving in London, Jacqui took part in her first orgy. She and her four housemates decided to push all of the boundaries of getting to know each other and fell into a prolonged session of group fumbling. They spent the following weeks relishing picking up the pieces and thinking about how they felt about themselves and each other.

Jacqui cannot remember how many people she slept with during her student days, something that she is only moderately ashamed of in the present day. She liked the consequences when they came, and was equally pleased when she got away with the things that she did. In her quest to become a better actress, she exposed herself to infatuation, over-indulgence, betrayal, poverty, submission, domination, infidelity, abuse and as many other set-pieces as she and her friends could muster. They treated feelings with little care and tended to do almost anything as long as it made them feel alive. She slept with older men and some of her tutors, and experimented with women. Countless times, there were at least three people involved. She helped people to cheat and she cheated on people in turn. She placed herself in situations where things were bound to happen. She wanted a huge range of human experiences to channel into her future as an actress.

Her life in London was also one of dinner parties and plays. All of them wanted to not just experience, but to network as well. They each desired to be a huge name and they strived to make their mark in their own way. Of course, as actors, they wanted to be infamous. She tried out many different things – vegetarianism, feminism and even a spot of fascism when she was auditioning for a rather gritty wartime play.

For Jacqui it was less about being perceived as something as it was about being free to do just what she wanted. She lost touch with her friends back home and tried to visit Morecambe as little as possible. She associated it with a sense of entrapment, as many children do when they first get let loose on the outside world. She would speak to her parents regularly, giving them a diluted version of her life, but not once did she make any attempts to contact Anne, and this worked both ways. Of all the things she had left behind, Jacqui was furthest away from her twin.

4.

Having decided that what she needed in life was a stable husband and a future, Anne set about it as if it were a military operation. She started to wear dresses and grew her hair. She wore make-up and smiled at customers at work. Her colleagues found her a more likeable person for it and started to invite her on work nights out. She made a few new friends and built up a rapport with the people that came into the bakery regularly. It didn't take long for her to put the hell-raising image behind her and to start giving off the impression of being more wifely.

She began to develop a relationship with her parents. Without the obvious competition there, she started conversations with her mother and even went for the occasional drink with Cyril. She became a suitable replacement for Jacqui, who came home less and less the more involved she became with life in London. As a fellow adult, she felt she could get on with her parents, even starting to view them as role models.

It was not uncommon for Anne to hear of former classmates getting engaged, or falling pregnant and moving in with their boyfriends. There was no transition between family life and settling down – you lived with your parents and then you moved in with the man you wanted to spend the rest of your life with. The few friends that Anne kept were getting serious with their boyfriends to different degrees, whilst she struggled to hold down a steady relationship.

Like much of Anne's life, it is hard to establish cause and effect. Did she struggle to keep a relationship going because she so wanted one, or was it that she was so desperate to succeed because she had so many failures? Either way, that was the situation. She would meet a man and usually scare him off within three weeks. She had many ways of doing this – declaring love after a first date, discussing baby names, or just getting drunk and trying to tell them all about her family. By actively deciding to get a man, it was condemning her to just the opposite.

Things never progressed much beyond a few dates and a couple of gropes. It always seemed to coincide with someone else's brilliant news, and left Anne despairing most of the time. She turned twenty genuinely believing that she would be on the shelf forever.

The more people settled down, the less they wanted to go

out, and Anne observed her social life ebb away to virtual nothingness. When she did get out, she placed even more of an emphasis on the arrival of her Mr Right. One glance from a gentleman at a bar and she was naming kids and decorating nurseries. By the time she realised that they had looked away, she was so far on in her head that she sometimes forgot to be disappointed. A chat up line would send her spinning, and she would accept it gratefully.

"Oh thank you. Thank you so much. That's really kind of you to say. Aren't you kind?" she would flutter upon being told that she was wearing nice shoes.

If things got as far as a date, she would ask relentless questions, as if she were conducting a survey. The questions hinted as to whether they wanted to marry, or have kids, or what their parents did for a living. She wanted to know about income and prospects, faithfulness and sexual history. It made her seem too intense to even have a one night stand with.

One or two stayed around for a few weeks. One, a young butcher named Martin, lasted two months. They had been together for six weeks when Anne mentioned sharing a flat. He had seemed a little bemused but had laughed the idea off. Anne started crying and then told him that she loved him. He panicked and told her that he loved her back, so she started circling flats in the paper and showing them to him. It took only two weeks of this, and an invite to a family wedding, to make Martin decide to join the Army.

People were always asking when she was going to settle down. When relationships broke up, she would often lie and say it was her decision. "No point in holding on forever," said Becky from work. She went on to have five children in five consecutive years with her new husband, who eventually cheated on her when she lost all interest in sex and ran off, leaving her with a large brood and struggling to make ends meet. At the time, though, she appeared settled and superior, and couldn't understand what Anne was waiting for.

These people put a lot of undue pressure on Anne, with their confidence that their way was the only way to live. Had Anne been down in London with her sister, she might have realised that she was still very young and could still have been almost anything she wanted to be. But tucked away in a seaside resort in the North West, her only prospect was to find a man, and it was a task that she was far from close to achieving.

The Hepworth twins only ever saw each other on the occasions when Jacqui returned from London. When she did reluctantly come home, she didn't receive a welcoming reception from her slightly younger sister.

Any reunions reminded Anne of how much she had hated life in the shadow of her twin. Jacqui was off experiencing the world, and each time she came home, she brought with her tales of the big city, and the weird and wonderful people she met. Each term brought a new achievement – a well received performance, an interesting course, or a chance encounter.

It became tradition, at Hilary's insistence, that the family be joined together for a meal on the first night of Jacqui's visits back home. The rest of the time she was free to come and go as she pleased but for one night each visit, they were expected to behave as a family. Jacqui would spend most of the meal sharing her news. It wasn't necessarily a conceited move because she was the one that had been away, and she was leading a much more interesting life than they were – even in the diluted form that she presented to them.

There would reach a point in each meal, however, when everyone would realise that they weren't paying Anne very much attention and Jacqui would ask her sister what she had been up to.

"So how's the bakery then?" a typical exchange would begin.

"It's alright," Anne would reply, knowing that nothing she could say would match meeting a famous actor on the underground, or being invited to the opening night of a West

End play by its director. Jacqui pressed on.

"Met any nice men?"

It always seemed that when Jacqui came home, Anne had been recently made single, making this innocent question more contentious than it should have been.

"We don't know what she keeps doing to them," Cyril joked at this juncture, and had received three frosty stares in return.

Anne's life was exhausted within two questions. There was nothing more to say. Everywhere she went, Jacqui was treated like a returning hero. People were dying to hear about her and her life, and she was happy to indulge them. They would comment to Anne about how well her sister looked, or how nice it must be to have her back, and she struggled to keep up her warm front. She would smile her way through it, always resolving even harder than before to find a man.

It was the Christmas of 1978 when Anne vowed to herself that she would be engaged by the time her sister graduated. That gave her seven months to find a man, make him fall in love with her and realise that he wanted to spend the rest of his life with her.

She went out each weekend – sometimes alone, but mainly with at least one friend – with an even more determined look in her eye, which made some men think she was crazy. If they seemed hesitant, she would approach them and wait for a line. If she didn't get one, she'd ask them if they were going to buy her a drink. This rarely worked.

Anne degraded herself on many occasions in the months that followed. Too many times she approached the same man twice on the same night, only to be told that he had turned her down only half an hour before. She spilled drinks down herself, fell over in front of men and laughed at inappropriate moments.

She got too excited when a man seemed interested in her. The anticipation was written all over her face and it was reasonable to assume that she might be a little deranged. Three months passed and Anne didn't even get to kiss one man. She was struggling to stay positive, and in the end her friends felt that they had to intervene. "Men can smell desperation," Becky informed her during a rare night out with Anne. She was usually looking after her kids, and was quite alarmed to see the way her friend was behaving. "I'm surprised they don't think you're a prostitute."

"It's not like that at all," Anne protested, but she could already see that it was.

"You'll never get a man looking like you'll die if you don't."

Anne laughed it off, but inside she was devastated; she didn't really know how not to scare a man.

When Anne tried to tone down her 'craziness,' she ended up seeming strange in a different way. Her parents were hearing rumours that their daughter was turning into a laughing stock, and Cyril was compelled to have a quiet word with her about the behaviour.

"I went out with this girl before I met your mother," he told her. "She was called Elizabeth. Lovely young girl, she was pretty and funny and had a lot of qualities. I looked forward to getting to know her. It only lasted a month, though. Her father told me that she had said I was thinking of proposing. Hell, that was the last thing on my mind, and I have to admit I scarpered. We're a fragile bunch, us men, and we're kind of like wild animals. We get scared if we think we're being trapped. Do you understand what I mean?"

Anne knew exactly what he meant, and was humiliated as a result. She was mindful of the advice of her father and her friend and decided that she had to tone it down.

Work nights out tended to be raucous affairs and one evening, only Becky and Anne were left standing by the time they got to their local club, Stars of Morecambe. Many people looked and sniggered as Anne walked in, her reputation three paces in front of her. They sat a table near the bar, looking uninterested whilst Becky scoured the room looking for the right man.

"You play it all wrong," she explained. "You walk in and go for the first thing you see. When he says no, you move to the second person. And then the third. You need to bide your time, make it look like you're here for more than a husband."

It took Becky an hour to give her friend the go ahead; a long hour in which Anne thought there would never be any takers. Unexpectedly, she spotted a man looking over rather intently and felt that this was a sure-fire winner. "Him, definitely," she hissed excitedly. "Make like you're going to the toilet and give him the chance to talk to you. You see which one?"

"I do," said Anne, who felt like she might wet herself with the anticipation. He was a good looking young man who was loitering with a couple of his friends not far from the ladies toilet. "I need to go anyway," she said and they both giggled.

She strode confidently across the room, looking as if she had no intention of stopping. "Excuse me, love," the man called out and Anne turned around. He wasn't as good looking as he had first appeared, but Anne was knocking twenty-one and didn't have the option to be choosy.

"Hi," she said. "Do I know you?"

"No, no, I've never seen you before."

Anne smiled. "But you're glad you have?" she asked as timidly as she could muster.

"I was hoping you might ask your friend to dance with me?" he said innocently, completely unprepared for Anne's face to crease up in the way it did. She burst into tears, took one look at Becky and fled towards the exit. In her haste to leave, and also due to her inebriated state, Anne clipped her heel on the top step leading to the exit and clattered down the remaining ones with tremendous force. She hit twelve solid steps on her descent, with the speed, force and relentlessness of a fleeing drunk woman. Those who saw the fall gasped with horror, and would be surprised later to discover that it hadn't been a fatal accident.

In fact, it did look much worse than it turned out to be. Anne was out cold for several minutes, and when she came round she was surprised to find staring back at her a man who would later introduce himself as Malcolm Lizar.

An Indecisive Man

1.

My father was born Malcolm Frederick Lizar on February 16th 1960. He was the second of three children brought into the world by Peter and Alice, who ran a bed and breakfast set back not so far from the seafront of Blackpool. They were devoted to their work, to the point where they ensured that they conceived in May, so that their children would be born during the off-season. After all, a heavily pregnant Alice could hardly be rushed off her feet. The children were born on consecutive Februarys from 1959 to 1961; Alfred first, followed by Malcolm, with Jennifer finally completing the family.

Peter and Alice hoped that their children would take over the family business in the long run, and they wanted them to become accustomed to B&B life as soon as possible. It was a rite of passage in the Lizar family when, at the age of seven, each child was introduced to the main guest house. Their parents kept them in their quarters until that time, as they were aware that some people did not find young children to their taste. Aged seven, they thought, the children were socialised enough through schooling to know how to talk to adults, and having the children around gave extra warmth to the place that encouraged people to return in the future.

The Lizar children talked to the guests quite freely and appeared to thrive on the conversations. Having new people arriving on a daily basis made life exciting for them, and they were much happier to stay at home than most children were growing up. No-one sees their upbringing as unusual until they reference it with the wider world.

The Lizar children did little to make themselves popular at school. Initially they had fitted in as any child does, but from the age of seven they each developed a complete disinterest in their peers and merely seemed to tolerate the schooling process. They seemed quite standoffish to the other children, who they only made superficial bonds with at best. In many ways they were just children who should have slipped under the radar. They withdrew from anything but modest interaction, but they weren't being snooty about it. It was plainly accepted at the time that there was something a little different about the Lizar children.

Their teachers were intrigued by them, mainly because it seemed that all three of them became exceptionally bright some time after the age of seven. This happened to Alfred first, and then to Malcolm a year later, with the same teacher. Peter and Alice would leave parents' evenings with swelled heads, having been filled with glowing platitudes about their gifted genes.

When Jennifer started showing the signs of the accelerated development experienced by her older brothers, the primary school head-teacher was compelled to speak to her parents. "We're amazed, it has to be said," he gushed. "There seems to be some sort magic about the number seven in your family. They all go from being a normal child to something of a prodigy. Do you give them a little something extra for breakfast?"

He had chuckled at this, but he did have to wonder whether there really was something that Peter and Alice were doing to their children to make them exceptional.

My grandparents thought they knew the answer. The only thing that changed in their children's lives when they turned seven was that they were exposed to the main guest house. They had a whole summer of mingling and chatting with guests before they returned to school, suddenly aware of foreign languages and enquiring about books that they wouldn't be expected to read until they got to high school. It was a change so rapid that it was impossible to ignore.

Over the summer Alfred, Malcolm and Jennifer conversed with tourists from all over the country and beyond. Young couples, war veterans, seaside performers and travelling businessmen were opening their minds to things that they just wouldn't have known otherwise. It gave them a whole new way of thinking that placed them far above their peers in such a short space of time.

They heard stories from the world at large, and they learned of interesting jobs and unusual lives, becoming all knowledgeable about various places in the country.

Although they respected the children's intelligence, their teachers struggled to hide their irritation when all three of them became chronically argumentative as part of this change. Through their varied social interactions with virtual strangers, the Lizar children learned all sorts of approaches to problems. It irked the teachers to be contradicted by a nine year old, but they remained in awe of how astute they all were.

The school was all for lauding the talents of the teacher that had overseen the birth of the children's rapid intellectual development, but they were deterred from this when they realised that it would seem unusual that only one family was benefitting, and chose to remain baffled by the phenomenon.

Peter and Alice were not pushy when it came to their children's academic progress. They would much rather have them talking to residents than hiding in their rooms doing extra study. They had a firm belief that the environment they were bringing their children up in was directly impacting their development in a positive way. They discussed their bright children on many occasions, as any proud parent would.

Before the children hit their teens, they were encouraged to take on roles in the guest house and this seemed to aid their development even further. They learned trades and the result was that they grew practical as well as intelligent.

Peter and Alice became used to the praise heaped on their children by most people they met. "What charming, intelligent children you have," guests would say repeatedly. "All three of them – what's your secret?"

There were only so many times people could ask them this question before they really started to wonder themselves.

2.

The Lizar Wider-Spectrum Theory of Development came about by little more than chance. Peter and Alice had started to run a Quiz Night at the B&B for their guests. They let their children join in, but they weren't allowed to compete for the weekly prize, which was usually a cuddly toy. No cheating was involved and there was no way for the children to know what the questions were going to be, but every week without fail they managed to return a top score. Often they would only have one or two wrong answers between them.

Peter and Alice knew that their children were special in this way, but it wasn't information that they could do anything with. They had spent their entire lives in Blackpool and only had a vague idea of what Psychology was. Without the appearance of Dr Tony Philpott, they probably would have done no more than wondered if they were onto something.

Dr Philpott was a Psychology lecturer from London. He was staying at the B&B whilst he completed some research on contentment in seaside resorts. He didn't favour the nightlife (or any part) of Blackpool and used his evenings to read. He did, however, grow to look forward to the Pleasant Rise Quiz Night during his five week stay. The first time he'd taken part merely out of boredom, but he had marked the

Lizar children's paper and been surprised at how well they had done, far exceeding his performance.

He swapped papers with them again the next week and was compelled to remark to them about how well they'd done. It was a difficult quiz, with Peter and Alice using particularly challenging books of questions, but the children had responded correctly on a whole variety of subjects.

"Who's the brain box?" he asked as he returned their sheet. The three children beamed back at him.

"We each do our bit," Alfred replied for them all.

"Quite remarkable," Dr Philpott said. During the next week he made discreet enquiries about the children to Peter and Alice and they started to wonder if the old man wasn't a little bit funny. Dad told me his parents thought about keeping the children out of the guest house until his stay was over. Then Dr Philpott revealed that he was a Psychologist, and they were more inclined to answer his questions.

Another stirring performance at the next Quiz Night told Tony that he was onto something. The children were as good at Greek Mythology as they were at Pop Music: real all-rounders. He stayed up late with Peter and Alice that night, asking them why they thought their children were so bright. They said they thought it was something to do with the guests they spoke to, but they couldn't really be sure. Dr Philpott asked repeatedly whether they had access to the questions, and was finally reassured. Over glasses of whisky and gin and tonic, a theory was born.

Dad was a little alarmed to suddenly be given a series of tests to do by one of the guests, but his parents told him that he had to. They didn't explain that he was taking part in the preliminary stages of a psychological study. All three Lizar children completed logic problems and general knowledge quizzes, alongside mathematics and map-reading. Dr Philpott was happy with the results, which showed that they were all performing well above average for their age.

Peter and Alice took Dr Philpott to their children's school to approach the head-teacher about furthering their research there. The plan was to prove that the Lizar children were brighter than those who had received the same education as them, which was exactly how they presented it to the school. Unsurprisingly, they were refused on the grounds that it sounded like a vanity study, and one that was designed to undermine the education system. Somehow word got out, and Malcolm and his siblings were teased for a good while about their arrogant parents. Malcolm didn't enjoy the attention, much preferring his anonymous role in school life, and informed his family that he would take no further part in the study. Alfred and Jennifer remained enthusiastic about the whole thing. My grandparents were not unkind people, and told Malcolm that he should instead focus on taking over the guest house when he was eighteen. They foresaw a glittering future for themselves that would leave them little time for the B&B. Malcolm became their back up plan, really.

They instead approached several other schools in the area, saying they were studying gender differences on a variety of tests. They were granted access and collected data on children that had had similar educations to the Lizar children. People were much more inclined to participate when they thought it was more than just the work of boastful parents. They also enlisted the children of other B&B owners, appealing to them by suggesting that they too may have remarkable children. Hundreds of children in the area completed tests that were sent to London for Dr Philpott's students to analyse. The study took about a year from start to finish.

The results suggested that children of B&B owners performed better on all sorts of tests compared to other children. The results hadn't been as significant as Dr Philpott had hoped for, but there was still a relationship. "This almost proves the theory without doubt," he informed the Lizars with glee. "We've done something very important here, people."

Malcolm was fifteen when the psychologist entered their lives. The research involved a lot of intensive work and all but Malcolm seemed to have little time for the B&B. They were often travelling to London to meet with Dr Philpott, or else entertaining him at the guest house. On other days they went into schools to oversee the tests, or around the B&B's getting more data from the children. Malcolm was far too young to be at the centre of operations, but he rose to the challenge admirably. He had lived this life for so long that he was efficient and knowledgeable in all that he did. Guests were often baffled to see how much the young man did whilst the rest of his family seemed to lounge about planning things. It was a little unsettling putting your holiday into the hands of a sixteen year old, but most guests left impressed with Malcolm, often forgetting his age completely.

He was developing normally. He had a healthy interest in women and managed a few flings with the guests around his age that stayed there. He quite liked the series of holiday romances he had whilst not being on holiday himself. It was convenient and he enjoyed the intense, but short-lived bonds that he had with these women. He appreciated the variety of friendships he made and strived not to have personal issues, thus relinquishing the need for any long term close buddies.

He lived his life by the B&B and this became apparent when his exam results came through. He later returned mediocre O-Level grades and only just earned admission into sixth form. He had severely underperformed, and the school were openly disappointed with him.

His parents didn't seem to mind, but they wanted to keep it quiet in case it had a negative impact upon the study. Malcolm didn't mind either. He didn't need qualifications for what he was doing – he had the experience. Not one to deviate from the path chosen for him, though, he went to sixth form to study business. The way things had progressed with his family dictated many choices for him, but Malcolm was certain that his future lay in running the family enterprise. His parents and siblings appeared confident, so he saw no reason to doubt them.

3.

Dr Philpott submitted an article to the *British Journal of Developmental Psychology* and organised a special evening lecture at his university to announce their findings to the world. He invited the Lizars to join him for the night. Against his better judgement, Malcolm was talked into joining them for the occasion.

"We're being gracious in allowing you to share our success, Malcolm," Jennifer told him. "You should at least be gracious enough to accept." Put in those terms, Malcolm found it hard to refuse.

He had just turned seventeen and it was the off-peak season again, so he was able to travel with the family without worrying about leaving the guest house. Having been in charge of most of the running of the business, he was quite possessive of it and saw it as his own. He was looking forward to getting college out of the way and had even started making plans for when the rest of his family shipped out to pursue their successful careers.

His rapport with the guests was second to none, and he was complimented daily on his efficiency. It seemed a common turn of phrase with the guests, "I'd happily give you a job working for me." To Malcolm it was just jovial banter, but once in a while he did day-dream about alternative futures. There was a part of him that wanted more than just stories, but he just didn't know where to start, which was enough to deter him. There was never anything that made him want to change his future.

The crowded lecture hall was a far cry from anything any of them had experienced before. It was packed with students, fellow lecturers and interested parties, keenly staring at the stage and chattering amongst themselves. Dr Philpott had been waiting a long time for such a triumph in his career and he had clearly been promoting the evening. After decades of poorly received papers, he finally had success in his sights and he wanted as many people to see it as possible. As he strolled onto the stage to a cautious applause, he looked extremely giddy, and, some would say, smug.

In comparison, the Lizar family walked on after him looking startled and lost. It was the night that they were to be introduced to psychological fraternity, and they just weren't sure how to behave.

Dr Philpott had opted not to include a speaking role for them, and thus all they were able to do once they arrived on stage was stare back out at the crowd. There were a couple of photographers near the front and several people taking notes, whilst many were sat with self-satisfied expressions, waiting to hear something undoubtedly ludicrous.

Up on that stage Malcolm started to wonder whether the B&B would become more popular as a result of this research. He didn't want to be running some sort of establishment full of patrons there solely because they were curious about the strange research that had emanated from its walls. Once his parents were too distracted by their research, he figured he could change the name and hopefully decimate the link. It would be easy enough, he hoped.

The moment Dr Philpott opened his mouth, it was plain to see that he was playing it like an inspirational professor from the movies. He pointed to each relevant Lizar when their name appeared in his story, and Malcolm realised that they were essentially a study aid – nothing more than live slide.

"Now, as you can imagine by the mere fact that I am here talking to you tonight, the results did indeed suggest something rather remarkable," he addressed the room. "Allow me to run you through our findings." At this point he rushed through the statistics and moved on to the implications.

"Beyond all reasonable doubt, it has been proven that children who grow up in guest houses are brighter and more equipped for educational success than children deprived of this environment. This takes us on a very exciting path of discovery when it comes to looking at nature versus nurture. It's proof that children need a wide range of support and they need variety in their lives. We need to look at other upbringings that may facilitate this development, and we need to look at bringing the Wider-Spectrum Theory into the classroom. I'm sure you'll agree, ladies and gentlemen, that we need to learn how to nurture our children with experience. This is only the first step."

He went on to explain that schools should bring in someone new each day to talk to classes about different things, just for ten minutes. This addition to the school day would broaden the minds of all children and in turn produce brighter citizens.

The lecture ended in rapturous applause, which Dr Philpott lapped up. The majority of the room were happily convinced by what they had been told. It all made sense and the statistics were there to 'prove' it – at least until someone else's statistics disproved it. Those seconds of applause and adulation were to be the highpoint in the career of Dr Tony Philpott.

The floor was opened for questions and answers. Most people wanted to talk to the Lizars, which unnerved Tony a little. Malcolm had headed off-stage, an act that was explained by Philpott as 'acute shyness'. Malcolm would be grateful in subsequent years that he wasn't in any of the photographs depicting the moment it all went wrong.

"Will the therapy work unless people really live the experience like your children did?"

"People can live it," Peter responded without hesitation. "By putting it in the classrooms on a daily basis, children would receive virtually the same amount of conversational stimulation as our children did."

"Do you plan to open up conversational development centres?"

"It's a possibility," Alice answered confidently. "We'd much rather see this research develop and move into classrooms. But if that isn't to be, then we would certainly consider running this as a private venture."

"Are you certain that there is no inherited intelligence at work in your family?"

"Quite certain," Alfred said. "Although my grandfather was a member of Mensa."

The hall fell silent, all eyes on Dr Philpott and his family of frauds. After several seconds of painful quietness, Tony could be heard hissing to Peter and Alice, "You never said."

"You never asked," Peter replied simply. It was true – Tony had assumed that they had got so far in their research by completely discounting inherited intelligence. It was basic common sense, and an assumption that cost Dr Tony Philpott his career.

4.

The Lizar family had their fair share of problems as a result of the fiasco, but some would say they got off lightly compared to Dr Philpott, who quit psychology and spent the final three years of his life as a full-time drunk, eventually dying alone in a park on Christmas Day. It was a fall from grace big enough to earn him a spot in the obituary sections, which was how Peter and Alice found out about his fate.

Alfred struggled to fit back in to family life. His parents had assured him that they didn't pass blame for what happened and it was just one of those things, but over time it became apparent that this was not exactly true.

He suddenly found Peter and Alice unwilling to talk to him. He had taken a year off after sixth form to work on the theory, and was now considering which university he should go to.

He tried to discuss this with both of his parents on various occasions, but they just told him that it was his decision. Alfred could tell that they resented the way he was looking to rebuild his life. He was given very few shifts working at the B&B and eventually took a summer job selling candy floss near the beach. He opted to go to Manchester University that September and didn't return for holidays.

Jennifer settled back into her work very quickly. She wanted to go to a top university that was far away from home. To be a seventeen year old girl with a reputation as a stuck up cow was difficult to live with, and she found making friends, or getting a boyfriend a real struggle. She was of an age where she would openly blame all of her family for what went wrong, as long as she wasn't to blame herself. Months passed before she started talking to everyone normally again, by which point she was just looking forward to the future beginning.

Peter and Alice sank into a deep depression in the wake of what some of the press were calling 'The Philpott Affair'. They felt a genuine grief as they pondered over what could have been. To suddenly only be guest house owners again left them empty. During this month they both listlessly contemplated ways of improving the research. They knew deep down it was gone; it just took them a while to accept it.

When they did emerge, however, they threw themselves back into their work in a big way. Almost immediately Malcolm was sidelined, with most of his duties being taken over again by his parents. "Looks like you won't need to take over so soon, after all," Peter said cheerfully on his first day back in charge.

That one sentence brought Malcolm's world crashing down around him. Over the past few years, his path had been made clear to him and he had blindly followed it, not really taking the time to consider what would happen if something went awry. Confidence had grown in the family as the research gained credence, and for at least a year they had all been completely sure that they wouldn't fail. Malcolm had believed this as well, and had accordingly not really tried very hard at sixth form.

Neither Peter nor Alice had paid much attention to Malcolm's education. He was working hard on his Business Studies A-level, but he had let the other two slip considerably. By the time Peter announced that Malcolm wouldn't be required, it was too late for him to do anything about it. As others matured, his intelligence was less remarkable, and at best he was a good student. But he hadn't been at best, and there was little chance of him getting a university place.

To be suddenly futureless terrified Malcolm. It wasn't the not knowing what he was going to do that scared him, but the prospect of having to make his own mind up.

After weeks of wonder and worry, Malcolm reached the only conclusion he was ever going to reach. He would let someone else decide. It was a familiar sentence from a guest that gave him the breakthrough he needed.

"I'd give you a job any time," a mechanic from Leicester complimented him on his last night of a week long family break in the resort.

"Thank you," Malcolm replied more enthusiastically than he had expected to. With that sentence came clarity. He vowed to himself at that moment that he would accept the next job offer he received, be it serious or otherwise.

Once he knew what he was working towards, Malcolm felt that he had a purpose all over again. He approached his new goal in the same way that he had taken over the B&B, by giving his life over to it. The thought of working there a moment longer than necessary filled him with a dread that he found hard to shift. Now that he knew that he needed to move on, it couldn't happen soon enough.

From that night on, Malcolm Lizar was very much on

display. He treated every customer as a potential opportunity. He was extra polite, extra courteous, and extremely interested in the lives of his guests, especially what they did for a living. He would ask them all sorts about their careers and make them feel that their lives were the most impressive thing in the world. He tied this in with exemplary service and waited for the comment to arise.

He impressed the guests, as ever, but after three months of waiting, Malcolm became despondent. After four months he began to despair. He couldn't understand what the problem was. After years of the words spilling out of guests' mouths so freely, it was an unfortunate time for it to dry up.

Peter and Alice had no idea what he could do, and they didn't like to raise the conversation in case the recriminations started. They knew they had let Malcolm down, they just preferred not to talk about it. The season went – Alfred had gone and Jennifer was making her university plans. Malcolm spent the off-season depressed and wondering if he was going to be stuck in the guest house forever. He tried to think of something that he wanted to do, but he got no further than thinking about thinking. He spent all of his time alone, listening to music and reading books – anything to keep his mind off his own decisions. He made no attempts to socialise with anyone, hoping that he wouldn't be around long enough to make firm friendships.

He dreaded the new season, as he feared he would be there for all of it. He didn't even have any education to distract him from what he was, a lowly waiter. Even his most modest of aspirations had been shattered and the more time went on, the more he believed he would just have to wait until his parents either died or retired so that he could revert back to the original plan.

When he had first resolved to take the next offer put to him, he had told himself that there would be a little discretion involved – that if it really seemed awful he could intervene in the decision making process. But when Martin and Ally Bickerstaff arrived in the first week of the season, Malcolm was prepared to say yes to anything.

5.

The Bickerstaffs were a couple of modest ambition. They ran a nightclub called Stars of Morecambe which satisfied them greatly. It was a popular venue, mainly because it was the only nightclub in the resort. They went to Blackpool once a year for a week to have a rest and that was all they wanted. Besides, the pair of them held a fear of the place being destroyed if they went further afield. They had seen too many news bulletins detailing seafront establishments being burned to the ground. They didn't mind going to the same resort each year, but they always made sure they went to a different guest house.

In 1979, they picked the Pleasant Rise Guest House at random. They spent little time there, but made sure they were around for meals. From the first evening they were enamoured with their waiter, who was a friendly and enthusiastic young man. Malcolm was still putting himself on the market, and although he felt terrible, he put up a façade for the guests. He hadn't entirely given up hope.

Over the course of the week they got to know Malcolm rather well. He had shown a lot of interest in the club, and said that of course he would head over there and have a look himself one day. Malcolm was doing the same with all of the guests, but Martin and Ally believed that they were the subject of some special treatment. He had certain feeder lines that he hoped would work, but to date had proved useless.

"Wow, I'd never considered a career in that," was one that he was fond of. He thought it was subtle enough to invite the comment.

Sometimes he preferred to flatter them a little more. "Oh that sounds so fulfilling. I would love a job as fulfilling as that." The Bickerstaffs didn't bite on either of these lines, or nearly all of the others that Malcolm used over the duration of their stay.

The one that worked for Martin and Ally came as a surprise to Malcolm. "Your staff must count themselves lucky to have bosses as great as you. It must be an honour to work for you."

Martin laughed politely at this and replied, "With charm like that, you'd be perfect in Stars." Ally chuckled at this as well.

"When do I start?" Malcolm asked without a trace of humour.

He left with Martin and Ally the following day as their new cloakroom attendant. They had offered him a room in their house until he found something more permanent. It was modest, and that was enough for Malcolm. Peter and Alice were shocked to see him leave so abruptly, and for such a lowly job, but they knew better than to try and stop him. They would always feel a certain level of guilt regarding their second son, and felt bound not to interfere. They couldn't help but show their disappointment, though. He received a cold hug from his mother and a manly handshake from his father and he had been on his way.

He quite liked disappointing his parents he had to admit, but the glory of moving on was soon tempered when he started the job. In all of the excitement of upping and leaving he hadn't really considered what he would be doing, which was to sit in a room, babysitting coats. It took him all of an hour to become incredibly bored by the work, and only another half an hour before he started to hanker after the B&B. He cursed himself for letting other people make his decisions for him, and vowed from that point not to let it happen again. His first own decision was to resign at the end of the night and find something else. Realising how dire his future could be, Malcolm was suddenly ready to take control of his life. His parents weren't around now, so he didn't need to react to them any more. He would just have to make choices like a normal adult.

"Excuse me love?" A drunk woman interrupted Malcolm's thoughts. He looked up and saw three ladies tottering on high heels, leering down at him sat at the table in front of two coat rails.

"Can I help?"

"Yeah, I just wanted to know if you're slow."

"I don't understand."

A wicked smile crept onto the woman's face as she looked back at her two friends and said, "'Cos you'd have to be thick to look after people's coats for a living." He flinched at the ensuing cackles.

To Malcolm it was a decision made. A drunken embodiment of everything he had been thinking. He didn't want to wait until the end of the night.

"Quite right, love," he smirked back. "And I'd be even thicker to imagine you won't die anything but bitter and lonely." He leapt up and marched from behind the table, leaving his post to go and search for Martin or Ally. If he couldn't find them, then he'd just leave and then rush back to their house and pack up his things.

The three gobsmacked drunk women watched him stride off, just as a fourth incredibly drunk woman clattered down the stairs at a pace and landed at his feet. As Anne lay unconscious, unaware of his existence, Malcolm looked down at her with curiosity, believing quite readily that he was in the process of falling in love at first sight.

An Unconventional Romance

1.

For both Malcolm and Anne, the auspicious circumstances in which they met seemed like fate. Malcolm was ordered by the Bickerstaffs to go in the ambulance with her to make sure that she was alright. She was conscious, but slightly delirious and they couldn't be certain whether it was concussion or drunkenness.

Malcolm was at Anne's side when she came to. They talked for hours whilst she waited for the all clear from the doctors, and discovered that they were just what the other needed. Malcolm was an available man who knew very few people. He had the potential to be dedicated. Anne needed a man who was unlikely to run away.

They found common ground when they talked about their families. Both believed that they were the least favoured child, and they joked about it in a way that they hadn't been able to do before. Malcolm was bred to be at ease with strangers and Anne was still drunk enough to be chatty.

Anne was discharged from hospital and Malcolm drove her home. They arranged to meet up the next evening and from there things moved very quickly. Malcolm skipped work several times to see Anne and was made simultaneously jobless and homeless. It was hard to pull sickies when you lived with your bosses. Martin and Ally expressed their bitter disappointment with him, and told him that he should return to Blackpool as he "clearly wasn't a Morecambe person".

Though they had only been seeing each other for a matter of days, Anne offered Malcolm a place in her bed. Both Cyril and Hilary felt that this was ill advised, but kept their silence as they were just pleased to see something positive happening in Anne's life.

Anne searched for work for her new live-in boyfriend and eventually found him a waiting-on job in a restaurant on the seafront. Malcolm had been hoping for something a little different to his past, but he was grateful to be pushed in any direction.

On the surface it appeared that everything had become serious very quickly, but at the same time the couple were not getting the chance to know each other. Anne got up for work at five in the morning, and Malcolm often only returned home from work at one or two, having stayed behind after work for a few drinks with his colleagues. He would have his days off during the week and Anne was free on weekends. There wasn't much time for them to be a couple.

Anne said she loved Malcolm because she wanted it to be so. She was in love with having a boyfriend at the very least. Malcolm told people that he loved her to justify the co-habitation. "It's just one of those things," he would lie to people.

They fell into a routine of unfamiliarity without giving it too much consideration. They didn't question anything because they were both essentially happy. Anne woke up with a man next to her and Malcolm got to feel settled. They didn't argue, and for their expectations this was enough.

Cyril and Hilary should have intervened when they noticed that Anne had taken down all of the photographs of her twin sister in the house, but again they felt that they didn't want to rock the boat.

Malcolm knew that Anne had an older sister, but he hadn't

been told that they were twins. It seemed that the older sister was a sore point in the family and he didn't wish to cause unpleasantness by bringing Jacqui into the conversation.

2.

During this time, Jacqui was completing her degree. She had wowed the examiners with a powerful one woman show depicting the life of an average wife as that of a black slave in the America of the past. She had a few weeks to kill before her graduation, so she decided that she would spend some time in Morecambe with the family. She needed to tell them that she was going to remain in London whilst she tried to carve out an acting career.

Her third year had been tumultuous to say the least. The games she played with her friends heightened as they reached the end of their university days and at times Jacqui had realised that things were getting out of control. She had fallen in love with her best friend, a fellow drama student called Neil. She had bonded with him whilst working on a university production the previous year. Summer had passed and she had managed to lure him away from his girlfriend. This had led to ill-feeling on campus and made the couple the centre of attention for a good week and a half.

Things got worse when Neil struck Jacqui for real during a performance. They'd had an argument just before show-time and Neil had seen red during a rather intense scene. He was thrown out of the university and exited Jacqui's life forever.

She responded to this trauma by having a lesbian fling with someone else on her course. This came to a sudden halt when Jacqui realised during an intimate moment that she was revolted by any vagina that wasn't her own. The spurned lover tried to get violent and Jacqui was compelled to tell the police. Some friends began to find her level of drama too much and actively dissociated from her. By the time her course was over, she was ready for a quiet few days back in her childhood home.

The Hepworth twins were reunited on a Friday night in June. Anne had asked her parents to keep Malcolm as a surprise for Jacqui. "I can't wait to see her face," she had said excitedly and they saw nothing particularly troubling in that.

It was a big thing for Anne. She was looking forward to Jacqui's homecoming meal for the first time ever, for at last she had some news to impart. Malcolm was working that night so he couldn't be there in person, but Anne was happy to make the announcement without him, once Jacqui had trawled through all of her news.

It would all have gone to plan had Jacqui not suddenly been overcome with emotion whilst trying to side-step the real story of her third year. She burst into tears and started to tell her family everything that had been happening to her in terrible detail. The meal as such came to a halt and they never did get round to hearing Anne's news. She was silently fuming that her sister had managed to steal her glory yet again. It didn't take much for all of those feelings of resentment to reignite.

The night came to an end when Jacqui was suitably comforted and their parents retired to bed to cope from the shock. They hadn't expected such a graphic account and were saddened to think that they could never think of their slightly older daughter in the same light again. Anne didn't wish to be left alone with Jacqui, and felt that the time wasn't right to tell her about her successes. Besides, she was doing a Saturday shift at the bakery and needed to get some sleep.

Jacqui sat in the dark, thinking over the past few years of her life and wondering what it had all been about. She got started on a bottle of her mother's gin and didn't notice how much she had drunk in the hours she sat there.

Whilst all of this was going on, Malcolm was drinking whisky with his colleagues after a busy night at the restaurant. They had done a great trade and felt the need to celebrate.

It was two in the morning when he thought to check his watch and decided to head home. Anne didn't say anything, but he did fear that he was testing her patience by coming home later and later as he got more involved in restaurant life. He staggered his way back to the Hepworths' house, the fresh air making him feel drunker than he had previously thought he was. That it took him three minutes to unlock the door was further proof, were it needed.

Jacqui didn't seem surprised when Malcolm fell into the hallway. She had been lost deep in thought, raking over all of the sordid things that she had done at university. Being sat in her childhood home made her feel guilty and rather dirty. She was coming to terms with feeling genuinely ashamed of herself, but she wasn't finding it easy.

A drunken Malcolm saw his girlfriend crying on the couch. Jacqui saw a kindly looking young man who was offering to comfort her. She didn't think to question it. Malcolm hugged her and asked her what the matter was. Jacqui fell into an embrace with him and just wept whilst he held her. The hug turned into a kiss, and Malcolm definitely felt something a little different about it. They say that things were different back then, and Mum had been through some interesting experiences, but I sometimes can't believe that she wasn't a little more concerned about this over-friendly stranger.

They had only met moments before, but within minutes Malcolm and Jacqui were in Jacqui's room undressing each other hurriedly.

Later, Malcolm and Jacqui fell asleep. Malcolm had been too drunk to realise that he was not in his usual room, and that he had slept with someone who looked just like his girlfriend, but was clearly not. Everything he did that night he attributed to how much he had to drink.

Jacqui didn't give anything a second thought until she woke up a few hours later with a strange man lying in bed next to her. She had been woken up by the sound of the toilet flushing in the bathroom. Anne was up for work and wondering to herself where Malcolm was. She didn't know whether to be worried or not. The last thing she wanted to do was scare him away by showing undue concern.

It only took Jacqui a moment to take in the situation and react in the way she should have done when she first met Malcolm. She emitted a piercing scream, which grabbed Anne's attention. The screams roused Malcolm, who instantly sought to comfort Jacqui. "Anne, what's wrong?" he asked her.

"Anne?" screeched Jacqui, just as Anne walked in.

The screams that woke Cyril and Hilary came from their slightly younger daughter.

3.

The hours that followed were rife with recriminations. There were many things that the Hepworth family had left unsaid to this point, but the misunderstanding (as Malcolm and Jacqui were keen to call it) opened the floodgates for everyone to say exactly what they were thinking.

Cyril and Hilary had to cope with a lot that day. They were unprepared for their daughters' love lives to be laid so bare, and they were beginning to believe that Jacqui had turned into some sort of deviant. They struggled to keep the peace, especially when the accusations turned their way.

Instantly, Anne adopted the role of victim. In her mind, she had been screwed over by her slightly older sister from birth, and this was just a hideous manifestation of her feelings. She felt it appropriate to scream at everyone, hurling abuse with the wild abandon that the blameless do.

It all spilled out in a series of tirades. After initially yelling at Malcolm and then at Jacqui, Anne had burst into tears and accepted her parents' comfort for a short while. She soon became angry with them and accused them of never loving her, and never putting up a fight for her. She brought up childhood incidents that the rest of the family had forgotten, or at least never considered to be significant. "Even now you're working out ways to make this not her fault," she snarled.

"Nonsense!" Cyril scoffed. "We love you both equally."

"Bollocks!" Anne shouted back. "You only wanted one child. All my life I've been the spare part of the family. Look at her life and look at mine. You tell me who's had the better one?"

It was a question that was doomed to be rhetorical, because Anne wouldn't accept anything that anyone tried to say. Jacqui knew there had been envy, how couldn't she? The ferocity, however, was a revelation. In her opinion they'd experienced similar childhoods, and had just developed different personalities. She simply perceived herself as the more motivated twin, and found it hard to grasp the sense of injustice that leaked out of her slightly younger sister with every new accusation.

Jacqui was too angry with Anne to be remotely sympathetic. She couldn't understand why Anne didn't tell her about Malcolm. She was also horribly hung-over and ill-prepared for such an onslaught.

"All of this, it's you. You brought it on yourself," she shouted when she'd finally had enough of being blamed for feelings that she had been oblivious to. "You have created this monster version of me, and you hid your boyfriend from me because of that. You know that if I'd been aware that he was your boyfriend, I would never have slept with him."

"Yet you'll sleep with a stranger who just walks into your house. You must have known he was mine!"

"If I'd known he was deluded enough to go out with you, I can assure you – "

Jacqui didn't finish her sentence. Anne slapped the remaining words from her mouth.

"Don't hit your sister!" Cyril said, with feigned paternal authority. These conversations were causing him great distress. He didn't like to think about his daughters in this way. He wasn't comfortable with such forthright sexual exchanges. "Now Anne, you have to admit that Jacqui didn't know."

And that was it. To Anne, Cyril had defended the favourite, and once again she felt vindicated in everything she said. The conversation went back into a circle, with Anne and her many insecurities at the very centre.

Malcolm remained quiet throughout most of the shouting. He wasn't sure how much the argument really involved him. He knew that he had been something of a catalyst, but the history being exchanged across the living room ran deeper than that. Once in a while, Anne would snap at him and he would bluster a little, but he was not the sort to defend himself.

Over these hours he developed an unspoken bond with Jacqui. They both felt like they had been deceived and they were joined in bearing the brunt of Anne's sizeable wrath. On a couple of occasions Malcolm was compelled to defend her, which made Anne either scream or cry. For most of the time, it was his role to remain silent.

It gave him a chance to think, and over the hours he assured himself that it had been an innocent mistake. He had been drunk and they did look basically identical. He was perturbed that Anne would keep her twin sister a secret from him, and he agreed with Jacqui when she placed the blame with Anne. He felt uncomfortable in and amongst this family feud, but it was also inappropriate to excuse himself.

The more she shouted, the more Anne appeared bitter and spiteful. If he'd had any true feelings for her, they dissipated completely over the course of the day. Within hours, she had gone from being his future to being a snivelling brat. He knew that he would be moving on.

Once in a while she would turn her attentions to him and ask how he could have not known. He generally stayed quiet, but eventually was compelled to break the deadlock. It was shortly before lunch time and they had been arguing it out for nearly seven hours. Malcolm had been ignored for a good half hour and Anne must have realised it.

"Do you have nothing to say for yourself?" she spat.

"Oh plenty," Malcolm said fiercely. "I'm sorry that I made a mistake. You've lied to me from the beginning and now I can see the real you and it's very fucking ugly. I can see why Jacqui here would be the favourite – she's far more endearing."

Cyril immediately asked Malcolm to leave, without really defending Anne in the process. Malcolm hadn't accumulated many things since his hasty move from Blackpool, so it only took him five minutes to pack.

He had been brought up to have manners and he interrupted the continuing battles of the Hepworth family to thank Cyril and Hilary for their hospitality. He smiled at Jacqui and didn't even look at Anne. By this point he loathed her.

It could be argued that this was the work of an actress, but Jacqui waited until Malcolm reached the front door before she shouted for him to wait. He stopped and turned around, just as he had been about to consider what on earth he was going to do next. "I'll come with you," she said brightly. "Or you'll come with me. Let's go to London."

And that's how my parents met. I'd love to have been there that day – it sounds like it was a lot of fun.

4.

Their first couple of weeks together were something of a dream for my mum and dad. Jacqui graduated with her new boyfriend proudly watching. Her family had opted to stay away, and although that hurt her a little, the joy of having Malcolm in her life was enough to compensate for this. Malcolm was welcomed by Jacqui's remaining friends and was able to enjoy the celebrations. He was caught up in the celebratory atmosphere of living with a group of graduating students. They were on the cusp of whatever it was that they wanted to do next, and now they were qualified they imagined that the world would promptly begin falling at their feet.

Malcolm saw no need to worry about his immediate future. He got caught up in sight-seeing and experiencing the city as much as he could. When presented with a world only known to him through television, he was much more interested in what he could do each day than considering what he should be doing long-term.

Mum felt the same. She was engrossed with her new love, not really thinking about her finances or what would happen next. She was aware that she would not just fall into acting work, but there didn't seem to be an immediate rush to jump before falling. The weeks of jubilation and celebrating the first days of the rest of their lives passed over and suddenly people were getting itchy feet. When the first of Jacqui's housemates announced their plans to move to Portsmouth, it suddenly struck the couple that the party had to end.

"I need a job, don't I?" Malcolm said sheepishly. It was the first time he and Jacqui had not been having fun since he arrived in London.

"I'd love to say no," replied Jacqui, "but I think we're nearly penniless. Have you thought about what you want to do?"

The answer was no, of course. He had ideas, but nothing even approaching a plan. Jacqui had direction; within days she had sought out an agent who had advised her to take on waitress work in the West End. He felt that she needed to be in the thick of the theatre sector, even if she weren't treading the boards. By working locally it made her available, and by being a waitress, she was upping the potential for chance encounters.

In his own job search, Malcolm assessed what he had to offer and realised that it just wasn't enough. Having not spoken to his family since he left Blackpool, he couldn't call on them for a reference. He hadn't formally resigned from the restaurant in Morecambe and he knew they would spare no good will for him. There were hundreds of careers out there for him, but not enough time to find the right one.

After a successful first night in her new job, Jacqui came home to find Malcolm staring absently around the living room, surrounded by the remnants of the classified section of the evening newspaper. Left alone, Malcolm found it very hard to work out what he wanted to do, and even harder to work out whether he was capable. Jacqui didn't wish to pressure him – she understood how confused he must be.

"I could ask my boss if there's any more work going," she suggested tentatively, having told Malcolm how much she had enjoyed her first night waitressing.

Every part of Malcolm wanted to run away from the catering industry, but the moment she suggested it, he knew that he had to comply.

"It'll buy you some time to work out what you really want to do," Jacqui added, but neither of them really believed it.

5.

The next years were spent getting by and falling in love. With their combined restaurant wages, Malcolm and Jacqui were able to rent a small flat near Shoreditch. Malcolm was an instant hit at the restaurant, proving adept at multiple orders and stacking plates in elaborate piles that drew admiration from customers and colleagues alike. Jacqui meanwhile pressured her agent into getting her work and after three months she was awarded a role playing a rape victim in a hard-hitting play that split the critics. Most of them agreed, however, that Jacqui's portrayal was the highlight of the show, and her agent saw that his client may have found her niche.

Those were years of incremental progressions. Within eighteen months Malcolm was head waiter of the restaurant, and Jacqui spent more weeks treading the boards than she did carrying plates. She was getting a name for herself depicting various victims of abuse, with more and more people finding her synonymous with tortured young women. She had never envisaged that this would be the direction her acting career would go, but she was shrewd enough to take the work until she was in a position to pick and choose.

They remained in the same flat whilst they started to earn more money. They made sure that they went out together at least twice a week; first and foremost they wanted to enjoy each other's company, and during the years of struggle they didn't lose sight of the reason they were doing it all.

They made contact with their respective families at Christmas and birthdays, but it was never suggested that they return home. It was a mutually unspoken agreement that they were all willing to keep. Both Malcolm and Jacqui felt sufficiently far removed from their childhoods to not want to explore them any further.

Jacqui's first lead role came almost three years after she had graduated. She was offered the only part in a one woman play called *Many Returns*. It was a gritty piece where a girl was preparing for her twenty-first birthday party and recounting the abuse from her father that had plagued her nearly from birth. The foul language and graphic speeches that littered the play caused quite a stir and as such brought interest from the press and paying public alike. The three week run sold out on word of mouth alone, and after strong first night reviews the run was extended for a further three months. It was not enough to make Jacqui famous on a large scale, but it did elevate her status in the circles that she was keen to move in.

By the time the play had finished, the plaudits were out in force for Jacqui as a leading lady and she was not short of offers. For the first time, she felt confident enough to abandon her increasingly casual hours at the restaurant. Shortly after she left, Malcolm was promoted to restaurant manager and things were looking bright for the pair. They were able to consider moving to a bigger flat in a more desirable neighbourhood with a view to eventually buying their own place.

It was the time of their lives that they wanted to freeze and remain in for eternity. Everybody has their halcyon days.

6.

The depression was not something Jacqui had anticipated.

It took Malcolm quite some time to notice the change in his girlfriend. He felt that he knew her well, and he had always counted his blessings with regards to how relentlessly happy they were in their early years. They spent a lot of the day time together before their work took them their separate ways, and they showed no signs of boring each other. The progressions they were making were enough to stop them worrying about the future, and they were able to enjoy times whilst they were good. Jacqui assumed that the ill-feeling that developed in her stomach with each suggestion was just a natural reaction to being on the cusp of getting what you always wanted.

Immediately after completing the run of *Many Returns*, Jacqui commenced work as the female lead in *In Sickness,* a play about a couple who both discover that they have cancer on the week before they are due to get married. The play was mainly constructed of monologues, where both of the leads try to work out whether it's worth having a future together if they're not going to have a future at all. Jacqui's character eventually reconciles herself with the idea of not growing old together, only to discover that her partner has committed suicide.

It crossed Jacqui's mind that she might become typecast, and she was a little perturbed that every character description pitched at her by Eric Biddulph, her agent, involved the word 'victim.'

"This is just the leg work," he informed her regularly. "In a few years you'll be able to pick the parts, and you'll look back and laugh at the 'victim era'." Eric tried to convince her of this every time she seemed reluctant to take on another tragic character. They were the same lines he had used on her when she was newly graduated, and with each passing year, the words seemed emptier and emptier.

But Jacqui didn't consider that it was the roles that were making her miserable. At first she just assumed that it was life that was numbing her a little bit.

It was during the fifth year of their relationship that Malcolm first detected a real change in his girlfriend, and he started to worry a little about his own future. It's a common human failing that we cannot see other people's problems from anyone's perspective but our own. Malcolm immediately concluded that he was responsible for any downturn in Jacqui's enthusiasm and good nature, which left him ill-equipped to help her.

For five years Jacqui had been playing victim after victim, sobbing her heart out on cue and trying to break the hearts of total strangers through agonised soliloquy. Over the years she spent countless hours in the minds of harrowed women; the ill-treated, battered and terminally ill. It was hardly surprising that after half a decade, her outlook on the world became more unabashedly grim.

She withdrew from friends and turned down many nights out. When Malcolm tried to make plans she'd say that she was too tired, and then when they didn't go out, she wondered if Malcolm didn't love her as much any more. With that in mind, she started to fear that she was losing him, and in response to this she withdrew from any intimacy.

During occasional bouts of wellbeing, she would pounce on her partner and suggest all sorts of wild things, but these nights would always be followed by days where she could barely look at him, let alone touch him. Each time Malcolm feared that he might have unwittingly violated her in the heat of the moment.

From this, she started to worry about her looks and her

weight. She began to feel unattractive in herself, and then grew concerned for her career. On stage, she was as stunning as ever. The performances seemed even more powerful to critics, and Eric had high hopes for where this was going. He didn't take time to notice the changes; as long as Jacqui was improving as an actress he didn't mind how withdrawn she seemed. That she was changing as a person seemed perfectly natural to him.

The prospect of a six month run playing a coma patient in *Life Scaffold* did nothing to improve Jacqui's outlook. She sobbed when she got the role, and her director just thought that she was an incredibly involved actress. Most people mistook Jacqui's depression for pretension, and that was part of the reason it took so long for anyone to show concern. The play was set around a woman lying in a coma. Various people come to her bedside to make confessionals about the way they treated her before the accident; her abusive father, her violent ex-boyfriend, her cold mother and the cruel bullies from her school, alongside a rapist guitar teacher and the current fiance who had cheated on her eight times. Throughout the play, Jacqui stood above the bed responding to the confessions with heart-felt monologues, detailing every ounce of pain and suffering that she had been through in her life. At the end of the play, the woman chooses to die rather than return to a world containing those people who had appeared at her bedside. The point is that she felt most alive during the coma, the safest place in a cruel world. The aim was for the audience to agree with her and want her to die as well, which in turn was meant to make them evaluate their own behaviour.

It was hardly a light play, and Jacqui appeared even more withdrawn than ever when she started rehearsals. She barely spoke and took to crying at nothing. Malcolm still believed it was all part of the acting process until opening night. He had been there for the opening night of all of her plays; it was one of his favourite things to do. Some of the lines Jacqui spoke that night he recognised; she had used them in arguments with him. It devastated him instantly.

He spent the night following the play sitting awake in the living room of their flat, wondering how he had managed to turn into the abusive monster from Jacqui's plays. Overnight he considered everything; he planned to leave her before she woke up so that she could continue with her life. He wanted to free her from the abuse that he couldn't quite grasp, but it was a decision that wouldn't sit well with him. After all, it was a decision he had to make himself.

It was only a lack of conviction on his part that left Malcolm still sat on the sofa when Jacqui emerged from bed the next morning. She was alarmed to see him still sat in the same position, and in the same clothes, as she had left him the night before. She leaned against the door of the living room, not knowing what to say, instantly fearing the worst. The pair remained where they were for nearly half an hour, both of them on the cusp of doing something, but neither of them knowing what it was they were meant to do. During the prolonged silence, for the first time in months Jacqui thought outside of her head. She tried to imagine how things were for Malcolm. Looking at things from that angle suddenly filled her with fear.

"Don't leave me," she blurted out suddenly and slid down the doorframe, landing abruptly on the carpet and bursting into tears.

7.

"No more tragic parts," Malcolm demanded.

"This is not shrewd thinking," Eric Biddulph countered. "To turn down these roles would be career suicide."

"Carry on the way she's going and we'll have a real suicide on our hands. Can't you see she's changed?"

"Actresses do change. The good ones do, anyway."

"But they're not meant to lose the will to live, are they?"

"She's signed up to *Life Scaffold* for six months. To pull out now would just send out the wrong signals. She may never work in theatre again."

"Then so be it." Malcolm wasn't used to being so assertive.

"It'll cost money," Eric warned.

"That shouldn't matter. You do alright out of Jacqui's talent, don't you?" He spoke in a manner that challenged Eric to defy him. "There'll be other plays, and if she's as talented as you keep saying she is… "

"And she is," interjected Eric.

"… then she'll have no issue finding work that isn't detrimental to her health."

Malcolm thought that Jacqui would be angry when he told her that he managed to lose her an agent, but she responded only with gratitude.

"You're amazing," she said to him with the first sign of genuine affection that she had shown him in months. "I didn't know what the problem was until a few hours ago and you've sorted it all out for me."

She and Malcolm sat on their settee holding each other with an intimacy reminiscent of their first few weeks together. It was reassuring to realise that there was nothing wrong with them.

Jacqui broke their embrace and Malcolm detected a look of reticence cross her face. "I think I might have wasted your time today," she said, looking mildly ashamed.

"I don't understand," Malcolm replied, immediately sensing further troubles.

"Well, it doesn't look like I would have been able to keep up the part anyway," she said. "I'm pregnant."

If such intimate discussion were acceptable, Malcolm would have joked with people about his potency. Jacqui had conceived her child during the one time in three months that she and

Malcolm had slept together. It had been on a night when she had felt especially alone and she had needed comfort. Malcolm had mistaken this for arousal and Jacqui had been too deflated to put him right on the matter. I was conceived out of misunderstanding and politeness.

He was thrilled, and because of this so was Jacqui. She hadn't planned for the child, but it was the perfect start to the next phase of her life. The pregnancy was enough to make her realise that she no longer wanted to be an actress, even if the roles were happier. Malcolm was earning enough for them to live a modest but happy life. He could certainly support her until the child was a little older and she could get to work on whatever career she wanted to go into. He assumed that they would stay in the same flat for the time being. He was keen to marry her as soon as possible. He didn't ask her immediately, but to himself he planned a small wedding with a few close friends and probably no family.

But from the moment she discovered that she was pregnant, a homing instinct manifested itself in Jacqui and she was overcome with the urge to return home and build some bridges with her family. She'd had plenty of fun in the capital, but she remembered a much calmer and happier time when she was growing up.

The prospect of starting a family of her own made Jacqui realise that she still needed hers after all. By the time she told Malcolm, it sounded like a decision made; and Malcolm was hardly one to challenge that.

No Grandparents Involved

1.

The couple found it surprisingly easy to tie up their loose ends in London. With Jacqui pulling out of the play, all it took was a month's notice both on Malcolm's job and their flat and they were pretty much ready to leave. They had decided to rent a house in Lancaster, so that Jacqui's family were nearby but not too close.

They informed both sets of parents by letter that they were returning to the North West along with the news that they were with child. If anything can bandage family wounds, it's the prospect of a new generation, and unsurprisingly the prospective grandparents were all keen to meet up. Peter and Alice insisted that they come and stay at the B&B and Malcolm felt it would be churlish to refuse. Enough time had passed, and enough had happened for him not to resent the way things had turned out for him growing up.

Jacqui was four and a half months pregnant when she met Malcolm's parents for the first time, and there was plenty for her to be nervous about. She had heard only negative things from Malcolm about his childhood, and she abhorred the part where his future was snatched from him. She was also worried that they might see her as the woman who took their son away from them for five years. There could easily be resentment on both sides.

Malcolm too was approaching the move back up north with a sense of trepidation. The last time he had seen Cyril and Hilary, they had hardly been making arrangements to keep in touch.

But the main concern that they shared was how Anne would react to them re-entering her life. They knew nothing of what had happened to Jacqui's sister from the moment they had walked out all those years ago. She was never mentioned in the few letters Jacqui had exchanged with her mother, which they both sensed to be ominous.

2.

Malcolm was shocked to see how much his parents had aged in five and a half years. From being middle-aged, they were suddenly so much older. Both had lost hair and their demeanours suggested two people heading towards their dotage. He hugged them both warmly and introduced them to Jacqui, who felt instantly at ease with them.

Malcolm was also surprised to find his brother and sister both staying at the guest house. He assumed that they would have moved on to bigger and better things after university, but it transpired that they had dropped out and were now taking over the bulk of running the Pleasant Rise Guest House. Malcolm couldn't say that he wasn't surprised; he was quite gobsmacked in fact. But he wasn't envious in the slightest. All he had to do was look at his pregnant girlfriend and he knew he was doing better than he ever could have hoped for.

The family gathered for a meal on the night of Malcolm and Jacqui's arrival. They all tried to cram nearly six years worth of news into one evening. Malcolm didn't tell them how he met Jacqui, and neither did he dwell on her depression.

Malcolm had changed in his time away. He had experienced a lot and seen a different world to his family, who he could tell had remained close and insular. Neither Alfred nor Jennifer were in relationships. Alfred had returned to Blackpool after dropping out of university and just worked in other guest houses. He never really escaped the life, and was talked into coming back by Alice when she said that she was keen to retire. Jennifer had lasted two terms before returning home for the beginning of the summer season, when she had promised her parents that she would never leave home again.

It made Malcolm uneasy to realise by the end of the meal that he held nothing but contempt for his family. He couldn't believe how much they lived outside of the real world and any affinity he had with them was gone. Being back in the B&B reminded him of the future he'd nearly had. Alfred and Jennifer still spoke with the same childish rivalry they had when they weren't grown adults. He could see them all dying in the guest house, living out their days serving tourists until they felt that their purpose was served, and that made him feel both sympathetic and relieved.

"We have to go," he told Jacqui in bed that evening. "I don't want to be here. They'll want us to stay – I can feel how oppressive it is already."

Jacqui, understanding exactly how he felt, put up no quarrel with this, and they agreed to go house hunting in Lancaster the next day. They were out of the B&B by the end of the week, with Malcolm vowing to keep his visits down to an absolute minimum. He only realised how little he had missed that life by revisiting it, and from that day on Malcolm struggled to remember any of his childhood fondly.

3.

Over a Sunday lunch in the restaurant that he had walked out on when he had fled Morecambe with Jacqui, Malcolm silently hoped that all future contact with Cyril and Hilary Hepworth would be as cordial as this. They had moved into their new house the day before, and had decided not to put off the reunion any longer. It was as if family were Jacqui's unique pregnancy craving, and it had reached the point where her need to see her parents outweighed the apprehension that the prospect of such a reunion held.

The catching up was more cagey than it had been with the Lizars, with everyone trying to avoid the more touchy subjects. They talked little about life in London and the events that occurred in the years that had passed between meetings, and they were well into their pudding when Jacqui finally raised the contentious subject.

"How's Anne?" she asked, instead of replying to a question about prams from her mother. The tension at the table instantly stepped up several notches.

Hilary placed her spoon in the bowl next to her half eaten apple pie with cream, and the look she gave Jacqui told her that she had ruined dessert. Hilary mulled over her response for a second whilst she chewed a bit of pie. It was an uncomfortable moment.

"She's doing very well," she replied. "She has her own flat now, and she's been made assistant manager at the bakery."

"Turned into a lovely young woman," Cyril added. Malcolm and Jacqui took this to mean that Anne was still single, and no further remarks were made on the matter. It didn't spoil the rest of the meal, which was played out with over-politeness and assurances that they would see each other again soon.

Jacqui was pleased that she had done it, and realised that she had missed her family more than Malcolm had. She knew there was history to work through, but as a first step it had gone well and everybody would be leaving on good terms.

"It's really good to see you both," she expressed as they were leaving, and the emotion of the moment finally got to her. "I really feel like I need my family around me now, in the best possible way."

Cyril touched her hand gently and smiled. Hilary wiped away a dry tear and Malcolm did his best not to spoil the moment by doing anything.

"Perhaps we could meet up again next Sunday?" Malcolm suggested, hoping that he wasn't pushing it.

"I think that would be nice," Hilary said, unexpectedly displaying her first real warmth towards him.

Malcolm considered, ever so briefly, suggesting that Anne come along as well, but he managed to stop himself well before he was close to saying it.

"Excuse me a moment, I think I left my spectacles at the table," Cyril said and moved away from them. As it turned out, these were to be his last words. On his way through the restaurant, Cyril found he had to sit down suddenly, and suffered a massive stroke that didn't do him the justice of killing him instantly. After six hours in hospital with his wife and slightly older daughter at his bedside, Cyril Hepworth passed away (aged fifty-six) without ever regaining consciousness.

It wasn't quite the perfect end to the perfect reunion.

4.

The boxes in Malcolm and Jacqui's new house remained unpacked for quite some time after they moved in. Sorting out their living quarters was very much an afterthought in and amongst the shock, grief and funeral arrangements. Hilary instantly came to rely on Jacqui to help her through the weeks after her husband died. Because they had both been there at the end, Hilary felt enough of a bond with her to want them to go through it together. Malcolm and Jacqui stayed over with Hilary every night between the death and the funeral.

Anne appeared once or twice, but she didn't seem too upset over her father's passing. Jacqui tried to give her time on her own with Hilary, but Hilary would then keep calling out for her to make sure that she was close by.

Whilst Jacqui and Malcolm had been in London, Hilary and Cyril had struggled to keep Anne on the straight and narrow. The rage she felt over losing her boyfriend to her sister sent her back to her old ways and she went through a spell of sleeping around and drug taking. One night, Cyril had come downstairs for a glass of water to find Anne indulging in a threesome in their living room. That was to be Anne's last night in the house, and she hadn't really spoken to her parents since. They would see each other in town once in a while and exchange news, but as such they led separate lives, and that was why Hilary hadn't thought to phone Anne the moment Cyril had the stroke.

Anne didn't greet Jacqui or Malcolm and only acknowledged them when they were discussing funeral arrangements or people who had been offering their sympathies. They all took the first car to the crematorium on the way to funeral, but nobody said a word. To anyone who didn't know them, they would have thought that it was quiet contemplation as opposed to awkwardness that kept them silent.

The service passed by without incident, although Malcolm did notice that Anne's lips tightened when Jacqui stood up to say a few words about her father.

The wake was held back at Hilary's house where over the course of the afternoon Malcolm overheard Anne complaining about the way her family had treated her to anyone who would listen. Although she now dressed in pastel colours and tried to make herself look as wifely and mature as possible, Malcolm detected the old bitterness straight away. The more she drank, the more details she tried to offer unwilling mourners about the things that had happened to her in the past. On at least three occasions, Malcolm heard her saying, "Of course, my father didn't love me the same way he did Jacqueline."

He could only hope that she would stay out of the way once the mourning was over and life had to return to a new normality. With Jacqui so heavily pregnant, Malcolm was keen to protect her from the wrath of her angry slightly younger sister, and he'd planned to talk to her about it after all of the guests had left.

Malcolm was clearing away some glasses from the dining room when he noticed an unexpected face by the door. His sister Jennifer silently stood there sporting puffy red eyes. Malcolm looked at her quizzically and she immediately burst into tears.

"Jen, what's up?" he asked, putting down the glasses he was carrying and rushing to comfort her. He had learned how to be affectionate over his years away, and was surprised when Jennifer tensed up with the contact. He'd forgotten how things used to be for him. She retracted from him and stopped the tears immediately, as if to prevent any further contact from her brother.

With a straight, emotionless face she said, "It's Mum. She's dead."

5.

Malcolm left Cyril's wake to go and mourn with his family. On the drive back to Blackpool, Jennifer explained what had happened. Alice had been out shopping in town, buying baby clothes for her future grandchild. She had been looking in a bag to admire the booties she had bought and had stepped out onto the road without looking. The driver that came hurtling around the corner at that moment had no chance, and in turn neither did Alice. She was killed instantly and died with a pair of knitted baby booties in her hand. It was these little details (recounted by the strangers who shared her last moments) that hurt Malcolm the most.

Most of the guests had found other accommodation whilst the rest were to vacate the following morning. Malcolm found his father sat in the darkened bar of the B&B with a bottle of whisky and a never quite empty glass in front of him. They sat up talking for a lot of the night. Alfred and Jennifer kept out of the way, preferring to deal with the business as opposed to the grief.

It was a surreal situation for both Jacqui and Malcolm, leaping from one tragedy to the next. The moment he discovered that his mother was dead, Malcolm had almost completely forgotten about Cyril. Jacqui stayed with Hilary for a couple of days before joining Malcolm in Blackpool. Anne had promised to check in on their mother in the evening, but it was certain that she wouldn't. Anne had only taken one day off work after Cyril's death and that was for the funeral, so it was unlikely that she would be even a little concerned with how Hilary was coping. As it turned out, these cynics were absolutely right.

"I feel like I'm in the same play I was in last week, just with a different cast," Malcolm said to Jacqui when they went for a walk. "Do you know what I mean?"

"I do," Jacqui replied with a grim smile. She had been thinking a similar thing.

"Everyone's saying the same things as if these simple clichés are enough to validate how we feel. People keep trying to tell me how she lived a good life, just like they were saying about your dad last week. It's all so fake."

"No, I think it's just people don't know how to act, so they just do what they can. We all yawn the same way, so why not grieve in the same way?"

"Sorry," Malcolm said. "Now's not the time. It sounds ridiculous, but I think it's made my mother's death seem less special."

"It's just a lot to take in," Jacqui assured him. "I don't think this happens to many people."

Malcolm and Jacqui headed back to Lancaster after the funeral and started to sort out their house. Everything felt a little empty now that the main grieving was over, and although it seemed inappropriate, it was time for practical thinking.

Malcolm needed a job and they had a baby to prepare for, which meant that although they were still very much suffering from their losses, it was time to move on as much as they could. This was made harder by late night calls from the parents left behind, and Malcolm once joked that perhaps they should set them up with each other. Humour aside, everyone was struggling with the sudden changes in their families. Malcolm and Jacqui had expected a difficult return to family life, but they hadn't anticipated this amount of tragedy.

Malcolm found work easier than he had expected. It seemed that having five years experience in a restaurant in the West End was enough to make him a clear candidate for any job he applied for. He had sent off applications to five restaurants and a hotel, all of which yielded interviews. He was in the enviable position two weeks later of trying to decide which position to take. Seeing him struggle, and knowing how hard Malcolm found decision-making, Jacqui told him to take the one that offered the most money and he accepted her advice immediately. Two weeks after his mother died, Malcolm was a restaurant manager in a hotel in the centre of Lancaster.

With frequent trips to their childhood homes, setting up their own home and the long hours Malcolm was working, the pregnancy flew by. There was always something going on and the couple had little time to make new friends in Lancaster. If either of them had been religious, they would have prayed for things to be less turbulent in the run up to the new arrival. Neither felt it was that much to ask for.

6.

My remaining grandfather shot himself dead on bonfire night in the shed at the back of the guest house. He had picked his night well. The crackles and bangs of November 5th disguised his actions, and he wasn't discovered until the next morning, when Jennifer had become concerned that he was nowhere to be seen. Alfred had conducted a search of the garden and it didn't take him long to find the worst thing that he would ever see. Peter had taken no chances and put a shotgun in his mouth and quite literally blown his brains out. It was a trauma no-one ever heard Alfred speak of, and from that day, people said he was half the man he used to be.

Malcolm had been at work preparing rotas for the restaurant when he received the news that he had lost his second parent in three months. He was told that his sister was in reception, and Malcolm said: "I wonder which relative has died this time." He had intended it as a grim joke.

And so it was back to the B&B for Malcolm, who insisted that at eight months gone, Jacqui was too pregnant to be dealing with a doubly bereaved family. "Call me if you need anything at all," he insisted. "Anything," he added to assure her that even at this particularly awful time, Jacqui and the baby-to-be were the most important thing to him.

Peter had left a note. He apologised to the person that found him. He said he didn't wish to be selfish, but Alice had been his life and he didn't want to live without her. He said he had made sure that Alfred and Jennifer were up to the task of taking over, and now he was certain there was nothing else for him to stay around for. He told them what a wonderful family they were, and how much he had enjoyed life until he had lost his soul-mate. Frequently he begged them all to understand what he had done, even though their acceptance would be irrelevant to him at this point.

His last sentences were enough to give Malcolm closure. "The Pleasant Rise Guest House is one third Malcolm's. In many respects, it should have been all of his. But Malcolm is bigger and better than that, in spite of us." Malcolm wept after he read that line; it seemed so unfair that his father should only open up to him for the first time in his suicide note.

Aside from that one brief outpouring, Malcolm shed no more tears for his parents. He kind of understood what his father had done, and with his mother's death still so fresh, it didn't feel like any extra pain had been added.

The suicide drew local press attention and subsequently some national coverage, when the full tragedy of Peter's death was realised. People started to assume that he had never recovered from the shame of their failed foray in the world of psychological experimentation, and that the cruel death of his wife had been the final straw.

The service was just the same as his mother's had been, and afterwards, everyone returned to the guest house, just as they had done a few months before. The mourners were even more sympathetic than the last time, but the words they said were exactly the same. Malcolm couldn't blame people for coming up with nothing original, but he was finding the whole experience extremely insincere.

The day passed slowly for Malcolm, and he kept on avoiding any conversations about the future with his brother and sister. He had overheard them in the days after Peter killed himself talking about trying to bring him back into the business as soon as possible. Even with all the grief and confusion flying around, Malcolm thought that it was a terrible idea. Rather than free up his family obligation, Malcolm feared that losing both of his parents might ensnare him more than he could ever cope with.

By the time Malcolm managed to speak to Jacqui, he was itching to get away, whilst still being extremely perturbed by his apparent coldness.

"Sorry I didn't call sooner," Malcolm said.

"I didn't know when to call," Jacqui replied.

"You didn't need to. I said I'd call," Malcolm reminded her.

"No, I didn't know when would be appropriate to interrupt," Jacqui said and then Malcolm heard her sob, and he knew exactly what was coming next.

7.

It is possible that Hilary Hepworth never found out that she was dying. She was found in her bed by the firemen that had battled to quell the blaze that had started in her living room some time after four in the morning. Initial reports were struggling to ascertain what caused the fire, but an electrical fault was eventually agreed upon at the inquest months later. By all means and rights, it just looked like Hilary fell asleep and died from smoke inhalation before she knew about it, but no-one can be sure. For years afterwards Jacqui was haunted by dreams of her mother lying in bed whilst the smoke filled her room, knowing that she could do nothing about it and just waiting for death to take her.

Jacqui found it much harder to deal with her parents' deaths than Malcolm did, or at least, she coped with it very differently. This was partly because of the pregnancy hormones, but mainly because she couldn't help but blame herself for making the last few years of their lives less than enjoyable. It hurt her that they would never see their grandchild, and it hurt even more that she had only moved back up north to be with her family. Each irony was just a bitter blow to Jacqui, who was hopelessly distraught from the moment she found out that she would never see her mother again.

Malcolm arranged the funeral after Anne refused to have anything to do with it. Jacqui had called to tell her what had happened, and Anne had simply said, "Then I have no family."

Hilary's death made Jacqui lonelier than she could ever have imagined. She had nothing to do but sit at home being pregnant and numbed by the shock of losing both of her parents. The deaths of Malcolm's mother and father had hurt her as well, as her unborn child was going to miss out on the experience of having grandparents.

There were times, usually just after Malcolm had left for work, that Jacqui contemplated phoning Anne. She had kept none of her friends from Morecambe, and so aside from Malcolm, she had no-one.

Whilst things were so strenuous, Jacqui hoped for, but didn't expect, some sort of truce with her sister; at least until the funeral had passed and she wasn't so heavily pregnant. But Anne had decided in the time since her father had died that she really had no need for her family and this spilled out in an angry phone exchange on the night before the funeral. Anne called to tell Jacqui that she wouldn't be in attendance.

"You'll regret it," Jacqui warned her.

"I have many regrets relating to this family," Anne retorted, "and attending her funeral is not one of them. I don't even know why I went to Dad's."

"This is your last chance to say goodbye."

"I said goodbye a long time ago, pretty much around the same time you stole my boyfriend and ran off to London."

"That's not how it happened," Jacqui started to protest.

"So you saw him first then?" Anne replied pointedly.

"Of course you can twist history – "

"It was pretty twisted to begin with."

"I did wonder how pent up you'd be after all these years. I hoped that there were some things more important than your bitterness, but clearly you're never going to be a big person in that sense." Jacqui was on the verge of tears and tried to control the desire to make hurtful remarks that she would struggle to take back.

"I feel free now, Jacqui. Free from my tart of a sister, and free from my cold, dismissive parents. I don't have that history any more. They're dead, and you were dead to me the moment you stole my boyfriend."

Had she not been so hormonal, Jacqui probably would have held her tongue and diplomatically tried to coerce her sister around. But this was all too much for her.

"Nothing will ever be more important than how you feel, it would seem Anne. From hereon you can only get older, lonelier and more miserable. You certainly can't make yourself any more odious."

It would be difficult to say who hung up first after that

statement, but it's a fair assumption that Jacqui was the only one reduced to tears.

8.

Alongside Jacqui and Malcolm, about fifteen of Hilary's closest friends and acquaintances filed into the crematorium. For a woman in her late fifties, Hilary had managed to keep only a few people close to her. That just one of her daughters was present made the occasion seem all the more sad.

The idea of raising her first child with no grandparental support terrified Jacqui. For someone who was nesting, such upheaval truly hurt her. From the moment she woke to the moment she slept, her mind felt no clarity, just a jumble of things to be sad and fearful about.

The last thing she needed upon her return from her mother's funeral was a poison pen letter. It had been hand delivered and the handwriting was hardly disguised. Jacqui didn't want Malcolm to see it, despite not knowing what the contents actually were. She felt he had enough on his plate – they both did – and it was a fair prediction that Anne had nothing nice to say. So she slipped upstairs to the bathroom and locked the door before she opened the letter.

Mystery was clearly not the point in this case – it was more about adding to her troubles. And it did. 'All of this is your own doing,' it said. 'These tragedies are just the beginning of a very miserable future. Fear for your child, Jacqui, for you will get what you deserve.'

This would make hard reading for anyone who wasn't recently bereaved and over eight months pregnant. But Jacqui was both of these things, and she sat down on the closed toilet lid and embarked upon a period of crying that would see out the remainder of the day. The only benefit of going to her mother's funeral that day was that she was able to pass the tears off as grief.

The following morning the fear had abated, but she felt no better. By not telling Malcolm about the latest development, she managed to make herself even more isolated. She worried about everything.

The messages were all quite simple; idle threats wishing Jacqui, Malcolm and their forthcoming offspring all the worst for the future, mixed in with intimations that things definitely wouldn't work out for them. With these letters came the prospect that Anne was now prone to doing anything. The resentment she had stored up had been much more vicious than Jacqui had first thought. She could happily cope with indifference, but the malice was a completely different prospect.

So during the final weeks of her pregnancy, Jacqui carried with her both grief and loneliness, combined with a fear of the unknown. It was possible that Anne would harm one or all of them. Mum entertained the idea of running back to London and escaping the terrible events that had dogged their return to Lancashire, but she knew that in a different way, life would be no better there. She wondered if Anne knew that she hadn't told Malcolm about the letters, because they always arrived when he was at work. She assumed that everything Anne did was deliberate, and with that she couldn't help but fear their intent.

Malcolm didn't press her to find out whether she was alright. Both of her parents had recently died, so of course she wasn't. She hid the real stress and only ever showed Malcolm her grief. There had been something about Malcolm's numbed reaction to his father's suicide that had worried her a little, and she was scared that he held the same indifference for everybody that he was supposed to love.

She knew the stress might be harming me, but she had no idea how to alleviate it.

There was no pattern – a letter would just appear – sometimes on consecutive days, and at other times upwards of four days apart. They were frequent enough for her to know that it wasn't over, and that whatever happened she shouldn't rest easy. It meant that she couldn't lie in wait for her sister, and even when a letter did arrive, Jacqui was so pregnant that she couldn't make it to the window in time to confirm that it really was Anne who was responsible.

It was by pure chance that when she went to put out an empty milk bottle one morning, Anne was crouching down to place her latest nasty missive through the door. The rain was pouring down relentlessly, and Jacqui was grateful that the front door was the furthest she would have to go that day.

The quite identical twins were as startled as each other. In Jacqui, this manifested itself through a gasp. Anne's response was to punch her sister in the jaw and force her way into the house whilst Jacqui tumbled to the floor where she struggled to get herself back up again. Anne slammed the front door and locked it, quickly checking to make sure that the assault had gone unseen.

9.

It was one of those situations where it seemed appropriate to ask why, but with the circumstances that had preceded the attack, it hardly seemed necessary. Jacqui, however, did feel that she should ask some sort of question, just to move things along. Anne had played her part – she had forcefully tied her slightly older sister to a chair and was very much strolling around in the manner of a hostage taker.

"Why now?" was the only question she could think of.

"I had no idea where to find you until now. Besides, this is the first time you've had sufficient things to lose." There was a philosophical tone to Anne's voice that implied she was fully assured of her reasoning.

"I understand how you feel… "

"I don't care whether you understand how I feel or not. Your opinion really doesn't come into this. But the three of you, you were all in it together. I realised that the moment Dad died and you were back by Mum's side as if no years had passed at all and you'd always been the dutiful daughter. Christ, for a while there you were the whore that had ruined their lives."

"This was all so long ago," Jacqui started to protest.

"Oh yes, and since then it's all been so fucking peachy for you!" spat Anne. "Here you are, all settled with a family. And after a nice little career as well."

"You know nothing about the acting!"

"Oh as if they weren't going to keep tabs on you. They had friends in London keep an eye out for you in the papers. There was quite a scrapbook in that house before the fire. They never stopped loving you and that was the problem! They wanted to blame you like I do, but it just wasn't in them. It was always about you for them."

"But you're doing all right for yourself, they told me that much."

"Assistant manager of a fucking bakery? It's not exactly the West End is it?"

"It wasn't perfect."

"Oh, I can imagine. Like you had to turn down invites to dinner because you were already going to an awards ceremony? I can only strive to conjure up the hardships you must have faced."

"You're being sarcastic."

"You're damn right I'm being sarcastic," Anne snarled, and Jacqui thought that she was going to hit her again. "Even the reviews of you were better than the reality of me for them. How do you think that felt? I was just trouble. I was angry, but only because you made me angry."

"I didn't know he was your boyfriend – "

"I'm not talking about that. I'm talking about everything. I'm talking about our lives. The more they loved you, the less loveable I became."

"So you're blaming everyone else entirely for the way you turned out? Pretty big ask."

This act of insolence earned Jacqui a cuff across the face, which was enough to silence her, concerned as she was about her bump. Anne was not someone who needing angering any further.

"I did what I could for you." As Jacqui spoke, she started to cry a little. "So many times I tried to include you and join in with things."

"Like when you took my place on the netball team?"

"I tried out for the team to try and spend time with you!"

"You did it to prove that you were better than me at everything! From the outset it was all about you."

Jacqui was suddenly taken back to the arguments that had followed her first encounter with Malcolm, and how Anne raged on, making the same point relentlessly. Back then she had been able to walk out, but it was obvious that Anne wouldn't be making this courtesy available to her this time. She thought about what she wanted to say, and when she did, she uttered it calmly.

"But only because I did those things. I didn't just get given acting roles, I worked for them. I tried out for school plays and for the netball team and I made the effort to make friends. I tried to be a likeable person. I had to do everything first, and at times that was terrifying. Sometimes I wanted to have someone show me how to do things."

"My heart bleeds," Anne shook her head and sneered. "Poor you. Even now, it's all about you."

As if to escape this conversational deadlock, at that very moment Jacqui's waters broke. Anne stepped back from the newly formed puddle and took a moment to look repulsed whilst she worked out what to do.

"Come on, Anne," Jacqui pleaded. "The baby's coming. Please untie me, and we can talk afterwards."

"You know I feel nothing for any of you. I went shopping

in town whilst the funeral was going on, and it didn't cross my mind the whole time. All of you, you mean nothing to me. God, you must wish you did right now. But I can leave you here, just like that, and I won't give it a second thought."

Anne was triumphant for the first time in her life. She gave a long, stony stare at her slightly older sister, sat there in labour, weeping and pleading for a bit of human decency. She had planned real physical harm, but this reduction of Jacqui was just perfect. Once satisfied that she had stared long enough, she walked across the living room, pulled the telephone cable out of the socket and carried it out of the house with her, making no further comment.

Jacqui let out an anguished but pointless scream for her sister to return. Now at least free from physical threats, she used her feet to drag both her and the chair she was tied to towards the front door. It was too much of a struggle to pick herself back up after the second tumble, and she was forced to lurch/crawl across the room and into the hall, where she felt a heavy contraction.

In her haste to leave, Anne had left the front door wide open. It was good fortune, for Jacqui would have really struggled to open it strapped to an upturned chair on the floor.

Once the contraction had passed, she made further attempts towards the door. When she was close enough, she began to scream at the top of her voice. There seemed to be no-one around. It was early afternoon and many were at work. The weather deterred people from spending unnecessary time outside, so it seemed that no-one could hear her screams.

Salvation came shortly after Jacqui had managed to get her head beyond the doorframe. Daniel Akers, a neighbour who was yet to meet Malcolm or Jacqui, was on his way home. He had been a postman for twenty five years and couldn't imagine working late into the day, and to that point the day had been very ordinary. It was only when he turned onto his street that he heard the screams emanating from one of the houses. He hopped off his bike and wheeled it down the pavement, getting ever closer to the grotesque wailing that he could hear.

He couldn't have expected the sight of a heavily pregnant woman lying half way out of her front door, tied to a chair. Daniel had seen many things in his time, though, and he wasn't easily fazed. Within minutes he had Jacqui untied and lying on a towel in the middle of her living room. He ran to his house and called an ambulance, and when Jacqui appeared to be temporarily comfortable, he asked her whether she had a partner and how he could be contacted.

Once he had called Malcolm at work from his own home telephone, Daniel remained by Jacqui's side, telling her to breathe and bombarding her with encouragement. The ambulance arrived shortly before Malcolm did, and I arrived shortly after that. The new family were whisked away to hospital, where the day finished without further event.

DANIEL

Pre-Memories

1.

And maybe that was the problem. From the moment I was born, things seemed to pass by without further event. My birth signalled an end to the drama as far as my parents were concerned. Their lives to that point had been tumultuous at times and they didn't want the same to happen to me. They didn't want me to be exposed to manipulation, anger and resentment. They vowed not to shout at me, or raise their voices in anger unless the situation really warranted it. They didn't want me to hear swear words from them or be exposed in any way to the harm that can be done to any child in their early forays into the world.

That was 14th December 1984, and that baby was me, Daniel Lizar. My name came from the man that helped my mother after my Auntie Anne attacked her. The police came and spoke to Mum about what had happened with Anne the next day. She told them everything she could and Anne was arrested immediately. She pleaded guilty to attempted murder and was sentenced to twelve years. There was no big trial, which meant that the ordeal was almost immediately over for my parents.

The joy of having a new child helped my mother through the weeks following Auntie Anne's arrest. After such a traumatic pregnancy, I was the best thing that could have happened to her. I don't think it arrogant to say that my arrival (something over which I had no control, and therefore can take no real pride in) stopped my mother from going down a very dark path. In effect she had lost all of her family in the space of four months, and it's hard to say how she would have coped if she hadn't been starting one of her own.

I'm a bastard. People my age don't really think about things like that any more. Quite a lot of us are bastards now, and there's no stigma about it. I have been called a bastard on countless occasions over my life, but I doubt that even once it's been because I was born out of wedlock. The fact is, I was born to two parents who loved both me and each other, and as far as starts in life go, that's not bad at all.

I would have been three months old when they married in a low key registry office ceremony, with Daniel Akers and his wife Celine acting as witnesses. Daniel was actually my godfather until he passed away peacefully after suffering a heart failure in his sleep when I was five. I remember very little of him, aside from the kind things my parents said about him. For my mother, the Akers were surrogate grandparents, and although they didn't spend much time together, they were quite close. Celine moved away to be closer to her family after my namesake died.

Mum was lonely. Dad was out at work for at least fifty hours a week, if not more. Those first weeks of my life were during the Christmas season, and it was only really when the January lull kicked in that my father was able to spend any time with my mother and me. Still pre-speech, and virtually pre-anything, I was a source of entertainment, but not exactly a firm friend.

The wedding was a good focus for the pair of them, and had my father thought about it a little more he probably would have dragged out the engagement a little longer. The whole process was over too quickly, and once again my mother returned to feeling lost and lonely.

Despite the joy that both my birth and their wedding brought them, my mother still felt that there was a lot missing from her life. Suddenly she started to feel about friends the same way that Auntie Anne had felt about obtaining a husband, just without the same deadly intensity. She should have learned from her slightly younger sister's mistakes, but perhaps it was one of the few twin things that she shared with Anne.

Taking me out for walks in my pram, usually just into the city centre, she would strike up conversations with other mothers, but talked to them just a little too much. She appeared edgy when they went to end the conversation, and in hindsight she admits that she must have looked skittish in that sense. It was hard for her to make friends when all she seemed to be doing was intimidating people a little.

Robyn, however, proved to be something of a godsend.

2.

Doing the maths, I would have been six months old when my mother met Robyn Proctor in the supermarket. I did the ice-breaking for the pair of them, and they told me on many occasions that without me they would never have become friends. It was one of those days where my mother was struggling to cope with the sadness that she often felt. Mostly her new family were enough to keep her happy and fulfilled, but occasionally she would stumble across a thought as she was drifting off to sleep and it would stick with her for some time.

The day that they met was one of my crying days. I was apparently a good child almost all of the time, but I would just have certain days where I couldn't be calmed down. I would eat food, and then carry on crying. Or I would fill my nappy, be changed and then start to bawl again. Toys would not deter me from my tears, either. So between the two of us, we made for quite a miserable duo.

My mother had planned for a quick visit to the supermarket and then home. I had other ideas, and my wailing distracted her to the point where she forgot what she had arrived for. She apparently stood in the canned goods aisle, on the brink of tears trying to work out why the hell she was even there. It was these moments that made her fear that she was losing it. Seeing another human at breaking point is usually enough to modify the behaviour of an adult, but as a six-month old infant, I chose this moment to piss myself and cry even harder.

Mum followed my lead. Well, she cried. She also closed her eyes, willing my noise to end. After a short time, she was forced to open them again because I had momentarily ceased crying. When she looked down, there was a woman she had never met before crouched before me in the trolley, whistling a lullaby. I think in the modern climate, the gut reaction of a mother would be to get their child away from the stranger as soon as possible. Back in 1985, though, people didn't just assume that anyone who showed a fondness for children probably wanted to abuse them. Strange to think of a time less suspicious than ours, really. Were it not, it's possible that they would never have become such firm friends.

"My God, are you a musician or a goddess?" Mum asked her.

"Teacher and mother," the woman replied and put her hand out for my mother to shake. "Robyn Proctor."

"You can't believe how pleased I am to meet you."

Robyn insisted that she buy my mother a brew. Mum was grateful for the respite from my wailing, but also for the company. By the time they went their separate ways, they were firm friends. Robyn told her that she had a one year old son named Alex, and that she was happily married to Charles, a man who at thirty-nine was ten years her senior. They were both at home while Robyn popped to the shops for a little bit of time alone, the few hours she took each week to keep her balanced. She was already back teaching part-time and explained that it was almost the perfect career path for her as a new mother.

Mum told me that she walked away from that encounter with the kind of thrill usually reserved for meeting a new love interest.

Robyn and her family brought a new focus into Mum's life that helped her move on from everything that had gone before. I've been told by my mother that all the way home, she kept telling me that we'd both made new friends, even though I was yet to meet Robyn's son. It's not a choice one gets to make aged six months.

My first ever social engagement was Alex Proctor's first birthday party, which took place two days after my mother had met Robyn. I'm told that Alex and I took to each other straight away. I presume we took to each other the way that two infants would take to each other – with inquisition and no real sense of emotion. Surely at that age everything is at least mildly fascinating. I can't imagine that there was anything that told our parents we were destined to be best friends. This has to be one of those stories where history has been rewritten in the name of spinning a good yarn.

The way I see it is that Alex and I became good friends because of the opportunity. He was the first other child that I knew, and he was the one I spent most of my time with in those pre-school years. He was the only person I knew when I started primary school. It was a chance thing as opposed to some personality match.

But as far as the family history goes, the Proctors and the Lizars became friends at first sight. Dad joined us at the party and he bonded with Charles immediately. He was the manager of a small restaurant in the city centre, which all sounds rather neat but that was the way it was. There was no question of my father working for Charles, for he could expect to manage much bigger restaurants. As they got to know each other, however, it became more and more likely that they would go into business together. Despite being fourteen years older than Dad, Charles found he had a lot in common with him and they developed a friendship independent of Mum and Robyn. That is, they didn't just spend time with each other because their wives forced them to.

The two families actively spent a lot of time together – meals, picnics, days out. There was usually something planned for each weekend. Whether it was that in many ways we mirrored each other that it worked, I can't be sure. All I know is that I grew up with a bigger family unit than most.

When I was three, my parents bought a house two streets away from where the Proctors lived, so our lives became even more interlinked. I'm told that some found the mutual reliance between our families quite odd, but the benefits were more than plain to see. These were friendships that shaped all of our lives.

3.

It would seem to me that in the years that followed my parents' move back up north, the time was spent trying to make up for the things my mother had lost. First it was her family, which was rectified by my birth and my parents' marriage. This was furthered by the arrival of the Proctors into our lives, which meant my mum had friends and the beginnings of a social network again. Mum met many people through Robyn, but I don't remember any of her friends from those days. I would say Robyn was the only important one.

Mum and Robyn were mutually beneficial friends. By the time Alex was nearly two, Robyn was keen to get back to work full-time, and Mum offered to look after him whilst she was at school. In return, Robyn said she would look after me during the day time when school was on holiday to give Mum a bit of break. It was sharing the load of motherhood in a way, and it obviously made it easier on both of them.

Robyn's lifestyle held great appeal to my mother. She listened to her talking about her work as a primary school teacher, and couldn't help but be infected by her enthusiasm. Since falling pregnant, she hadn't given all that much thought to what she would do instead of acting. Occasionally she considered trying to get some theatre work in Lancaster, but even the idea filled her with a sense of dread that she hadn't felt since her last performance.

When my mother mentioned that she might like to give teaching a try, Robyn was overjoyed. A degree in drama was enough to get her onto the relevant course, and with the dual-family system in great shape there would be plenty of time for her to get studying and pass the course before it was time for me to go to school.

Dad and Charles enjoyed drinking together, and often would arrange to have the same evenings off as each other. Charles was really the first true friend that my father ever had. There had been acquaintances in London, mainly through work, and people that they had associated with, but this was the first bond my father had felt towards someone outside of his immediate family. Being in the same industry meant that they had lots to talk about, and on a personal level they found that they could laugh together. As men, they just wanted someone to hang around with and be comfortable. It's a small ask, and because of that, they found their friendship easy to manage.

And me? Well during these years I followed a pretty standard pattern of development. I was crawling at around six months, made attempts at speaking some time after my first birthday and I was toddling shortly after that. I was well looked after, by all accounts, and my parents haven't really told me much about those years; nothing of interest, at least.

We had days out in theme parks that I can't remember,

and we went to the zoo and on trips to the seaside. I didn't fall into ponds, or go missing in crowds, or even fall over in an amusing fashion. I didn't injure myself notably, or do anything remarkable. There are plenty of pictures – Christmas, birthdays, family walks, me sitting on a potty not looking as disturbed by the situation as I should have done – but they all point to an uneventful infancy.

My first memory is of trying to chase some birds in a wildfowl centre. I'm not sure how old I was, but there was snow on the ground and my memory tells me that I was wearing mittens. I remember tottering towards them and being pulled back by my hood. Story over.

Having heard more about my parents' lives growing up, I can see how that influenced the way they behaved with me. My father was present, but often quite distant. We interacted and played and had fun, but there was no real emotion to him. He didn't hug me or tell me he loved me, but he made up for it in general enthusiasm. He used to call me his little mate. He just didn't know how to really do the emotional stuff because it had been so absent in his family. He often seemed passive to me whilst I was growing up, but that was just because he didn't want to push me in any direction. He was keen for us to have different childhoods.

Mum, on the other hand, was very protective. She had seen first hand how cruel the world could be, and she was keen to keep me on a close rein. Even though Auntie Anne was in prison, she could never quite relax. Anne was a lesson to her in how favouritism can damage a child, and for that reason she didn't want to have any more children. She wanted me to feel loved and she also wanted to guide me through the world. Her biggest fear was that I would turn out as damaged as her sister.

4.

When I was four I started to learn a little about my family

history. Alex would often go off to visit his grandparents, which left me confused as to why this was a trip that we weren't to join them on, as it was one of the few things that we didn't do together. I remember this, vaguely, because it was only when I got to school that I found out that it was unusual for me to have no grandparents. I just thought that grandparents were something special that Alex had.

I asked all of the questions that an innocent four year old would. What happened to your mummies and daddies? Did they not want to meet me? Why was Alex allowed grandparents but I wasn't? It never really made sense to me, but I was aware of the sadness these questions caused my mother, and how my father became tense whenever the subject was brought up. I understood that not having grandparents was a negative thing, even if I wasn't to feel too sad about it.

At that age you just ask questions with no sense of tact, but on the whole you just accept the way of the world. There were times when I thought Alex was my brother, because people said we were just like brothers, and I had no concept of similes back then. As they were best friends and had plenty of time to talk, Robyn was fully aware of our family history, and my mother always placed the emphasis on how much being separated from Auntie Anne had shaped their futures. They were concerned what a similar divide would have upon Alex and me, even though we weren't related.

Alex was born in July and I in December, which was a clear age gap that meant we should have been at school a year apart. Neither of them wanted me to feel inferior, and Mum had enough bad memories about being the trail-blazer to warn Robyn about the impact it could have on Alex. As a teacher, Robyn had heard of children being held back for certain reasons, usually illness or some other extenuating circumstance. It seemed the only logical way to keep Alex and me together, even if it was morally questionable.

So Robyn just lied. She said that Alex was too ill to start

school that September. She told them, and these were her bosses, that her son was undergoing tests at the hospital and that she felt that he wouldn't be well enough to start school with all of the other children. I don't know if she even specified an illness, but Alex and I were happy to be told that we would be going to school together.

I spent a lot of time with the Proctors during holidays, when my mother would catch up on her teacher training work. She was completing it as a night course at a local college. Twice a week I went over to Alex's for the evening whilst Mum studied. She started when I was two and was qualified by the time I was ready to go to school. We would both start school in September; me as a pupil in reception, Mum as a high school drama teacher.

We spent Christmas Days together, so it really did feel like we were one big family. Dad and Charles would be out working during the day time, so Mum and Robyn would cook dinner at one of their houses whilst Alex and I played with our new toys. We were given matching gifts with the parity that parents usually only show to siblings.

There would be six other celebrations in the year, one for each of our birthdays. This would take the form of a meal, or a small gathering for us kids, where a whole bunch of other kids would come out of the woodwork, bearing gifts and parents that I had never met before. We'd play games, eat lots of food and listen to nursery rhymes. Then they would go. These events were traditional as well, with the only deviation being the alternation between the birthday boys.

It was quite an insular start to life. Other kids came by to play, but not often and their names didn't stick. Neither Alex nor I went to nursery, so by the time we were due to start school, we were the only other kid that each other knew. But that's better than most – I don't think many people start primary school with a best friend.

There were no childminders drifting in and out of my life

because between them, our parents had it covered. If they did things as a foursome, they wanted to include us as well. Our parents were a constant presence in our lives, and as such I got to know a small number of people very well.

Obviously I didn't go visiting my Auntie Anne in prison. Her existence was kept from me. I think I went to the Pleasant Rise Guest House about five times during my early childhood and I remember nothing of these short visits.

And that's what happened to me in the years before I started school. Nothing to write home about. No character shaping dramas, or incidents that took me away from anything but a normal path. I was growing into a happy child with a very secure family around me.

When things go wrong, people always seek to blame the parents, but shy of imprisonment, there is no way to protect your child forever. There's only so much you can do.

5.

Initially school confused me greatly. As I say, there had been other children who entered my life, but none that I can remember. Having not been to playgroup or nursery, the sight of hundreds of children congregating in a playground fazed me somewhat.

Robyn and my mum both took us down to school on our first day. I wasn't nervous about the whole experience until I got there. I hadn't even the beginning of a clue as to how many people there were in the world, but the playground alone was incredibly daunting. Most of the children were bigger than me and they all seemed to know what they were doing. They ran about, or fought a little, and made a lot of different noises. The majority didn't have their mothers with them, and to me that seemed incredibly grown up.

I held onto my mother's hand, and Alex did the same with Robyn. This must have been the last time either of us acted without any sense of social awareness.

"You look like new ones," a kindly looking older lady said as she approached us. "We're all gathering over there." She pointed to a corner of the playground I had been yet to study, where a gaggle of children my age were stood with a variety of parents.

School had been explained to me at great length by my parents, and also by the Proctors, but I had lacked the imagination to give much thought to what it all meant. Robyn had clearly prepared Alex for the whole experience, for he instantly exuded all of the confidence needed for meeting new people. He looked inquisitively at the other children and waved at a few here and there that he seemed to recognise. He must have paid more attention to the other children at those parties than I had. I shrank by my mother's side and waited to be told what to do.

The gathered parents were asked to say goodbye to their children, and for the next five minutes the crowd turned into shambolic display of kisses, hugs and tears – from parents and children alike. The lady who had led me over introduced herself as Mrs Paige, and she told us that she would be our teacher. I remember little of Mrs Paige, aside from the fact that she used to wear knitted sweatshirts with animal patterns on them. There was one particular one, a gaudy red number with rows of white sheep stitched into it, which will remain with me for the little forever that I have left.

I watched as my mother left me in the playground, feeling utterly betrayed. I hadn't asked for this big change, or this new world. I was happy as I was, and it made no sense that I had to come here when there seemed to be no valid reason for me to do so. Robyn walked into the school to go and sort out her new class, but at least Alex knew that he had a parent to hand. Without any concern, he followed Mrs Paige and the rest of the class into the school. Even the ones bawling their eyes out knew that they had to follow the strange new lady. Lacking the knowledge to do anything else, I trailed behind them.

I was quite the talker until that first day of school. Within the small circle of people that I knew, I was encouraged to converse both with Alex and all of the adults. But the moment I was sat in a classroom, I went mute. I just didn't know how to adjust immediately.

Such were the demands of reception class, we spent most of that first week getting to know each other, or at least trying to remember each other's names. We sang nursery rhymes and attempted the alphabet. Whilst Alex would shout out answers, I stayed silent in the seat next to him, hoping that no-one addressed me. Whenever I was forced to answer a question, I did so with a shaky voice that invited no further interrogation.

Other kids would talk to me and I would do my best to deflect the attention. If I was older, people would have just written me off as rude, but for now I was deemed shy by Mrs Paige, who spent the first few weeks of my schooling life trying to convince me to interact with the other children.

But after the initial culture shock, it wasn't acquired shyness that was keeping me to myself; it was pure intrigue at all these other people. The way they spoke and the things they said enthralled me.

During my second week, we were all asked to say one interesting thing about ourselves, be it our favourite colour, favourite pet or any other fact that a young child can provide about themselves. One child, one of many whose names I have forgotten over the years, said that his mummy and daddy didn't live together. At that moment I feared that my head would explode. I had not been introduced to a reality where people's parents could live anywhere but in the same house.

Other kids knew what they wanted to be when they grew up. It was usually what their parents did, but the options sounded fascinating. Some even had hobbies and interests, like toy trains or computer games. I did things, but I hadn't formed an opinion on what I liked the best.

As Mrs Paige went around the room, I became more and more aware that I didn't know what I would say about myself. I hadn't considered a favourite colour, or a favourite animal, and my parents lived in the same house, like normal parents did. It was the day my egocentrism was shattered once and for all, and everyone else appeared to be so much more exciting than I was. It was this revelation that rendered me almost wordless during my first weeks of primary school.

6.

Without Alex it's possible that I wouldn't have made any friends during my time at Gregson Lane Primary School. I was too busy observing people to engage with them. I listened to Alex when he spoke to them, and kids that age say incredible things to each other, such is their combined misunderstanding about how the world works. The school brought together children of different backgrounds, and although it was hardly multi-cultural, it was certainly comprised of a socio-economic diversity.

We were a mid-ground family, but one on the rise with the addition of Mum's teacher's salary. The Proctors were considered quite well off, and soon we would be thought of as the same. The children from poorer families were the most interesting to me. They appeared to be more worldly wise than I was. The children who seemed most like me were also the ones that seemed to lack any real knowledge of the world. I was less drawn to these classmates.

One of the most fascinating of my classmates was a girl named Lauren Bell. Of all the kids in the classroom, she spoke with the most authority about a whole range of topics, and for that reason she proved popular with most of us in the class. Her mother was a hairdresser, and Lauren had spent the weeks leading up to school with her to save money on child-minding fees. The things she spoke about were fragments of things that she had heard whilst sitting in the hairdressers.

Most of her observations would not stand the test of time, but in those early weeks, she was an oracle to us.

There were numerous occasions where I would go home with some information from school that I had heard from Lauren and one of my parents would have to dispel it for me. I don't recall it being anything serious, or even contentious; it was just things that she had misheard and chosen to pass on to her new school friends.

Of all the new people that I was observing, it was her that I wanted to make my friend. My social awkwardness was the only difficulty I had to overcome. Alex was my bridge in that respect.

Our classmates had drifted towards Alex when they realised that his mother was one of the teachers. At that age, teachers were equivalent to God in our eyes. Somehow this made Alex anointed in the eyes of our peers, and he was confident enough to rise to the challenge.

He was a loyal friend and kept me close at hand, however quiet I may have seemed. This is how I got to learn things about people, because Alex worked the room and I was his shadow.

I began to understand a little about hierarchical structures and the benefits of reflected glory. It would have been so easy for me to have fallen under the radar at an early stage and become something of a nobody in the Gregson Lane community. I was saved from anonymity by my best friend, the son of a teacher no less. People wanted to be his friend, and part of that meant wanting to be my friend as well. When given the chance to make some friends out of all these potential candidates, I knew I would be able to speak comfortably. But for those first weeks, I just didn't believe I had anything interesting to say.

7.

In my weeks of observing my classmates, I saw many of them

cry at some point, be it due to tumbling over in the playground, pissing their pants or just missing their mummies. Dad explained to me that I should try and cry as little as possible, as people would think me weak. He also said that there were times when people just had to cry, but that you could tell when those were. I used to tell my parents everything about school so that they could help me understand it a little better. Just knowing that they knew about it was a comfort for me in some way.

When I saw others cry, I thought of that as fake crying. When Lauren Bell started crying during register one morning, I could tell that it was real. It wasn't genuine empathy, which would have been beyond my nearly five years of age, but mere inquisition that troubled me about Lauren's sadness. Mrs Paige took her out of the room for a short while and when they returned Lauren was smiling a little and returned to her desk without saying anything else. "Why was she crying?" I whispered to Alex, which meant that we would find out at playtime.

"My daddy moved out over the weekend," Lauren explained, trying hard not to cry again in the playground.

"Why did he do that?" Alex asked.

"I don't really know," Lauren replied matter-of-factly.

"Oh. So where has he gone?"

"I don't know," Lauren answered. I scowled, thinking to myself that she didn't seem so clued up after all.

"Is he coming back?" Alex persisted. Children lack all of the social graces that adults wish they could once in a while. They have no sense of what is a touchy subject and when questions are becoming too probing. Perhaps with that child-like honesty, we'd get more done as adults. It's certainly worth considering.

"I don't know," Lauren said, clearly not realising that it was all she was saying.

"Daddys don't just leave for no reason," I blurted out, the

first time I had spoken without being asked a question, and Lauren stepped back in surprise. Alex seemed a little startled as well. It was a huge breakthrough for me, and I couldn't hide how pleased I was to be talking to someone properly. My smile was deeply inappropriate, considering the conversation.

Her home situation meant that Lauren had something new to tell us every day. Although I could see these events were upsetting her, it crossed my mind that at least it was a little bit of excitement. Lauren was aware that I liked the interesting stories, and that I said very little when nothing had happened at home. She also enjoyed the exclusivity of me talking to her, so when she had nothing new of her own to offer, she would try and find things out about our classmates to entertain me with instead.

It came to be that the three of us would spend plenty of time together, and my shyness started to evaporate. I began to engage with my classmates more and even got a line in the Nativity play at Christmas, saying 'Look, a star,' while dressed vaguely like a King. If Lauren found something interesting out about someone, I was inclined to try and talk to them at playtime. My actions would have appeared contrived to anyone older, and I'm sure I would have considered them some sort of deception, but it wasn't like that. I just liked hearing stories about lives more interesting than mine.

8.

Lauren brought me two types of stories over the course of my reception year – real and fictional. She never told a lie, and the leads she gave me with regards to people were never wrong.

It might have been the revelation that a classmate lived on a farm, right through to the discovery that one boy had two fathers. Each story made my life seem even duller, and Lauren's the very definition of enviable.

The fictional stories were the ones that came from the television. Since her father had moved out, Lauren's mother had started to let her watch an Australian soap on tea-time television, and each day Lauren would come in and tell us the latest goings on. We didn't understand what it all meant, not even Lauren, but these tales would occupy a lot of our time. We were aware that men and women kissed each other, and most of the stories seemed to revolve around who kissed who. There were other things that they argued about, and the story always seemed to stop at an exciting moment, which we would have to wait at least a day to find out about.

At home, I was limited to watching a select few cartoons. Dad saw television as mindless and didn't want me exposed to anything beyond a few innocuous kids' shows. Even my television life was uneventful!

At some point Lauren's father returned, so her lunch time bulletins focused more on the fictional. The lives that Lauren described did seem interesting, even if I wasn't sure exactly what it was they were doing. Things like running away from home and being trapped in a burning building all made some sense to me, but it would be hard to say that I truly understood them. It's much easier to say that I began to crave them.

'Til Death Do Us Start

1.

My mother's first year as a drama teacher had gone very well, to the point where she wanted to open up a summer school to teach a bit of drama to those children who had not taken it as an option in school and might have regretted it. As it turned out, there were plenty who were in this very position, having been forced into taking more sensible options by their parents.

In order to do this, Robyn offered to look after me during summer school, which was the first three weeks of the summer holiday. In recognition of our advancing years (Alex was already six), we were allowed to go play in the park unsupervised, but only in the bit visible from the Proctors' house. To us that was freedom, and we made that area our own, which in reality meant climbing a tree and making games up around that. Occasionally we'd take a football along, but it wasn't that much fun with just the two of us kicking it to each other. Making games up was much more entertaining. Usually it would involve us emulating something we'd seen in a cartoon or kids' show, like I would pretend to be a cat stuck in a tree and Alex would be the fireman. Or the world would be flooding, Noah's Ark style, and it was down to Alex and me not to fall into the water (the park). Give two young kids a couple of props and they'll come up with a whole array of ideas.

One day we made a sign and put it on the tree. It read 'Danex'

– an ingenious amalgamation of our names. The tree became our fort and we would climb it, looking out onto the street for potential invaders. It was a harmless game, where we would try and not be detected in our tree. Occasional variations involved using a water pistol on the 'invader', or shouting something puerile out to them and trying not to laugh as they looked for the source of the insult.

Another game we would play was to stay out longer than we were meant to, and we would use the tree to keep an eye out for Robyn coming over to see if we were alright. When she entered the park, we would drop down from the tree and nip through the railings and back to Alex's house before she did. Robyn learned to find this game amusing, but apparently we scared her on several occasions.

We were on lookout the day that Robyn came rushing out of her house with more urgency than we were accustomed to. We observed her as she made her way towards the park, and from our positions in the tree branches, we could see that she was moving quickly. A challenge, in other words. We waited for her to get in line with the tree, and she continued to the gate, we dropped to the ground and made a run for it. It was the usual procedure, but for the first time in my life, I heard Robyn bellow at the top of her voice.

"Stop right there!"

It was a noise serious and piercing enough to stop us in our tracks. She rushed over to us, and we thought that we were about to get in serious trouble, but there was a calmness about her that we would learn was the way parents approached bad news.

She crouched down so that she was face to face with Alex. "We've just had a call from the hospital, it's your grandad," she said seriously but kindly to Alex. "We have to go now. Daniel, your parents are still at work, so you're going to have to come with us."

I nodded at her solemnly. I didn't really understand what

was going on, but I remember thinking that it all seemed terribly exciting.

2.

That was my first experience of being in a hospital, and I think I can remember it pretty well. The grandfather in question was Robyn's father. It was all was very chaotic, but I remember us being ushered into Robyn's car and being driven away without the usual caution that she would exhibit.

Alex's grandfather had been rushed straight into A&E, which was where Robyn had been instructed to go by the lady who had phoned her from the nursing home. I know now that he had suffered a stroke shortly after getting out of the bath and he had arrived at hospital unconscious. By the time we located reception, all they had was bad news. The receptionist asked for Robyn to wait whilst a doctor came to see her. She knew what that meant and started to cry.

Lucky for Alex and me, who had no idea what was going on, Charles arrived only minutes after we did. He rushed into the room with a sense of urgency and immediately hugged his wife. She cried more and he did his best to comfort her. A doctor came over and took them to a room, whilst the receptionist was instructed to keep an eye on us. Alone, we tried to make sense of what was going on.

"Where's your grandad?" I asked him, and he shrugged. I always turned to Alex for information about new things – his six month age advantage and his elevated school status was enough for him to be the leader of the two of us back then. We couldn't see inside the room where Robyn and Charles were, so I just tried to guess what was going on.

Charles emerged first, and I'm sure I could hear Robyn crying from within. "Go and see your mother," he said to Alex who walked with the correct level of caution in the room, where the door was shut behind them.

"Better get you home," Charles said to me with a forced cheerfulness.

"What about Alex?"

"He needs to stay here for a while."

"Is he sick?"

"No, no, he's fine."

"Is Robyn sick?"

"No, she's fine too. She needs to stay here as well. I'm just going to drive you home."

"Is Alex's grandad dead?" I asked.

When I got home, my father was already waiting for me. He thanked Charles and told them that if they needed anything, we were there. Charles made a hasty exit, and my father popped on a cartoon to try and make things a little more light-hearted. He made no attempt to explain what had happened, but I still had lots of questions that needed answering.

"What does dead mean?"

3.

Death was the first taboo subject that I learned about. When Mum returned from her summer school, she was taken into the kitchen and given an update on what had happened. When she and my father came back into the living room, they both looked grim-faced.

"We need to talk to you," Mum said softly, so I knew that I wasn't in trouble.

And that was how I started to learn a little about life and death. "Alex's grandad has gone to heaven," Mum explained. Dad told me more recently that he had not approved of that part of the conversation, what with us not being a religious family. I asked the usual types of questions as I tried to get to grips with the concept. I needed assuring on several occasions that it was very much a one-way trip and that Alex's grandfather would not be returning.

"Does he not want to come back?" I persisted.

"It's not that he doesn't want to come back," Mum replied.

"He can't," Dad added. "It's not something we have a choice on."

"Is Alex's grandad with my grandad now?"

I suppose they'd hoped that I wouldn't get round to these questions, the concept of death being enough for any five year old in one sitting. But that was the main thing that was on my mind – Alex's grandfather might not be here any more, but mine had never been there as far I could tell.

"Yes," Mum told me. "He's in the same place as all of your grandparents."

"How many do I have?"

"You had four."

"And they are all with Alex's grandad?"

"That's right." I imagine Mum began to falter at this point.

"And where's that?"

I think even the non-religious parents must use heaven to try and soften the blow of mortality when trying to explain it to a young child. I don't know what she said to me, but my first perception of death was that it was a very nice thing to happen to you that left everyone else feeling miserable. I imagined clouds and blue skies, and I think somewhere in this description was my first encounter with God and religion. I remember not feeling sorry for Alex and his family any more.

"So why do people get sad?" I persisted.

"Because it means they don't get to see that person ever again."

"Unless they die?"

Dad stepped in at this point, presumably because he feared that I may try to kill myself if they glamorised death too heavily.

"In a way, yes. But only when it's their time to go."

"So you can't make yourself die?"

"No, it's not an option," he said firmly, and for years I

didn't question it again.

They continued to explain to me how normal death was, and how lucky I was in a way not to have been around when my grandparents died. That didn't make sense to me.

"Why?" I asked. It's only as we get older that we feel the need to complicate questions.

"Well, it made us all very sad," Mum took over from here.

"But shouldn't you be happy for them?"

They changed the subject shortly afterwards, but it wasn't something I was going to let lie for long.

4.

Mum cancelled the last two days of her summer school to be with me whilst Robyn grieved, and I'm sure she must have regretted it. I persistently asked her the same questions about death, and her vague answers didn't satisfy my curiosity at all. I must have been a nightmare. I didn't want to play games, or go out in the garden on my bike, and any suggestions of trips out were declined by me.

My interest turned towards other members of my family. I knew of my Uncle Alfred and Auntie Jennifer, but I had never thought to ask Mum before. "Do you have any brothers and sisters?" I asked, moving the questioning away from death for a short while.

"No, there's just me," she replied without a thought.

"That must make you feel very lonely," I said tactlessly. Mum was clearly tiring of me.

"You could work for the police with your interrogation skills," she said to me weakly at one point. I didn't know what she meant and assumed that she was missing the point again.

On the second day after Alex's grandfather died, I must have driven her to distraction. Mum was quite well adjusted after everything that happened to her; she didn't leap into therapy or try and take the past out on anyone else. After nearly two days of almost relentless inquisition, though, she caved and popped the television on in an attempt to distract me.

Because the television was something of a rarity in my life, it seemed enough of a treat for me to cease my questions and watch with my mother, who was clearly happy to have subdued me at last. We went through the initial run of children's television programmes, which in themselves were enough to keep me happy. At some point during an art and craft programme, Mum drifted off to sleep.

I think to me this was the equivalent of being left in a toy shop after dark. At 5pm the television would normally have been switched off, as even the teen dramas and the kids' news were deemed a little too worldly for me. I guess it was right that my mother might not wish me to see family breakdowns, hostage situations and dramatic lives. She also knew first hand how acting had made her feel on stage, so perhaps the drama just reminded her of the tough times.

I sat as still as I could, hoping that I wouldn't wake her up. I didn't dare change the channel lest it rouse Mum, so I just sat there consuming the programmes that came on. First of all there was a teen drama based in a secondary school. The kids all looked much older than me, and I remember that the main storyline had something to do with someone taking up smoking. There was lots of shouting. Then there was a short kids' news bulletin, where I got my first glimpse of war. I suppose that would have been the first Gulf War, but all I can remember were a couple of explosions and some people crying in the street.

I could hardly contain my excitement when the Australian soap that Lauren had been telling us about came on. Despite having never actually seen it before I felt a familiarity with the characters and their predicaments. Suddenly I had the correct visualisations for the things that Lauren had been telling me about for at least six months, almost like being able to see after being blind for a while. The episode ended with a brick crashing through a window and a close up of someone as they fell to the ground. Then the credits rolled and I realised I was holding my breath. This was even more exciting than Alex's grandad dying!

My mother rose from her slumber, and it took her a moment or two to realise what was going on. "Daniel, you know I don't want you watching things like this," she said wearily. "Why didn't you wake me?"

"You didn't tell me to," I answered simply. It's lines like this that can slay a parent when they are irked with you. Just be a bit cute. It all seems so obvious now, but at the time there was nothing deliberate in my comment. It was just the truth. Again with no awareness of what the consequences would be, I started to tell Mum all about the things that had happened in the programme. I used words she didn't think I knew and explained concepts that she could never have expected me to know about.

"Wow," she said, and I was still a little surprised because I thought she would be annoyed with me for watching television without her permission.

So with all this extra time together, Mum saw an opportunity to try a little experiment on me.

The way Mum looked at it was that she had never seen me more animated than in the wake of watching that soap opera. I was explaining relatively complex plots to her, and doing it in a way that not only made sense, but showed some signs of real intellect. If she'd asked me about the stories that Mrs Paige had read to us in class then I would have struggled to get everything right, but this was something else. It was multiple parallel plots, a whole cast of names and also interpreting the things that had happened before it.

So during those weeks, we watched television together. Because Dad worked late, it meant that we could watch programmes right up to the watershed; the soaps, and dramas about the emergency services. It was a real eye-opener for a five year old, all these exciting things condensed into a short space of time, and as far as I was concerned it was as real as anything or anyone I had encountered to that point.

Mum asked me questions after each programme, and she was surprised by how much I retained. I was following the plots well and making some assumptions about what I saw. It also sparked a lot of questions in me, questions that Mum was happy to answer, as most of them veered away from probing about my absent grandparents.

She tried me on different things. With the soaps she wanted to see whether I remembered characters and storylines on a day-to-day basis, and with the dramas she wondered if I had any ideas as to what would happen next. Usually I was wrong, but she could see that I engaged in the plot and treated it with a fascination she hadn't seen in me before.

She enjoyed it as well. Her drama training had taught her to treat television as a lesser art-form, but she saw something in those programmes that she hadn't allowed herself to see before. I know she enjoyed them because we continued to watch those programmes long after the summer holidays had finished.

I loved it. I didn't understand that it was play acting, but I didn't consider them documentaries either. Just stories, like the ones Lauren told me, but just more real. The medical dramas were the best because they had the big action sequences. The police dramas were more of the same, and by the end of the holidays I was adamant that I wanted to be a police officer when I grew up.

I also wanted to be a robber for a while, and an ambulance driver. I certainly learned lots about different types of people. Living in a predominantly white area, multiculturalism was not something I had been introduced to, and so the tokenism on television helped me to understand that not everybody looked like me.

"You're not to tell your father," Mum reminded me each

evening before I went to bed. It would have been at around eight o'clock, so I can assure you that she wasn't introducing me to programmes that were entirely unsuitable for someone my age.

I always promised that I wouldn't say a word, because I wanted to keep watching these shows. In a way I started to live for it. Fickle as a five year old is prone to be, I was quite saddened when the Proctors stopped grieving and Alex returned to play games. I kept it a secret from him as well, liking that I was learning things about the world that he couldn't ever have dreamt up. I felt that in those weeks I grew wiser than he did, and things altered between us once and for all.

This, in the grand scheme of being a child, meant that I made up all of the games that we played.

Having been parted from my best friend for a fortnight, I was pleased to have him back, but at the same time I knew that I had been having plenty of fun in his absence.

Alex became a barrier between me and the world I had recently discovered. When he went home (or when I came home from his), Mum and I would settle down for some dramas and the occasional bit of news. Mum was educating me by asking me questions about the things I had seen, and she did treat it as if she were teaching me. There's no way she would have relented on the television watching if she hadn't seen the benefits.

Things went back to normal. When at Robyn's, we would go over to the park and play in the area by the tree, but instead of being a tree, it was often a house. This would be a house where dramatic scenes occurred. "Let's pretend," I would say, "that we're married and you've had an affair."

"What's an affair?"

So I would explain as best I could – never revealing my source, of course – and then we would play the game. All of my ideas for games that summer stemmed from something I had seen on the television, and I wonder now if Mum would have been so keen for me to continue watching television if she had seen me slap my best friend across the face and call him a cow in my best cockney accent.

Other times the tree would be the perfect set-up for an accident, usually with me falling out of it and Alex pretending to be a paramedic, or we'd run around it, one us of playing policeman, one of us robber.

"Let's pretend that I'm in the house and you throw a brick through the window."

"Why?"

"Because you hate me."

"I don't hate you."

"Let's pretend."

Compared to Alex's suggestion of pretending to be brum-brum cars, my concepts were genius.

Robyn was mildly amazed by the games that Alex told her we played. "Son of a drama teacher alright," she would laugh.

Mum told me that Robyn praised me for weeks. I think my mother saw that as success enough and she was not discouraged from letting me watch more programmes, but always in moderation.

I wasn't exposed to anything gratuitous – no sex, no real violence, and only the most minor of accidents. Looking back I always imagine it was more than that, but Mum was still keen to protect me from the things that a five year old shouldn't be aware of.

I didn't stop engaging with the world or wishing that I could spend all of my time watching television dramas. There was nothing like that, it was just that I knew that these were my favourite hours of the day.

It's easy to try and piece your history together to fit the story, but this was not a series of revelations or dramatic changes. I just took to television well, and it enhanced my development somewhat. All kids have to have an interest, don't they?

The Dominic Effect

1.

From that summer, I was nothing if not inquisitive. I went through the 'why' phase with some gusto, badgering my parents, teachers and anyone older that might have some information to impart to me. Once I started to think, my mind went into overdrive and I just wanted to know, and understand, everything.

In the second year our teacher was Miss Pawson, who I regarded as 'really old'. She was a stern teacher, very much of the Victorian mould: thin spectacles resting on an ample nose, permanently arched eye-brows and a shrill but menacing voice. She had served her time as a teacher and clearly had no love for it anymore, so I can understand how I could have rubbed her up the wrong way from day one.

It had hardly been an auspicious start. She was calling out the register and referred to me as 'Daniel Lizard'. Some of the more aware children sniggered, but I quite innocently ignored her.

"Daniel Lizard," she repeated and looked around the class. "Is Daniel not here today?"

"He's there, miss," someone pointed at me.

"Then why aren't you saying 'yes miss'?" she turned to me.

"My name is Daniel Lizar," I said with a matter-of-fact tone that clearly irked her. "You said Daniel Lizard."

"Surely you must have known I had made a mistake," she replied.

"No, I thought there might be a Daniel Lizard starting today."

Some of the other children were laughing heartily by this stage, aggravating our new teacher even further.

"But they're almost the same name," she persisted, not wishing to lose face in front of her new rabble of infants.

"Yes, Lizar is like Lizard, but different. My name is Daniel Lizar."

My card was marked from that moment. Miss Pawson wrote me off on that first day, and I subsequently did nothing to make myself appeal to her.

I wanted to know why the alphabet needed to be in a certain order, and why we needed numbers at all. Why was blue called blue? I wanted to know about languages and other types of people. Sometimes I would have questions relating to things that I had seen on the television that I didn't think Mum would tell me about.

Miss Pawson just saw me as disruptive. I was in a way, but disruptive in the right direction. I wanted to learn, it wasn't like I wanted to stop everyone else from learning. I just wanted to make sure that I knew everything.

"Well if it isn't Daniel Lizar with another question!" she often sniped. Teachers like that can alienate a child from education forever. Luckily I was made of sturdier stuff, and continued to ask my questions. My need to know outweighed her reluctance to tell me as far as I was concerned.

I can see why she was annoyed. Second year infants are not meant to go around asking provocative questions that could possibly embarrass the teacher and/or the rest of the class. I don't think I was asking about sex or violence, but death was something that played on my mind. That was the taboo that I was really interested in.

When my questions annoyed her, it told me that I was onto something interesting. By shooting me down she should have shattered my confidence, but it strengthened my resolve and my desire to know. It was an irony lost on both of us at the time.

A typical exchange would involve Miss Pawson teaching us something and me raising my left hand whilst trying to contain myself in my seat with my right hand. I would lean and stretch and make little noises so that I couldn't be ignored. I wouldn't put my hand down until I was addressed, and as the year progressed this waiting time increased.

"Who made up the letters of the alphabet?"

"That's not important."

"Why isn't it important?"

"Because I'm teaching you about words, not letters."

"But aren't words and letters the same?"

"No. Words are groups of letters put together to make sense."

"Were words and letters invented by the same person?"

"It isn't like that."

"How is it?"

"Daniel, this is not helping Miranda learn to pronounce 'church'."

"You've said it for her now. Can you answer my question?"

"It's not what I'm here to teach you."

"Do you not know? I thought you were a teacher."

It was inflammatory lines such as that which would make her explode and send me into the corridor. If a teacher walked past, they looked at me with suspicion. Even though I was just asking questions, Miss Pawson was building up a reputation for me as a trouble-maker, which meant that when I went into successive classes, the teachers expected me to be naughty and were ready to send me to the corridor at the slightest provocation.

She was an important figure in my life. My first enemy.

2.

One day Miss Pawson came into the classroom looking sadder than usual. She insisted that the class quieten down, and we all obeyed. We all feared Miss Pawson; her anger was very intimidating when compared to the gentle approach of Mrs Paige the year before.

"I have some bad news," she told us. We all looked at each other, unable to predict what she was going to say. "You'll notice that Dominic Austen isn't with us this morning. His father called to tell us that his mother passed away last night."

"What does passed away mean?" I asked with my typical eagerness, not ascertaining the macabre nature of the situation.

"It means she's not with us any more," Miss Pawson answered, much more kindly than normal.

"Is she dead?" I asked.

"Yes, Daniel, I'm afraid she is."

I felt a familiar rush of excitement. "How did she die?" I asked bluntly.

"She was involved in an accident."

"What kind of accident?"

"It was a car accident." To this point, Miss Pawson was showing much more patience than usual. I guess it was the situation.

"What happened?"

"I don't have any more details, I'm afraid Daniel. Not that it's polite to ask too many questions at times like this."

For once, I knew when to shut up, but that didn't mean I wasn't completely fascinated.

All day, playground talk was about death and in particular the death of Dominic Austen's mother. Many mistruths were being passed around about what happened when cars crashed. The children in older years were spreading more graphic rumours, introducing us to terms such as drink driving and decapitation.

I had a lot of questions for my own mother when I got home.

"You're not going to die are you, Mummy? You're not going to visit my grandparents soon are you?"

"I certainly hope not," she said, not really comfortable discussing her own demise.

"Does that mean you're not planning on visiting them and leaving me?"

"It's not something you choose to do."

"But I thought your mummy and daddy chose to go to heaven."

"No, no. It's not like that."

"Does that mean I could die at any moment?"

How do you explain that to a six year old?

With difficulty. Mum tried, but I wound up more confused than before. I now knew that death was definitely a bad thing and that my mum was not happy that her parents had died. I knew that it was possible for me to die, and I knew for sure that no-one was happy that Dominic's mother was dead, even if she was in a better place. But I still didn't grasp as much as I wanted to.

By the end of our Q&A session I was sufficiently terrified of death. Mum must have been concerned by her performance because Dad sat me down for a longer discussion the next day. He made more sense. He explained that at some point we would all die and that although it was a sad thing, it was a fact of life.

"Why do people get all upset when they hear that someone is going to die?" I asked him.

"Because we don't want other people to die. We don't want to die ourselves."

"It's very exciting, isn't it Daddy?"

"That's one way of putting it."

"Were you upset when your mummy and daddy died?"

"In a way," he replied, and he too shut up.

I realised at this stage that it was alright to talk about death providing I didn't mention my grandparents.

3.

It was two weeks before Dominic came back to school. The

day before he was due to return, Miss Pawson sat us down and explained that we were to be as kind to him as we possibly could.

"He's going to need you all to be supportive. Don't ask him questions about what has happened, but if he wants to talk about it, let him."

"How will we know?" I asked.

Miss Pawson ignored me and carried on addressing the class. "If he appears upset, offer him some comfort but come and let me know."

"Are we allowed to mention death to him at all?"

"It's probably best not to, Daniel," she sighed.

"But if he mentions it – "

"I very much doubt he'll be mentioning it," Miss Pawson replied unsurely. I was growing accustomed to reading hesitation in adults. It was like when my parents talked about my grandparents, I knew that there was something missing. So from Miss Pawson's voice, I ascertained that there was still a chance that Dominic might wish to talk about it.

I sat there quietly, but privately I was looking forward to Dominic's return.

I loved the way the classroom went quiet as Dominic's father led him in the next day. They had decided to reintroduce him after morning playtime, probably so he didn't get accosted in the yard when we were all out there.

"Dominic! Lovely to see you!" Miss Pawson said as if it were a complete surprise. She was unnervingly jovial and Dominic told me later that he knew that she was just pretending to be nice to him because his mummy was dead. The class remained quiet until Miss Pawson told us to carry on with whatever we were doing.

I couldn't help but look at him. There was something so magnificent about the grief that I could see written all over his face. Dominic had always been a fairly quiet, anonymous member of the class. But he came back looking different – slightly ravaged by a wider world that we knew nothing about.

"I don't think he's alright," I said to Alex quietly. "He definitely needs a friend."

Dominic had a couple of close friends in the class, both of whom appeared ill-equipped to deal with what had happened to him. He sat on their table with them, but they had taken Miss Pawson's advice too literally and barely uttered a word to him.

All of my conversation was about Dominic that morning, and I think Alex tired of it. Such is the attitude of the seven year old, that he probably thought he was going to lose his best friend. He was certainly more reluctant to approach Dominic than I was, but he joined me at my behest.

We went to see him after we had eaten lunch. I remember this being my idea, because to have gone and had lunch with him might have seemed too obvious. It's strange to think back on my actions at that age as deliberate, but there was definitely a motive and a plan behind what I was doing. It was a crude and contrived plan, but it was certainly the right one. It was one of the few times that I approached a classmate without Alex leading the way.

"How are you, Dominic?" I asked him. "We were very sorry to hear about your mummy."

Dominic's eyes instantly welled up, but he managed not to cry. "I'm sorry too," he said simply. "It's really weird without her."

"It's very sad," I concurred, struggling with what to say. "Alex's grandad died last summer."

In adulthood, such shameless use of a friend's bereavement would have been condemned without any further thought. In the laws of infant school, it was a valid method because it worked. Dominic and I bonded that lunch time, and he talked to us about what had happened and how things were at home. A dinner lady tried to intervene at one point, but left us alone because she could see that it was actually doing some good. It would have been terrible for him to lose his mother, and then to return to school and be treated differently by all of his friends. That we weren't ignoring what had happened to him was enough for him to want to hang around with us.

It was such a successful approach that Dominic asked whether he could be moved to sit with us in class that afternoon. Naturally, Miss Pawson agreed, although I can imagine that she was hesitant about letting my influence anywhere near him.

4.

It all sounds so deliberate and calculating – it must be the way I'm telling it – but the reality was slightly less sinister. My interpretation of the dramas that I watched with my mother was that they were exciting moments of life that were presented to us for entertainment. They were different to cartoons because they contained real people, and in my mind this meant that it was all completely genuine. I had no reason to suspect that these people were acting, and I had no idea that the whole thing was scripted. I didn't trouble to think how these depictions of real life came to be.

By becoming Dominic's friend I was trying to get in on the action, and had I been right I would have earned myself a lot of screen time. There were many incidents on Dominic's rocky road to normality, although most of them just involved him crying when something reminded him that his mum had just died.

I was by his side when he called a dinner lady a "stupid cow-face" after she enquired as to why he wasn't eating his pudding. I looked on in horror as he kicked Hannah Forsyth in the shin when she wouldn't share her crayons with him. I was sent out to talk to him after he burst into tears during story-time when a character was called Pam, just like his mum had been. I spoke to him on the telephone for five minutes each night, making sure that he was alright.

Both of my parents were impressed with the level of compassion I was showing towards my new friend, and they must have been thrilled at the prospect of a morally sound son. They encouraged the friendship and showed a great deal of sympathy towards Mr Austen.

"Can he come over and play after school one night?" I asked my parents one evening. I liked Dominic, but the main reason for me having him over was so that I would get an invite in return. I was itching to see what life was like for him outside of school, and I was even more desperate to see where all of the action was taking place.

After a successful evening at my house, I was invited back to Dominic's. I was so excited over the course of that week; it was as if I were heading off to Disneyland. In my mind I had all sorts of ideas of how things would be. The house would be dark and untidy. Dominic's father would sit in the living room, unshaven and drinking whisky straight from the bottle. His sister would sit in her room crying, and Dominic would wander from room to room looking lost. Arguments would erupt from nowhere as everyone took Mrs Austen's death out on each other.

I was viciously disappointed to find a family moving on with their lives. The fish fingers were prepared with motherly expertise, and Dominic's sister didn't even have puffy red eyes. The place was tidy and the atmosphere pleasant. There was no threat of an argument. In fact, the family seemed extremely close in light of the tragedy. Mr Austen didn't even flinch when I asked him whether he missed his wife.

Being at Dominic's was no different than being at any other house, and I felt quite put out by this. It was like getting to Disneyland, and discovering it was just another Wacky Warehouse. I was disappointed in Dominic. It tarnished the way I viewed our friendship.

Real life just wasn't packaged the same as television, and

I was starting to see this. Nothing of my friendship with Dominic had lived up to my expectations, and I just saw him as a huge let down. I'd decided to dissociate myself from him well before my dad came to pick me up.

5.

When you're in infant school, it's not that easy to get rid of your friends. You have years left of being in the same class for a start, and even with the limited social awareness that I had, I knew that it wasn't right just to ditch the kid whose mother had recently died. Six year olds don't go through the gradual drift that adults do – either they're friends or they hate each other.

I initially tried to ignore Dominic, which made him cry and, in turn, Miss Pawson angry with me. For a few days I carried on as if nothing was wrong, whilst I struggled to work out how to stop being his friend.

The answer came to me from television. One evening, Mum and I were watching one of the soaps. I remember that it was on at half past seven because I always had to get into my pyjamas before it started so that I'd be ready to go straight to bed when the credits rolled. For three nights a week this would be my bedtime story and each day would end on a cliffhanger that I could hardly have understood.

In the programme there was a fight in the pub, preceded by the silence that real drama commanded. The fight was caused by one man saying something horrible about another man's wife. Mum liked me to ask questions about the things that I saw as it backed up her belief that these dramas were educational. She had become engrossed by the soaps herself and would have struggled to stop watching them if I'd suddenly lost interest.

Dad still had no idea that Mum and I did this. He was busy working at the hotel in the evenings and setting up a restaurant with Charles Proctor during the day time. I saw him often enough, but my time was predominantly spent with Mum whilst he went out to build a life for us all. It was harmless, but Mum just didn't think that Dad would approve, especially as they had strived to keep me away from television during my infancy.

"Why are they fighting?" I asked.

"Because that man was mean to him," Mum explained. "Not that you should do that, even if you hate someone."

"Does he hate him for what he said?"

"Yes, because he said something that he knew would hurt him."

That was my eureka moment.

I went into school the next day armed with a plan and a killer line. I said little to Dominic all morning, pretending instead to be fascinated by everything that Alex and Lauren said. Understandably, by morning play-time Dominic was a little concerned and asked me if I was alright.

"I'm not sure I want to be friends any more," I told him, exactly as I had planned to.

Dominic's eyes welled up as he asked me, "Why not?"

"I don't know," I shrugged and said nothing else. Dominic turned to walk away from me before he started to cry properly. "That's right," I called after him, "go tell your mummy!"

Upon hearing my line, Dominic turned from distraught to implacable in seconds. He ran at me and began hitting me in a flailing fashion that came from nothing but pure rage. Someone yelled 'fight' and suddenly seven years' worth of schoolchildren were gathered around to witness what could only have amounted to some wrestling and a couple of kicks.

Mr Poulton – who would be my third year teacher – was on playground duty that morning, and it was he who broke up the fight before sending Dominic and me to the head-teacher. We received stern words, but there were no serious repercussions.

I insisted that Dominic must have misheard me and the dressing down was diffused. We shook on it and promised to make friends, make friends, never ever break friends, but this was merely an aesthetic gesture. Dominic and I had little else to do with each other for the remainder of our time at Gregson Lane Primary School.

I felt no sadness about what had happened. All I could think about was the fight. The fight! It had been something special. It was my introduction to aggression, and the first 'bad thing' that my parents had been unable to shield me from. Walking back from the head-teacher's office, my heart was pounding and I was grinning from ear to ear. I tried to compose myself as I went back to class.

"I think you just love the drama," Miss Pawson sniped at me. I didn't quite know what she meant, but I liked the sound of it.

Tendencies

1.

When you're young, you take on the world with the opinion that you know everything until proven otherwise. Of course, we can't remember most of our misconceptions because they're replaced with facts. We believe in all sorts – tooth fairies, men in the moon, talking toads and badgers. We believe that the world is no bigger than our hometowns and that Wales is abroad. We take Bible stories literally and assume that our school friends will be our friends for life. We've had to learn everything we know, but it's hard to say how and when we learned most things. We believe as we see unless we are told otherwise, and that was how it was with me and television.

Long before television was deluged with every feasible combination of reality programme, I thought the fiction I saw was the truth. It was this side of life that engaged me, rather than inane, everyday happenings.

I loved the stories on television, and as a result I started to enjoy reading books as well, which pleased my parents no end. By the time I reached the end of infant school, I was reading books that were designed for kids in high school. They were fundamentally different to television stories because I had to do all the imagining myself. So books were fiction, but television was reality.

The more I write about it, the more it seems peculiar that

we kept this from Dad for so long. He did genuinely dislike television – he thought that it rotted the brain – but he wouldn't have forbidden Mum and me from watching it. He didn't threaten me when I was growing up, or really get mad about stupid things, but the way I'm telling this story, you would think he was a threatening force. When he did find out, he really wasn't angry at all. Not about that, anyway.

He probably would have been concerned had he asked me what I thought about television at the time. He would have heard me say that it was the best bits of life put out to entertain everyone. Then I would have said how much I wished that life was like television because television was exciting, and my life was boring. I'm sure parenting is just full of ironies like this.

Perhaps if I'd known about my dead grandparents' remarkable collective demise, or about my psycho Auntie Anne, then I wouldn't have been so enthralled by the dramas occurring on television. At least I would have known that life can be *that* exciting. But enough of the excuses. I promised myself I wouldn't litter this with excuses, and I don't think my parents put a foot wrong in my upbringing. Sometimes I just struggle to make sense of it all, and that is just one of many 'logical' explanations I have for my life.

2.

My perception of television was altered forever when I made a childish faux pas in front of my mum. We were watching an Australian soap, which ended abruptly with one girl trying to choose between two boys.

"They can't just stand there until tomorrow," I said as the credits rolled. "Will they sleep?"

In and amongst her hysterics, Mum managed to inform me that it wasn't real.

"What do you mean?" I asked irritably, as if she were saying the most ridiculous thing I'd ever heard, which at that point it was.

"They're actors," she told me. "It's just a drama."

"I know that, stupid," I replied precociously.

"Dramas aren't real. They're like the school play, but with proper actors."

"Actors are people that are filmed for television," I said by means of contradiction.

"And act on stages. It's basically playing a game. That's what I teach children to do."

"At school?"

"And in the summer, when you spend more time at Alex's house."

"Do you act, Mummy?"

"Only for school these days. I used to act on a stage."

"Do you sometimes act now, Mummy? Are we ever on television?"

It took many more questions before I fully understood, by which point acting sounded like something I wanted to do.

I pleaded with Mum to let me go to her summer school that year, so that I could hang around with the actors. She eventually relented but said I could only watch, and not get involved. That was enough for me. Alex came along to keep me entertained, not that I needed entertaining.

It was a low key affair, but the point of the programme was for the kids to come up with a play by the end of the course. They had to write it, cast it and perform it. At the end of the three weeks they received a video of the play. It was aimed at the children heading into their GCSE years, to give them practice at big drama projects, but it attracted children from all five years of the high school.

No acting took place on the first day. It was all about getting to know each other and brain-storming. So they did ice-breaking in the morning and then Mum got them thinking about what sort of a show they wanted to put on. They all sat in a circle whilst Alex and I sat observing from the stage of the school hall. Mum had told me to pretend that I was a man who couldn't speak for the duration of the school. I knew she was trying to trick me, but I was more interested in just watching the process of creating drama.

The group decided upon a play about bullying. I remember the older ones being more vocal about what should happen than the younger ones, who seemed to just get swept away in the excitement of creating something. They wanted to target the people who see bullying but ignore it for whatever reason. One child played a victim, and they would be on their own in a playground. Hanging around in the background, silently observing, were fifteen of the young actors. A group of three children bounded on stage and commenced bullying the victim-child. One by one, each of the silent observers joined the group to throw an insult at the victim-child, who was visibly getting more distressed. He cried out more and more until he finally shouted out "Nooooooooooo!" The lights went dark and when they returned, the child was on his own, with the observers back in the background, this time with their backs to him. One by one, they turned around, and looked to see if the bullies had gone. When they realised it was safe, they crowded around the boy and tried to help him, saying that the bullies were horrible.

"By then it's too late!" booms a narrator. "Don't turn your back on bullying."

It was very cheesy, but there have been worse government infomercials over the years.

The three weeks building up to the play were a frenzy of activity and excitement. Alex and I watched every day as they developed scripts, and held auditions, and gave roles back-stage to the particularly talentless ones. Between them they built a set and developed a play. The older children took the lead roles, whilst the younger ones were the observers, each trusted with one line each. Mum even taught them how to do lighting to make sure it looked like a proper play.

It was a thrilling few weeks for me and Alex, and we became the mascots of the room. They'd talk to us when they were having breaks and I guess it was my first brush with celebrity. I was in awe of them. They were all so grown up and I was being given an insight into how drama was made.

Parents were invited to an early evening showing of the play to prove to them that it was worth handing over a sum of money to keep their children entertained over the summer holidays. There was an audience of about forty gathered; it seemed like a large and buzzing crowd to me, though.

Alex and I were allowed to hang out backstage, which was really just the corridor to the PE department. People were getting nervous, trying to be like real actors I imagine. It was fun to be around them and feel part of it. Confusion started to build when the child-victim didn't appear. Mum asked around and no-one had heard anything. Eventually the child-victim's mother appeared and told everyone that her son had fallen ill and wouldn't be able to make it.

Everyone started to complain and ask what they should do. "Does anyone know his lines?" people started to shout out, but most had been concentrating on their individual parts and hadn't thought to listen to the rest of the play. Mum hadn't cast an understudy – a matter she wouldn't forget in subsequent years.

"Daniel does!" Alex piped up and all eyes on the room turned to me. "He can say the whole thing." It was true. I had been glued to the rehearsals and was word perfect on the play from start to finish.

Mum didn't look too sure, but there were twenty-five people in that room fighting my corner. Within minutes she was won round and all of a sudden I was about to take the lead role in a play.

I don't remember being nervous when I took to the stage.

The curtains had been drawn so the room was pitch black, bar the stage lighting and the small red lights emanating from recording camcorders. I knew all of the directions and exactly what to do. I had three Christmas plays under my belt, so a room full of expectant parents didn't faze me in the slightest.

I went through the beginning of the play, wandering around innocently. Then the bullies appeared and they seemed so much bigger all of a sudden. One by one, more and more children gathered to shout abuse, and I started to forget what I was meant to say. I'm sure my memory exaggerates the silence that filled the room as I struggled to remember my lines.

I couldn't tell whether the children were acting angry at me, or whether they were getting angry because I was forgetting my lines. I felt alone and scared and I couldn't see my mum out there in the dark. I was seven years old, and suddenly all these bigger kids were menacing, so I wet myself onstage in front of all those people. Realising my mistake, I ran off in a flood of tears to the sound of sympathy from the audience and giggling onstage.

Somehow, they got to the end of the play. One of the other children stepped in and improvised the rest of the lines, and they all got a standing ovation. I seem to recall being told that someone slipped in my puddle of piss, but I wasn't there to see it. I was sat crying outside the PE block, believing that my entire world had collapsed. Alex came out to look after me, and soon after Mum was there as well. She called for Robyn to collect us and I was taken away without ever having to face those people again. I didn't care about the parents, but I had enjoyed hanging out with the older children. It made me feel like a grown up, and I knew that I had done the most childish thing in front of them. They had laughed and I had lost their respect forever.

I wouldn't take part in drama until I was at high school. My parents wrote to the school and requested that I not appear in any more Christmas plays after I spent nearly a week having tantrums on the matter. That experience scarred me enough to never want to do it again. It haunts me to think that there are still possibly twenty-five people out there that possess a video of me pissing myself.

3.

From then on I spurned the limelight. I have never craved popularity and I've only ever wanted a small but amazing group of friends. Other people didn't really interest me unless something exciting was happening to them. As that was almost never, there didn't seem much point in trying to enamour myself to classrooms full of kids. I lay low for the summer, engrossing myself in a reading scheme for children at my local library, spending my days enjoying the lives of others instead of mine.

Word got around about the pant wetting incident in a way I can't explain. I assume it involved word of mouth from the older kids to their younger siblings and eventually back to my school. Or maybe Alex just told people. This meant that I wasn't deemed cool as we entered junior school. Quite lucky that I didn't want to be popular, really. As far as school went, Alex and Lauren were good enough for me. Nothing special, just a boy friend and a girl friend. It was nice and balanced.

Junior school entailed more work than infants. I was an attentive pupil this time, but no less inquisitive. I'm sure the teachers must have talked about me in the staff room, and word had come from the infant teachers that I was something of a little shit. All of my junior school teachers treated me warily and tried to control my questions in the early stages of the academic year. Fact is, though, that I was a good pupil and they couldn't be seen to be stifling an enquiring mind.

I started to enjoy creative writing the best, as it was my opportunity to write stories. I was writing them at home, so it kind of felt like extra leisure time in school. My stories were all simple. No more than two hundred words and they were all direct rip offs of things that I had seen on television.

The stuff I wrote in school was toned down, as we were restricted in what we could write about. It was usually 'What I Did Last Weekend', or 'A Day at the Zoo'.

A Day at the Zoo
By Daniel Lizar (aged 9)

Last week me and my class went to the zoo. When we got there we went in the entrance and there were lots of animals. There were tigers and lions and camels. We ate a packed lunch on some grass. It rained. Then we saw a seal do tricks. It was very funny. Then we all got on the bus and came home. I had a great day and so did everyone else. I liked the zoo.

I still have some of my creative writing books from that time, but I only have one or two of the stories I wrote at home. This was one of them.

The Boy Who Ran Away
By Daniel Lizar (aged 10)

There was a boy called Mark. He was fat and sad and no-one liked him. He was picked on at school and he had no friends. He was stupid as well. His mummy and daddy argued a lot. Some nights they threw plates at each other. One night Mark woke up and he heard his mummy and daddy having a fight. He went downstairs and he saw his daddy hit his mummy. Mark was frightened so he ran away. He ran across a busy road and hid in the park. When his mummy realised she called the police and started to cry. His daddy went out looking for him. He ran and shouted for Mark and Mark heard him but he was frightened of his daddy and hid behind a bush. It was dark and Mark was frightened. But then a man came and asked Mark if he would like some sweets. Mark was hungry so he took the sweets. Then the man asked if Mark would like to get into his car. It was raining so Mark said yes because he was scared of his daddy. Mark went to the stranger's car and no-one ever saw him again. All that was left was one of his shoes and a patch of oil from the stranger's car.

I've amended the spelling, but changed none of the words. I knew my teachers would be cross with me if I wrote these stories in school, but I really enjoyed writing them. As I progressed through junior school, I became disenchanted with the creative writing we had to do in the classroom. Like most of life, it just seemed boring to me.

4.

It's strange that it took me so long to rock the boat with regards to my stories. I was writing at home from my second year juniors, and managed to keep my bleaker tales away from my schoolbooks for many years. The problem is that most kids don't really want to write many stories, and they certainly don't want to challenge themselves as writers. They were quite happy to write about their weekends or thrill themselves with a scary yarn about a witch. That wasn't enough for me.

I liked telling proper stories and making up characters, and in turn making bad and dramatic things happen to them. This wasn't the sort of thing that you did last weekend.

By my last year, though, my rebellious streak was starting to kick in and I had finally bored of the system. It was a traditional project for the children in the top year of juniors to prepare a short story book for the children in the top year of infants. They had an A4 sheet of coloured card folded in two as a cover, with a picture stuck on the front on slightly smaller white paper, and on the back was a short blurb. Something like 'Erica the Witch wants to play, but she has no friends. What will she do?' Inside were sheets of paper with words on one side, and a picture on the opposite side that opened up and read like a proper book. The whole affair was held together with treasury tags and probably looked quite rubbish in hindsight.

I was assigned to a boy called Martin, who I remember being some pasty little ginger kid of the anaemic variety. He was very scrawny and I'm sure that he wouldn't have made it through high school without catching the eye of a bully or two. I met him before I wrote the book to find out what sort of things he liked. I had to take three things he liked and put them into the story. He liked cars, rockets and his mummy.

Knowing that anything beyond a charming tale would never make it past the scrutiny of the teachers, I had to be a little bit devious in my approach. In school, I joined in with my classmates in creating a fluffy story with a happy ending. At home, I was working in parallel, making a second, edgier storybook. In my years of soap watching, I had encountered many concepts, especially about the things that generated misery. Some of them I understood quite well, like affairs and stealing. Others were more grey areas, but I knew the terms and I knew what shocked my mother.

I took double card, and double paper, and double treasury tags and put one set into my bag. I told Mum and Dad that I was just doing my homework for school. I told them they couldn't see the book until it was finished, and because they thought I was being cute they had no reason to question me. I don't think I was being malicious; I was just trying to save them the effort of being angry at me.

The school version involved a ginger boy who built a car that when it got really fast it turned into a rocket, and he flew to the moon in it with his mummy. I believe it ended by them flying back to earth and having fish fingers for their tea. I was told that it was great and that Martin was going to love it. I smiled back at them, and allowed myself a mischievous grin when they looked away, just like I'd seen them do on television.

That was the way I saw the plan – it was just a little something I was doing. It was a plot with characters and a deception, and something of a climax. The climax was to be the last day of the Easter term, when we were to go and read the story-books to our infants. My alternative storybook was in my bag, and it wasn't difficult to swap them over once Mrs Proctor had handed them out.

Of all of my junior school teachers, I liked being taught by Robyn the best. She knew me better than all of the others and she didn't treat me with the indifference or annoyance displayed by most of her colleagues. She was used to my questions and we had the rapport resultant of her being there during the entirety of my life. It was a good year at school for me; on the whole I got in less trouble than I had in previous years and Robyn never sent me out of class.

They had decided that the most beneficial way to do this was to make my class read our stories to the infants as a group, so we each were to take it in turns with our tale, telling the class who it was for and what things we included in it.

One by one my classmates sat at the front of the room with their infant and read their stories. They involved racing cars, or going to the beach, or having an adventure with friends. They all involved happy endings with the one loose end holding the story together all tied up. I watched on with bored indifference, just knowing intuitively that I had the most exciting story.

My turn rolled around alphabetically and I stepped up. "My story is for Martin," I announced and Martin stood up and came and sat at the front of group. "Martin likes rockets, cars and his mummy and these things are all in the story.

"Once upon a time there was a boy called Martin who lived at home with his mummy and his daddy. He was happy and they were all happy." I turned the book to show everyone the first picture – a boy, a Mummy, a Daddy and a house. "Every night Martin's Mummy drove him home from school," I looked up to Robyn and Mr Poulton at this point, pausing to show that I had subtly included another one of Martin's favourite things. They looked on approvingly as I showed the class the picture of the car, and I continued. Martin was smiling giddily, so happy to be the star of his very own story.

"When they got home Martin would have spaghetti shaped like rockets on toast for his dinner and rocket ice lollies for pudding. Martin loved rockets. Martin loved to draw rockets and he wanted to be a rocket driver when he was older. He wished his mummy would buy him a rocket for his birthday." This was accompanied by a picture of Martin with a rocket inside a thought bubble.

"On the night before his birthday Martin's Mummy said she had to go out to the shop. I know, thought Martin, she's gone out to buy me a rocket." This picture was similar to the last, but this time Martin had an exclamation mark over his head. "He sat in the living room with his daddy excitedly waiting for his mummy to return with the rocket. His mummy was gone for ages and Martin's Daddy started to get worried. Martin thought that the rocket must be hard to get into the car." The picture here was of a rocket on top of a car. This was the part where Martin was meant to get a toy rocket for his birthday and live happily ever after.

"When she came home Martin's Mummy came in crying. I've been raped, she said," and I looked up to show my picture of Martin's Mummy crying. The whole classroom was staring at me with looks of abject horror, just knowing that I had said something bad, even though the majority of us had no idea what rape was.

5.

I admit it – I fucked up. Things were going well for me if I thought about it. I was on the cusp of leaving primary school and becoming one of the big boys, and as the years had passed, my quality of life had been getting better and better. Dad and Charles' restaurant had proved to be a huge success, and whilst I was in juniors, they opened two more – one in Preston, and one in Southport.

When I was in Year Four we moved into a four bedroom cottage in Galgate, a village just outside Lancaster. It meant moving away from the Proctors, but only for six months. They snapped up a property just round the corner from ours. The fortunes of our families were running in tandem.

Living in a village meant our parents gave us more freedom to roam. We were allowed to play out on our bikes and I would always make up dramatic adventures for us to act out. They were usually emulations of scenes that I had seen on the television, especially the Australian soaps where the more weird and wonderful things tended to happen. We'd pretend to be trapped in burning buildings, or in earthquakes or land-slides. In the woods we would pretend we had been kidnapped, or lost in the bush, or we'd pretend the stream was a dangerous river that we would have to cross. It was the sort of place that facilitated these games. When Lauren played, the stories would take a romantic turn, whilst never explicitly leading to Alex or I kissing her.

"Let's pretend that Lauren has been cheating on Alex with me and Alex has just found out. We'll walk over there holding hands, and you'll be on the other side of the road and you see us and shout 'You bastard!'"

They were simple but dramatic little scenes and I could happily spend hours arranging them. Many days were passed this way. I couldn't just sit and write little stories all of the time. Playing football or other sports was of no interest to me, and the general playground games like hop-scotch, tig and conkers seemed banal compared to the things I came up with. Normal pursuits just didn't appeal to me like they did with a lot of other kids.

Nothing of interest really happened to me. My family didn't

struggle for anything. We took increasingly nice holidays where we saw plenty of things and met some new people, but I came back with no out of the ordinary happenings. It was a normal childhood in every way, from what I can tell. It's hard to know what compelled me to try and spoil things like that.

6.

My parents were called to the school immediately. Robyn had made the call and insisted that it was urgent. I had been whisked out of the class shortly after she had composed herself sufficiently to respond to what had happened.

"What's raped?" Martin had asked.

Robyn grabbed me roughly and I was taken into the corridor, with Mr Poulton close behind.

"Daniel, where did you learn such a word?" she asked, firmly but not angrily.

"You filthy little brat!" Mr Poulton bellowed at me (he'd always thought I was trouble). "What am I supposed to say to that class?"

Realising I was in serious trouble, I started to cry.

"No tears, Lizar, not this time," Mr Poulton continued. Pupils like me were a perfect excuse for him to vent his frustrations. "You'll be going to the head-teacher and you'll be telling him exactly what you put at the end of your story."

"I'll take him," Robyn said.

"If I find out he's got off lightly, I'll be lodging a complaint," I remember him saying. "I know you're friends with his mother." With that he strode back into the chaos of over fifty children wanting to know what rape was.

Robyn bombarded me with questions on the way to the head-teacher's office and I gave her very few answers. I said I didn't know where I had heard of rape, but really it had been on a soap only a few weeks before. Some woman had been coming back from the pub on her own, when a shadow stepped out from an alleyway. Minutes later she was seen stumbling through her front door in tears, and for weeks afterwards she would cry and tell people that she had been raped. It seemed like a pretty bad thing to happen to a woman, so I guess I was right in that respect.

This was definitely the angriest I had seen the head-teacher. Robyn explained to him what had happened and he just got redder and redder. It was a hard story to explain, and Robyn struggled to get the last bit out.

"What did he say at the end of the story, Mrs Proctor?"

"He said, that Martin's Mummy came home and said she had been raped," the same silence filled the room. The silence that preceded thunderous anger.

"Eleven year old boys should not know about rape! Call his parents now!"

And that was when Robyn called Mum and Dad. I was made to wait outside the head-teacher's office whilst he and Robyn talked about what had happened. I heard him shouting occasionally whilst I fought back the tears. I was terrified this time. Never had my parents been called down to the school before.

I was waiting for a good forty-five minutes, which was excruciatingly long for an anxious eleven year old. I felt no better when I saw the concerned look on my parents' faces as they approached the office.

"Mrs Proctor brought Daniel to me today to show me the storybook he made for one of his schoolmates in the infants," the head-teacher said when we were called in. "This was a school project and he used the opportunity to make a book full of obscenities."

My father asked to see the book, ready to leap to my defence. I watched as he and Mum read through the story, not finding anything to be outraged by. Then they opened the last page and I assume that the word 'raped' just leapt out at them. Until that moment, I had counted on their support in this matter, but like the colour from their faces, their solidarity drained away very quickly. My mother let go of my hand, which she had been holding covertly since we had sat down. She looked at me briefly and I looked away.

"Where the hell did you hear a word like that?" Dad said to me, much more firmly than I was used to. I didn't answer; I just looked away from him as well.

"Is it a word you hear the children use very often?" Mum asked innocently.

"Not really, I have to say that your son is the first," the head-teacher sneered.

"He didn't get it from us," Dad replied. He sounded irked, but kept his cool well.

"Well it certainly isn't part of the curriculum at Gregson Lane," affirmed the head-teacher.

"Where did you get it from?" Mum asked me. Then I think it dawned on her.

"I just saw it on the television," I said. I was defeated completely and this was my only line of defence. "I don't know what raped is."

My parents and the head-teacher agreed that I should be punished for my actions in the school. I had to apologise to both classes and explain that I shouldn't write about horrible things that I didn't understand. The teachers had the Easter holidays to hope that all of the children had forgotten about rape by the time we returned. I was banned from sports day, which wasn't exactly a punishment for me, and I was given two weeks' worth of lunch time lines.

My father assured the school that I would be punished further at home. He was disappointed in a way that was completely novel to me at the time. The moment I said that I had seen it on television, he knew that he was misguided in defending me so vehemently to the head-teacher. "I had no idea that Daniel was watching those sorts of programmes,"

Dad informed him, as if they were suddenly on the same side. "I don't get to spend much time with him in the evenings. I'm afraid that side of things has been left to his mother."

Mum looked as guilty as I did. Nothing was said all the way home. I could tell that there were many things that Dad wanted to ask, and I knew that I had ruined mine and Mum's little secret, so I hoped that the silence would last as long as possible.

Repercussions

1.

By the time we got home from school I knew that the day's troubles were far from over. I was sent to my room the moment we got in.

"I'll talk to you later," my father said. I slunk upstairs with no further protest, and lay on my bed with the door open, listening to them row for the first time.

"I just don't understand," I heard Dad shout. "Why all the secrecy?"

"I didn't think you'd approve," Mum answered.

"I wouldn't have approved, you're quite right, but like everything else we could have discussed it."

"I know, but I didn't tell you at first and then I didn't know when to tell you."

"How long has this been going on for?"

Mum paused for a long time at this point. I don't know whether she was reluctant to say, or whether she had to work it out. Eventually, she answered tentatively, "About six years."

Dad exploded. "Six years! You've been subjecting our son to images of rape and violence for six years?"

"No, it wasn't like that. Most of the episodes are pretty tame. It's been helping with his learning. It raises questions."

"For example, what is rape?"

"He usually asks about the tricky stuff."

"We're meant to be in this together. That's how we said we were going to be after all that stuff with our families."

"You're making too much of this."

"Of you lying to me? I ask you about your day, every day, and at no point did you think to say, well Daniel and I watched a woman get raped for entertainment this evening. You could have spoken up about this at any point, Jacqui."

"I know, I'm sorry. I didn't think it was doing any harm."

"Or was it that you enjoyed having a special relationship with him?"

"Oh I have that already," Mum suddenly turned. "It's not like you're around for him most of the time."

"I've only ever been out there trying to make something of this family."

"I know, I shouldn't have said that." The flash-point was quickly diffused. "But because I've been the one doing most of the raising, and certainly taking control of the emotional interaction, I've had to make certain decisions."

"I wouldn't have been unreasonable."

"Now it's out there it seems so stupid," Mum said, and they began to talk reasonably like they normally did. I had to move to the top of the stairs to hear them, ready to launch back into my room if the situation required it. Mum explained how it had started.

"And most people would have approved of that, wouldn't they?" he asked and I could sense the conversation turning again. I guess Mum nodded at this point. "But I'm not exactly one to approve of home-made models of child development, am I?"

"Don't blame yourself," Mum offered, rather foolishly really. "On some level at least it was to protect you. You clearly have issues with your childhood and your family, that's why you keep Alfred and Jennifer at arm's length."

"I don't see you taking Daniel to visit Anne in prison, do I?"

"That's different and you know it."

"We both drew a line under the past when Daniel arrived, and here you are using it against me."

"Oh come on, Malcolm, we both know you're repressed. You can't honestly believe that you haven't changed since your parents died?"

Things went quiet from then on. When I ascertained that there was nothing else to hear, I went back to my room and lay on my bed, waiting for the trouble that was still to come. My head was awash with all of the things that my parents had alluded to in their argument. It was a shame I was in no position to ask questions.

2.

After a couple of hours of now calm conversation, Mum and Dad remembered that they had left their son stewing in his room, awaiting an almighty bollocking. It was Dad who came to me, and I remember wishing that it had been Mum. I sensed that she was on my side, mainly because she seemed to be in as much trouble as I was.

To my surprise, Dad was the same as he always was when I did something naughty. The change I had noticed in him seemed to have dissipated and I knew to expect a calm explanation.

"Daniel, you know you did something bad today don't you?"

I nodded.

"Do you know what that thing was?"

I shook my head and started to cry. Dad placed a hand on my arm, and I remember thinking how unusual it was for him to make contact with me.

"You put a bad word in that book. You understand that, right?"

I nodded, and grizzled a little.

"And you know what that word was?"

"Raped?" I replied.

"That's right. Raped is a bad word. It means to rape someone."

"To beat someone up?"

He took a breath. "No. It's to have sex with them without them wanting you to. Do you know what sex is?"

I didn't. I had heard the term both in the playground and on television, but I had no idea what it meant. Dad explained it to me without hesitation or embarrassment. He explained that it was how babies were made, and it was an act of a man joining together with a woman. I got some crazy notions at this point about a literal joining together which Dad put me straight on immediately. He said that whilst men had penises, women had vaginas, and that a man puts his penis into the vagina, and that was what he meant by joining together. I asked why on numerous occasions and he gave me lots of candid answers. By the end of it I had a basic grasp of what sex was, and to be honest I thought it was disgusting.

"Men and women should only have sex when both of them want to," Dad moved on to the main point. "If one doesn't want to and the other one makes them, well that's against the law. That's rape. So in your story, you said that a man forced his penis into Martin's mother's vagina when she didn't want him to. If that had really happened, it would be incredibly upsetting, and you shouldn't write stories about it."

I understood. In a way that had been the point of my story, but I hadn't known quite how horrible I was being. I had wanted to shock everyone and create a stir; I just didn't want to get into trouble for doing it. When I heard about it, though, rape did sound horrible and I was very sorry that I had included it in the story. I thought that between us we had established that I wasn't really to blame for what happened because I didn't know the extent of what I was saying. I wanted to do the right thing and hopefully avoid trouble completely. I figured that Dad would tell the school I was innocent and they would all realise that there was no harm done.

"Should I say sorry to Martin's mum?" I asked.

"I think it's best not to make contact," Dad assured me. "But you are going to be grounded for the Easter holidays."

"What?" I protested. "But I didn't know what raped was!"

"No, but you did know that you'd put a bad word into your story on purpose," Dad pointed out. "You knew that it would upset a lot of people, and you've caused a great deal of trouble. And you won't be watching those programmes any more, either."

That was a real sucker-punch, and I was about to wail a series of protests, but I was interrupted by the door-bell ringing. Dad left me immediately to go and answer it. I walked downstairs as he answered the door in front of me in the hallway. I was surprised to see Lauren's father stood there.

"Would you care to explain to me why my daughter came home asking me about rape this evening?" he spat.

3.

Mr Bell was really angry. He always looked quite angry; I had noticed that about him. I used to think he was angry because he had been kicked out of home once and men didn't like to be kicked out of their homes, but I think he was just that sort of person. He wasn't well educated, but he had made some money in business, so he was kind of stupid but powerful, which manifested itself in aggression.

Dad invited him in and Mr Bell barged past him. He stopped in the hallway when he saw me stood on the stairs, looking tearful, and by this point rather frightened.

"There he is! You dirty little shit!" he bellowed at me and I let out a small whimper. Angry and stupid as he was, Mr Bell was a truly terrifying proposition. "What the fuck do you think you're doing going around saying things like that to my daughter?"

"Now listen, you can't just barge in here like this," Mum rushed out from the kitchen.

"Your son said he was going to rape my daughter!" Mr Bell shouted at Mum.

"Daniel, did you?" Mum asked me straight away, and I was offended by the implication.

"No. I only said raped once," although by now, I had said it many, many times.

"I think Lauren's been exaggerating," Mum said to him. "There was an incident, but Daniel has threatened no-one."

Mr Bell was not placated by the tamer reality of the situation. He had come round to our house to get mad, and he was determined not to leave disappointed.

"Whichever way you look at it, my daughter came home tonight asking me about rape, and that's because of your fucking son's filthy little mouth," he snapped.

"Mr Bell, you have sworn three times since you stormed in here, so I think you should be careful exactly what you criticise my son for." Mum said pointedly. I'd never heard her sound like a teacher before, and if I had been Mr Bell, I would have been a little scared.

"You don't speak to me like that," Mr Bell shouted back. "With jellyfish for parents, no wonder the boy is turning out to be tapped."

"Now that's enough!" Dad insisted. "You've said your piece and we're sorry if your daughter was upset by what happened."

"Irresponsible bloody parents. You need your kid taking away from you. When eleven year olds are bringing rape into the playground, there is something very, very wrong with the world. I'll be asking the school to expel the little scrote for the last term, and Lauren is going to be going to an all girls high school. And you," he turned to me, "will never see my daughter again."

It was enough of a victory for him and he strode out of the house, slamming the front door in his wake.

"Oh God," Dad sighed, "that man's going to make us notorious."

"He was very rude," I said.

"Go back to your room, Daniel. I don't really want to look at you right now," Dad said to me bluntly and he walked into the living room.

4.

I returned to my bedroom in a state of confusion. The day was taking so many twists that I was finding it a struggle to keep up. Mum and Dad closed the living room door, which meant there was no point in me trying to listen. I didn't know how long it would be before one of them came to see me again, so I decided to get out one of my exercise books.

I had three or four pads full of stories that I had written over the course of junior school, which contained the sum total of my private literary output. They were mainly stories about the children in my class, often written at times when they had annoyed me. That might have been some playground rudeness or someone getting to answer a question before me. More often than not, though, the stories were about children as a force of good versus the evil of teachers. This meant that most of my stories ended in some misfortune befalling the likes of Miss Pawson and Mr Poulton.

It was a simple process. Part one was to choose the character. The second part was to replicate something I'd seen on the television in a story form. This involved lots of people being punched, cheated on, hit by cars, murdered, collapsing, being electrocuted and so on. They were nothing more than a simple set up and a dramatic event on each story. Some stories required two or three parts, each with their own cliffhanger. That was how a story had to end for me, in a big dramatic moment.

There was one where Miss Pawson went into a coma after a car crash, and another I had written when I must have been cross with Alex about something. That had him falling off a cliff and being washed out to sea. Many of these stories ended in maiming, amputation and death.

I didn't bother to disguise the names of people, for as far as I was concerned they would never see them and therefore there wasn't a problem. I must have written a hundred of these stories whilst I was in junior school. Sometimes my selections weren't revenge. If someone cried in class, I would often think up a story that would explain why they were crying, be it divorcing parents, dying relatives or burglary.

Only two or three of these stories were written on loose sheets of paper. These were stories I had written when away on holiday. I didn't take the books with me in case anyone asked to see them.

Sat in my room leafing through the pages, I knew that my writing days were coming to an end, and that was almost as sad as being banned from watching television. I didn't feel that the day could get any worse, but then I didn't notice Mum entering the room.

5.

"What are those?" she asked.

I had made some feeble attempt to throw the notebooks under the bed when I noticed her, which just drew more attention to them. "Nothing," I lied the most hopeless of lies. Then I tried to distract her. "Does Dad mean it? About television?"

Mum nodded. "Your father is angry with both of us. He didn't like that we kept it from him."

"But he wouldn't have understanded," I replied. I was at least thirteen before I discovered that understanded wasn't a word.

"I think he would. I should have told him. I think he would have been right to have been concerned. Daniel, what you did today – "

"I know," I interjected. "It was stupid."

"Why did you do it?"

"I don't know," I said. And that was the truth by that point.

"Your father's angry because he thinks television is bad for you, and you've kind of proven that by doing what you did."

"But it was my fault, not television."

"Were it not for hearing it on television, you would never have used that word in your story."

"But I didn't know what raped meant."

"You knew it was bad. And you normally ask me about these things."

"But I heard it in the playground," I said, forgetting that I had already blamed television earlier that day.

"Don't lie to me, Daniel," Mum said firmly, but without raising her voice. I could sense the disappointment, though, and it's a special kind of guilt generated by a mother's disappointment. "It was on television only the other week. How would you have felt if someone had written that about me?"

Suddenly my thoughts turned to my smoking gun; the notebooks sticking out from underneath my bed. I must have cast them a guilty glance, because no sooner had I thought about them, Mum asked me again what I was hiding.

"Nothing."

She knelt down next to me.

"I hoped you and I were friends," she said to me, looking genuinely hurt.

"We are. We have fun together. You're a cool Mum."

"If you thought I was a cool Mum, you wouldn't lie to me," she said. There was nowhere left for me to manoeuvre. I passed her the notebooks.

We sat in silence as Mum read the first story. She looked at me with a mixture of confusion and disgust when she finished it. She read another story before flicking through the book and picking out another at random. She picked up another book and again chose a story at random, all the time not saying a word. She put that notebook down and didn't select another one. Instead she just looked at me, as if she were seeing me for the first time.

"I have no idea what your father is going to say about these. Daniel, these stories are horrible."

I started to cry again. "Please don't tell him," I begged desperately.

"I'm not going to keep things from him again. Daniel, this is a real issue. How long have you been writing these for?"

There wasn't a right answer and I was all out of lies, so I told her that it had been a few years.

"Oh, Daniel."

She just didn't know what else to say. Where was she supposed to start? To discover that your assumedly well-adjusted son has been writing poisonous stories about everyone he is irked by is a lot for a mother. It raises all sorts of questions.

Eventually Mum stood up, gathering the notebooks as she went. "Mum, no," I pleaded, but she said nothing and walked towards the door. Just for a fleeting moment the thought passed my mind that I should push her down the stairs to try and stop her, but I think some sense must have got to me, because I did no more than entertain it. I just called after her loudly; another error on my part as it alerted my father to the situation even sooner than he would have been.

"What's all the noise about?" he snapped, completely beyond being superhumanly calm. He looked at the notebooks in Mum's hands, and then up to me, bawling away at the top of the stairs. "Oh fuck," he said, and the curse-word hung in the air for quite some time.

I was sure that I was going to get hit, and I was pretty sure that I deserved it. It could have gone either way. He looked at my mother, who seemed ready to try and defend me, and I think that was it for him. He gave us both thunderous glances and stormed out of the house.

The silence after he left was louder than the one experienced between the three of us. Mum, I think, wanted to comfort me, but to absolve me from blame was completely beyond her.

6.

I went back to my room whilst Mum went into the living room to cry. I heard Dad's car drive away, and lay there in the dark waiting to hear him return.

I feared the worst. I feared that I had angered Dad so much that he wouldn't come back. I foresaw my parents divorcing and neither of them forgiving me for ruining their lives. I became convinced that they would have me adopted, or send me to live with some distant relative.

Dad could go speeding off and in all of his anger, he could crash his car. He could die. Or he could get mad and vengeful and set fire to the house. He might run off with one of the neighbours. I kind of understood betrayal, and how it led to other betrayals; in the heat of the moment, people were allowed to do regrettable things that they wouldn't usually get away with.

Then I started to imagine blue lights flashing through the curtains of my bedroom window, followed by an authoritative knock at the door. There would be two policemen and they would be bringing bad news with them.

I didn't even notice Mum come into my room with a bowl of soup and a couple of slices of toast.

"Here you go," she said, with the same flat tone she had been using with me since she had looked in my notebooks. The very same notebooks were under her arm. "This stops now," she said with a deadly seriousness that told me that defiance wasn't an option. Very slowly, she started to tear pages from the notebooks, not taking her eyes off me for a second.

She ripped up the stories in no particular order, taking special care to tear each page into at least four pieces before letting them drop to the floor. There was nothing I could say. I had already known that I would never see those stories again, but it was the end of years of work for me, and I struggled not to start crying again.

With near perfect timing, the last cover of the last notebook was sashaying to the floor when we both heard the sound of a car on the driveway. Mum's expression changed, and when she looked at me, it was with a fear that told me we were both in it together again. It was obvious neither of us were expecting Dad back. We breathed in unison, waiting not for the sound of keys in the door, but the sharp knock that would bring us the worst.

7.

We were so relieved to hear Dad walk through the door that we nearly forgot that he was angry with us. We rushed to the top of the stairs, but he had already made his way into the living room.

"Go to bed, Daniel," Mum said sternly to me, and our alliance was once again severed. I did exactly as I was told, mildly irked that I was to play no further part in proceedings.

It took me a while to go to sleep, as I was too busy listening to what my parents were saying in the living room. It was a conversation that filled me with horror. First of all Dad told Mum that he had been up into the hills for a drive and a think. Mum told him how worried she was, and how irresponsible he had been. Dad mocked the accusation, telling her that she didn't have much place to be calling him irresponsible.

The confrontation was quickly dispensed when Dad started making his demands.

"I want to see those stories."

"You can't, I ripped them all up."

"Protecting him again?" Dad replied.

"I just needed to do something. I didn't want them intact."

It was upon hearing this that I looked down to the fragments of my literature lying on my carpet. Hopping out of bed, I started picking through the remains. I realised very quickly that it was a futile effort; Mum had been very thorough in destroying my work. I was about to give up anyway, but when Dad suggested I go and see a psychiatrist, I immediately stopped what I was doing.

"Isn't that a bit drastic?"

"What was in those stories?"

"Lots of things. Attacks, murders. Just things he's – "

" – seen on television. I know. Do you realise you might have destroyed our child? I think he needs help."

"Perhaps we should see if we can help him first," Mum suggested, and that idea was laid to rest.

I fell asleep whilst they were still discussing what could be done with me. They were both lost for ideas, and I think I stopped listening before I actually drifted away for the night. The consequences hadn't even begun to start, and I was scared by what would happen next. Things had changed – irreparable damage had been done.

It had been the single most eventful day of my life. Monumental things had happened to me in a series of cliffhanger moments. I don't think I could have known at the time that it was a defining moment of my life. I doubt I was capable of that level of introspection. But part of me had loved every second of it.

DANNY

A Strategic Re-Birth

1.

Danny Lizar was born on September 3rd 1996 sitting on the downstairs of a double-decker bus heading out of Lancaster city centre, surrounded by screaming schoolchildren clambering over seats, hitting each other and shouting at the tops of their voices. He was born from necessity, from the will to shed his skin and leave some of the past behind. It was a small gesture, a slight name change, but it marked something of a cleansing.

I had to start somewhere.

Now that they knew what I was capable of, Mum and Dad were keen to make sure that I stayed on the straight and narrow. During my last term at primary school, my bag was checked on the way in and out of the house. They also performed random searches of my bedroom to make sure that there were no new storybooks being filled. I was forbidden to have writing material in my room and any homework that I had was completed in the living room and checked by Mum or Dad before it was placed in my schoolbag.

Alex supported me without hesitation. He had witnessed the whole thing and failed to see how it made me a bad person. He still wanted me to come round and play, although it was notable that the television was never switched on when I went over there. I was heavily supervised and Alex and I weren't even allowed down to the park on our own. These were my dad's stipulations and Robyn and Charles adhered to them rigorously.

The repercussions extended much further than the family home. Things didn't improve when I returned to school for two weeks of lunch time lines and formal apologies to both my classmates and the children in Year Two. Several of the children had been instructed by their parents not to play with me, and it was a social exclusion that the school could only condone. I was officially trouble, and the school knew that they would be rid of me at the end of term, so they left me to weather the storm with very little support.

There's something about a smart child with behavioural difficulties that people find hard to take. If the stupid kids were naughty, it seemed to be expected. The children with parents poorer than mine could start any number of fights and not experience the social stigma of what I had done. I think people were shocked because I was from a respectable family. Were it not for Alex's blind loyalty, then I would have been completely alone during my last weeks at primary school.

There were several rumours doing the rounds during the last term. Alex used to tell me what they were at my insistence, and it seemed that many of them were stemming from their parents. There were comments made about my family, most of them outlandish lies. There were things said in school that weren't so far off the mark, but I was yet to learn that. There was definitely talk of a relative in prison, but I didn't check any of the stories out with my mum and dad. I didn't want them to think that things were worse than they already were, mainly because I thought it would get me in even more trouble.

My woes were exacerbated when Lauren didn't return after the Easter holidays. Her father hadn't calmed down and insisted on home schooling her until high school, where she would be far away from my corrupting influence.

It was probably guilt that compelled Mum to make me change schools instead of Lauren. She called Mr Bell to let him know what they were doing, but he didn't change his mind. He had decided that boys in general were trouble, and that it would help Lauren immeasurably if she were kept away from them. It also coincided with his brick-laying business making some real money and my parents told me later that they thought he was just keen to prove he had cash.

Irrespective it remained that I was to head to Albany Cross High School, a few miles beyond the other side of the city to me, where the only person I would know was me.

It's a measure of Alex's friendship that he asked to be moved as well. His father told him not to be so stupid, but Robyn could see something in the idea. My parents didn't disagree, thinking that it might be incredibly damaging to send me away completely alone. It was the only leniency showed to me over those months, and I was cheered to discover that my best friend would be coming with me.

Some would say I never deserved Alex, not even then.

2.

There was nothing monumental for me about leaving primary school. The last term was an awkward formality that had to be played out. Most of my class were moving on to the same high school so there weren't many farewells to be had, and certainly no-one came up to me to say that I would be missed. I was happy to be leaving these people behind as they had always been pretty insignificant to me. Lauren left a huge gap in my life, but I had to accept that she was gone and I think I adjusted within a few weeks.

Although my grounding was long complete, the summer holidays loomed with the dread of week after week of sheer boredom. With all the supervision and the general wariness about my mental health, it wasn't to be a summer of exciting games and new adventures. When I was at Alex's we played computer games, which was fun in a way, but it always seemed unreal to me, just like cartoons. I generated excitement from things that I could relate to, and shooting baddies wasn't something I could associate myself with.

I missed the soaps like they were estranged best friends of mine. All of their plots were up in the air when I last encountered them and I feared that I was losing touch. It bothered me to know that their lives were continuing without me. The cliffhangers from the various programmes I had watched plagued me in my sleep, and this enforced separation was, I think, the hardest punishment for me to take.

Ever determined, I managed to pick up on one point of contact that my parents had failed to account for. This oversight was the magazine that came with the Saturday newspaper. In light of the television ban, it became my only source of keeping up to date, and I was rewarded with piecemeal details about what was going to happen.

I had been watching those programmes for years and I'd cottoned on to certain conventions that held them together. I was surprised to learn that I could read about the story and pretty well conjure up a portrayal of the events in my head. During those holidays I only looked forward to Saturday mornings, where I would soak up the information and spend considerable time imagining how these fragments of information played out on screen.

On the whole it was a tiresome and long summer, and I was terrible company for Alex. I was constantly miserable and rude and was forever telling him how boring everything was.

Every detail I heard about my new school filled me with dread. The seventy-five minute commute each way, the lime green uniform, the bigger kids who seemed like grown ups to me. My new school was evidence that my punishment was ongoing and I felt like I would never be rid of the memory of what I had done, which seemed less and less significant to me as the months went on.

I was told that I would need to get up at half past six every morning in order to catch my first bus into Lancaster at twenty past seven. The second bus left Lancaster bus station at 8am and traversed several housing estates on the way before finally arriving at the school at twenty to nine. School finished at half past three and I could expect to be home no earlier than quarter to five.

I made tearful pleas to my parents on a daily basis to be given a reprieve, reiterating how sorry I really was and how I deserved a second chance.

"This is your second chance," Dad would reply.

3.

The morning of my first day at high school was fittingly grey and I took no pleasure from Mum admiring me in my new school uniform, trying to get tearful and telling me that her little boy was growing up. I spited her by refusing to kiss her goodbye as I went to get the first bus, picking Alex up along the way.

I asked him if he was nervous.

"Not really," he shrugged. "You?"

"I dunno," I replied. "Kind of. It's going to be weird not knowing anyone."

"It can't be any worse than primary school, though," he said and I had to admit he had a point.

The first bus was alright, because it was mainly humans instead of schoolchildren. But waiting at the bus station for the second leg, I was suddenly surrounded by older, more unruly people. There were children who were only a little bit older than me, who were sprouting tufts of facial hair and developing deeper voices. Some faces were marked with tiny scabs from picked spots, and some of the girls walked around with the tops of their skirts rolled up. In some corners, the older ones were smoking.

Strangely, though, in and amongst this crowd of strangers I sensed a new beginning. I saw an end to being in trouble and realised that if I could prove myself trustworthy, then I might be allowed to watch television again.

Alex and I made our way onto the bus and went to go upstairs, but we were hauled back by some older kids. "First years stay downstairs," they spat at us by way of introduction to the high school hierarchy. It was only the more daring third years and the older kids who were allowed on the top deck – the first two years were meant to know their place, and from that day we did.

Aside from Alex sat next to me, this was complete anonymity and I was starting to revel in it.

"Hello," a skinny kid with white-blonde hair said from the seats next to ours. He looked permanently alarmed and clutched onto a briefcase that he must have known would get him bullied eventually. "Are you two new as well?"

"How did you guess?" I replied, rather abruptly, deciding that I wanted a go at being cool.

"You looked nervous too," he said and that knocked the wind out my sails a little. "What are your names?"

"Alex Proctor," Alex said, and offered a friendly hand in a gesture I recall as being surprisingly grown up.

"Danny Lizar," I beamed.

"Danny?" Alex was perplexed.

"Yeah," I said. "Danny Lizar. Like Lizard, just drop the d."

At that moment I thought I was cool as fuck.

4.

Upon arrival at Albany Cross High School, I was presented with the world on a wider scale. There had been no more than a hundred and seventy five pupils at Gregson Lane, whereas my new school boasted fifteen hundred.

Instead of being one building, the school was spread out over several blocks, with massive playing fields and two playgrounds. It was huge compared to what I was used to, and now that I was Danny Lizar, I was looking forward to getting stuck in. Best of all, it looked just like the high schools on kids' TV dramas.

Now that he had a name, he also needed a personality, and I was keen for my new self to come across in just the right way. I'd had a taste of being a problem child and I knew that it got me into trouble, so I wanted Danny Lizar to be just part of the crowd. He needed to be a trustworthy grown up type who was allowed to watch television again. I had a lot to prove to myself and my parents.

Over the first few weeks, I developed Danny Lizar into a fully fledged character. I was polite but enthusiastic, trying to talk to all of the children in my tutor group to make new acquaintances. Each night I spent longer than necessary on my homework and made it clear that I was enjoying it. I knew I was bright, and so did my teachers, so it was very much apparent that I was to aim to be in the top sets when the year was segregated by intelligence instead of random selection.

My tutor was the music teacher Miss Lawrence, who was recently qualified and seemed younger than the other teachers on the whole. Because she was young, she was deemed cool by a lot of the other kids and I struck an instant rapport with her. I answered questions and offered to help, although only enough so it didn't look like I was a teacher's pet. I hoped that by impressing her, she would spread good words about me in the staff room.

I still had no desire to have a big group of friends, but Alex and I did hit it off with two other boys from Morecambe called Mark and Philip, who seemed very similar to us. It was nice to be part of a small gang and I revelled in the acceptance.

My parents also adjusted to calling me Danny. I explained that it was for a fresh start, which they wholeheartedly supported. They wanted to encourage my rehabilitation in any way they could and were clearly impressed by the efforts that I had been making.

I settled into a nice normal life – neither Mark nor Philip had any discerning characteristics about them aside from them being nice kids. Between us we fell into a happy mid-ground in the high school infrastructure.

My marks were great and my first term report card was glowing. Mum and Dad were delighted and it felt like things were improving. The tension between them had dissipated and Dad even started making romantic gestures with things like flowers. I saw this as a sign that Danny Lizar was proving to be something of a success, which made me bold enough to suggest that if I carried on doing well, television should be allowed back into the house.

Mum wasn't adverse to the idea, but was reticent about suggesting it to Dad. Things had been going so well that she didn't want to rock the boat. I persisted a little and she said that she would mention it at an appropriate moment.

He wasn't happy about the proposition, but I was surprised when Dad agreed that we could have a television back in the house if I got through my first year of high school without transgressing. I was elated and immediately agreed to all of his terms.

If I had been gifted with introspection at the age of twelve, I might have started to see a problem with the way I played things out in my head. The deal I made with my father was a real challenge in many ways, and I knew that I was going to be deserving of the reward should I make it through.

It would be like telling me now to give up cigarettes for a year. I'm not sure I was addicted to causing trouble, but to behave impeccably was something I felt incredibly restrained by.

So I spent the beginning weeks of my deal with Dad in a state of terminal boredom. High school was opening a whole new world for me, one where I moved from classroom to classroom and met a variety of teachers, where everything was structured into a real timetable. There were so many other children, all of them going through exciting changes that had only been briefly explained to me in my last year of primary school. Some smoked, or had crazy hair, and they were nothing like the children I had previously encountered.

There was talk on the buses of sex, and I was introduced to all the swear words I would ever need to know just by walking down the corridors between classes. I had to avoid detention and remain on my best behaviour, which meant that I couldn't really get involved in the dynamic microcosm that I had stepped into. I strived to be mediocre, just like my parents had wished.

If I couldn't do that, then I at least had to make it look like it wasn't my fault.

During the second term of Year 7, Mark was taken sick and didn't come to school for nearly two weeks. We were told that it was flu, followed by a stomach bug, but none of us had heard from him and we were duly concerned about his welfare.

I started to seriously consider what it was that was keeping him off school for so long. I ruled out measles because it was a boring solution, and started to imagine broken limbs or something more serious. Cancer, in the end, seemed to be the most salient solution. It was the illness I had the most experience with, through the series of scares and deaths that I had seen in various dramatic guises. I didn't know much about it, but I knew that the mere mention of the word could reduce people to tears.

"When's Mark coming back, Miss?" I asked Miss Lawrence during one registration.

"Next week we hope," she beamed back at me. I loved that smile.

I clung onto the 'we hope' element and started to speculate.

"Do you think it really is a stomach bug?" I asked Alex as we walked on to our next class.

"I think so," Alex replied. He didn't get suspicious about stuff unless I brought it up first.

"Usually people are only off for a while if they've broken a leg or if they're… " I purposely tailed off.

"If they're what?"

"Dying," I said with perfect dramatic effect.

It takes very little to generate a rumour in high school and before long Alex had started to make enquiries about Mark's health. This meant that people asked him why he was asking and Alex wasn't one for lying. I don't know who he first mentioned Mark's potential cancer to, but within three days the head-teacher – Mrs Owen – had to call an assembly to insist to the children that Mark was not dying from cancer and would be back with his class-mates early the following week.

I was amazed how quickly word had got around. It was an intricate network of children that held the school together. Take the school bus, for example. Kids from all over the school are mixed up based on geographical location, so things get overheard and dispersed like dandelion seeds. All it had taken was a couple of questions and I had generated a huge buzz that had taken the school by storm.

When Mark returned the next week he was greeted very enthusiastically. He later found out that everyone thought he had cancer, but he had remained touched that people would care. I couldn't help but be intoxicated by the whole incident – I had created a real moment where no-one got hurt and no-one got punished. Although I had vowed to leave such thrills behind me with the death of Daniel Lizar, I managed to tell myself that this was somehow different.

5.

It took very little to assure me that I wasn't causing any trouble by creating waves through suggestion, and it was this that saw me through my television free year without imploding from the boredom. Alex became my stooge, however unwittingly. Without being asked, he always passed on my pieces of speculation to someone in our classes who would treat it like the hot news it was intended to be. By the time the rumour had hit fever pitch, it was completely untraceable.

There was a girl called Pippa in my tutorial group. She was one of the cooler kids; she seemed to act in a mature manner at the time. Thinking back, all she did was imitate her mother's behaviour and act like she was at least twenty years older than she was. She was good at sport and very bright, thus guaranteed popularity throughout her high school life. It goes without saying she was pretty. Most of the boys said they fancied her, not wishing to look any less developed than the other boys in the year.

Her one downfall was that she was unnaturally clumsy. She'd trip over all the time and was well known for knocking over her Bunsen burner in Science classes. On any pitch she seemed graceful and focused, but if there was no sport involved then she just seemed to struggle with coordination.

On one particular weekend, she had been out biking with her family and had crashed into a tree. She caught the side of her face on the trunk and had a nasty looking black left eye, with some bruising on the cheek as well.

"Do you think her dad hits her?" I said to Alex after she had explained to the whole class how she had injured herself.

"Maybe," he said, pondering it. "But she did say she crashed."

"She would say that," I replied with a self-assurance that was hard to challenge.

"That's true."

"We need to find out," I said. "We can help her if we know what's going on."

Alex was then dispatched to many people to make vague enquiries about her father and what he was like. I was often there to ensure that the conversations went to plan. Pippa's friends were worried about her, of course, and would then start asking discreet questions of their own. These conversations were overheard and started to spill out beyond our tutor group and into the rest of the school. It was a rumour that Pippa fed merely through her own clumsiness. People started to notice that she often had bruised arms and knocked things over a lot, as if she were jumpy.

Her friends became convinced that she was being beaten up and told Miss Lawrence, who told Mrs Owen, who called in a social worker alongside Pippa's parents. The family were apparently mortified and threatened to sue the school. Pippa strenuously denied that anything was going on, but people remained suspicious of her. It wasn't my intention, but I caused a huge dent in her potential popularity. Having an impact appealed to me, I must say.

6.

The reward for my good behaviour was the return of the television, just as the summer holidays started. I had completed my first year of high school without getting (myself) into trouble, and I had been placed in top sets for every subject. I'm sure Dad was reluctant to keep his side of the bargain, but I had done everything that he had asked of me.

It wasn't without conditions, of course. Mum had to watch with me at first and talk to me about anything contentious that arose. If it looked like the programme might contain unsuitable material, then it was to be switched off. Dad preferred me to watch children's television and game shows. The soaps were at my mother's discretion. I agreed to all of this and soon there was a brand new television in the house. I was going to suggest getting Sky at the same time, but I think I knew not to push my luck.

Dad joined us on that first night and watched some programmes. He made the point that this was how it could have been in the first place, which polluted the cordial atmosphere a little.

I felt like I had turned everything round in a year, and considered my Danny Lizar project a success. I much preferred being called Danny, and it seemed that he wasn't half as much trouble as Daniel had been. I think my dad liked Danny a lot more then as well.

If he wanted to keep an eye on my television watching, it was fine with me. I was in high school now, and there was so much about me that he just couldn't know. I was doing things that I was sure they could never find out about. By the end of that first year, I was punch drunk on power, and really, it could have gone in any direction.

Blurring

1.

I wonder what my life would have been like if Princess Diana hadn't died.

2.

Summer 1997 was spent catching up with old friends. We had been estranged for over a year, but the moment I tuned in again, it felt just like old times.

One thing I've learned over the years is that little changes in the world of soaps. People come and go, but they remain essentially the same. If one type of character leaves, they are soon replaced by someone who holds the same basic characteristics, and life continues.

It's only after the ban that I can recall picking out characters as favourites. I favoured edgy characters, generally the interesting teenagers who I suppose I could relate to. Their issues seemed like things that could possibly happen to me, and I remember being most enthralled with their storylines.

The Australian soaps focused more on the younger characters, and the scrapes they got into were attention-grabbing. They got lost in places and fell out with their parents ('the olds'). They were often disobedient but essentially good on the inside. They were preoccupied with romance at a time when I was becoming sexually aware, and it was the girls on these soaps that sparked my interest in the opposite sex.

Little had changed whilst I'd been away. The events that happened on these shows seemed to have less long reaching consequences and were generally forgotten about, so it felt like I had missed out on less. But whilst these programmes appealed to me with their shiny imagery and simple, satisfying plotlines, it was the British soaps that had the power to compel me with their story-telling.

The summer of 1997 was not only notable for the untimely demise of the posthumously styled Queen of Hearts, it also marked a time when the nation was gripped by a major 'whodunit' in everyone's favourite London soap opera, *Jubilee Line*. For those not initiated, it's a show set in the area around a tube station somewhere south of the Thames. The action takes place in the street that the station is on, which includes some market stalls, residential housing, a pub and a scattering of shops and other conveniences. A couple of years earlier, a nightclub had been built on what had been a playground. The locals had protested at the development project, some to the point where they had been arrested, and this had made the arrival of club owner Darryl Clough far from welcome.

Before I had been banned from watching television, Darryl had been making himself unpopular by kissing other peoples' wives and sacking people from their jobs. He picked fights with the local hard-men and was doing a good job at drawing business away from The Three Crowns, which is the local pub and epicentre of activity on *Jubilee Line*. I believe he was involved with drugs as well, but that side of his life remains hazy to me.

I'd kept up with his antics through the television guides. As a result I knew that he had done more cheating, hit a girlfriend and murdered a business rival. When I first tuned back in, Darryl was making plans to buy the community centre and turn it into a block of flats. He was clearly the most hated man in the soap at the time, and his death was leaked to the press well in advance. I was quite excited when the ban was lifted, knowing that I was about to witness a massive storyline.

Darryl was murdered at the end of my first week back watching the show. He had spent those episodes infuriating just about everyone. His mother had disowned him when she discovered that he had murdered one of her old classmates in a breaking and entering gone wrong. His girlfriend had finally walked away from their harrowingly violent relationship and he had blown up her car in revenge. He had also clashed with protesting residents over the community centre development, whilst bribing and angering others with his cheating ways and wheeling and dealing. As the week unfolded it seemed that everyone had a motive.

The tension reached fever pitch on the Friday with a party being held to celebrate the nightclub's birthday, which was well attended in spite of all the ill-feeling towards Darryl. He made a telling speech to the party about a promising future, whilst numerous characters in the crowd glowered with intent. Several confrontations occurred in and around the club, and I remember expecting him to die at any moment.

Darryl made it through the party and I was beginning to tell myself that perhaps the papers had got it wrong and he wasn't going to die after all. But he was walking to his car carrying a suitcase full of takings when he turned around to face an approaching shadow. In the darkness there was the sound of him being knifed to death before the credits rolled silently, denoting a truly dramatic moment.

Six suspects were identified in the episodes that followed Darryl's death. Each of them had a strong motive to kill Darryl, and they all had very little by way of an alibi. Nobody, however, knew whether it was his mother, his ex-girlfriend, his assistant manager at the club, the pub landlord, the gambler who owed him money, or the husband of a character he had recently seduced. Each possibility seemed just as likely.

Over five weeks the story played out, with each suspect looking shifty at every opportunity. Clues were dished out, evidence was hidden and lies were told. Occasionally someone was arrested at the end of an episode, and the police were in almost every scene, but no evidence seemed to be conclusive. It was a true mystery.

The storyline had more impact on me than anything I had seen before. It wasn't because of the break I had been forced to observe, it was the magnitude of the thing. It wasn't just a dramatic plot, it was something that spilled out of the episodes and into everyday life. 'Who killed Darryl Clough?' was the question on everyone's lips during the summer of 1997.

Each week, all of the television magazines in the newsagents ran cover stories on the plot as it unfolded. Tabloids were filled with headlines stating that they knew who the killer was, although they could never be sure. There were stories of power surges after episodes as the nation collectively put on their kettles, and others about the latest betting odds as people predicted the outcome as if it really were a sport. The magazine shows on television were also full of *Jubilee Line* features, and the cast were interviewed on a variety of programmes. It was strange seeing the actors out of context, but it made them more real to me.

For my part, I took the whole thing extremely seriously. I was glued to every episode, demanding silence throughout, and then spent a considerable amount of time after each viewing discussing with Mum about who we thought was the killer. She always emphasised how terrible murder was, and I humoured these moral lessons, as they beat having no television.

Sometimes I taped the episodes and watched them again the next day, looking for clues that I might have missed on the first viewing. There was never really anything there, but I paused scenes with a lot going on in the background, just in case a tell-tale sign had been included, and I apportioned meaning to who ended each episode with a guilty expression. I was so desperate to catch the right killer that I had a chart in a notepad, with reasons for and against each character being the perpetrator listed with great care and thought.

Each day I went to Mum or Alex with a new theory on who I thought the killer was. I changed my mind after most episodes, hedging my bets right up until it was finally revealed. Dad expressed his concern in how interested I was in the story, but I countered that a lot of people were doing this. He had to agree as he had heard little else from the staff in his restaurants during those weeks. I remember that he was particularly vocal in his disapproval of the storyline featuring on news programmes, which he felt was a step too far.

He was satisfied that I wasn't causing any trouble and that I had earned the benefit of the doubt. Danny Lizar was gaining his father's trust, so nothing more was said on the matter.

Whilst most things in my life were going smoothly, the one thing I had been lacking was money. There are many things a twelve year old boy suddenly needs in life; namely stickers, cinema tickets and sweets. I received £3 a week pocket money, and by the time the summer of Darryl Clough kicked in, I was more than aware that it just wasn't enough to satisfy me. I wanted to go bowling with my friends, and get accessories for my bike that my parents wouldn't just shell out for on demand.

Although we were pretty well off, I wasn't spoiled. I've heard many times that only children are meant to get over-indulged, but not giving in to my material needs was part of Mum and Dad's desire to raise a normal child. Throughout my childhood, presents were limited to birthdays and Christmases, with the occasional modest treat in between.

The idea of earning my money was ingrained in me from an early age. Alex and I often went washing cars during the summer holidays when we were at primary school, a time when £1 seemed like real treasure. I did odd jobs for money here and there, but if I got too demanding my parents would threaten to charge me board and lodgings. I liked the idea of having a job of my own.

As part of my fascination with the Darryl Clough storyline, I used to go down to the newsagents in Galgate each day to buy a twenty pence mix after browsing through the newspapers and TV magazines. It was quite cheeky of me, really, and it didn't take the newsagent long to cotton on to what I was doing.

"Magazines cost more than a twenty pence mix," he said grumpily, making me jump and drop the soap magazine that I was leafing through.

"Sorry," I replied sincerely, sensing unwanted hostility. "I didn't realise it wasn't allowed."

I must have appeared genuinely sorry, because he instantly took to me after that. He asked me a little about what I was reading and then he asked me: "So how would you like to earn some money so you can buy those magazines?"

I left the shop in gainful employment. That morning a paperboy had failed to turn in and he wanted someone reliable to replace him. I jumped at the opportunity without consulting my parents, who were both very keen on the idea as it turned out. I felt very grown up that day.

Everyone knew exactly when the killer was going to be revealed as blanket advertising kept us in the loop. It was all over the press and the one hour special was previewed frequently on the television and plastered all over billboards as well. Even Dad was at home to watch it with us, although he said it was just coincidence that he had taken that evening off. It's possible that he wanted to check up on me, but I like to believe that he was just as susceptible to the hype as the rest of us.

It was on the news that the cast were gathering for a special screening of the episode, and several were interviewed upon arrival as part of the bulletin.

"I don't care what you say," Dad moaned. "This is not news."

"Oh shut up," Mum joked and I shushed them impatiently. It was a warm moment.

Most of the cast members interviewed said that six endings had been filmed so no-one knew who the killer was, which made the whole thing that little more exciting. I also looked out for guilty faces in these interviews. Out of character, I thought that they had more chance to slip up, but none of them provided me with any discernable clues. I waited until just before the programme was about to start to make my prediction – the assistant manager. He was emotionally stressed and acting more suspiciously than most in recent episodes.

Mum disagreed and said that she thought it was Darryl's mother because she had hardly grieved for him at all. In fact she had been quite cold hearted about the whole thing.

"He did kill her friend," I said.

"He's still her son," Mum replied, and I thought on that for a moment and felt reassured.

"You're wrong," I said confidently, just as the programme was about to start.

I know Dad must have been keen to find out 'whodunit' because he didn't say a word throughout the programme. Mum and I gasped at moments when we thought a character was about to confess, but of course the reveal didn't happen until right at the end when the pub landlord sat alone in his cellar, staring at a knife with dried blood on it, weeping next to a bottle of whisky. A stunned silence purvaded my living room for several seconds.

There was a sense of anti-climax to knowing the truth. The fun had been in the mystery and in those first seconds of realisation, but all of a sudden there was no puzzle to solve.

My summer holidays had been dominated by this story, and I felt a sense of loss when it was all over. I knew the following episodes would be boring in comparison, and all the other soaps seemed second rate. I did genuinely worry about what I would do to occupy my time on the day after the Darryl Clough mystery was resolved.

3.

I loved my paper-round. I liked being out of the house before seven in the morning, before most people were awake. It felt like I had a head start on the day, and I liked having the village almost to myself. On different days I would meet different people on my travels, and it gave me a real sense of community. I had a role to play in delivering the news to people, and that was something I took pride in.

My route covered half of the village, the opposite side to where my family and the Proctors lived. I liked having that side to myself, as no-one over there knew my parents, or Alex. It was mine for the discovering. I enjoyed finding short cuts between streets and reducing the time it took me on a day-to-day basis. And then there were those who I came into contact with whilst out and about. Many were those I delivered to, when they were up early enough to receive their newspapers. I often heard little pockets of conversation in the seconds it took for me to push the paper through their letterbox. There was one house I delivered to where the couple who lived there always seemed to be arguing. Over the weeks I developed all sorts of theories as to who they were and what it was they argued about.

The two main parts of my route were separated by a park, where I would sit down mid-round and search through some of the newspapers and magazines for features on *Jubilee Line*. I became more aware of Princess Diana this way as she was often on the covers of the tabloids being criticised for going on holidays with men when she was supposed to be looking after her children. On a Tuesday, all of the television magazines were delivered as well, so my paper-round that day would take even longer.

The morning after the climax of the Darryl Clough 'whodunit,' I sat in the park and looked at the papers with the sad realisation that the news coverage would all but dry up over the following days. I didn't know whether I'd still enjoy the paper-round without the added incentive, and the days were going to be bleaker anyway without my main point of interest any more. I've heard reports of people becoming grief-stricken when a series of Big Brother ends, and I can believe it. I was on the cusp of a similar depression on that Saturday. I remember feeling quite lost for a short time, but then events overnight changed all of that forever.

4.

I was well adjusted to waking up early for my paper-round, but I did like Sundays the best because I only had to get up at seven. Getting up so early meant that I was always awake before my parents, so I was a little concerned when my mother walked into my room just before my alarm went off on Sunday 31st August 1997. My first thought was that I had made a mistake and overslept, especially when she told me that Mr Taylor the newsagent had been on the phone.

"What time is it?" I asked, both bleary and alert.

"It's Diana," Mum said to me, which I thought a strange answer to the question. I looked at her curiously, so she qualified her statement. "She's dead." I didn't need to ask which Diana.

When the accident happened, many newspapers had been recalled to include details about the crash. This meant that they hadn't been delivered to Mr Taylor and therefore I couldn't start my paper-round. Dad was sat downstairs in his pyjamas, watching the news with little interest. It was barely more than the repetition of the few things that were known, intertwined with speculation about what might have happened, who knew and how people might be feeling. There were endless showings of the car wreckage, and the hospital where she had died. The newsreaders seemed at a loss for what to say, knowing that people were tuning in every second. "The Princess of Wales has been killed in a car crash," they announced every other minute, looking as perplexed by events as my parents were.

That morning, nothing else mattered. Everything but Diana's death had ceased to exist, just like it had for Alex's family when his grandfather had died.

When I was given the go-ahead to collect my newspapers, I was disappointed to be leaving all of the excitement. Mum had started to cry a little and my father was reluctantly comforting her. He later said that he didn't really see what all the fuss was about. The 'Diana thing' soon became one of his favourite gripes.

I rode down to the newsagents and was surprised to find an abnormally large queue. It wasn't a big shop, but even so I had never seen it particularly full. Everyone had at least one newspaper under their arms and they were all talking to each other about what had happened in Paris that morning.

"I knew that Dodi was trouble," one woman said.

"Lynda Lee-Potter was saying how irresponsible Diana was being in the *Daily Mail* only last week," someone else offered. "Still, she didn't deserve this."

"Such a tragedy," Mr Taylor said sombrely to a man and his son who were at the counter. Both of them were nodding. I couldn't quite understand how everyone knew just how to behave, as if they had been prepared for dealing with a nationally important death. "Those poor kids."

"I can't stop thinking about those poor kids," another woman piped up.

Mr Taylor spotted me and his tone changed. "Hurry up

Danny, we're already running late today," he said like it was my fault. I wanted to protest, but it would have appeared churlish on such a day. I left with no further word.

I realised quite early on into my paper-round that everyone was feeling the impact of the news. Maybe it was just because I was out much later than normal, but I encountered a lot more people over the course of my deliveries than usual, all of whom seemed desperate to talk to me for one reason or another.

There was one man in his mid-twenties who was just fascinated by the whole thing. He was clearly someone who liked football, as he took two tabloids each day. He came to collect them from me and quickly glanced over the back page of one before turning to the more pressing matter. He looked at the other paper, and then held them both up next to each other. Some papers had gone to print announcing that Dodi was dead and Diana was seriously injured. Others had obviously held off a little longer and were able to announce that she had died as well.

"More on the ball, these guys," he said to me, pointing at the newspaper reporting Diana's death. "Don't know if it's worth reading this onc if I know it's not true. Not that there's much truth in these in the first place." He seemed quite jolly about the whole thing, which amused me a little.

The next person I encountered was far less cordial as he came to berate me at his door. He was overweight, his cheeks were red, his hair thinned and he had big bags under his eyes. "What time do you call this?" he barked at me.

"It's because of the news," I replied. For that day many of us just referred to it as 'the news.'

"I couldn't give two shits," the man shouted. "It's barely worth you bringing it at all."

"Do you want me to take them back to the shop then?" I asked completely innocently.

"Don't be so bloody cheeky!" he exploded.

"The papers were held back to be reprinted," I explained

sternly. "Everyone else seems to understand. This is a national tragedy."

"Like fuck it is," he snapped, then snatched the papers from my hand before storming inside, slamming the door behind him as he went.

I was shaken by the encounter. I hadn't had anyone get that angry with me since the 'raped' incident and confrontation always got to me more than I wanted it to. My heart skipped a beat as one woman opened her door when I was pushing her paper through. She was in her forties, and looked quite shocking stood there in her dressing gown, sporting bedraggled hair and staring blankly at me through her unmade-up face.

"Sorry I'm late," I said to her, anticipating another bollocking.

"It's not your fault, love," she replied and burst into tears. "It's just awful isn't it? She was such a lovely woman." She pulled me into a tearful embrace, which I wriggled out of as soon as seemed appropriate. I think she was instantly embarrassed as she went back into the house without a further word.

Shortly afterwards I was stopped by a man and his wife, who were out walking as I rode past them. The man asked me if they could buy a paper from me because the newsagents had completely sold out.

"I'm sorry," I said, "these are all taken." It was a shame that the angry man hadn't refused his papers, because then I would have had surplus.

"I'll give you a tenner," the man persisted. His wife just stood there expectantly.

"I'm really not allowed to," I said, despite the temptation. It took me a week to earn ten pounds.

"Lynne won't believe it until she reads it," the man said to me as if it were a perfectly reasonable sentence. His wife nodded when I looked at her.

"I can let you have a quick read of one," I suggested, not knowing really what to do. I looked away whilst they devoured the tabloid headline, but I heard Lynne let out a little sob followed by a full cry. Her husband handed me back the paper and ushered her away, glancing at me frostily like I had made his wife cry.

The whole world had gone mad.

I didn't want my paper-round to end. It was like I had woken up in a parallel universe, one with only a single topic of conversation. Complete strangers were talking and comforting each other on the street, sharing in the collective shock. Two weeks later, these people would pass by as if nothing had ever happened, but in the wake of the accident, everyone was pulling together.

I dropped the paper-bag off with Mr Taylor, who was still busy despite all of the papers being sold out. I wanted to stay a little longer to see what other crazy things people would do and say, but I was conscious of missing out on the developments being reported on the news.

Mum and Dad hadn't moved whilst I was out of the house. I quietly joined them for the next several hours of reports from the crash site, and outside Harrods, Buckingham Palace and Sandringham amongst other places. Dignitaries and friends issued statements and the movements of the Royal Family were closely monitored. Not much really happened, but it didn't feel that way.

It would have been inescapable, had I wanted to escape from it. Many channels had been turned into news channels out of respect, and the ones that didn't ceased transmission and directed people to the news. All normal television was cancelled until the evening at the earliest – it was something I had never experienced before. It was a day we all played a part in.

5.

I was allowed to stay up late that evening. I didn't head to bed until I was sure that there was nothing else to be said. I know it sounds bad, but it had been an enjoyable day for me, and

I looked forward to seeing what the newspapers said about it the next morning.

Television had spilled out into real life. When I stepped out of the house, it was like going behind the scenes. Everyone I had met that day had felt something about what had happened in one way or another. The tireless news coverage was padded out with reactions from civilians all around the country, and it was just the same as the things I had seen that morning. Being on the paper-round had given me a part to play, and I guess I felt like I was more involved than most.

Thinking of anything else that day wasn't an option, and so it followed that I dreamt about it that night. Most dreams – even the most vivid ones – get lost to time very quickly. But I remember the dream I had that night so well that I still wonder if wasn't in fact a vision. I've never had a dream like it since.

It started with me on my paper-round; I could see myself riding around on my bike with some music going on in the background. The music stopped with a screech of my brakes and I could see myself walking down a driveway. I usually remember my dreams in the first person, so this was unusual already. I recognised the house as that of the woman who had cried and hugged me that morning. In the dream she came to collect the paper from me and gave me a grim but meaningful smile. I wished her a good day and carried on. There was no hug.

Instead of following me down the path, though, the dream went back into the house with the woman. She leaned against the door and slumped down to the floor, resting her head on the frosted glass. A man appeared in her living room doorway and just said: "I'm sorry." The woman looked away from him just as a tear rolled down her face.

The action returned to me riding to another house. I was on the driveway of the house of the two tabloid man.

We exchanged greetings and commented briefly on what was going on. I was more articulate in the dream than I had been during the day, and I seemed to know just the right things to say. I said goodbye and carried on, leaving the man to skip through the Diana news and find the racing section in the middle of the paper. He wandered back inside and immediately started to look around for a pen. The voice of a woman called out his name – Ben – and he threw the newspaper down on the couch guiltily.

The woman who appeared was my form tutor, Miss Lawrence. "Come back to bed," she cooed in a way that I had witnessed innumerable times on television.

"Not now," Ben said seriously. "Haven't you heard? About Diana?"

"No," Miss Lawrence said. "What about me?"

Ben pushed the racing section back inside the paper as he passed it to Miss Lawrence, who put her hand to her mouth as she looked at the headline.

Then I was back in view, looking at a front page as I walked down a driveway, shaking my head sadly at 'the news'.

I looked up when I was startled by a loud, "Oi!" It was the man who had bawled me out for real that day. "Buy your own fucking paper!"

He swiped the tabloid out of my hands and pushed me to the ground before storming back inside his house.

"It's supposed to be a fucking morning newspaper," he muttered angrily. He looked out of the window to see me cycling down his driveway, looking visibly shaken. He smiled a wicked smile, and took a swig of some alcohol from a well-filled tumbler and leaned back into his chair.

"Did you just push the paper-boy?" said someone who had just walked into the room. I recognised her as Jenny, a girl from my tutorial group at school. It's hard to say how she had ended up in my dream.

"Go back to your room," the angry man shouted.

"You can't go pushing – "

"GO BACK TO YOUR ROOM!" he bellowed and Jenny

darted back up the stairs as though she were on the return leg of a bungee run. She sat in her darkened room and cowered, listening out for noises from downstairs.

The action moved back out onto the street with a close-up of two pairs of shoes in transit down a pavement. The view panned out to reveal a man and a woman talking as they strolled along.

"I just won't believe it until I've seen it," the woman said.

"You won't see it," the man said, and I recognised them as the couple who had stopped me on my paper-round. "There are no papers left in the village."

"Then let's drive to town," the woman I remembered as Lynne said.

The man sighed, and was about to say something when he was distracted by something over the road. "Lynne, look," he pointed.

It was, of course, me making my way down the road.

"Oi!" the man called over to me and a look of fright flashed across my face. What followed was a faithful replication of what had happened in real life that morning, right down to me letting them look through the paper. At the end, though, I rode off and they remained on the street. Lynne sat on the kerb and burst into tears, clearly upset by something more than Diana's death.

The dream cut first to the Angry Alcoholic, and then to Ben with the gambling problem, both leaving their houses. The Angry Alcoholic took a swig from a whisky bottle as he left and Ben picked up the racing section of the paper. The images alternated between them as they climbed into their cars and sped away. Ben just drove quickly, whilst the Angry Alcoholic was more erratic.

Occasionally I would appear in shot riding down the road with my empty paper-bag over my shoulder. The shots of their driving grew more intimidating, with close ups of wheels and gear-sticks predicting the impending drama. There was some dramatic music playing in the background – a bass-heavy string instrument going at the rate of an adrenaline fuelled pulse.

Unexpectedly, Ben's car drove around me and I watched as he headed to the junction that led into the centre of the village. The Angry Alcoholic's car hurtled down the main road, swerving to avoid Ben, who had absent-mindedly pulled out of the junction. The Angry Alcoholic lost control, and then it was from my viewpoint, watching his car hit the kerb on the other side of the road and mount the pavement to collide with a young pedestrian, who disappeared under the car upon impact.

Everything fell deathly quiet as the image homed in on my shocked face, frozen in the aftermath of the crash.

I woke with a start moments before my alarm went off for the Monday morning paper-round. Everything carried on naturally from there.

6.

I had tried in the past to recapture dreams that had ended abruptly, but there aren't many out there that can control their minds to the point of making accurate sequels to their most exciting dreams. As I showered, dressed and made my way to the newsagents, I thought of nothing but the potential identity of the run down pedestrian in my dream soap.

The victim had to be important to the dream me, who I considered to be like a character on television. It clearly wasn't me in that dream, but me playing someone else. That was why he was more articulate than I was, and behaved in ways different to the way I had the day before. I was merely a figure in a vision, an actor in my own dream.

I mulled over the possibilities. My first thought was Alex, but I quickly took him out of contention, along with anyone I actually knew. Making a victim out of someone real was a different matter completely, and history had taught me that creating these subversions, even fictionally, was inappropriate behaviour.

On my way to the paper-shop I stopped at the exact place where the dream had ended. I could picture the incident playing out in front of me just as it had in the dream, and instinctively I decided that the victim had to be my younger brother.

There weren't exactly many people around at half past six in the morning, so I knew that no-one would see me as I ran about. I dropped my bike on the tarmac and dashed over to where the car had mounted the pavement. I crouched down to where I imagined the body lay, his head lolling out from underneath the boot of the car. "Paul," I muttered, christening my new brother. It was a quiet time of day, so I didn't want to make too much noise in case someone saw what I was doing.

I acted out the scene in the street, imagining everything that was going on around me. Ben stopped his car and ran off to call an ambulance, whilst I remained crouching, whispering lines to my pretend little brother as he lay on the ground. More people rushed out to see what was happening, including Mr Taylor, but no-one dared approach Paul and me.

The ambulance arrived very quickly, and I guess the scene was over in about three minutes. I imagined that someone shouted cut and I stepped out of character and walked back to my bike. I rode on to the newsagents, thinking about what could and should happen next. I used the paper-round as planning time; I couldn't do any filming whilst I was actually making deliveries, as continuity-wise I had only just completed my round. In the game, it was still the day of Diana's death.

After returning the empty paper-bag to Mr Taylor, I went back into character and pedalled home as quickly as possible, maintaining a distraught expression as I prepared to break the news to my parents. When I got in, Dad had already gone off to work and Mum was in the shower, so I was free to play out the next scene without the fear of getting caught. I was aware that this stuff would seem weird to the untrained eye, and exercised caution right from the beginning.

As soon as I checked the coast was clear, I went out the front door and walked back in again, this time in character. It was classic soap opera stuff as I hurriedly told my parents what had happened. They reacted as they should and soon rushed off the hospital, leaving me at home. I even ran out onto our driveway, miming "Mum! Dad!" as they drove off.

Mum was dressed and downstairs when I walked back in. "I thought you came back earlier," she said to me.

"I was just making sure I'd put my bike away," I lied. As she was around all day, I had to play the rest of my game more covertly. At one point I performed a phone conversation with my 'parents', who were ringing from the hospital. Mum was in the kitchen, so I just mimed my improvised lines into the handset. I was told that Paul wasn't doing well, and the conversation ended abruptly when 'Mum' was called away by the nurses. "No!" I whispered into the dial-tone, by means of a cliffhanger.

I had woken up that day, started a story, and I was gripped by it. I asked to be left behind when Mum was heading out to go and sign a book of condolence in the supermarket in town. She wouldn't let me, so I trailed along and stood in a queue of proxy-mourners, planning out what would happen in the next instalment of my game.

Diana's death wasn't interesting to me any more. My own story was far more compelling, and I found something annoying about the way people were behaving. All of this crying over a stranger had been unusual at first, but now it seemed like they were play-acting more than I was.

It was whilst Mum was penning her message of condolence that I decided my little brother had to die. It would lead to grief, blame and drama, things that I had become more than familiar with whilst watching the soaps. I knew by this point that many more episodes had to follow.

7.

The game developed rapidly after that, and it was a process with very little reflection involved. The last day of my summer holiday was spent working out exactly what was going on and with whom. I decided that my soap opera was to be called *Morning Delivery*, seeing as all the characters being on my paper-round held it together.

Morning Delivery focused on the lives and loves of five households in the village of Galgate, all bound together by the paper-boy who delivered to each of them.

Sheila and Jimmy Parr lived at number 15 Yew Tree Avenue with their son, Mark. I imagined here that my school-friend Mark was their son, as he would be easy to incorporate into the plots. Jimmy had been having an affair, which Sheila had found out about on the morning that Diana died. That was why she had been crying in my dream.

In the early episodes, Jimmy moved out and Sheila struggled to cope with Mark's reaction to the whole thing. As I walked to Alex's house each morning to collect him on the way to the bus stop, I would play out conversations with Mark about what was happening in his family. Often I would hold my part of the conversation in whispers, but if there were people around I would just think it out instead.

It also made sense to have Philip in the show, so he became the son of Lynne and her husband who had stopped Danny in the street to look at his paper. They lived at 8 Orchard Grove, and Lynne believed that she had foreseen the death of Princess Diana, which marked the beginning of a mental decline for her. I decided to name her husband Kevin, and the mental problems would be their first major storyline.

The Angry Alcoholic I named Arthur Robson. He was the villain of the show, a single father who had been made unemployed. I imagined that he was arrested in hospital after the crash and the subsequent death of my little brother. He was refused bail, which meant that my classmate Jenny was without either of her parents. Her sister Cathy returned to the village with her boyfriend Rick to look after her, just in time to stop her being taken away by social services.

It was artistic license that allowed me to do all of this. I pretended that my school was in Galgate, but it was just filmed in a location on the other side of Lancaster. I pretended that my friends and my teacher were all local, when in reality they were all miles away. As Miss Lawrence had taken the role of Diana, I imagined that she lived at 49 Hill Street with her boyfriend, Ben the gambler. It meant that there was someone from my tutor group in each household, so it made sense as the dust settled to centre the action there.

The third episode was devoted to tying everyone together through school, which I filmed during the first day back after the summer holidays. This meant using choice moments of real conversation to lead into scenes that only I imagined took place. School was too busy for me to act out scenes, so these ones stayed largely on the inside. I tried to guide my friends and teacher as much as possible by being as like 'Danny' as possible, but I had a lot of work to turn real life into drama.

As it was all in my head, this wasn't really a challenge. That first day back seemed so much more entertaining now that I had my game to play. I felt so much more enthusiastic about life than I had done the year before, with the best part being that I was having fun whilst no-one got hurt.

It was a pretend show on a pretend channel, but by the time Diana's funeral came around a week after she had died, I was pretending that we were all mourning the passing of my younger brother. I comforted Mum as we watched the funeral, and assumed that the Church could be superimposed on afterwards. Elton John was going to be billed as a Very Special Guest on the credits, and it was written in that he was so moved by the tragedy that he had insisted on coming.

This was the beginning of a much bigger story, one that I

knew wouldn't end with the funeral when the rest of the world returned to normal and immediately forgot their grief. More importantly, I had no desire to see it end either.

For The First Time On British Television…

1.

So, this game. Imagine people play-acting out a soap opera but remove all of the other people. Weird, right? It wasn't how it felt, though. It was a compulsion; a fun thing that I just felt the need to do. It was like being in a drama company where every other player was fabricated. It was me and a network of pseudo-imaginary friends doing a soap.

It was a series of thick and fast plotlines emulating the dramatic bits I'd seen in all of the soaps on TV. There were countless times when I saw something on screen and was infected by the urge to have a dramatic showdown. I'd excuse myself and go to my room to film something that had been inspired by what I had just seen. It wasn't copying as such, but I would carry the emotion of the programmes with me and inject it right into my game. Every episode was high drama.

My character was kidnapped at least three times. Once was by the Angry Alcoholic, I recall, who I murdered to both escape captivity and to avenge my brother's death. He subsequently came back from the dead to wreak revenge and Danny experienced a nervous breakdown. That was pretty much how all of my plots panned out – drama, then tears, then falling apart, and then moving on without further consideration.

Fidelity had little place in my game. Like the soaps, everyone was at it, and my family was ripped apart in the show by my dad sleeping with a waitress from his restaurant, and later by my mum having an affair with Charles. Often I'd only 'do' the climaxes of the storylines, assuming that the build up had already been filmed. Seemingly irreversible events always came with elaborate caveats that allowed things to return to normal the moment I was bored with a particular storyline. Each of the teenage characters ran away from home at some point, usually as a solution to a corner they were backed into (standard shoplifting or smoking stuff, really).

Several plots were written off as dreams – like when Danny witnessed the Angry Alcoholic murder Jenny, and when Ben torched the bookies with Danny locked inside (I acted this one out in the garden shed, which was private enough for me to perform openly and loudly). Danny died in the fire, which was all a dream to make Ben see the error of his gambling ways. The Lizar family spent a few weeks at the heart of a harrowing domestic violence storyline, which culminated in Mum murdering Dad (this was around the time that I discovered *Brookside* and realised just how grisly soap could be). I downgraded his condition to a coma and he was eventually forgiven when it was discovered that he had cancer, which was offered as an explanation for his sudden ill-behaviour.

Believe it or not, these were the lucky plots. Many stories were wrapped up without further thought the moment I grew bored of acting them out (which meant I'd done all the big scenes that were fun to film and didn't really want to do any more with them). Lynne's post-Diana depression suffered such a fate, although she did later commit suicide when she realised that Kevin was sleeping with Miss Lawrence. I imagined the tension between Philip and Miss Lawrence in tutorial for weeks around that storyline, with clashes and walk-outs happening most days in my head. They weren't hallucinations; I just imagined how they would play out. Sheila Parr was involved in a hit and run incident which I duly forgot about in favour of breaking up her marriage and kick-starting a huge custody battle plot.

My interest in storylines only lasted as long as I could be involved with them. I contrived ways for Danny to be present for all the big moments. If you were able to see all of Danny's scenes back to back, I'm pretty sure that ninety percent of them would have been climaxes to storylines.

I did big disasters with a regularity that even the American soaps would have balked at; bus crashes, house fires, explosions, hurricanes and floods were staples of my game. I'd do most of these scenes in the woods near my house, or at home on one of the rare occasions that my parents left me unsupervised. School was too conspicuous for me to do more than blend my acting into everyday life. Lots occurred there on the show, but almost exclusively in my head.

So what did all of this look like? To the casual observer, a big explosion would have looked like me ducking down on the street and moving on. It was a stumble, at best, but I'd imagine it playing out on screen like a full-blown dive. A chase scene with gangsters would just seem like I was running around the park haphazardly, or a public showdown would be me stood somewhere muttering and making indistinguishable hand gestures.

No-one saw me in my room when I pretended to be trapped in a house with burglars prowling around, or when I simulated falling down the stairs. The scenes that I couldn't pull off effectively I said were performed by a stunt double.

Some people might have seen me mouthing to myself in class once or twice, and my parents may have wondered why I spent complete days playing in the shed, but on the whole I have to assume that I was relatively discreet.

Even then I knew that all of this was a bit weird, but it was too enjoyable for me to let it perturb me.

2.

There's something to be said about the way I felt my life improved from the moment I started playing *Morning Delivery*. I didn't get bored like I had done before. My game entertained me and hurt no-one. I wasn't writing vicious stories or starting rumours about my classmates, I was just making my reality a bit more fun.

I didn't believe in what I was doing, as in I didn't think it was real. That's never been the issue. It was a more sophisticated game of let's pretend that I used to enhance a rather uneventful life.

Stuff happened to other people in school that I'd capitalise on. It was mainly scuffles and bollockings, but I always managed to incorporate them into the storylines. Ambulances appeared in playground once or twice, which would fuel some disaster scenes in my head. I was adept at thinking up a tragedy on the spot.

Without the show, my life was tame, a series of innocuous happenings like birthday parties in bowling alleys and troublesome maths puzzles. Imagining exciting events and acting some of them out was my way of relieving the boredom. I wasn't allowed to watch 'too much' television and computer games didn't grab me. In general I was too old to play games but too young to be getting stuck into smoking, drinking and rebelling. My show wasn't the only option, but I can see how it quickly became my primary preoccupation.

I often went into daydreams when an idea took hold, falling vacant in class, or during dinner, or on the bus when Alex was trying to talk to me. I can see that this was a huge waste of my thoughts and energy. It was a quintessentially futile endeavour, but it beats growing up connected to the internet, like kids are these days, never bothering to have any imagination.

My alternate reality gave me additional friends and the power to pull the strings. I was hardly a megalomaniac, but I did enjoy controlling my hypothetical world. I contextualised it to a fairly elaborate degree. I gave it a half past seven time slot (despite all of the post-watershed themes and language) on a major television channel (Channel 4, I felt, was gritty enough for the show) and thought a bit about how the media responded to it. I could picture my face on the front of TV guides, looking gloomy, with headlines like 'REVENGE!' and 'FAMILY TRAGEDY!' emblazoned underneath. I made it a popular show with critics and viewers alike, and imagined myself to be a household name, whilst never actually believing that I was.

I really did see it for what it was, though. I can't emphasise that enough. If I truly believed it was real, I would have been more dedicated to playing out each storyline to the bitter end, rather than forgetting completely about characters and events. It was highly unsophisticated and completely disjointed. I guess that was why it eventually left me dissatisfied.

3.

Where I went wrong was in the improvisation. My game occurred spontaneously and although I tried to think of the bigger picture, I often got bored with what I was doing. With death, I had no patience for prolonged bouts of grief. Crying scenes only entertained me short-term, and when anything stopped being fun to film, it was nipped in the bud instantly.

There were times when I had lots to do and I didn't get the chance to film for a few days, by which time I'd lost the thread of what was happening and was inclined to start all over again. My cast were too disparate and I had little real contact with them, leaving me with too much to imagine. Most of the time I had to say that I was only concentrating on my storylines to account for the fact that I forgot where each character was up to. I started too big and frequently lost control of my game.

Ironically, I was so fascinated by making my own imaginary television programme that I ended up appearing more well-adjusted to others than ever before.

Looking back, I can't help but be impressed by how intricate the plots were in *Morning Delivery*. Put together, they made for a web of overlapping storylines, but at the time it was just me running with every idea that I came up with. It was really just a mish-mash of all the programmes I was watching at the time. A meta-soap, if you will.

So much was abandoned over the months I played *Morning Delivery* that I struggled to remember what had gone before, even for my own character. If I could have included more people and turned it into a group game, or an acting club, then it might have gone the distance. Nine months in, though, and I was seeking a fresh start. The shackles of the soap I'd created were too much to disentangle myself from. Not seeing my cast regularly meant that I grew tired of imagining them into my show.

I'd heard of cast culls in the newspapers and thought about killing off all but the people I actually knew from the programme. Even those familiar to me had horrible baggage, though, and I wanted fresh starts for all. I'd already admonished many of my storylines as lame and was sure that I could do much better if it was executed differently. So I axed the show. Just like that.

It would have been a perfect opportunity to leave this game behind, but that didn't cross my mind, not even briefly. My only thoughts were on how to enhance it.

One Man Show

1.

I imagined the fevered media response to the decision to axe *Morning Delivery* was heightened when it was announced that Danny Lizar was signing up to appear in a brand new programme. I planned a weekly show charting the life and loves of a teenager from Lancaster, and the people who were in his life. It was special because the cast would be playing themselves, but acting out dramas on-screen.

The idea came when watching *The Truman Show* one day when I was round at Alex's for tea. I liked the idea of how a whole drama could be built around the life of one individual. It was precisely what I was looking for. With me as the main character, it gave me the control without the difficulties of managing a relatively disparate cast. As these people were all in my life, it was easy to imagine exactly what was going on with their characters. It was a simpler show, in many ways, but I felt that it was the beginning of a new mature direction for me.

Naming my new project was something I found troublesome. I didn't want to start filming until I had the right title. This decision delayed the launch of the show by a couple of weeks, which was when something appropriate finally presented itself.

We had a stand-in science teacher for a week around this time. He was calling out the register when he made the common error of calling me Danny Lizard.

"It's Lizar," I corrected him automatically. I had learned to take it in my stride, and when I put people right, I aimed to do it in the most aloof way I could, so my response was well rehearsed. "It's almost Lizard, but you drop the d."

"Well I'm very sorry, Mr Almost Lizard," the supply responded with the most immaculately deadpan tone, and the whole class erupted into fits of laughter. It was a name that stuck, for a week or two at least. People enjoyed calling me Mr Almost Lizard or The Almost Lizard, and the more I heard the latter, the more ideal it sounded to me.

I wanted *The Almost Lizard* to begin strongly and get better from then. On numerous occasions I picked a day to start and would go through the motions of making the first few episodes before deciding it was all wrong and wanting to start again. A day in school gone wrong – through bus crashes, fires or abductions – just didn't feel special enough for me, and the ideas just fell flat. Creatively it was very frustrating. It took until the summer holidays before I made the opening episode that befitted my expectations.

The Lizars and the Proctors were headed somewhere on the Costa del Sol that year, and it felt right that things should begin there.

On the soaps, characters frequently head abroad to find someone: a missing loved one or estranged family member. This was the first plot that came to mind and I stuck with it, planning in the weeks building up to the trip exactly what would happen.

The Almost Lizard actually began without me, although I was present on the journey to Spain when I imagined that it was being filmed. Everyone in our party commented at some point on how quiet I was being at the airport, on the flight (my first flight at that) and then on the coach to the resort. I could hardly tell them that I was just pretending I wasn't there.

Despite all of my preparation, I didn't really know what

Danny was going to be doing in Spain, aged thirteen and on his own. It seemed most likely that he would have run away from home, but I wasn't entirely sure why he had run away in the first place, or what he would be doing in the same hotel as Malcolm, Jacqui and the Proctors.

With me, the storylines are only ever planned to an extent. Improvisation was another unique selling point of *The Almost Lizard*. In this first episode, I arrived with only a location and the fact that I had run away, but I had faith that the idea would present itself.

Alex and I were sharing a room on one of the top floors of the hotel. We were so high up that we could see almost all of the resort, and definitely everything on the sea front – a string of British-oriented restaurants and bars, which led into the city centre where the nightlife allegedly took place.

I was itching to be involved the moment we arrived. Whilst Alex unpacked, I locked myself in the bathroom and filmed Danny's debut; me splashing water on my face and looking worried. It was a relatively quiet start, but I remember getting a rush of excitement as I put the first scene in the can. From there, the rest of the story started to tell itself.

I was helping Dad carry glasses to the hotel bar on the first evening when I decided that Danny was working as an underage barman. I covertly filmed a few scenes under that guise. For the remainder of the night I made like I fancied one of the barmaids and insisted on clearing all of the tables around us when people left and taking them over to the bar, much to the hilarity of the rest of our party. It meant there were plenty of scenes of me as barman, which I imagined I was doing in the background of the scenes being filmed by my parents and the Proctors.

There was limited appeal in this for both me and the audience, so on the way back from the toilet later in the evening, I pretended to spot the others and hid behind a wall. It was an act that was essentially subtle and didn't draw any attention to the quite strange thing that I was doing. That was a small plot development completed and I returned to my table temporarily satiated.

A little later I excused myself, saying that I wanted to get something from my room. I took the lift to the correct floor and then ran to the room, fumbling with the lock in a panicked fashion, and once inside, ran around throwing my things together, saying 'shit' repeatedly and generally looking stricken. I grabbed my invisible holdall and ran out into the corridor. I dashed to a lift and looked around in a frenzy as I waited for it to arrive, repeatedly pressing the down button to illustrate my impatience. Throughout these scenes, though, there was no-one around, so I could act freely, which always made it feel more real.

The lift arrived empty, which meant that it was able to contain my unwitting parents. My expression turned to abject horror at the sight of Mum and Dad. I stepped away from the lift and ran back to my room, slamming the door and slumping behind it in a way I had viewed many times. I imagined someone shouting cut for the night and I became Danny Lizar the actor again. I passed a couple of remarks to crew members and signed off for the night, returning to the bar with no further scenes to film. This was definitely the opening I was hoping for.

For the remainder of the holiday I snatched minutes alone here and there to piece the first episode together. Most of this happened in my hotel room when Alex was elsewhere, or when I wandered a little way away from the group on excursions and muttered my lines. At other times I would go on short walks to the shop or to the beach, where I could mumble to my heart's content.

In these scenes, I was talking with my extended family, who tried unsuccessfully to talk Danny into coming home, and it was during these scenes that I decided what had happened to make him run away to Spain in the first place.

Danny had run away because he thought that he had accidentally killed his auntie. It was Alex who informed him that his auntie had died in a car accident that had nothing to do with him, something that Danny refused to believe. He remembered tampering with her brakes in an act of revenge, which he knew must have led to the crash. Malcolm told him in some Spanish village where Danny had supposedly fled to (this was just a day trip) that the brakes weren't the issue. Robyn found him at the swimming pool and gave him a sharp lesson on the damage he was doing to his parents and Charles pinned him up against the wall of his hotel room and demanded that he do the decent thing.

On the last day, the storyline needed tying up. We were having a relaxing final day by the pool when I looked up at the balcony of my room and saw my first cliffhanger. Episode one of *The Almost Lizard* ended with Danny staring up at his mother, who was preparing to leap off her balcony. I decided immediately that episode two would be wholly devoted the dramatic stand-off between Danny and Jacqui.

My opportunity to do this justice came about very easily, when everyone else headed down to the seafront to pick up some last minute souvenirs. I said I was happy just lying by the pool. I gave them five minutes to come back for anything they may have forgotten and sprang into action.

Episode two began exactly where the first had left off. Instead of the close-up of Danny's shocked expression, it was a wider shot of the swimming pool area.

"Mum!" I mouthed and leapt off the sun lounger. I had nothing with me, so I was able to abandon my spot in the way I would have done if my mother really had been about to throw herself off a hotel balcony. The sight of a teenager legging it around a resort hotel was not something that aroused suspicion from anyone. On the spur of the moment I took the more dramatically sound option of running up the stairs. A dash was much more fascinating if it involved running instead of willing a lift to go faster. I imagined shots cutting between Jacqui on the balcony and Danny pelting it up flight after flight of concrete steps.

I was out of breath when I burst into my room, which I was pretending was Mum's. With the door closed and no-one around, I could do exactly what I wanted. The episode was a lengthy heart to heart between Danny and Jacqui, building up to Danny saving her from suicide by promising to return home. I utilised having the room to myself by being loud, angry, violent and hysterical at different moments. The time was filled with recriminations and mud-slinging, as Danny explained how he killed his auntie. Jacqui put him right on many things, so Danny told her he had moved on from his family. "I can't go back to that hell," I remember fake sobbing at one point. I always struggled with the fake crying.

Danny told his mum he didn't love her in one angry exchange, and she blamed him for ruining her life and being selfish. The centrepiece of the episode was when Jacqui turned from her position on the railings to shout at Danny and she slipped. I ran to grab her hand, leaning over the side and holding my hand out into the air. We were at least nine floors up, so I doubted that anyone could see me doing this. It was my most prolonged filming to date, and possibly the most free to act that I had ever felt. After a short struggle, Danny pulled Jacqui onto the balcony and I let myself fall onto the floor.

The episode was completed in one take, and by the end of it I had a real sense of who Danny Lizar was as a character: passionate, emotional and dramatic. I liked him. I felt genuinely drained as I hugged my invisible mother, promising to return home, just as the door rattled, indicating that Alex was about to enter the room. By the time he walked in I was looking out over the resort from the balcony, as if I had been in this contemplative position for some time.

2.

Danny returned to the UK and took on the bare essentials of my life over the next few episodes. He got a paper-round, went to my school and lived with my parents. We shared the same friends, the same form tutor, and many of our personality traits were highly interchangeable. He became my own imaginary friend, part me, part fantasy.

The setting for the show chose itself; it was essentially all the places that I was able to go. Characters came and left as and when I needed them, which usually fitted conveniently with how they featured in my life. The great thing was the actors didn't mind being sidelined to background characters for months at a time if they drifted out of my life and the storylines. They were just happy to be part of such a vital show.

A lot of the storylines were relatively short-lived, but I always tried to make sure they were completed. As the show only went out once a week, a plot that took me three weeks to film would only amount to three episodes. After a couple of months, I felt the show was doing well enough to go up to two nights a week, which doubled the number of cliffhangers.

The last scene of the episode was the one I always enjoyed. A good twist that was over-used in the early months of *The Almost Lizard* would involve me suddenly collapsing at the end of an episode, or pretending to crash my bike, or knocking myself out. These mild health scares were easy to film and provided immediate suspense. By the end of the next episode I would usually be fully recovered, but the point was that the incident would make one character or another feel guilty about how they had treated me.

Others would also fall victim to minor accidents, and I would often discover people unconscious just when they needed rescuing. It was melodrama imported from the Australian soaps, but it was a rich source of action for me.

As in Spain, I had to film the big drama alone, but that

didn't stop me involving others as often as I could. Sometimes a scene just had to be made public.

During a storyline about a dying grandparent (Danny, unlike me, still had at least one grandparent left), I decided to run out of class suddenly to go and have a fake cry in the toilets. It was during a geography lesson and our teacher Mr Peters was attempting to introduce us to plate tectonics when I started to drift into a daydream. I often tried to think like Danny, and I started to reflect on the worry of having a dying grandparent. It reminded me of how I had no grandparents, and that made me well up a little, alongside the thought of a family member dying.

I was immersed in the moment and was pretty sure I was on the brink of actual tears, so I didn't think before I leapt up and dashed out of the classroom. I felt a surge of excitement ignoring Mr Peters as he shouted after me. I rushed into the boys' toilet and locked myself in a cubicle, completing the scene with a few sobs before imagining the credits rolling. Only then did I consider what I had just done and how I would need to make up a reasonable excuse.

Keeping this to myself has been big part of the game. Having this world that exists beyond that inhabited by everyone, a world bigger than reality, one controlled only by me and my whim – it's exciting. I have always thrived upon keeping it to myself, and the potential for getting caught is a thrill in itself.

Mr Peters was one of the nice teachers and was more concerned than angry, so he sent Alex to look for me. He knocked on my cubicle and I let out a big sniff to tell him that I was there. I counted to ten, flushed the toilet and opened the door, dabbing my eyes with tissues.

"I've just been sick," I said gravely. "I really don't feel well." I didn't question whether he believed me for a second. The payoff for my lies was being sent home ill, leaving me with the house to myself to film in peace for the afternoon.

It started well; I could do better. Christmas was approaching and I knew that the festive episodes had to be extra dramatic. I chose to mark the occasion with a kidnapping storyline that I just knew would grip the nation. Characters were kept interesting by the skeletons in their closets, and these revelations often led to really exciting events. I started thinking about the Christmas plot in October, and the idea came to me quite quickly. From thereon, the show was all about building up to Danny getting kidnapped. I started to drop hints in the plot about what was to follow, referring to how mad my old boss was when I left Spain.

Having a long-term storyline to prepare gave me a sense of purpose, more so than when I just went with whatever I thought up next. I planned where I would go to film certain scenes, and exactly what needed to happen in each episode to make it a good storyline. I selected a site for the kidnapping, and worked out how I would film the episodes where I was being held captive. The script remained improvised, but everything else was well thought out.

Throughout November, Danny became convinced that he was being watched, and on several occasions voiced his concerns to his family and friends, who told him not to worry about it. I did a few of these conversations for real with Alex, Mark and Philip, and they really did tell me not to worry, mainly because I made it all sound so casual.

All three of them were quite dismissive, with Mark in particular telling me that I was paranoid. His character would live to regret that bitterly.

I chose the park on my paper-round as the right place for the kidnapping. It was dark at that time in December, especially as I didn't get home from school until five, which I know angered some of my customers as they liked to have their evening paper there the moment they got in. People are very particular about their newspaper deliveries, I discovered during my years as a paper-boy.

It was a simple scene to co-ordinate; just me pretending that someone had pushed me off my bike and looking fearful at a shadow looming over me. It was dealt with very quickly, and from thereon, I just had to film my Christmas scenes in a corner of our garage.

In the run up to Christmas, I made my excuses on any occasion when I was bored and headed out to the garage. A lot of the time my parents were out and I didn't even have to think of some elaborate reason for me going there, but from Christmas Eve onwards, they were both around more, along with several passing guests and well wishers, which complicated things somewhat. It didn't make it impossible, though.

Danny was to escape in the Christmas Day episode. It injected something into a storyline that I was starting to find tedious, as repeatedly filming scenes of being gagged and bound held only limited interest to me. When it was revealed that Danny's old boss was the kidnapper, I had to sit silently whilst I imagined him explaining his reasons for holding me captive. He had lost his own son in a car accident, and had grown to view Danny as a replacement. He was clearly a madman.

We were having a shared Christmas lunch with Alex, Robyn and Charles in the afternoon, as was tradition, so I decided to get all my filming done in the morning. I remember thinking that it would also give the production team extra time to edit the episode before transmission as well. Crazy, huh? I told Mum and Dad that I was heading out to look for a missing decoration that I was sure was in the garage.

I sat down on the concrete floor and filmed myself breaking free from the rope that I was tied up in, and making my escape through the window. I hadn't intended for it to be literal, and only meant to motion throwing the garden gnome I had found nearby. I remember too well the gut wrenching sensation I got as the window smashed.

Dad was first out of the house, with Mum not far behind him. I looked at them guiltily through the broken window, unable to think of a good lie on such short notice. I received a very unseasonal bollocking for that act, which annoyed me. After over a fortnight held captive I thought that they might have been a little more welcoming. I corrected myself and accepted the punishment. Besides, a month without pocket money more than made up for the added realism I'd brought to the Christmas Day episode. I concluded that I had done what was best for the show, and that was to my credit as an actor.

3.

The Almost Lizard was working out well, but I did start to feel a little dissatisfied with flapping my way earnestly through yet another heartfelt argument with an empty room. I had a real cast and I wanted to use them. I figured that if I did less filming alone, it was an improvement of sorts. It was my concession to that fact that there was something abnormal about my game.

I had to assume that what I was doing was unusual, but part of me liked to think that it was something that everyone did secretly. 'It's perfectly natural and everyone does it,' the problem pages informed me of masturbation, and I hoped that this was the same sort of thing.

A lot of things are like that when you're fourteen, when you privately hope that you're growing the correct amount of pubic hair and you pray that you've got the difference between a BJ and fingering absolutely correct.

There are so many questions you want to ask, mixed up with the insurgency of hormones that seems to make almost everything a little romantic. It was an age where I thought I was too old to be asking too many questions in case I showed some blinding naïvety that would ruin the limited social status I had. I liked being left alone by the hierarchy, and generally I strived to keep it that way. There was so much that I didn't know about others at that point that I could treat it as feasible that making up television shows was just another of those things. For a while I became convinced of it and starting making some discreet enquiries around school. I recall being obsessed about getting some reassurance from somewhere.

It's safe to say I trusted Alex more than anyone else in the world – even more than my parents. He never let me down, and I knew him well enough to ask him the right questions without giving myself away. He was the natural choice for first person to ask whether he ever played TV dramas on his own.

We still spent a lot of time together in the evenings, as well as at school. We were in all of the same classes, so we'd do our homework together. It was important for Danny Lizar to have a strong friendship at the centre of the programme, and the kids on TV always had someone to do their homework with, so I had come up with the innovation of being 'study buddies' shortly after starting work on *The Almost Lizard*.

Through his time spent with me, Alex had been subjected to a lot of soap operas and at some point he must have conceded and started to show an interest. We'd often do our homework in front of the television, which could go on for hours at a time as the programmes I like rolled on, one after another.

It was whilst watching a teen drama that I courted Alex's opinion on the merits of play-acting. A couple were getting in trouble on-screen for snogging in the canteen, something that I would have loved to get in trouble for.

"Don't you wish school was like this?" I asked.

He looked at the screen for a second and then back at me. "No," he replied.

"But don't you wish it was more exciting?"

"The work can be a bit dull," he replied, and I struggled to contain a sigh.

"I just think it'd be fun if more stuff happened," I said, largely to myself. "I just like to pretend that life could be more fun."

Alex went quiet and looked at the screen. I waited for

a response, but after a few moments I realised that the conversation was over and joined him in staring intently at the screen. I didn't dare court anyone's opinion after that.

4.

I remember the comedic elements of *The Almost Lizard* much less than the high drama. In shows like mine, comedy storylines could only last a few episodes at the most before the idea grew tired and stopped being funny.

I also found comedy was the best way for me to introduce other people into the game, which made it invaluable to my progression. There was a time in my third year that I remember very well, and I blush even to write about it. We were all becoming 'young men' as our sex education teachers liked to tell us. I mentioned before about the rumours and the pretending to know about things you felt you should know about. By the third year some of the more extroverted 'young men' were openly admitting to masturbation and discussing it as publicly and as often as possible.

I wasn't entirely clear on the subject. I still wasn't sure that it was as perfectly natural as everyone kept telling me it was, thinking that if I admitted to doing it, everyone would just burst out laughing, call me a wanker and tell me that I was the only one. I had the same fear about my game, so I guess I was pretty pent up with all the things I chose not to divulge about myself.

Whilst I felt uncomfortable discussing it, I always listened intently when others bragged about it in class. This tended to involve them boasting about the record number of wanks they'd had in one day, often citing double figures which I soon discovered to be an impossible feat. I'm sure some deviant out there could prove me wrong, but in my experience it begins to hurt a lot after four.

These were the tales passed down from older brothers and

particularly cool uncles. I remember once sitting on my right hand for more than half an hour because I was told it would go numb and feel like someone else was doing it for me. I failed to replicate this myth, as all I got was pins and needles in my hand, and a libido lost in the preparation.

Another thing I heard one evening on the bus was the description of something known as the danger wank. For those who don't know, this involves masturbating in a place where others are nearby, traditionally at home when your mum (or other suitable house resident) is at home. You shout for your potential victim and the goal is to try and ejaculate before they get to you. I heard this one day and immediately knew that it was a way for me to get someone else acting out *The Almost Lizard*.

I was at home a couple of nights later. Dad was working, of course, so it was just me and Mum in the house. I was in my room under the covers and decided to give it a go. By way of build up I had filmed a couple of scenes during the day that indicated that Danny was feeling a little horny, imagined conversations with good looking girls and a couple of covert glances at my crotch, really it was very unsubtle.

I waited for the moment where it would be a close race between Mum coming up the stairs and into my room and me coming all over my bed-sheets, and I shouted for her at the top of my voice.

The plan was for her to nearly catch me and for me to try and cover up what I was doing in a comedic fashion, eventually asking her, "What's for tea?" Soaps didn't talk masturbation, so I was hoping that it was going to be both hilarious and ground-breaking.

My mistake was not seeing my limitations, namely not knowing how to stop yourself at the moment your mind goes blank. Mum walked in when my face was contorted with concentration, whilst my right arm still pounded away under the covers. I let out a groan, and she let out an "Oh!" before quickly vacating the room.

I opened my eyes and fell back against my pillows, cursing repeatedly and burying my head in my hands, which I had forgotten contained my cooling ejaculate. It was excruciating for me personally, but I remained in character regardless.

"Sorry love, I thought you called for me," Mum said through the door. She was either unnerved or she was struggling not to laugh, because she sounded shaky. Part of me was dying inside with the embarrassment of it all, but it had been extremely authentic.

Over the next couple of days, Mum and I did several scenes with us skirting around the subject, purposefully avoiding referring to what had happened. It took her over a week before she could bring herself to look at me directly. Dad was dispatched to give me a quick refresher course on the birds and the bees – another hilariously awkward scene I got to film with someone else – and then I moved on to some other plot. The personal humiliation was hugely outweighed by the greater good of the show.

5.

Spurred on by the success of the danger wank scenes, I set about bringing more people into my fabricated dramas. I had little desire to film more embarrassing sexual incidents with my parents, and found a more plentiful source of footage from manipulating my friends into falling out with each other.

Me and my friends were quite volatile as it was and only needed a little goading into petty disputes. I had no trouble convincing Philip that Alex fancied his older sister, which caused a rift for a couple of days. On another occasion I made Alex think that Mark was saying things about him behind his back. It yielded a good confrontation, and I was able to bring myself into the action by helping the warring friends patch things up.

At other times, though, I liked to be more directly involved and do the falling out myself. A potential storyline emerged when Mark confided in Alex that he had taken a liking to a girl in our year called Jemma. He knew her from our maths class, and I remember her being both pretty and quite popular. She was the sort of girl who spent most of her time around the boys, but was a little too feminine to be an all out tomboy. I believe she lives in London now, trying to make it big with her indie band. That's the sort of girl she was.

The potential conflict was obvious to me the moment Alex let it slip that Mark fancied her. Nothing was a secret between Alex and me, which made it much easier to organise the things I did. Mark had told Alex when they had gone bowling in Morecambe. I wasn't allowed to go bowling in Morecambe because Mum and Dad told me I might get in trouble. They told me Morecambe was rough and I wasn't allowed to go there unsupervised. It was a source of mockery with my friends and I had filmed an outburst the week before when they had joked about my mummy not letting me out to play. I asked Alex about the trip when we were on the bus home, and it wasn't long before he told me what Mark had said. Instantly I thought: love triangle.

It wasn't tough to bring about, either. I had many more lessons with Jemma than Mark did, so from the day after I heard about Mark's crush, I made a concerted effort to get to know her and covertly steal her away from him. I talked to her more in classes, making a scene out of each encounter as the storyline developed. I bought her a CD single of some band that I pretended to like as much as she did, and then managed to get myself in the same group as her for a history project we were working on.

With this contact, we started getting on pretty well. I made her laugh and she really thought the CD was a sweet gesture on my part. When Alex told me that Mark was planning to get her a Valentine's Day card, I knew exactly where the climax to the story was coming from. These things were just instinctive, half of the time, and were they not just going on inside my head, I like to think that I would have been lauded for such a skill.

I made sure Alex went to help Mark pick the card, and then got a full report on the type that he had bought. Alex was suspicious already, having noticed my sudden interest in Jemma, but I convinced him that I was just getting in there to talk Mark up. Thinking it was a noble cause, Alex readily helped me out. I took this information and picked out a far more expensive card to go with a box of chocolates that cost me a weeks' money from my paper-round.

The night before Valentine's Day, I suggested to Alex that Mark should slip the card in Jemma's bag during maths, and reminded him that he couldn't sign it. "It's meant to be a mystery, that's the fun of it. He also needs to address it to My Darling Valentine," I added. Alex didn't say much, but I knew that he would pass the information on at the first opportunity. After maths was history, which meant I was sitting next to Jemma with ample opportunity to remove Mark's card from her bag. I replaced it with my more expensive one and the chocolates, pretending that I had dropped my pencil on the floor. It was a slick operation, and I stuffed Mark's card into the nearest bag to Jemma's, which just so happened to belong to Louise, a girl with a chronic musty odour about her.

As it turned out, Louise discovered her card first and let out a shriek of delight. The card was passed around the class with a stunned amusement, no-one but Louise believing it was anything but a joke. When it got to me, I couldn't resist the moment. "My God," I said, with the whole class playing extras, "this is Mark's handwriting."

By lunch time, word was out that Mark fancied Louise, confirmed by the girl herself when she spotted us in the canteen. "Hi Mark," she said, skipping gracelessly towards us.

"Hi," Mark said, struggling to think what her name was.

There was an awkward silence and I could see that Louise was losing her nerve. More eyes turned to the table as people eagerly waited for what they knew was going to be a crushing blow to this socially unacceptable schoolgirl.

"Thanks for the card," she said, and Philip spat out some of his drink in mock horror. It was a great supporting performance.

"What?"

Louise produced the card from her bag.

"That wasn't for you!" Mark snarled cruelly. Alex and Philip were laughing, but I had chosen to play it straight for this scene. "Do I look blind?"

It took a few seconds for Louise's face to crumple, and when it did, she flung her tray onto our table and dashed away in a lumbering fashion. Unsurprisingly no-one ran after her and, amidst slight pangs of guilt, I mentally congratulated her on portraying such a tragic figure.

Mark continued to protest between mouthfuls of school issue cottage pie, but he failed to contain the mirth of Philip and Alex. He had given up eating completely when Jemma strolled up to the table and started talking to me without even acknowledging him.

"Those chocolates look expensive, Danny," she said. I loved that moment, the second that the penny dropped and the climactic scene kicked in. "Thank you so much."

Mark turned from red embarrassed to red angry within seconds, and I caught him fuming out of the corner of my eye as I tried to act all sheepish around Jemma.

"No worries," I said quite coolly for me. "I hope you enjoy them." She didn't let me down gently on the spot, which made my storyline an even bigger success. Mark waited until she had left the dinner hall before lunging angrily across the table at me.

"You fucking twat!" he grabbed me, but then realised that everyone was staring and let go, knowing that he couldn't actually hit me. Order was restored and I was amazed to have orchestrated my first crowd scene with relative ease.

A simple lie got me out of trouble on that occasion, telling Mark that I didn't know that he liked her. I said I had no idea how his card had ended up in Louise's bag, suggesting that she might have just found it on the floor near her bag. "Perhaps it fell out when I was putting my card in," I suggested. "Listen, mate, if you like her, I'll back off. I'm really sorry."

Louise received no such explanation, and I didn't think to try and make her feel better about herself. She was off school for the next week, but I chose to think that it was flu and nothing that I was to blame for. Jemma told me two days later that she didn't see me in that way, but by that point the storyline was over and I really didn't care.

Alex sat there and kept quiet about what I had done, just like I knew he would. Not only was he loyal, but he had told me about Mark in the first place, so to some extent it was his fault. But I had burnt him, and he expressed this on the bus on the way home. "Sometimes you do these things and you don't care who you hurt. It's a little weird."

"You're a little weird," I replied and started to laugh.

6.

I tried not to dwell on what Alex had said, but I was concerned that my friends were getting wise to me orchestrating fall-outs amongst the group. There had been quite a few in a short space of time and if they had really put their heads together they would have noticed that I was central to almost all of our recent disagreements. I was scared of losing the few friends I had.

I also thought it would be good for the show if it didn't descend into just a constant series of fallings out, which I assumed must have been getting a little boring for the viewers. It was time to bring some other characters into my plots to liven things up. Besides, I was ready for another major storyline.

Almost three years of high school plays and assemblies had taught me the dramatic potential in bullying. The teen dramas I watched were proof that such stories could run and run, and I wanted a long-term plot that I could really get my teeth into. One day I imagined being interviewed by someone from a day time TV show, who had picked up word of a dramatic new storyline in *The Almost Lizard*. "This is the biggest thing I've done to date, definitely," I told the reporter. "I think people will get to see a whole new side to Danny."

My bully was easy to find. It was well known that Nick Armitage was the hardest lad in our year. He already smoked and it was rumoured at the time that he had already had sex with five women, including his stepmum. Geeks feared him whilst the tough kids revered him. The cool kids didn't like him, but they knew well enough not to cross him. He had all the benchmark characteristics of a school bully: a broken home, a stud in one ear and a permanent air of menace.

I knew that it wouldn't take much to make an enemy out of Nick Armitage; I just had to decide how I was going to do it.

I first thought of telling the teachers he was smoking, but I was saddened to realise that they would probably respect my confidentiality and he'd never find out that it was me who ratted him out. I was also trying to make Danny Lizar a bit more innocent in this story than he had been in the recent love triangle. I wanted him to be popular with the audience.

In my timetabled school week, I knew that I passed Nick on corridors several times, and it was just up to me to pick the day I wanted the storyline to start. I was impatient, and only waited a couple of days before filming commenced. The new episode began on a new morning, with a scene of Danny being happy at home, and then being content in his first two lessons, even mentioning how he finally felt pleased to have come home from Spain.

Towards the end of our German lesson, I purposely untied

a shoelace in preparation for the big scene. I had an eye for routines and I knew that I was due to pass Nick on the corridor on my way to maths after German. The corridor that linked the humanities department to the maths block was much thinner than most in the school, and there had been several times when teachers had to be called out to bring order to the sight of up to a hundred high school kids inextricably wedged in a corridor, seemingly with no means of escaping. I had never been caught in one of these crushes, but I had seen the traumatised faces of those who had. It happened to Alex once, and he said someone had grabbed his privates in all the kerfuffle.

I was apprehensive because I only had one take to get it right. I made sure I was absently talking to Alex when I tripped over my untied shoelace and slammed into Nick much harder than I had anticipated, sending us both crashing to the floor.

"Shit," I muttered. Swearing was more than acceptable on *The Almost Lizard*. "Nick, I'm so sorry." I picked myself up and offered my arm to help him up.

He stood up unassisted and leaned in to me, eyeball to eyeball. "You, fuck-stick, are dead," he growled. Two of his friends were with him and I knew that Nick was angry about being shown up in front of them.

All of my friends had decided not to stick around, having clearly decided that they didn't want to get caught up in my trouble.

"I'm sorry Nick, I tripped," I tried to explain with an obvious quiver. Nick responded by cuffing me around the side of the head. It hurt quite a lot, and that was even without him really trying.

"That's just for starters," he assured me and carried on down the corridor with his friends in tow. I looked around as everyone made themselves look busy, refusing to meet my gaze. The scene ended with me clutching my face, standing a little shell-shocked in the corridor. I couldn't have asked for it to go any better.

After filming the incident scene, I adopted the 'condemned man' look and made my way to Maths. I took my seat next to Mark and whispered, "Thanks for your help there." Mark couldn't quite bring himself to look at me, and I liked it. Everyone was playing their part just right. I spent most of the lesson looking distracted and worried, purposely avoiding the gazes of my friends, who wanted to know how angry I was with them.

It took him most of the lesson to speak to me, but eventually Mark said: "What do you think he's going to do to you?"

I'd been asking myself the same thing. It was the part of the story that was out of my control, which was unsettling to say the least.

"Whatever it is, I'm sure you'll be hiding round the corner, watching from a safe distance," I said cruelly. Lashing out was important to the plot. I wanted to isolate Danny from his friends a little more to heighten the seriousness of his plight.

"Oi, fuck-stick," I heard Nick shout in the playground the next day. "Think you're fucking hard do you?" He walked over to where I was stood and pushed me. I went straight into character and said nothing, portraying the pacifist in this scenario. "I said, do you think you're fucking hard?" he repeated twice as loudly.

I remained silent and Nick took a swipe at me. I fell to the floor immediately as all of my friends evaporated into the background. He kicked me once in the stomach and then walked off with his merry band of sycophants shadowing him. I lay foetal on the floor for a few seconds and imagined the credits rolling. I was feeling some pain, but it all was just method acting to me.

Frequently his friends would verbally abuse me on the bus, which kept the storyline ticking over during the days where Nick didn't barge me in the corridor, or pin me up against the lockers, arm across my throat and demand my lunch money.

Another time he stole all of my clothes and towel when I was in the showers after PE, and on several occasions he just emptied the contents of my bag onto the floor before trampling on them and walking off. And then sometimes he just hit me.

I had underestimated my fellow pupils. In and amongst the fear and indifference I had imagined that someone would show sympathy and try and help me. I thought there would be some act of kindness from a stranger, or a friend stepping up to help. I felt Danny Lizar was popular enough to earn that. But as the bullying storyline played out during the summer term, it became increasingly clear that no-one – teachers included – were planning on jumping to his rescue. Nick would make threatening comments in the hallways in the earshot of adults, but nothing would be said. No warning, no admonishment; the truth was that most of them were scared of this unruly fourteen year old, knowing how humiliating it would be to be beaten up by a pupil.

I supplemented the school scenes with moments I filmed in my room of Danny struggling to cope with the increasing pressure of the situation. I fake cried myself to sleep on a few occasions, and found cause to be snappy with my parents. I lashed out at Alex, Mark and Philip routinely, but I think they tolerated it because they felt quite guilty about being so weak. Both in and out of character, I felt betrayed by my friends, and as the weeks passed, my resentment towards them became more real than scripted.

The story was starting to take over the programme, as I tried to show how bullying takes over a life.

It says in magazines how actors often feel emotionally drained when filming the tougher storylines, and several weeks into the bullying plot I had to admit that it was beginning to take its toll. Nick caught the same bus home as me one evening after school and pushed me down the stairs from the top deck just as we were pulling into town. The tears I disguised as I lay on the floor were very real, and at that moment I wanted it to end immediately.

I hate losing control.

7.

I said nothing to Alex on our second bus back to Galgate, not even a goodbye when we parted. I had been lucky not to sustain any serious injuries in the attack, but I had picked up a few bruises. As much as I was genuinely scared, I knew I had to keep the storyline going, and I went home to film some denials with Mum over the course of the evening.

I didn't find it difficult to be snappy with her, either. The lines were being further blurred between me and my character. I had a go at her when she asked where Alex was and stormed out, and it didn't feel like acting any more, although I knew it made for a great scene. I sat in the dark and wanted to cry, not just for dramatic effect but because I really wanted to cry. I shared his fears because they were real, but they were also completely fabricated.

I had started to skip meals already, sometimes for effect, but more often because I really didn't feel like eating. My stomach had shrunk with the worry, and the thought of eating often made me sick. I pencilled in an idea for a potential bulimia storyline once the bullying was over.

The next day was the last before half-term, and I resolved to bring this plot to a swift conclusion. If not, then I was looking forward to respite for a week. I knew Nick wouldn't go to the trouble of persecuting me at home, and for once I was grateful for living so far away from school. With only a day to prepare, I had to admit that I had no idea how to get him off my back. I didn't know how to end the storyline.

I sat away from my friends during registration, having avoided Alex on the bus. They looked towards me intermittently. I pointedly avoided their glances, thinking bitterly about how weak they were. Other people knew what was happening to me, people who I would have called acquaintances, but I couldn't be mad at everyone so I just focused on the few that I really cared about. Nick Armitage was a big name in the school; any third year that could beat up ninety-five percent of the fifth form was going to instil fear in everyone.

I had turned a blind eye to his behaviour in the past, having seen other people suffer in the same way I was now. It seemed easier to ignore it than to intervene, but now I was on the wrong side of this apathy, I couldn't help but take the stance of the victim. This storyline was giving me an insight into human nature and how bloody awful we all were.

My three closest friends gathered and approached me at the end of the class. "Danny, are you alright?" Philip asked.

A thousand spiteful comments formed on my lips, but I managed to contain myself.

"Do I look alright?" I demanded. "Or are you too busy running away all of the time to see how I look?"

"It's Nick Armitage, Danny," Philip said. I let out a bitter chuckle.

"Which makes it perfectly acceptable to turn your back on your friend," I said and looked away from them. I wasn't sure if I was going to cry.

"We don't know what to do," Mark admitted. "We want to help."

I snorted, but said nothing else.

A silence ensued that became too loud for me. I grabbed my bag, jumped up and pushed past them. I ran out into the corridor and crashed into a fifth former.

"Dickhead," he said and pushed me out of the way. I was shaking for real. I looked down the corridor and realised that everyone scared me at least a little.

I didn't think twice as I ran to the front entrance and thumped through the doors. I dashed across the playground and out of the main gates, not looking behind me once as I sped up the road.

I ran for three more streets before I dared to stop. I sat down on a kerbstone and let out a strangled cry, one of happiness, knowing that I was at least safe for a week. I couldn't say whether I thought the storyline was going well, or going too well.

Skeletons

1.

The Almost Lizard had been putting a strain on my friendships with Philip and Mark long before the bullying storyline, but my lashing out had added to things considerably. They made no attempts to contact me over half term, and beyond that things were cagey at the very least. Philip told me further down the line that I was troubled, a line that formally ended our friendship. The rot set in with their apathy towards my plight, though, and I don't think I could have ever forgiven them anyway.

Despite the years we had shared together, I would have given up on Alex as well had he not redeemed himself so spectacularly. Whilst Mark and Philip willingly kept their distance from me, Alex was round at my house the day after I had run out of school, full of concern and information.

I had been hiding out in my darkened room for the morning when he turned up. I had already skipped breakfast and pretended that I was asleep when Mum called me. She was a little cautious about entering my room again after the danger wank storyline, so if I didn't reply she thought it better to leave me be.

"Alex is here," she told me through the door. I had been privately hoping that someone would show some interest in what was happening to me. When I stepped into the living room he was sat with Mum drinking tea.

"Hi Danny," he said brightly, but I could tell that he was nervous.

"Hi," I returned, minus the enthusiasm.

"Have you had some breakfast?" Mum asked.

"Yes thanks," I lied, turning away from her towards camera in order to give the required deceptive look.

"I've got some washing to be getting on with," she excused herself. Her departure added tension to the room.

"Are you alright?" Alex cut in, just as I was about to ask him how he dared show his face around here. "We were worried about you when you ran off like that."

"I had to get away," I replied matter-of-factly.

"I understand," Alex said.

I felt a monologue coming on. "Do you? Do you really understand?" I demanded and continued without waiting for an answer. "Do you wake up scared each morning wondering what the hell you did to deserve all of this torture? Do you walk around every corner expecting to get attacked? Do you fear catching a bus in case you get trapped upstairs with row after row of people who are after your blood? Do you understand what it's like to wonder if you'll get a lunch each day, or whether you'll just have to go without because someone's stolen your money?

"Do you understand how it feels when even strangers can't look you in the eye, or when you realise that your best mates don't care enough to at least try and help you? Do you?"

I was surprised and quite impressed to discover that I had started to cry over the course of this unrehearsed outburst. Alex looked like he was on the brink as well. I sat down on the sofa opposite to him and looked away, hoping that he would come over to comfort me – I felt it was what the scene needed.

He did. A few seconds later he stepped across the room and put a conciliatory arm on my shoulder. I moved into heart-to-heart mode.

"Danny, I'm sorry," he said. I still refused to look at him. "Nick told us he'd make things worse for everyone if we grassed him up, especially you."

"How can things get any worse for me?" I asked flatly.

"I really want to help," he said, his voice quivering with emotion. I finally turned to face him.

"I don't think it's something you're capable of."

"I told Miss Lawrence," Alex blurted out. I hadn't been expecting that at all, a plot twist that I hadn't accounted for.

"You did what?"

"Mr Eccles wanted to know why you weren't in RE, so he asked her in the staff room. She'd already spotted that you weren't quite yourself."

"You could have covered for me," I said. There was a lot to discuss, and I knew that this was a quality two-hander episode.

"I was sick of being helpless," Alex told me. "It seemed like the right thing to do. No, it was the right thing to do, no doubt about it."

"But Nick said he would make things worse," I reasoned. "You just said so."

"And you asked how things could get worse," he bounced back at me. "That was the conclusion I reached yesterday. At least if all of the teachers know there's a problem they can keep an eye on things."

I studied Alex for a moment, wondering whether he was playing his own game at the same time. There have been times with many people where it has crossed my mind that we're both acting out scenes for our own programmes simultaneously, mainly because people do seem to act like they're on television at certain moments.

"What did she say?" I asked.

"She was shocked. She kept asking me questions and asking me whether I was absolutely sure, so I showed her this." I hadn't noticed until then that there was a notepad on the coffee table, which Alex picked up and passed over to me.

It was a school exercise book; each page had been turned into a neat table with columns entitled 'Date,' 'Act Committed,' and 'Severity (out of ten).' The incidents went back to the first time Nick had hit me on the corridor and continued in detail up to the bus incident two evenings before. I studied each page carefully, welling up with the memories of what had happened, but more than anything completely touched by what Alex had done.

"I knew someone would have to know at some point," Alex explained, "but Nick gets away with this stuff all of the time, so I came up with this. Miss Lawrence photocopied it and gave it back to me. She told me to keep it safe."

My character and I were equally moved by what we were hearing.

"By the time we go back, they might have decided what to do with him. Miss Lawrence thinks he could be expelled this time."

"I don't know what to say," I said, and I really was struggling for a good line.

"I'm sorry I didn't help sooner, but I really didn't know if it was the right thing to do. I should have stood up to him – maybe between us we could have twatted him?"

"I doubt it." I couldn't help but smile at the thought.

"I nearly hit him when I heard him say those things about your aunt."

"Jenny?" I was curious.

"Not Jenny, no," Alex replied. "Anne?"

"I don't have an Auntie Anne."

"Just shows how ridiculous he was being then. I thought it sounded like lies."

"What was he saying?"

Alex seemed unsure whether to speak, but I looked at him sternly, giving him the impression that if he kept this information from me then he wouldn't be forgiven, in spite of everything.

"He said you had this crazy Auntie Anne who wanders around Morecambe trying to pick fights with people. He said his mum said she had been big news a long time ago, now she was just a sad nutter. That was the last straw for me. I couldn't let it continue."

"Alex, I think I love you," I said and hugged him. "You might have saved my life." It was a touching conclusion to the episode, and Alex didn't seem to mind that I remained in the embrace until sufficient time would have passed for the credits to roll over the screen. It was the sort of ending credits you saved for special episodes, and this had certainly been that.

The bullying storyline was coming to an end, and the relief was visible on both mine and Danny's faces. At the back of my mind, though, a much more interesting development had materialised.

2.

The possibility of an absentee aunt was a tantalising proposition for me, and for the show. By the time Alex left, I was already planning out a swift conclusion to the bullying storyline so that I could move on to the new prospect. In the weeks to come I would learn of Nick's expulsion and enjoy the complete eradication of my bullying problem. By the time I was told that my ordeal was over, I was firmly in the throes of my new plotline.

There was something about what Alex had said that seemed to fit a little too well. I couldn't instantly dismiss it as vicious nonsense. There had been a smattering of clues over the years. In the second year of high school, Alex had told me that there had been talk of taking me out of Albany Cross and placing me somewhere more local. I assumed at the time that it was because I had proven myself to be well behaved and my parents were just considering ending the punishment.

There was another time when I was nine or ten and out for a

meal with my family and Alex's when the conversation turned to siblings.

"You're a twin aren't you?" Robyn had said to Mum and then she suddenly clamped her hand over her mouth.

"No, I'm an only child," Mum had replied and the subject was dropped immediately. The meaning had been lost on me and I'd forgotten all about it until Anne's name was mentioned to me.

It certainly explained why Mum and Dad didn't want me going to Morecambe on my own. I thought lots of things were unfair at that age, so it had been nothing to get suspicious about. In context, it was all so obvious.

Mum went to the supermarket and left me on my own on the second day of half term, making sure that I was alright several times before she left. I insisted that I was, regretting the impact the bullying storyline was still having on the family. Mum and Dad had felt terrible when I announced my terror during a heart to heart that I believed was deserving of numerous accolades.

The cameras rolled as I watched from the living room window until she was out of sight. I immediately went to my parents' room and cautiously worked my way through their wardrobe, stopping only to consider a few photo albums that were in the bottom. There was nothing in them that pre-dated my birth.

Undeterred I moved on to Mum's drawers, sight checking all of her letters to see if there was something more personal in and amongst the bank statements and electricity bills. There was nothing in there that alluded to a secret sister.

I hadn't even considered the possibility that this anonymous sibling might belong to my dad. I knew his family, so there seemed no reason to suspect that he may have hidden one. It just had to be Mum.

After three quarters of an hour I ran out of places to look

aside from the loft, which I decided to leave until I had more time. I didn't want to unravel the storyline too quickly, and the suspense would build if I waited until the next opportunity arose.

I was left alone again a couple of days later, this time with Mum more satisfied about my well-being. I waited until she went to have coffee with a friend and made my way up into the loft, a place I hadn't really visited much. It was a disappointing haul, though, with the only clues lying in a box of paraphernalia Mum had kept from her acting days in London.

The mystery kept my mind off my impending return to school. By then we were fairly sure that Nick wouldn't return to torment me, but my inner victim wasn't so sure. I lost a bit of sleep about it on the night before going back, but the moment I was told that he had been expelled I drew a line under it and worried no more.

My holiday was extended when I was told to stay away from school whilst they formalised Nick's expulsion. Dad insisted on staying home with me for those two days, so I found myself in the unusual position of spending time with him alone. It could have been a nice chance to bond with him, but instead I spied an opportunity to probe into our mystery family history. Dad suggested a game of Scrabble; I presume because it was time consuming and would occupy me for a while.

We shared some jokes over words that we didn't agree on, and then I made us a cup of tea. I hesitated before talking a couple of times for dramatic effect, and then started digging. "What was Mum like when you met her?"

"How do you mean?"

"Well I look at girls at school and I wonder how I'm going to meet the one that I want to spend the rest of my life with," I lied.

These poignant father-son moments occurred rarely during my teens, but I could tell that Dad got something out of them when they did. He considered the question for a while before speaking. He told me that he had met her by chance in Morecambe shortly after he moved there, some bollocks about sharing the last table in a café.

"She made me an offer I couldn't refuse," he said and smiled. A smutty thought popped into my mind and ignited a smirk, so Dad qualified the statement. "Dirty sod," he smiled. "We hit it off and she invited me to live with her in London. It was totally out of the blue, I'd only left the North West once before. I felt so alive." I detected a sadness in him, and I wanted to ask him why he didn't feel alive anymore.

"You just did it?" I asked. The story was fascinating to me, even if it wasn't the one that I was aiming for.

"There was no reason not to. I wasn't really getting on with my family at the time."

"Why not?" I asked. Usually I don't think the conversation would have gone any further, but Dad felt sorry for my recent torment and decided to open up. He told me all about his childhood in the Pleasant Rise Guest House; about growing up with the guests and being unusually clever, and about the arrival of Mr Philpott and the damage done when the study was presented. The game was abandoned as Dad told me about the life he had mapped out for himself, and how it was snatched away when his family failed to make the amazing breakthrough they thought they had.

"I've always strived to make sure that things were different for you," he said. "I've always wanted you to be yourself and to make your own choices. I want you to be whatever you want to be and I'll be proud of that."

"You're an amazing dad," I told him. "You've not pushed me at all, only provided."

I couldn't tell him that I loved him, I didn't like the mushy stuff and even praising Dad had felt a bit forced. I suddenly remembered the point of the conversation and decided to take control of it again.

"Didn't Mum miss her mum and dad when you just ran off?"

Dad pondered over the question for too long. I was onto something.

"She'd been away at university for some time already," he said.

"And what about when they died? How did she feel to be left with no-one at all?"

"There's nothing really more to say."

It wasn't an outright lie, but it wasn't the truth either. I decided to change the subject, whilst inside every part of me squirmed with excitement. I couldn't believe that she was real. This was bigger than I could have hoped for, and there was no question in my mind that I had to meet her.

3.

The night I found out that Nick had been expelled, Dad had gone to work and Mum and I were on our own. I started out with an innocent enough question.

"What's your maiden name?" I asked her. It did seem odd that I had never thought to ask before, but then I'd never been curious about her history before. It shows how well she concealed it that I hadn't probed the matter.

"Hepworth," she said.

"You don't look like a Hepworth. You're definitely a Lizar."

"Thanks," she said, looking at me a little strangely. I left it at that.

Alex was by my side for most of my first day back. Mark and Philip said hello to me in the morning, but kept their distance for the rest of the day. We ate lunch together almost silently, with Alex's attempts at making conversation falling flat on every occasion.

I broke away from him for a short while to film a scene by the pay phone. I leafed through the phonebook, which was for the Morecambe area. Nick had been accurate about the existence of my auntie, so I assumed that he was right about her living in Morecambe as well. I had to assume that she was called Anne, otherwise I had very little to go on.

I looked around suspiciously to show that I was up to something private, and thumbed my way to the H's. There were four A. Hepworths listed, with the beginnings of their addresses next to them. It made sense for me to go and visit them rather than call, as there was only so much dramatic potential in a series of phone conversations.

Everyone at school felt bad about what had happened to me, either just because it sounded horrible or because they felt guilty about doing nothing about it. This gave me a window to get away with a thing or two, liking skipping a few afternoons by claiming I was unwell. No teacher would refuse that request and I used it once to go home just because I didn't fancy being in school, and twice to go and hunt for this mysterious auntie.

So on two afternoons I made my way into Morecambe to meet these A. Hepworth's in the order that they had been listed. I had taken an A-Z from home to assist me, so I knew exactly where I was heading.

The first address turned out to be an old people's home on the seafront, and the second place I went to was empty. It was a sad end to the first day of looking, and the episode ended with Danny despondent. About a week later I bunked off again to find the last two potential A. Hepworths in Morecambe. My A-Z took me to an estate a little bit outside of the centre, and to be honest it came as something of a shock to me.

I can't deny that I'm a sheltered middle-class boy, and until that point I'd had no cause to go onto a council estate. It was a far cry from my quaint village and I noticed a difference in the people there. Like the area itself, with rusting cars on front lawns and beer cans and kebab wrappers in the drains, the residents seemed a little bit dilapidated and uncared for. There was harshness on the faces of people that I passed, a 'don't mess with me' stare that I found intimidating.

It was the perfect place to find a missing relative. On the soaps, people were often discovered festering in tower blocks, living a life far away from the safety of the community at the centre of the show. I played it wide-eyed, walking briskly and trying to avoid trouble.

After fifteen minutes of taking wrong turns and going down weathered cul-de-sacs with broken gates and 'beware of the dog' signs, I found the street I was looking for. A. Hepworth lived in a ground floor flat, which looked inhabited.

I looked around and breathed in before finally pressing the doorbell. I waited, and then rang it a second time. There was no sign of life so I turned away and walked down the pathway, wondering what it was that made A. Hepworths so difficult to get hold of.

"Can I help?" a voice called out behind me. I swung around and saw a woman stood in the doorway where I had just been standing. She looked like a downtrodden version of my mother, so I knew she was who I was looking for.

The cameras continued to roll, but I stood in a freeze as one episode ended and a new one (an hour long special, I decided) started from where the other had left off. To begin, I looked the woman up and down. She was quite portly, with greasy bleached hair and lots of dark roots. She wore an ill-fitting and cheap looking summer dress, and I could tell that she smoked.

"My name's Danny," I said. "Danny Lizar. Like Lizard, but without the d."

4.

"I know who you are," Anne said and insisted that I go in immediately. "I know the surname well. Are you related to Malcolm?" she asked hesitantly, as if she didn't know whether to expect friend or foe.

"I'm his son," I replied and she smiled in a way that I considered to be warm.

"Then you must have a cup of tea," she said and went into her kitchen. I sat on the sofa and looked around at the drab and anonymous living room. It made me feel extremely middle-class and I was grateful that I didn't have to live in such conditions. I hadn't really experienced such a place outside of television before, which says a lot about my upbringing.

Anne was more composed when she came back into the living room, clutching a tray in her hands with a pot of tea and an open packet of malted milks. She was very polite, asking if I took sugar and pouring the tea into a chipped mug for me. I warmed to her during this exchange, enjoying being treated like a grown up even though I was still wearing my school uniform.

"Did Malcolm send you?" she asked when we'd settled down.

"No," I replied, "my parents don't know I know you exist."

The look that flashed across her eyes when I said this made me feel a little uneasy, but I wasn't suspicious of her at all.

"That makes sense," Anne said after a few seconds. "She must still feel very ashamed."

One thing I hadn't learned about myself was that I was just as fallible to manipulation as everyone else. "Why would she be ashamed?" I asked, reading from Anne's script.

"I'd hate to speak out of turn," she began. For the next hour, Anne talked to me in detail about the history she shared with Mum. I thought up flashback scenes, telling the story of the Hepworth twins, portraying things just as Anne recounted it.

She told me of a childhood where Mum was pushed to greatness by my grandparents, whilst she was systematically ignored. "They held me back from school for a year on purpose so that Jacqui could progress without having to deal with the burden of me," she explained.

I heard about the endless times when Mum went out of her

way to ruin opportunities for Anne, like when Mum joined the netball team just to make her feel inferior. Mum, as depicted by Anne, convinced her sister that she would fail in her exams, breaking her spirits to the point where it became a prophecy. "She was as determined as my parents that she would succeed and I would fail. I didn't stand a chance," Anne said.

Then she told me how she had finally stepped out of her sister's shadow when Mum had gone to uni. "I just wanted to find a man I could settle down with. When she found out about me and your dad she came back to Morecambe almost straight away and told me that she could steal him away from me within the week."

Anne became tearful at points, so I was certain that she was being sincere. Jacqui didn't really sound like the woman I knew to be my mother, though. I had never seen her behave in a malicious way. "She was prettier than me, more successful than me and she wooed him with tales of London and the bright lights. Your father didn't stand a chance," she sobbed.

When she composed herself, she continued to tell me how Mum ripped her family apart by running off to London with my dad in tow. "The rest of us struggled to get over the scandal. I was ashamed because my sister had stolen my boyfriend, and my parents felt that everyone thought we were trash. We all drifted apart because of the things we couldn't say.

"Then she turned up out of the blue, pregnant with you. It broke Dad's heart all over again to see the girl who had destroyed the family. It reminded him of all the pain. He hated your dad for what he'd done to me as well, and I think pretending to be happy that they were starting a family was just too much for him. He died suddenly. Did Jacqui tell you about that?"

She hadn't. My family history had remained completely taboo, but Anne filled me in with her side of the story, of my broken-hearted grandfather, killed by the exploits of their wayward daughter in London. I heard how my grandmother perished in a house fire, on a night when Mum had promised to visit but had failed to do so. Anne started to cry again when she said, "If she'd gone round, the pan wouldn't have been left on and the fire wouldn't have happened. I would still have a mother."

"That doesn't sound like Mum at all," I said, shaking my head in exaggerated disbelief.

"I can imagine," Anne countered knowingly. "The last time I saw her was at Mum's funeral. I told her that I didn't blame her for killing Mum, and she said that from then on, I had no family. She pointed at her stomach – at you – and said, 'You'll never get to be an auntie.' And that hurt more than anything."

Danny Lizar was not beyond family loyalty, however, so I spat, "It's lies!"

"Remember," Anne replied, "your mother is an actress."

It was an amazing line. One that spun me out completely. Although clearly underprivileged, Anne seemed like a fundamentally good-natured woman who had been the victim of a life littered with tragedy. Hers was a story you had to sympathise with. At the same time, my parents had been so coy about the family history that everything she told me couldn't be instantly written off. She cried at all the right moments, as if she were playing her own game. She directed that episode, no question about it.

I didn't know what to say in response. The cameras kept rolling, homing in on the dilemmas written across Danny's face. It came to mind how I'd heard of her in the first place. "Is it true that you went to prison?" I asked.

"Did your mother say that?" Her confidence faltered a little after that.

"No, someone at school – that's how I heard about you."

"It's playground lies, dear," she assured me. I was more inclined to believe her over Nick Armitage any day.

She asked me about school and I started to think that she was keen for me to leave. "You and Mum should really meet up," I suggested. "All that was so long ago."

"I don't think so," Anne replied. "I think we're both happier without the other one. I think your mother's done enough for me."

"She's not like that any more," I said, words that must have told Anne that she had played a blinder. "Given the chance, I'm sure she'd apologise."

"I doubt that very much. I know you mean well, but I know Jacqui. Trust me."

And I did. When I said I had to go, I didn't think twice when she asked me to come and visit again. It didn't cross my mind that she might have been conjuring up her own revenge storyline. I was blinded by all of the things I had discovered about my family.

The episode ended with Danny running from the house, shell-shocked and clearly unsure what to believe.

5.

I decided that for the next episode, Danny would try and act normally around his parents, ending most scenes with a suspicious expression of some sorts. These faces are used in all soaps to denote dishonesty within conversations. They can express evil intentions, or insincerity in a conciliatory hug, and it's as close as a character gets to talking directly to the audience.

In the scenes that followed the meeting with Anne, I pulled several faces that suggested Danny just couldn't believe his parents. I forced them to lie to me about the past so that I could justify keeping my visits to Anne a secret.

A month passed before I felt ready to face Auntie Anne again. I fell into a bit of a depression caused by the breakdown of my friendships with Philip and Mark. It had turned a bit nasty once in a while – just barbed remarks, but it was during this time that I realised that they wanted nothing to do with me at all. That coupled with my parents' lies sent me into a darkened room, listening to a compilation of angst-heavy rock music and not communicating with the world too much.

In that time I told Alex everything, just for the support and the scenes that such a confession yielded. He backed me up immediately, so I insisted that he come with me next time I went to see Anne.

I spent a lot of time thinking and as the memory of her began to fade, I started to wonder whether Anne was just misguided in her opinions. The more I saw my mum and dad, the more I sided with them. Then little things would remind me of their duplicity and I would become desperate to see Anne again. The problem was that I was still at the age where I had to account for all of my movements, so getting away was not the easiest of tasks. That added to the cloud that hung over me, a mixture of hormones and real torment.

Alex and I picked a Saturday when we were both free and told our Mums that we were going shopping in Lancaster. My auntie was more charming on the second meeting, probably because I was less of a surprise this time. She was very composed and nothing I said threw her. She didn't even appear affronted when I went into my interrogation the moment I sat down. I had lots of questions and a general idea of how I wanted the scenes to go, so I didn't give her much chance to divert me with pleasantries.

I asked her to tell me everything in depth, and in return she painted a truly tragic childhood. Alex had been providing plenty of advice on the way there, thinking up ways to try and catch her out by asking about her more recent life. He was on my mum's side and found the idea that she would hide something like this completely preposterous.

"Where do you work now?" I asked her at one point.

"I'm not working," Anne said confidently. "I had to leave my last job due to stress."

"What was the job?" I pressed.

"Just in an office," she answered. "A law firm. I had some trouble with one of the partners. Wandering hands, y'know?"

It's hard to continue to grill someone when they even so much as allude to being the victim of a sexual assault. I was also beginning to feel genuinely sorry for the woman. But there were scenes to think about, so the little matter of social decency was brushed aside.

"And you've lived in Morecambe all of your life?"

"That's right."

"It's very strange that you live so near but your paths have never crossed," Alex piped up.

"I don't tend to leave Morecambe." She didn't skip a beat.

"But Danny's been to Morecambe loads of times," Alex said.

"It's just chance," Anne shrugged. "And I'm pretty sure that if your mum and dad had seen me they would have turned the other way. Would you like a biscuit?"

I ceased with the questions and we ended the afternoon by telling her about school. She showed a real interest in our stories and laughed in all the right places. I was feeling comfortable with her and it didn't seem at all false to promise to visit her again soon.

"She's the real deal," Alex said on our way back home. I agreed, and it annoyed me that my parents had kept her from me. They might not have wanted me to have an auntie, but I decided that it wasn't their choice to make.

"We should just keep this a secret," Anne said to me as we were leaving. I couldn't have agreed more.

6.

My loyalty to my parents was obviously a fickle thing, as from that second meeting my default response was to believe Anne's version of events almost implicitly. She was a virtual stranger and my parents had been nurturing me for nearly fourteen years. They earned my distrust with one act, which was probably guided also by my wish for the best plots possible. 'A terrible secret threatens to rip the Lizar family apart', I imagined the listing read for one episode. 'Danny struggles to believe his parents', read another.

I always had an idea of what the plot synopses for episodes would say. Just before the Nick storyline came to a head, the TV guide said, 'Danny hits rock bottom and doesn't know who to turn to'. Strange that I remember these fleeting thoughts so well. I sometimes think in these terms now.

It's not unusual for fourteen year old boys to treat their parents like they are the enemy, but it's usually over curtailed liberties or insufficient spending money. Rarely is it over a history shrouded in lies and mystery, so my secret turning against Mum and Dad felt like it was more justified than the things most kids in school complained about.

The summer holidays provided me with ample opportunity for covert meetings with my new relative, and I tried to meet up with Anne twice a week, interrupted only by our family holiday. We spent ten days in Greece with the Proctors that year, and I had originally planned the location to be the place where I would reveal everything that I knew. When we got there, though, it just felt too soon.

I was also bowled over by a surprise holiday romance with a girl from Slough called Katy. Her parents started chatting to the grown-ups on our table and as a result Alex and I befriended Katy, and a whole host of other holiday friends that she had already made. She introduced me to a world where people have large groups of friends and feel popular all of the time. As the hotel brat-pack, we were cool by default, and this new group warranted a series of special episodes.

From the beginning she singled me out as a favourite and when the group played truth or dare, she admitted that she would snog me. Her next dare was to do just that and although I was embarrassed I was also ecstatic. This romance had come from nowhere and I got through my first kiss without too much worry. We kissed several more times that night and she briefly let me touch one of her fledgling breasts, much to the cheers of the group. These weren't my kind of people, but it was nice to pretend for a week and a half.

My dalliance with Katy ended when I saw her snogging a German in the resort swimming pool. The brief heartache that followed made for some good viewing and cliffhangers, and a first romantic plot for my character. I considered another balcony moment, this time with me on the precipice, but chose to imagine a showdown with Katy that left her humiliated. The reality was that I just didn't speak to her before she went home and she left my life with no fanfare whatsoever. I didn't even get to call her a bitch, apart from in *The Almost Lizard*, where I ripped her apart articulately with a few choice put-downs. It helped give me closure.

Upon reflection, though, I'd had my first kiss that holiday and that was a big moment for both Danny and me.

When we returned, Mum was straight into her summer school and Dad immediately spent every hour of the day catching up on the ten days he'd just taken off. On our first day back, I went straight over to Anne's as soon as I had finished my paper-round.

We walked into town and down on the beach before going for a coffee together. She asked lots of questions about me and didn't bring up Mum and Dad at all. I was flattered by the grown-up way in which she spoke to me – occasionally swearing and sharing a mucky joke or two.

"Who was that man who was at your place last time I came over?" I remember asking.

"He really was no-one," she smiled. "Not a keeper." We both smirked.

We moved on to my recent romantic encounter.

"Sounds like a slag to me," Anne surmised. I found it impossible not to be charmed by her. The time flew by and soon

I was looking at my watch and making noises about getting home before Mum did. Anne understood and suggested that we go bowling next week, her treat.

"Totally," I beamed. "You're like Mum, you know, but cooler."

Leaving Anne, I decided that there were no more scenes to be filmed until I could get home and regard my parents suspiciously again. I liked to give myself times when I was off duty, so that I could behave more like a child actor on downtime. I gave myself the occasional holiday from the show to make sure that people didn't get too bored with Danny being in it all the time.

My bus stop was on the other side of town and I made my way there along the seafront. I don't remember what I was thinking about, but I was minding my own business, perhaps thinking of getting an ice cream or preparing my excuses for when Mum asked where I'd been. I wasn't looking for any trouble. I wasn't expecting to see my father walking ahead of me. Hand in hand with Robyn Proctor.

Christmas Showdown Shocker!

1.

The sudden cliffhanger left me in an involuntary freeze for a few seconds, mouth agape. I concealed myself next to an ice cream van where I could watch Dad and Robyn move slowly down the promenade, with no sign of letting go of each other's hands. It was possible, I thought, that there was some reasonable explanation for all of this and I waited for a sign of Dad comforting her, a valid reason for him to be holding Robyn's hand. Even if neither of them was looking particularly distressed, an affair was not something I was prepared to accept without conclusive proof.

Dad removed any ambiguity from the situation by leaning in and kissing my best friend's mother.

I wasn't consciously filming at this point, but afterwards I knew that everything I did and saw in those minutes would be included in *The Almost Lizard*. There and then, though, I could only think of things in real terms. Dad and Robyn as a couple was such a ludicrous proposition that I couldn't have possibly believed it were they not kissing less than forty metres in front of me. It was crazier than Mum having a secret sister.

Dad was a dependable force in my life. I portray him as distant and unfeeling at times, but he was by no means absent. Mum just happened to be around more. I'd never doubted that my father loved me and my mother, and I respected the fact that he had eventually grown angry with us on a couple of occasions.

Secret sister aside, my family had been a rock solid unit and the kiss I was watching was nothing short of a detonation. I had grown to rely on my family to be uneventful; it was how everything had started in the first place.

They pulled out of their embrace and smiled in that smug way people do when they're in love. My head filled with thoughts that made me run away.

Presumably I made my way home on the bus, but I don't remember it at all. Mum was out when I entered the house. I was home much later than I had planned, but I had virtually forgotten that I'd even seen Anne that day. I walked upstairs, climbed into bed and lay there fully-clothed with my eyes closed. I think I fell asleep, but I can't be certain of that.

I opened my eyes when Mum came into my room a couple of hours later, making noises about me wasting my holiday by staying in bed all day. I grunted and nearly protested that I had been out and about, but instead I remembered.

Dad.

Robyn.

And going further back to lunch time, Anne.

I told Mum that I wasn't well, and I was grateful to her for leaving me alone after only a few questions about what was wrong. I lay there in the dark thinking about Dad and Robyn, imagining them together, going through the motions of an affair. The illicit kiss, followed by the denial, then by the crumbling of morals where everything got too much and they started to pull at each other's clothes before disappearing below the camera line. The guilt and the decision to do it again, the scenes of them in bed together, or one of them getting dressed to return to their families. These things had played out in the corner of my living room countless times. A soap always had to have some sort of ongoing affair, and it was a fate I had written for characters away from my own family many times.

When combined with the average levels of teenage angst I was already experiencing, my anger and confusion progressed in the direction of conspiracy. I started to think more of Danny and of the show.

It hurt more that it was Robyn, the woman who had defended me when everyone else was speaking out in condemnation of my behaviour at primary school. I had a great deal of sympathy for Charles, but by default I assumed that he was probably hiding stuff as well. All adults are liars, I thought frequently that night, feeling like I had touched on something bordering philosophy.

Some moments were spent thinking Mum deserved everything she got, that it was a fair punishment for her own lies. They were both deceitful people, but I knew that what Dad was doing was much worse. The more I considered things, the further I felt detached from my parents, and with that detachment was a propensity to do something to hurt them. It was the biggest thing to happen to me both on and off-screen.

These lies were something I had to keep to myself until the time was right. As it stood I knew nothing and it wouldn't do the storyline justice if I wasn't completely prepared. How would I know the best course of action without all of the facts?

Experience had taught me that when families were destroyed, it was usually on Christmas Day, when months' and sometimes years' worth of secrets spilled out over the course of a turkey dinner. For years, Christmas Day had been marked by a series of births, marriages, deaths and devastating revelations from the continuing dramas in the corner of the room. It was a staple of the festive season, a time when each programme tried to outdo its rivals by going for the most dramatic culmination.

Having experienced little of a tumultuous life to this point, I had nothing to go on when it came to conflict and revelations, so I took television as my guide. By the time morning came and tiredness got the better of me, it was decided that this story just had to build up to a Christmas climax.

2.

I had nearly five months worth of plot to create before Christmas, which required a substantial amount of planning to keep things interesting in the build up to the big showdown. It gave me time initially to try and make sense of all the crazy things I was finding out, and then decide exactly what to do for maximum impact.

The first stage of the plot involved Danny struggling to come to terms with the shocks from his parents, and with a plan underway, his battle to conceal his new found distaste for Malcolm and Jacqui. I was seething with betrayal and having to quell the urge to shout "Fucking liars!" in their faces every time they tried to make small-talk with me. They looked different to me – there was now an edge to their expressions that oozed deceit.

In any other situation, I could have gone to Alex's and talked things through in the strictest confidence. I knew he didn't repeat conversations with me to his parents, who therefore couldn't feedback to my parents. My extended family became very claustrophobic, with all the people I wanted to talk to suddenly being unapproachable.

I spent a lot of time on my own when I could, and managed to endure the time spent with Mum and Dad. That was where the acting came in – Danny and I shared the same deception, so it was easy in some ways to play the scenes where he was pretending that things were normal with his parents. I saw a lot of Alex, of course, but these times were tarnished with the secrets I knew could destroy him.

There was no reprieve from what was in my head. If I wasn't thinking about Dad and Robyn, I was trying to work out whether or not Mum really did destroy Auntie Anne's life.

The more I considered it, the more likely it seemed that Anne was a wronged woman. Of all the adults in the equation, she was the only one who hadn't lied to me, so she was ahead in my fickle estimations by default. So it was her I turned to when I had enough of brooding.

A week or so after my discovery, I took the opportunity to go and visit Anne. When I arrived she was warm and friendly and made me endless cups of tea, which made me cry for the first time since my family started falling apart. She asked what was wrong and I was compelled to tell her through broken sentences exactly what I had seen. As I spoke of my father's infidelity, I could tell that she wasn't surprised, and it was a viewpoint of Dad that I hadn't experienced before. It was also one that closely matched my revised opinions on him, and I knew that Anne had been the right person to turn to. When I finished, she gave me the motherly hug that I needed.

"This must be awful for you," she sympathised. "Most kids don't get to see this side of their parents. Most of them are allowed to think that their Mum and Dad are near enough perfect."

"I didn't think that," I answered. "But I didn't think Dad would do that, and with Robyn of all people."

"He didn't seem like the cheating sort to me, either," she replied without malice. "He's quite the charmer. I don't like to say this Danny, but Robyn might not be the first."

She said it so kindly that it was impossible to think of it as a vindictive statement. She was agreeing with me, and she was talking about Dad with the same distaste I felt towards him. She touched my hand and gave me a reassuring smile, and it seemed like we were in this together.

3.

To really progress things I needed to find out more about Dad and Robyn than I already knew. Every time he left the house

– be it to go to work or otherwise – I was suspicious. Moving out of the moping stage, I started to test him.

I hadn't noticed how often Dad seemed to leave papers at one of his restaurants. To the untrained eye he must have appeared forgetful, but in light of what I knew every errand or task that he remembered he had to do at the last minute was just an excuse to go and see his lover. I started offering to go places with him, showing an interest in the restaurants and hinting that I'd like to work in one of them when I was old enough. Other times I said I was just a bit bored and fancied a trip out. In response he blustered for a few seconds whilst he tried to think up a legitimate reason for me to stay at home. I could see the defeat in his eyes on the occasions when he couldn't think of a reasonable lie and consented to take me along.

When he did get away, I'd wait twenty minutes and then call Alex for a chat, casually asking whether his mum and dad were in. It was an innocent enough question, and Alex didn't notice that when I asked his mum was always out. Sometimes she had yoga classes or some other contrived reason to be out of the house, but there were other times when she'd just 'popped out.' It all added to my dossier.

I had no covert means of tailing Dad and Robyn, being too young to drive and rather conspicuous on a bike, which limited my investigations somewhat. I had to be a bit more creative than that.

My opportunity to intervene came one evening when Dad had clearly lied to me on his way out. Now that I knew what was going on, it seemed almost inconceivable that I hadn't detected that something before. Lying didn't come naturally to him and the mildest of inquisitions sent him into a fluster. After he left I called Alex up at his house and just asked in passing whether his parents were in. It just so happened that Robyn had gone to her yoga class, so I invited myself round.

We watched some television for a while and I waited until he was fully engrossed in whatever was on before I nipped off to the toilet. I sneaked into Charles and Robyn's room and I removed a pair of knickers from her underwear drawer. I stuffed them down the back of my trousers, hoping that they wouldn't fall out unexpectedly, leaving me in the slightly difficult position of explaining to Alex why I was trying to walk out with a pair of his mum's undies.

I left soon afterwards. Dad was home late that night and I was annoyed that no part of me could believe that he had just been at work. I thought about where it was they went – was it a hotel, or did they just do it in the car? No kid really wants to think about their Dad having sex, do they? If you're reading this and thinking, well, kind of, then have a word with yourself. And this is a judgement coming from me, so you know how weird it must be.

He went straight to his room and I heard him talk briefly with Mum, then things went quiet. I waited for half an hour to pass without so much as a floorboard creaking, and it was only when they were both snoring that I crept downstairs and popped the knickers in his jacket pocket. I had thought of placing them down the back of the sofa or in his car, but this was an act aimed solely at fucking with his mind and it didn't suit me for other people to know. I wanted Dad to be scared and, if possible, I wanted him to blame Robyn for playing a sexy trick on him.

Alas I have no idea how he reacted to that because I wasn't around when he found them. I heard nothing else on the matter and just had to hope that my plan had the desired effect on him. At the very least it must have given him a hell of a fright and instigated a hefty bout of paranoia. Mainly I wished I could have seen the look on his face as the security of his secret was momentarily challenged.

There was another time when Dad told us he was having dinner with his accountant. He was looking shifty so I took swift action. As he ate breakfast I helped myself to his cash cards from his wallet and threw them down a drain on my way to the bus stop. Suffice to say dinner was cancelled and I congratulated myself on a successful interception. The victory was made sweeter when I went over to Alex's that evening to see that Robyn was in. Her yoga class had been cancelled, apparently.

For Robyn, a simple letter was the best I could come up with. She needed unsettling as well and I had no idea whether Dad had confronted her about the knickers. Television had taught me that anonymous notes were most effective when written with newspaper cuttings, and keeping the message short was the key.

I cut out the letters I, K, N, O, and W from various magazines and filmed a few scenes of me preparing the letter, which I posted to Robyn's work. It felt good to put it in the letter box (definitely an episode ending moment) but then nothing happened. I asked Alex how his parents were a couple of days later and he just said that they were fine. He would have told me if anything had been said, so I had to rely on the fact that the letter had scared her.

I only had the chance to see Dad and Robyn together when the two families did something en masse. These occasions fascinated me, and I spent the whole time surreptitiously looking for tell-tale glances between the two of them.

We gathered at the Proctors' house for a barbecue in early October, one of those surprise warm weekends at a time when we should have been getting the thick coats out again. Dad and Robyn were so obvious. They often glanced sideways at each other when they thought no-one was looking, but it was very rare that their eyes met. When they did, though, they exchanged a brief smile. Again I had to wonder how the hell I hadn't spotted something sooner.

I made a point of being quiet and sullen all evening, because when I spoke the ache in my throat made my voice shaky and I didn't want people asking me whether I was alright. I had promised myself that I wouldn't let this situation make me cry, but that barbecue was a challenge. It reminded me that I wasn't being evil. I was scorned and that was a different matter entirely. As the hours passed I came close to blowing the whole thing there and then in some spontaneous ugly scenes. I wanted to shoot down every jocular remark with a barbed retort, but it didn't feel right. I had faith in the Christmas showdown.

Any hesitancy about my storyline was killed off that evening. It was the final confirmation for me. I slept very little as I started to work out the next ten weeks in meticulous detail, episode by episode.

4.

I'd made a rod for my own back in trying to stretch it out until Christmas and at times the wait became almost too much to bear. I didn't want the viewers to be bored with how slow-moving the storyline was and I felt the added pressure to make the pay-off extremely satisfying. In the meantime I had to make sure that the tension was always mounting. There had to be lots of little 'moments' occurring, some of which I contrived, but most of them happened reactively.

Alex and I were talking to an acquaintance one day during a Domestic Science class. We were joking around because we weren't much interested in cooking and it was more fun to ridicule each other's attempts at making Mississippi Mud Cake. We got to talking about cooking disasters from previous lessons, exchanging tales of dropped apple pies and nuked scones, when Alex said: "My mum's a great cook, though. Saves me having to worry about it!"

"Your mum's a slag," I snapped back without consideration. I said it so fiercely that it was impossible to laugh it off as a joke.

Alex struggled not to react. I imagine he was counting to

ten silently. He was well brought up like that. “I don’t know what your problem is,” he eventually said. “Were you not the centre of attention for a second or something? I thought you were looking uncomfortable.”

“What’s that meant to mean?” I was very much immersed in my role as victim of the piece and didn’t like being spoken to as if I was in the wrong.

“My mum has always been good with you. Why the hell would you call her that?”

A better person would have kept quiet to preserve Alex’s feelings. I kept quiet to preserve my storyline. It would have been a great scene, though. A silenced Domestic Science class watching on as I bellowed, “Because she’s been shagging my dad for months!” But it wasn’t to be. I apologised for going too far and remained ominously mute for the rest of the lesson.

I skipped the afternoon and went to see Anne. She had been my rock, letting me call her to talk whenever I liked and always welcoming me when I appeared on her doorstep. I liked the deviousness of sneaking out to call her from the telephone box in the village, looking out for people that I knew and who might get suspicious. Were I doing the storyline now, I could be sending sneaky texts right in front of the people I was talking about, but I think the classic telephone box call has its merits.

It was whilst I was pouring my heart out to Anne, a twist to the storyline came to me unexpectedly.

“There’s another reason why I’m here,” I improvised. “I told Mum about you last night.”

I could tell Anne was briefly thrown. I liked that. It meant her response looked natural on screen. “Really?”

“Yeah. I guess I couldn’t keep all of the secrets in,” I replied as if it were a real confession.

Anne contemplated the twist for a second, bouncing it around in her head whilst she thought of what to say. I tried to read her, wondering whether this was what she wanted or not.

All I could tell was that it was very interesting information for her.

"And what did she say?" she eventually asked.

"She was shocked," I lied. "She obviously didn't expect me ever to speak of you. You could tell she didn't know what to say at first. I told her how I'd heard of you and met you."

"Did you tell her what we talked about?"

"No. The things we've talked about are between me and you, right?"

"That's right," she agreed, the confidence returning. "Did she say anything else?"

"Yeah. I was shocked really. She asked quite a few questions, asked how you were and where you were living these days. She said she was sorry for keeping you from me. I don't think she'd realised what she had done until I brought you up. She said she'd had to forget about you."

"Oh."

"But she wants to see you," I added quickly.

"Really?"

I nodded eagerly. "I was stunned too. I did have to talk her into it a little bit. I said I wanted my family to get on. She might have been feeling guilty about keeping us apart. She might even be ready to apologise for what she's done." I was getting very good at on the spot deception. It didn't look like I was lying, I'm sure.

Anne must have been trying to work out what was real and what was fake. It's possible that she had lived with her own version of the past for so long that this turn of events seemed perfectly logical to her. Maybe Jacqui did feel guilty and maybe she did want to make amends. She was clearly a little suspicious, but I must have done enough to earn her trust. The intrigue was possibly enough incentive, or perhaps she saw a way of getting at Mum again.

But she agreed and that was the main point. I pushed it a little.

"Christmas is the perfect time for a reunion, don't you think?"

To be fair, if I'd been her I would have been a little suspicious at this point, so in some sense she only had herself to blame.

5.

I had expected to feel nervous when I woke up on Christmas morning, but if anything I was unerringly calm. It didn't really feel like Christmas Day at all – my mind wasn't on presents, which had to be a first in my lifetime. All of the childish excitement of Christmas had dissipated now that the day meant something so much more than that. I'd expected to at least wake up with my stomach in knots, though. I told myself, rather ostentatiously, that I was beyond feelings by that stage, numbed by my parents' secrets. I can only imagine the sort of poetry I was writing in English at the time.

There had been talk that year of not having Christmas dinner with the Proctors, which would have been the first time in my living memory. I made great protestations about tradition and how a big extended family Christmas was the best. Alex had unwittingly joined my cause and between us we persuaded our parents to carry on as normal. I imagined plenty of scenes with Dad and Robyn plotting over this one. They could only have been worried about feeling awkward and guilty, so it was satisfying to know that the reality would be so much worse for them.

Things had been different with Anne once she agreed to come for Christmas dinner. Thinking that Mum knew everything, she started talking reconciliations and fresh starts. She continued to criticise Dad, knowing that I wouldn't challenge her on anything she said, but she regarded Mum much more kindly.

When Anne talked about things getting better, I humoured her to make sure that she turned up for the Christmas special if nothing else. I didn't want to see her hurt because she had been extremely supportive of me during these lonely months, but I had mapped out a storyline and it was vital for me to make sure it went as smoothly as possible. I deserved this vengeance regardless of any innocent victims I might pick up on the way.

Justifying everything was a very simple process for me at the time. All I had to do was remind myself that my life was a lie and it seemed fair that everyone should pay, innocent or otherwise.

Christmas Eve had been all about the anticipation, Danny wandering around looking ominously at the people who were about to face the worst day of their lives. Alex had been over at ours rattling on about how much he enjoyed Christmas and how cool it was that we got to spend that time together. He said it with a poignancy that always seems contrived on television.

Elsewhere the day had been littered with the hopes and dreams of the festive season that most people share; the chance to have a guaranteed nice day and a good rest. Mum had been busying herself with food preparation and making sure the house looked nice. Dad finished work quite late, but he was at the Lancaster restaurant and had returned home at a relatively reasonable time. It seemed everyone was looking forward to Christmas, aside from Danny Lizar, who had foreboding written all over his face.

I lay awake as it got light. The episode started with a series of overhead shots of all the central characters lying in bed. Danny stared at the ceiling, breathing in and out slowly, just waiting. Malcolm and Jacqui were blissfully asleep in the half-light. Anne was sat up smoking a cigarette and looking pensive. Robyn was also sat up, thinking to herself whilst Charles snored away next to her. She looked at him with a look combining guilt and disgust. Alex was wide awake, fidgeting excitedly just because it was Christmas.

I couldn't wait any longer and went downstairs at about

eight and started to prepare myself a glass of cordial in the kitchen. The movement was enough to rouse Mum, who entered the scene shortly after me, full of festive joy. There was a buzz about Mum at Christmas.

I gazed suspiciously in the direction of the camera when she walked in and then turned to face her, the picture of innocence. "Merry Christmas," she said brightly, taking me into a hug.

"Merry Christmas," I said back and returned her embrace. I grimaced towards the camera. I expect Mum retained the same enthusiastic grin she had walked in with. A bittersweet moment for the viewers, I thought.

"I'll go and get your dad up for presents," she said after she had put the kettle on. I was left in the kitchen drinking cordial and looking more apprehensive than I felt.

I felt no pangs of guilt as I opened my presents, which included my own computer set up in the corner of the living room. It was the biggest haul I had ever received. Compensating, I thought, but feigned gratitude.

In an earlier episode Danny had gone out and purposely bought Christmas presents for Malcolm and Jacqui that were going to seem more meaningful once the day was out. For Mum I found a leather-bound book of memories, and I bought Dad a photo frame, in which I placed a picture of the three of us on holiday. Combined, they cost three weeks' paper-round money, but they were worth every penny for the bitter irony alone. They both said that I was very thoughtful, which confirmed what I already knew; that they didn't suspect a thing.

We watched TV together, animations about plucky reindeers and Disney favourites saving Christmas. We were all far too old for such shows, but again I liked the peace and wellbeing that was flying around the house. It was all about the calm before the storm. People have to seem really happy before something terrible happens, otherwise it just isn't as devastating.

The Proctors arrived at their traditional time of two o'clock. Drinks were served in the hour before Mum put the starters out. I watched with interest as Dad kissed Robyn on the cheek and wished her a merry Christmas. It was a glaring omission of mine not to have put up some mistletoe. The scene wasn't wasted, though, as I adopted a disgruntled look for the viewers. I glanced at Mum, Charles and Alex in turn, envying and resenting their ignorance. Most of the day must have been spent with me making faces for the benefit of hypothetical people and it's a surprise someone didn't ask me if I had developed a nervous twitch.

The conversation before dinner was, to be fair, very boring. There were no telling comments or any sly glances between my dad and the woman I had given the moniker 'the slag', so I excused myself a couple of times and went to the bathroom to film a couple of pep-talks.

Dead on three – as always – Mum called us through to the dining room for our starters. She didn't think much of the Royal Family as a whole, a feeling exacerbated by the way they responded to the death of Diana, and I'm sure she made us eat dead on three so we could avoid the Queen's speech. I started to feel a little bit sick as the reality kicked in. I'd set too many things in motion not to go through with it, and I was at the mercy of the improvisational skills of my fellow cast members.

So we sat down, pulled crackers, exchanged shit jokes, laughed at the tackiness of the prizes and tried to adorn hats that ripped upon first contact with human hair. More wine was poured and everyone looked on at the food with anticipation, safe in the knowledge that we'd all have a great feed. It was a soup starter, which was ideal for my somersaulting stomach. I was able to eat it normally and thus not draw attention to my nervousness.

I was facing the clock on the dining room wall, which I referred to at least twice a minute. I had told Anne to arrive at four o'clock and I expected to drop my bombshell shortly before that. I hadn't planned out exactly how I would break the news, but I was on my guard for an appropriate moment to throw it out there.

"This is lovely soup," Robyn said and I rolled my eyes for the viewers. I tried to think of a way to turn the statement around, but it wasn't my cue. The moment passed.

It was half past three when Alex and I hopped up to clear away the starters. Mum followed us in and the next fifteen minutes were spent delivering steaming plates of vegetables, stuffing and gravy, and finally a small mountain of sliced turkey. Each new dish generated coos and hand rubbing from the hungry diners. Everyone clamoured to say what looked good and what smelled the nicest. Again, no-one said anything provocative enough.

"I love your Christmas dinners, Jacqui," Alex beamed. "They're so much nicer than when Mum makes it."

Everyone laughed as Robyn pulled a face of mock indignation. I joined in half-heartedly, and briefly glared at Robyn before turning my attention to the roast potatoes. The meal was my nemesis temporarily, an insurmountable challenge made even worse by the knowledge that none of us would make it through this course. Months in the making, this was the climax of the story and I can't deny that my ball-sack had severely contracted at this point.

By that point the situation was no longer in my hands.

Alex was seated next to me and eventually sensed my anxiety to the point where he felt he had to raise it. Everyone looked straight at me when he asked whether I was alright, so I projected an innocent smile. "Yeah, great," I replied to the room. "I can't wait for this." I hoped the viewers appreciated the remark.

A further glance at the clock told me it was ten to four and I had to get things moving along. Despite my relatively meticulous planning I had expected the conversation piece to present itself over the course of the meal, but with time ticking away it fell to me to contrive something quickly. I saw the scene slipping away. It was a one-take job with absolutely no room for fuck-ups.

I thought quickly, ignoring my plate and focussing on regaining control. The success of the episode rested in my hands and I felt a pressure I was sure no other actor had gone through, not with so much personally at stake. I started to chew on a piece of turkey to keep everyone's attentions away from me. I was shaking inside so much that it was impossible to believe that I wasn't doing so visibly.

I resolved to respond to the next thing that came out of Robyn's mouth, but to my frustration, nobody spoke for a painstaking two minutes. It was approaching five to and Anne was under strict instructions to be punctual. The room echoed with the deafening smattering of smacking lips and cutlery scraping across plates. I have subsequently grown to despise those noises, and all loud eaters in the process. Reaching panic stations, I thought of just launching my lunch across the room and screaming that I couldn't take it any more.

Robyn intervened.

"This really is delicious, Jacqui," she said and everyone murmured their assent out of politeness.

"Is it better or worse than sleeping with my father?" I asked. Dad dropped a fork and everyone else stopped eating. Robyn's mouth fell open and Mum glared at me with a venom I had never seen in her before. Alex and Charles both looked bemused, glancing at each other and around the table for answers. The moment stretched on just as I thought it would.

"I don't know if you think that's funny," Mum spoke first.

"I don't," I answered back.

"You can go to your room right now."

"Okay. But only if you ask her if it's true."

Charles bowed his head towards the table and I could tell that he believed me already.

"Don't even think about dignifying that with a response,

Robyn," Mum said. "He's just attention seeking. We hoped he was over all that by now."

I looked away from her with disdain and turned to my father. "Tell them I'm lying, Dad," I said emotionlessly. I was saddened to realise that I wasn't enjoying my revenge as much as expected, but I had a duty to see the episode through.

"You nasty little shit," Dad growled. Then bellowed. "Get out of here! Now!"

"I saw you!" I snivelled at him. "Months ago, I saw you. I know it's true."

"Malcolm?" Mum piped up unsteadily. These scenes had been played out hundreds of time in my head, and there were many ways I had foreseen the moment of realisation. At the more vindictive points of my plotting, I had looked forward to the moment that her face crumbled with the shock of an unforeseen betrayal. It had been one of my main motivations, but I took no glory from seeing it happen for real. In the few seconds it took Dad to answer, this affair had gone from being a ludicrous proposition to an absolute certainty. It made her mouth quiver in a way that broke my heart on the spot. In the seconds that crushed her, I forgave Mum all of her lies and realised that she didn't deserve any of it, that I should have talked it out with her and given her the opportunity to explain things to me before going all out to ruin everything she had built up.

Then the doorbell rang.

Nobody stepped up to answer it and I silently hoped that Anne would just turn around and leave if we just ignored her. I looked at the floor, guiltily hoping that everyone could just forget the whole thing.

"Can someone just deny what Danny is saying here?" Mum said to everyone. Robyn and Dad both avoided her gaze and she let out a little sob, consolidating how wretched I felt.

It was too much for Alex, who had remained silent throughout. He threw his chair back and went to run out of the room.

"Wait," I grabbed his shoulder. He swung around and pushed me to the floor. I went with a clatter, taking a couple of table ornaments with me for effect.

"Don't you dare touch me," he blustered and darted for the front door. The remaining five of us froze in an impromptu tableau; everything was seemingly revealed but no-one quite knew what to say. It was down to Mum and Charles to react, or for Robyn and Dad to offer up apologies and excuses, but everyone seemed lost for a next line. Charles continued to stare into what remained of his dinner whilst Mum scanned the room with her eyes, seeking an ally. Dad and Robyn looked at opposing walls.

"I'm not late am I?" Anne asked from behind us, stood in the doorway clutching a bottle of wine in her left hand. She'd obviously tried to dress for the occasion but she still looked like a bag lady. Mum looked at her, horrified. "Danny didn't tell you, did he?"

Mum shrieked then. She looked at me and she instantly knew everything. She turned back to Anne.

"Get out," she shouted. "Whatever he's told you, you're not welcome here. Get out!"

A plate sailed across the room, shattering on the doorframe above Anne's head. Years of hatred returned in a second, and Anne launched the bottle of wine she'd brought straight back at Mum, who dodged it rather effortlessly. The bottle exploded on the sideboard, spilling some shards of glass onto Charles' dinner plate. It was enough to make him look up.

"Regardless of who you are and what you're doing here," he said calmly to Anne, "that was very fucking rude. You have just interrupted the worst moment of my life, and it would make me very happy if you were to return to whatever jumble sale you limped in from and leave us to it."

Charles' stern tone should have been enough to put Anne off, but with her expectations dashed I was introduced to the woman my parents had tried to protect me from.

"I see everyone knows about Malcolm's latest indiscretion," she said to the room cruelly. "I'm Anne, by the way. Jacqui has told you about me I hope."

Mum sat down. I think her legs gave way. Not something to be proud of, making your mum's legs give way. Stood in front of her were her husband and best friend, who were having an affair, and her son and estranged sister, who had been secretly colluding. I wished that we could at least cut to an advert break and someone would walk in and congratulate us on some amazing scenes, but instead we had to play this out until the bitter end.

"Perhaps, Robyn, we should go and have a little chat back home. Thank you for such a public humiliation, Danny. Perhaps next time you could do me the decency of having a quiet word in my ear instead."

Charles sounded so matter-of-fact that it crossed my mind that he might be feeling alright about everything. It gave me the confidence to look up, and I saw that he was completely expressionless, save for the tears streaming from both eyes.

"Charles," Dad said and made to walk over to him, then thought better of it.

"Mal, thanks for having us over. It's been memorable," Charles said before punching Dad square in the jaw, forcing him out of his seat and under the table in an undignified heap. He destroyed Dad in one blow and then marched out. Robyn scurried after him, saying nothing to Mum for fear of a similar assault.

Anne was smirking. "Nice to meet you both," she said as they brushed past her. "Merry Christmas."

"I can't imagine why Jacqui hardly speaks of you," Charles stopped and said to her. "Were you this charming before prison?"

Charles stole the scene in those few minutes. His dialogue was scorching hot. I imagined plaudits and awards, were it a real show he was filming and the not the decimation of his own family. The remaining Proctors exited, leaving Jacqui, Malcolm, me and Anne.

"Time to go, Anne," Malcolm said. "There's no place for you here. I don't know why Danny brought you to us – "

"Doesn't look like you have much place here either," Anne interrupted.

"Why don't you both leave?" Mum suggested, holding back the tears.

"How about it Malcolm? For old times' sake?" Anne erupted into laughter at her little joke and it was obvious to me how vicious and hideous she really was. All of my sympathies lay with Mum, but it was too late for that.

"I think you should go," I told Anne.

"After everything your mum did to me? We talked about this, Danny," she said for the benefit of my parents. Her smirk had vanished, though.

"What rubbish have you been poisoning his mind with?" Mum demanded wearily.

"I know it's your fault my grandma died," I blurted out. I think it was a justification, but it didn't sound that way.

Mums eyes sparkled with anger as her mouth curled into a swear word. She launched herself at Anne and the Hepworth twins fell to the floor and started scrapping in the hallway, pulling down the telephone table in their wake. Given time, Anne would have won that battle, but Dad grappled her away and pushed her through the front door, slamming it behind her.

I was the only one left in the dining room, listening on as Anne hurled obscenities from the driveway. Mum remained on the hall floor and Dad leaned against the front door. Not one of us could look at the other.

A rock plunged through the living room window, adding decibels to the screaming and hollering coming from my new-found Auntie. "You're cancers, the lot of you! You deserve everything you get. I should have killed that monster growing inside of you when I had the chance, Jacqui."

I peered out of the dining room window. It was nearly dark, but I could see net curtains twitching from neighbours' windows all over the street. One or two stood in their doorways, alarmed by the unseasonal fracas and wondering whether to intervene.

Moving back to centre stage and taking control of the episode, I walked past my parents and out into the street to face Anne.

"You said she wanted me here," my Auntie spat at me. "You're just like them… "

"You're right, I am," I replied, feeling a monologue coming on. "I'm not all lonely and pent up and spiteful like you. I don't know what really happened in the past, but you're a liar. I can see it so clearly now. You used me when I was vulnerable. Now you get yourself out of here or I'll say that you touched me inappropriately."

The last part I whispered in case any of the neighbours were listening.

"You're your mother's son alright," Anne sneered and went to slap me.

I don't take pride in the fact that I hit a woman, but I was confused and also angry at her for having deceived me as well. I slapped her across the right cheek and she fell to the floor. I was frozen to the spot as a police car swung into the street seconds after I belted her. For a while it seemed like they had come for me.

I was relieved that they picked up Anne and not me. The officers told her that she was in breach of a restraining order, and then charged her with trespass and criminal damage.

I couldn't have predicted that episode at all. No amount of planning could have made it as powerful as it was. The critics would bleat that it was charged with emotion from a stunning ensemble cast. It would win awards.

The episode ended with Danny sat on the driveway, as his estranged Auntie was driven off in the back of a police car.

Two more officers went in to speak with Malcolm and Jacqui and Danny burst into tears again.

It was my best and worst episode to date, a real ratings buster. I wondered if I could still call it a game when there wasn't an ounce of fun left in it.

6.

There was enough going on in the wake of the revelations to justify a new episode of *The Almost Lizard* each day between Christmas and New Year's Eve. The fallout only really began the moment that Anne was carted away in the police car. A good portion of my year had been spent preparing for those scenes with little thought to what would happen afterwards. It wasn't something I was in a position to control.

In all truth I expected a few weeks of tears and arguments followed by reconciliation and all of us moving on with our lives. In soaps, affairs don't always mean the end. Something often happens to inspire forgiveness. I hadn't planned that part, but I guess I'd always intended to repair the damage once things had calmed down. It's hard to imagine that I wanted to see my family ruined forever.

Anne had shocked me with her sudden character change. She had won me over through kindness and opportunism, but she had revealed her true nature in a harrowing performance. It was clear now why Mum had kept her away from me and I regretted my actions bitterly. A few days later I was told my parents' history in great detail, but on Christmas Day I only had an inkling of how awful I had been.

I sat quietly with Mum as she gave her statement to the police. Dad had spoken to them first, and then Mum had politely asked him to leave. I gave my statement last. This was the first time I'd had real police on the programme. Any involvement with the law in the past had been imagined and so doing those scenes was still quite exciting despite the churning guilt in my stomach.

My statement was more a monologue directed at my mother, recounting how the school bully who ruined my life had told me about my crazy auntie, who had duped me with lies about my own parents. I played it young and impressionable. I told the police that I wanted to make Christmas special by healing the family rift, but it had all gone horribly wrong. The police believed my well-meaning act far more than Mum did.

We signed statements and the officers wished us a season's greetings with heavy irony. I showed them out, whilst Mum remained firmly in her seat, suddenly paralysed. She'd held herself together through the formalities, but when it was over she dropped the pretence and started to react. Or not react, more accurately. She just sat and stared into space under the inadequate glow of the fairy lights from the Christmas tree. Occasionally a tear rolled down her cheek, but aside from that she was essentially comatose.

The house had been decorated to the nines for the big day, but each festive touch had become tragic in light of what had taken place. The discarded wrapping paper on the floor, the cards hanging from the wall, and the Quality Street and nibbles that littered the coffee table, it all looked so trite and pathetic that night. From that day I've always seen Christmas as a hopelessly optimistic time, an opportunity to paper over the cracks of how bloody awful life can be at times. It's not a bad delusion to have. We all need something to look forward to. For many, Christmas and a summer holiday is all the anticipation required to make it through each year. Who am I to judge?

I was in bed by eight o'clock that evening with nothing more to film. Neither Mum nor I thought to watch the soaps on television. I heard her trudge wearily up the stairs some time after nine and the sound made me cry. Not in the way a kid cries because he knows he's going to get a bollocking for knocking over a vase, but in a way that told me I had done something truly terrible and I felt very sorry for doing it.

Downstairs in the dining room, Christmas dinner congealed and decayed. Three days later Mum threw it all away in a rage, along with the crockery, silverware and table ornaments. It marked the end of her period of wallowing. Instead of finding a bat or a similar deliverer of destruction, she reached for the duster. She looked me dead in the eye, no love lost, and said, "This house is a shithole."

"Are you okay?" I asked.

"You're going to put the vac round every room in this house," she informed me. "Then you're going to clean the bathrooms."

I naively believed that from this point everything would start to go back to normal.

I had a Boxing Day showdown with Alex. Mum was virtually catatonic and I needed someone to talk to about what had happened, and Alex was the only one I could realistically consider. I was a little surprised when he agreed to meet with me.

We convened at the park. He was there before me and the moment I caught his eye I knew that I was in for another gruelling scene.

"What a mess," I opened and watched Alex try to suppress a violent outburst. "This has been a nightmare for me, Al, let me tell you."

That was enough to provoke a reaction. "Oh I fucking bet," he spat caustically. "How long were you plotting that one?"

For a second I thought he knew. I panicked and stumbled over my response.

"Why couldn't you have told people normally instead of making such a scene?" he demanded. Alex could be fierce at times, but it had never been directed at me before and I was a little intimidated.

"I couldn't keep it to myself any longer," I spluttered.

"Shut up!" he barked back. "You timed it just for when your

auntie turned up. You can't say it was a complete coincidence."

"What do you mean?"

I waited for him to show his hand.

"I mean you wanted to get back at your mum and dad to maximum effect. You waited until everyone was happy so you could cause the most damage. You're a shit, Danny. Our lives don't need livening up by one of your melodramatic performances."

I stood there exposed, lacking a response that anyone would understand.

"I was angry," I offered lamely.

"At who?"

"My parents. Your mum."

"And what about me and my dad? Did we deserve it as well?"

Totally subservient I replied, "I didn't think."

"That's just it. You're totally thoughtless."

I nearly told him he sounded like my dad, but it didn't feel appropriate.

"I was hurt."

"You're just cruel. We should have been in same boat and supporting each other through this, but now I hate you more than I hate my mum and your dad."

This was the scene where it dawned on Danny exactly what he had done. Alex stalked out of the park, and so ended one of the strongest double acts in the short history of *The Almost Lizard*.

Dad booked into a Travelodge on the other side of Lancaster, not giving anything away as to how he was feeling. He emerged for clean clothes a couple of days before the New Year, ringing the doorbell like a visitor. Mum was still engrossed in her cleaning binge and was dusting the hall lampshade at the time. I appeared in the doorway and regarded him silently but judgementally.

"I think it's time we talked," he said. I snorted and Dad glared at me, wordlessly warning me against being too sanctimonious about this. I glared back, indicating that his opinion meant nothing to me.

"Does this mean she doesn't want you?" Mum asked casually.

"I've not seen Robyn," Dad replied. "She's not important."

"I suppose I should hear the details," Mum said and just dropped the duster on the floor. She motioned for Dad to go into the living room. I moved out of the way and then followed them in. I was only a little bit shorter than Dad by that point, and I remember considering whether I could take him in a fight.

"This is just me and your mum I think," he said to me.

"I think Danny has as much right to hear this as me," Mum piped up unexpectedly. "You cheated on him just as much as you cheated on me." She went out to pour herself a gin and tonic whilst Dad and I shared an uncomfortable silence until she returned.

Dad said that he didn't know where to start.

"How about telling me how you ended up shagging my best friend?" Mum asked.

Sheepishly, Dad took his story back nearly four years to when I was getting in trouble for the story I told in class, and when he had discovered about the secret television watching. Mum was suitably incredulous. Not wishing to steal the scene, I remained mute.

"I was so angry with you and I didn't know what to do. I went back to the school to see her. I wanted to know if everyone knew that you were watching television behind my back – "

"Do you know how ridiculous that sounds? I wasn't sleeping with the bloody television!"

"It was a betrayal, Jacqui."

"And one good betrayal deserves another," she rallied back.

"Robyn calmed me down and helped me put it in perspective.

She hugged me and I kissed her back."

Mum flinched.

"We kissed once or twice, and then Robyn pulled away. I knew it was wrong immediately. She looked angry and told me to leave."

"So you came back to us?" Mum looked amused. She was playing a part, I swear. "We were so worried about you that night. We thought you'd driven off and had a crash."

Dad continued. He told us nothing happened for a long time after that, but there was always a hint of unfinished business between them. They managed to contain their lust for two years until one night Robyn came into the Lancaster restaurant looking for Charles, who was over at the Southport branch. She arrived clearly distressed, following a particularly acerbic PTA meeting where she had been branded a liberal and accused of irresponsible thinking for wanting the year five children to be given some very basic sex education.

"When she realised Charles wasn't there, she broke down in front of me. I only took her into the office because I thought she was disturbing the customers."

As Dad told the story I shared the flashback the viewers were being treated to. I could picture it all so clearly. They shared a couple of drinks and Dad managed to cheer her up. Mum let out a little 'huh' at that part of the story. They had a little more to drink after Dad locked up the restaurant. Left alone, they succumbed to the ongoing flirtation and desire, right on the floor of the restaurant.

"We thought it would get it out of our systems once and for all," he said in his defence.

"But we know it didn't turn out like that, don't we Malcolm?"

It wasn't like that, apparently. Afterwards they had both felt extremely guilty and tried their best to avoid each other as much as possible. They hid behind their spouses and went out of their way not to be left alone. The way Dad described it they were just victims to an uncomfortable attraction, and that as good people they held off having sex until they absolutely had to.

After this they found themselves getting into arguments at home and needing to storm off. It just so happened that they would turn to each other for shoulders to cry on and soon sex was the only option. It was tea, sympathy and a shag in a motorway hotel by all accounts.

"It sounds almost unavoidable," Mum said. Her amusement gave her power, I think, and it was the justice the viewers would want to see Jacqui experience.

"We've ended it now," he added. "It's over."

"I can imagine it's a lot less fun when it's out in the open. Takes the shine off the sneaking around. We could pretend though, couldn't we? You could come home and pretend to be off to some work emergency, and I could pretend to believe you. I don't care whether it's over now, you arsehole, we're over! That's the point!"

"We can sort this out," Dad said lamely.

"You can pack your stuff and get out," Mum answered tonelessly.

"At least let us talk a little more."

"I think we've heard enough."

"I think you should let Danny speak for himself," and Dad looked at me for only the second time since he had arrived, just when I had convinced myself that I wasn't really in the room, perhaps only directing this scene. I had been happy to have no lines, but thinking up something dramatic off the cuff was not really a challenge.

"You're dead to me," I answered and stared at him intently until he had to look away.

Half an hour later, his car was packed up and heading back to the Travelodge. However united our front was in the presence of Dad, it fell apart the moment he drove off. I went to my room and she carried on cleaning and we didn't speak again that day.

My final set-to of the week was with Robyn. She caught sight of me as I left the newsagent having completed my paper-round for the day. She had been in her car and had gone to the effort of pulling up and marching across the street. I stood and watched with interest as she shouted and bawled and made her way over to me.

"Are you proud of what you did, hey? Do you see how many people you've managed to hurt? Was that what you wanted?"

Street rows were a staple part of programmes like *The Almost Lizard*, but something I rarely got to film for real.

"I'd have preferred it if you hadn't slept with my father at all," I bellowed back to her.

"Did you think what you'd do to your mother?"

"Did you?" I countered loudly, ensuring that the spat remained public.

"You have a short memory, Danny. I defended you when people thought there was something wrong with you. They wanted to pump you full of pills to make sure you turned out to be normal. Do you remember? They were going to call in a shrink to get all the badness out of you, and I told them that they were the insane ones."

It was an awesome speech, but it stung to be on the receiving end of it.

A smattering of villagers had gathered to watch what was going on from a safe distance, close enough to hear but so far as to not look overtly nosey.

Danny was in the right and deserved to win the argument. Robyn had done more wrong and needed shooting down. Programmes like this survived on a sense of eventual justice. My voice was a little too shaky to deliver the lines the way I really wanted to, but armed with Dad's side of the story I had the perfect response.

"You mean the night you first kissed my father? The night all this started. You defended me and ripped my family apart at the same time."

"You're a damaged little boy and don't you forget it," she hissed and went to hit me. I grabbed her arm.

"A slapper in more ways than one," I said and pushed her away. She stormed back to her car. "Home-wrecker!" I yelled after her as she drove away. I stood in the street for a while looking despondent, reminding the viewers that Danny warranted sympathy.

I thought of Anne shortly before midnight took us into a new millennium. I was sat at home with Mum watching television silently. We'd given up on communicating with each other much earlier in the day when I realised that she couldn't speak to me unless it was unpleasantly.

I thought of Anne because she used to listen to me and I missed that. If I hadn't got her locked up she would have been dishing out sympathy at a time when that was all I needed. I thought of where she was at that point, locked up and awaiting sentence for the charges she'd been coerced into pleading guilty to. There would be no trial, no formal exit for Anne. Her character had left the show in the back of a police car, never to be seen again.

Midnight came and I was thinking up new credits for the show to mark the new millennium. Mum and I wished each other a half-hearted happy new year. Then she told me to go to bed.

7.

And after that? Nothing.

This is the difficulty with trying to emulate television drama in the real world. Real time. In the soaps, the ends are tied up as much as possible and everyone is in a position to move on to other storylines or have a quiet patch. Take the standard divorce procedure, there are a few weeks of recriminations and fallout followed by a rest period until one character moves on or divorce proceedings kick in, or maybe a meaty custody battle to keep things ticking along. Then there will be elements of moving on – new love interests, a new job, and some sort of new lease of life for one or the other.

January came and went with no showdowns and no plot developments to speak of. Dad stayed away, Mum remained frosty and the Proctors made no contact. Alex showed little evidence of thawing and sat purposefully separate from me on our buses to and from school. He spent his time with the acquaintances he had kept on standby throughout his high school career.

As a result I spent all of my time between lessons on my own, sat quietly near to people that I kind of knew from classes, nearly being part of what they were doing. On other days I whiled away the time in the library, reading novels and doing extra research for my coursework.

Word was out about what I had done to Alex and due to his relative popularity, people were inclined to side with him and give me more of a wide berth than they did already. I could tell I was being actively shunned rather than just going unnoticed, and it was an unpleasant development. It added to my already considerable angst.

In her quest to move on, Mum was working longer hours doing after-school activities and had joined a theatre group. When she was in, we didn't speak beyond the functional, idle small talk about meals and washing. When we were in the same room we watched television in silence, but usually I remained in my room whilst she sat downstairs.

When we were in the same room and speaking to each other, I invariably said something that made her shout at me. She's just lashing out, I assured myself. I also understood that it had to be this way, that she had every right.

Mum was being strong, and to do that she had to distance herself from me. I was too young to be kicked out, so I was endured at best. She was moving on and it seemed that she was moving away from me in the process. All around me people were moving on but I felt cornered. I had no option but to spend January moping in my room and going on internet forums to start arguments with strangers. There was nothing happening that added to the show apart from Mum snapping at me, which grew tedious rather quickly for both me and the viewer. I attempted some internet based storyline, but me typing on my computer failed to capture the imagination.

So the characters were rested for a while until something happened. The others had little bits of action, but it was a clear month off for Danny, and I hoped the viewers would be really pleased to see him when he did return. I didn't have it in me to fabricate anything at that time, not when I knew what I was capable of. It seemed for a while that nothing would happen again, ever.

Then Robyn and Charles got back together.

Charles had been Mum's official rock in the aftermath of the revelations. They had gone for dinner and drinks a few times and I suspect they might have slept together at some point. I know that they talked a lot on the phone, bound by this shitty experience that they had in common.

I was in one night when I noticed her looking at the phone a lot and it occurred to me that it hadn't rung in days. Over the next few days she asked me routinely whether Charles had called and when I said he hadn't she looked at me like it was my fault. We were both getting suspicious.

"Why don't you call him?" I asked one day.

"If I wanted your opinion I would have asked for it," she snapped back. I tried my best not to inflame things, but I always seemed to uncover new ways of irritating her without even trying.

The day after that little spat, Alex spoke to me for the first time since Boxing Day. "By the way, Mum and Dad are back together. You didn't get to ruin everything after all," he said to me at the bus stop. An episode ended there and then.

I fumed about Robyn's second chance all day, walking around with thunder on my face and a 'don't fuck with me' gait that must have been laughable. I told Mum that evening, thinking that I should probably not keep things from her. Learning from my mistakes, see.

"Well that's just fucking brilliant!" she raged in response. "Thanks for that, Danny."

"What did I do?"

"What did you do? What did you do, Danny?"

I knew I was in trouble when she started to say my name a lot.

"I'm forty-one years old and my only son has made himself instrumental in destroying my marriage. That smarts for a start. And now I'm stuck here with you whilst the woman who screwed my husband gets to keep her family together. Thank you very much."

I acknowledged that I was filming my first decent scene in ages and responded.

"Well perhaps if you'd tried a little harder to keep Dad interested then absolutely none of this would have happened anyway."

Mum slapped me like I hoped she would. I recoiled and stormed out of the house, deluding myself that I might just not return. It gave me a rush to be involved in something dramatic. I'd missed it during my weeks away.

This was a new low for Danny. He was falling. I didn't know where to take him or what would happen next. I caught a bus into town because I didn't know what else to do. I was worried that I was writing myself into a corner with no-one to interact with.

I wondered whether it was time to leave the show.

When characters hit rock bottom they have to react to keep things moving on. Sometimes they have to make things worse just to ensure that something happens. If there was nothing for me to do then how could I justify a place in the show? I thought back to *Morning Delivery* where revenge was best served with a brick through a window, and when I got off the bus in town I found myself gravitating towards Dad's Lancaster restaurant. The *ChaMal* chain had proven popular from the start and I wondered what would happen to it.

I found a small piece of rubble in an alleyway near the restaurant, which was situated near the river in a small strip of eateries. As I walked towards it I allowed everything to pass through my mind, montage style; my broken family, my ex-best friend, the misery and boredom, the loneliness, the arguments, the silence and the being left behind.

Smashing the window was a textbook cry for help from Danny. He was desperate to get in trouble to try and get some attention, especially from the father he was sure had abandoned him. I played out the scene to maximum effect, mentally debating whether or not to do it before touching the spot where Mum had slapped me. Post-edit, this scene would be sound-tracked by snatches of dialogue from the past that demonstrated how low Danny had sunk. A little bit of Robyn's tirade, then Dad reliving his first time with Robyn, and Alex's little character assassination, then a snippet of the row with Mum.

"Fuck you all," I muttered then released the missile. It was an impressive stunt, the window showing Danny's reflection before collapsing underneath itself, sweeping away the image of the wronged teen in a landslide. An eerie silence followed the shattering before the alarm went off.

I was tempted to remain where I was but I wasn't quite sure if Danny was ready for consequences. I fled the scene without direction, running a safe distance without knowing what I would do once I got there. When I was clear of the shrieking alarm I dropped to a walking pace and moved inconspicuously through the centre of town. It was only eight o'clock but it was dark and seemed much later. I hadn't been out late at night before. In my fifteen years I hadn't made too many demands for freedom from my parents, and I'd had no reason to be in town after dark.

Smashing the window had given me a brief sense of euphoria, but it soon faded. I didn't want to be out and about any more and decided to head home. Danny had hit rock bottom and had a realisation just in time.

As I approached the bus station I tensed up again when I noticed Steve Etches and Callum Shay stood by the entrance engaged in a chip fight. They were friends of Nick Armitage and had been instrumental in my torment on the school bus during the bullying storyline. Since Nick's expulsion and subsequent disappearance to a Young Offenders' Institute they had reverted to not acknowledging my presence at all, but out of school and quite late into the evening I didn't know whether I would enjoy the same indifference.

I kept my head down in an attempt to shrink myself as much as possible, but it came as no surprise when a chip bounced off the top of my head. Ignore it, I thought, not wanting to enter that particular scene at that particular moment. Then I thought, fuck it.

I looked directly at the pair of them. I was feeling pretty edgy at that point, having engaged in a criminal act only minutes before, so I found I had the confidence to storm up to Steve and grab him round the throat. He was a little taller and definitely bigger than me, but I was full of rage and that seemed to even things out.

"Don't fucking mess with me," I snarled and I'm proud to say that I managed not to sound as terrified as I really was.

In the ensuing silence I had moments to reflect on what I was doing and the fear started to creep in. By all means and rights Steve should have pushed me away and kicked seven shades of shit out of me, so I was shocked to find him attempting to placate me.

"Calm down, Lizard. Sorry. We was only messing around," he said, slightly asphyxiated. I loosened my grip and waited for the onslaught of punches. Steve reached into a bag they had been keeping on the floor and produced a can of lager, which to my surprise he offered to me.

LIZARD

Wild Child

1.

I couldn't help but feel a little proud of my hangover the next morning. It was my first and it was on a school morning. Mum woke me up with some aggressive words and my head hurt before I even opened my eyes. To my credit I made it all the way to the toilet before I puked and managed a few mouthfuls of toast ahead of catching the bus to school.

Having called in sick for my paper-round I was able to leave on time. Away from Mum I allowed myself to feel as bad as I looked. It was a self-inflicted illness of the kind I hadn't experience before. I was groggy and it was bitingly cold. All I wanted to do was close my eyes and go back to sleep.

I had followed Steve and Callum to a bench in a churchyard near town, half expecting them to mug me at any moment. I was both nervous and perplexed which had made me drink my can very quickly. Over the course of the evening we got through six more between us, which was more than I had ever had before. My prior drinking experience had been a couple of stubbies on holiday and a little something on New Year's Eve.

They asked me what I was doing out and about and that was enough to set me off raging about my broken home, littering my speech with more expletives than normal. They empathised with my ire; Steve's parents had split up years ago and Callum didn't even know who his father was.

I had gone through life believing that I had nothing to say to their sort of person. God, they'd made my life hell only the year before. They weren't people I was born to associate with, let alone identify with, but there I was talking with them about what a dick my father was and them empathising with my rage.

I knew just enough about football to hold a bit of conversation on the matter and Callum remembered that he'd seen me at a couple of Lancaster City matches. He mainly sat there and smoked and laughed when Steve said something amusing. He told me that his mum had a duty free scam going on, so she didn't notice him routinely stealing packets of fags from her stash. He was enthusiastic about cars, football and girls and completely mute on almost any other subject. His area was brawn; he had a stocky frame and a permanently angry look on his face. Even his happy laugh was menacing. He gave off an aroma of violence at all times, but reserved a look for his mates that said, 'You're alright.'

Steve was the talker and had the air of a leader about him. He dished out the beers only when he was ready and when the conversation didn't interest him he talked about something else until the original subject was completely forgotten. It was like he couldn't let a moment go without sharing his view on it.

It was Steve who said, "You're alright, Lizard," as I staggered away at the end of the evening. I can't overstate what a thrill that was for me.

Waiting for the bus the next morning, though, I knew not to hope for anything more than one peculiar evening. I stayed away from Alex at the bus stop, but I'm sure he witnessed me throwing up into a hedge just before the bus arrived. I kept my eyes shut all the way to town. I think I might have fallen asleep briefly on a couple of occasions. When I got to the bus station, I leaned against a wall and tried to will myself into feeling better. I was incapable of thinking anything coherent, even in my mind I was just a series of groans.

Again I thought about turning back and going home, but I knew that Mum would find out and I didn't want to enrage her further. A little humility was needed to get things back on track at home. I had fallen through the door some time after eleven the night before, incapable of disguising my drunkenness.

"Where the hell have you been?" Mum had screeched.

"Leave it out," I slurred back.

"Have you been drinking?"

"Have you been drinking?" I asked in return. I barged past her and fell up the stairs towards my bed. I was pretty dizzy by then, ricocheting off the walls with almost every step.

"Don't you dare think about going off the rails!" she shouted after me. I smirked, knowing full well that going off the rails was exactly what I was planning to do.

It didn't feel like such a great idea the next morning, though, with the prospect of another lonely school day ahead of me, this time with the added pain of a hangover and an irate mother.

Alex caught my eye briefly, just long enough for me to register his disgust.

I saw Steve, Callum and two others walk into the bus station. I didn't try to acknowledge them, accepting that I got lucky the night before but not to expect anything of it. I pretended not to see them and started looking for nothing in my school bag.

"Alright Lizard, how's your head?" Steve slapped me on the back and I jumped skittishly. I couldn't have been more surprised.

"I feel fucking terrible," I said and we both laughed. Callum joined in and so did the two that I didn't know.

By the time we pulled up outside school I had been formally introduced to the other two. Russell and Lee were very similar to each other, simple in their tastes and perennially bored. They had less of a range than Callum even, and I seem to remember them predominantly talking about porn, wanking and which girls (famous or otherwise) they wanted to get into.

Any female judged to be above the status of pigdog were fair game for wolf whistling and vulgar heckling.

In a way, Steve was the only one with a truly distinct personality. He was the clear leader of the group and the other three were non-descript followers of his cause. Callum, Russell and Lee all had skinheads and in their spare time wore variations of the same tracksuit almost exclusively.

I think Russell and Lee were as surprised as I was to find me infiltrating their gang, but they made no attempt to challenge it. Steve introduced me as Lizard and they nodded and accepted that I would be there from now on.

They all had nicknames. Steve was named Ste-Bo, which I thought sounded a little like J-Lo, but I didn't say anything. On account of his propensity to fight, Callum went by the moniker Knuckles, which was often abbreviated to Knucks. Lee was L-Dog, his rapper name, apparently, because he thought he was a champion beat-boxer. He wasn't. Russell was charmingly known as Boner because they said he had a permanent erection.

I caught Alex looking over once or twice but I pretended that I hadn't noticed. He must have been stunned by what he was seeing that morning. All of a sudden I didn't need him and I was moving in a new circle. These events had storyline potential and I saw Danny being given a new lease of life, something that had seemed impossible even twelve hours earlier. Alex definitely heard Ste-Bo tell me to come and find them at lunch time. We were walking right in front of him when he said it. My hangover dissipated with the excitement of the offer.

2.

It was strange that my parents' separation made me cool to people who would have hated me otherwise. Not one of the group lived with their fathers, each with their own tales of abandonment and ill-treatment. As a group we all held our families and their messy lives in contempt. We were wise enough to see that they were unworthy of respect. They were all fuck-ups and they deserved to be treated as such.

I went from having absolutely no-one to having four new friends very quickly. They weren't my kind of people but I was lonely and willing to change. I could be their kind of people.

I pictured a television guide article introducing the four major new characters to the show. All of them were added to the opening credits, cementing their place at the heart of the cast.

They could have been playing an elaborate trick on me, but I was in no position to be suspicious.

Ste-Bo invited me to a party that weekend and I accepted calmly, disguising my urge to skip around with delight.

I hadn't been to a proper party before. Until that week I hadn't been the sort of person who received invites to anything other than tame parentally supervised birthday bashes, and even those were few and far between.

This was a real party invite. Knuckles' Mum was off on a fags and booze run which left him home alone with Kerry, his seventeen year old sister. It wasn't the sort of thing I was exposed to as best mate to Alex Proctor.

I told Mum rather ambiguously that I was staying with friends, knowing full well that it wasn't that simple. Already my new friends were the source of rifts between us on account of them getting me drunk a few days before. Mum was still touchy about Robyn and Charles reuniting and leapt at any chance to launch into a conflict. It didn't take a lot to create a scene.

"Do you not remember me telling you that you were grounded?"

"I remember," I answered cockily.

"Then you're not going out," she answered.

"Try and stop me."

There was a silent stand off for a moment or two when it

was decided that Mum wouldn't challenge me. I watched her expression go from caring to ambivalent, and then she shrugged. "Don't expect to be welcomed back here tomorrow," she said and I was a little troubled that there weren't more cross words.

"Don't expect me to want to come back either," I retorted and slammed the door on my way out. I stalked down the drive muttering that she was a fucking bitch, imagining that she was inside filming her real sadness at being outdone by Danny. I knew full well that she wouldn't kick me out, however strained our relationship was.

The party was an event worth dedicating an entire episode to. There hadn't been a proper party on the show before. Knowing these people only a little, I headed into town with wild fantasies about what might happen over the course of the night.

I can't say I had a storyline mapped out in my head at this point, but I knew that the sort of people I was fraternising with were only going to be a bad influence on me. I was happy to have a storyline again, and even happier to have new friends even if they weren't strictly speaking my kind of people. I had nothing to lose and had decided to do whatever the storyline threw at me.

I imagined another TV guide article where I explained the reasons for Danny's new direction. "Danny has been through a lot in recent months. His family has fallen apart and he seems to have lost everyone he cared about," I revealed. "This is after the bullying and the shock of finding out about his long lost aunt and his dad's affair with Robyn. He's feeling very low and suddenly this unlikely bunch of people take an interest in him. He's desperate to fit in with them, which means he's capable of anything.

"I'm very excited about this plot," I continued. "It's really changing the character of Danny and I look forward to each script, finding out what he's going to do next. Can I reveal what's in store? Nope, even I don't know what's going to happen!"

I met Ste-Bo in town. I didn't own a tracksuit so I was

wearing what I considered to be the least middle-class items of clothing in my wardrobe, which were a pair of scruffy jeans and a t-shirt with a sportswear logo emblazoned across the front. I let myself down by wearing my school coat, but I didn't have any other. There had been no need until now for me to consider my sartorial qualities and how un-cool I was.

"Y'alright," I grunted at Ste-Bo. I had to remind myself not to look too enthusiastic when I met up with them. It wasn't how they worked.

"We're gonna need something to drink," Ste-Bo replied without returning the greeting. I'd been paid that day for the paper-rounds I had completed and offered up the only tenner I had. "Don't be a prick, Lizard," he said, not unkindly. "You look about twelve. You're not going to get served anywhere."

I flushed a little, as I did many times during this part of my life when my naivety shone through.

"Besides," he added, "it's no fun if you pay for it."

It was here that I found a use for my relative innocence. It made me perfect accomplice material. Ste-Bo led me to Sainsbury's where we wandered around for ten minutes, browsing at biscuits, washing powder and magazines before making our way to the alcohol aisles. There was a lady there stacking shelves, so Ste-Bo sent me to go and ask her where I could find something.

"Like what?" I asked, clearly panicked.

"I dunno, fucking tampons or something," he said and smiled at me. Surprisingly I didn't blindly obey him. I opted for Garibaldi biscuits, for some reason it was the first thing that came to mind. I was glad Ste-Bo didn't hear me because I'm sure it would have been the source of great ridicule. The woman told me and I thanked her. She smiled at me, which would have made me feel guilty were I not in the middle of some impromptu shoplifting scenes.

I walked back over to Ste-Bo who told me I needed to go and buy some chewing gum. I was a little confused. I had assumed that we had come to the supermarket to steal some booze but it seemed we were just there to legitimately buy chewing gum. Perhaps it was a test of my character, I thought, but I was still a little disappointed that things hadn't worked out as dramatically as I thought.

"Good work, Lizard," Ste-Bo said when we'd left. I looked perplexed until he produced a sizeable bottle of whisky from inside his jacket. "You're a brilliant decoy."

Danny had been shoplifting. It was my first major transgression of the storyline and it had given me quite a glow.

Knuckles lived on an estate in Skerton, over the river from town. Although Mum wasn't really the heirs and graces sort, she would have been more than concerned if she knew that it was where my new friends were from.

Ste-Bo and I drank directly from the bottle as we walked towards Knuckles' place. Ste-Bo gulped whilst I took baby sips. I assumed that if we were both getting pissed he wouldn't notice that he was consuming the lion's share. It was hard enough not grimacing every time I tasted it – it was my first crack at whisky and my initial impression was that it was foul and burned in your throat. I was pretty drunk by the time we'd walked to the party, even though I could have drunk no more than the equivalent of a double measure.

"This is good whisky," I commented at one point. It was cheap supermarket whisky, but I didn't know the difference at the time.

"Booze is booze," Steve replied. "It tastes good because it's free." At the time that sounded quite profound.

"That's what I meant," I slurred and then tripped on my shoelace.

We got to the party a little bit before seven when there were only a handful of people in the living room. Knuckles introduced me to his sister, who told me she was studying to be a beauty technician at college. I didn't know what it meant so I made a couple of cooing sounds and moved on. She had two friends with her already, Mel and Hayles, who didn't go to the trouble of introductions or trying to say anything. I thought they looked very grown up with their scraped back hair, micro-skirts and nuclear orange skin. They remained in the background looking at each other's nails. I pretended I wasn't interested in them either, but frequently stole glances down their low cut tops when I was relatively sure they wouldn't notice. I was drunk and told myself that I'd like to fuck all three of them.

"At once," Boner would have added if I'd spoken my mind.

I sat with my new friends and ignored the girls. We passed the whisky around our little circle and I continued to take tiny sips when it was my turn. Knuckles passed around cigarettes from his mum's stash and I nearly declined, but remembered just in time that smoking was the epitome of rebellion.

Smoking isn't easy to do when you don't know how and I'm pretty sure that most people can't enjoy their first tab. There's a certain amount of dedication in becoming a smoker, plenty of retches and head rushes to get through before you really start to look forward to your next one. For my first, I only knew that you had to inhale and did so with gusto, taking in far too much and descending into an unflattering coughing fit in front of everyone.

I'd only been at the party for forty-five minutes when I puked for the first time. I'd consumed no more than four shots' worth of whisky, but the experience of my first cigarette tipped me over the edge. My vision blurred and my eyes streamed for the fifteen minutes that I slumped over a toilet bowl. For a while I thought I might never stand up again.

By the time I was able to leave the bathroom the party had started. The lights had been mainly switched off and the stereo had been cranked right up. Most of the people there were older than me and not one of them was a familiar face.

"Where've you been?" Ste-Bo asked. "Puking?"

"Nah, having a shit, innit?" I replied and everyone laughed. I was portraying Lizard well, I felt.

I remained drunk all night with only the smallest amount of a top up on the whole. Knuckles had raided the drinks cabinet before the party started and kept a stash up in his room. He told me to nip up and help myself at any point. I only went up twice, and on the second occasion there were at least two people having sex in Knuckles' bed. I watched for a few seconds then darted away when I thought I was detected, so I didn't even manage to get any booze that time.

I'd never seen anyone having sex before then, and it was possibly the first time sex was shown on *The Almost Lizard*. It displayed brilliantly how rock and roll this party was meant to be.

I found that by drinking less I was more capable of dealing with smoking. With more people there I was less conspicuous and not as worried about inhaling correctly as the night wore on.

The night played out to the sounds of happy hardcore at intolerable volumes. The house got smokier and in it was mixed the smell of something I just knew had to be cannabis. Aside from me and the gang, everyone else in the room was of college age and they all seemed so grown up. They swore a lot and there were play-fights and outbreaks of slanging matches and testosterone contests. I spent most of my night feeling very intimidated. We all seemed so young and unimportant by comparison.

Most of the lads in the room smelled of violence and looked prepared for a brawl at the slightest provocation. I didn't speak to anyone in case they turned on me. I didn't want to see Lizard beaten up.

Once in a while something got smashed and I'd jump and realise how far removed from my natural habitat I was. But it was right for Lizard. For Danny. For me. If it was a little scary, it was still new and there is something to be said for new things. My first party, my first whisky, my first shoplift, my first cigarettes and the first time I'd had a hand job administered by someone other than myself. But the last one was later.

As the night wore on, people started to talk a little to me and my friends. They'd avoided us when they were sober because we were of school age and only there out of necessity. When they came over I nodded in the right places and tried to look like a sound bloke, concentrating more on neither throwing up nor passing out.

Whoever had been at it in his room must have finished because Knuckles came down with a bottle of vodka and the intention of playing drinking games. I'd just about stopped being blind drunk at this point but was uncontrollably hammered again by the end of one round, which concluded with a surprise shot of tequila each.

It was too much for my stomach. I stood up wordlessly to go to the bathroom, but the queue was half way down the stairs and I knew I wouldn't make it. The first burst of vomit shot into my mouth. I swallowed it back lukewarm, which made me feel worse. I stumbled through the living room and out into the back yard, where I threw up repeatedly next to a wheelie bin. I was relieved that it was February and no-one was congregating in the garden to see what a lightweight I was.

I crouched near my vomit to compose myself before going back in. I decided that drinking until you were sick was actually a very cool thing to do. Geed up, I stood to go back inside and noticed a girl at the back door.

"Y'alright?" she asked.

I wiped the snot off my nose and nodded at her. "Tequila has never been my strong point," I laughed.

"I'm Vicki," she said. "With an I. Two I's really, but you know what I mean."

"How unusual," I replied condescendingly.

"You still at school? One of Call's mates?"

I nodded again, slightly embarrassed to have only been born fifteen years earlier.

"I'm not fussy," she said. "I think some lads your age are far more mature than the ones at college."

I smiled gratefully and then suddenly we were kissing. Within seconds she'd reached into my trousers and less than two minutes later I had ejaculated onto her top. She smiled, sympathetically I think, and then I heard the cheers. My new friends had gathered in the doorway expecting to find me throwing up everywhere and had instead witnessed my first vaguely sexual experience.

Vicki went inside without another word and I was left to do my trousers back up, wondering whether they'd seen my cock. Half an hour later I saw Vicki crying in a corner of the room. I found out off Knuckles a few days later that she'd been chucked by her boyfriend at the party and I'd been on the receiving end of a rebound hand-job. She may have been upset, but I was elated. I hadn't expected to be filming my first sex scene (with another person). Better than that, the act had given me credibility with my new friends.

The party ended in the early hours of the morning with the shouts of a burly neighbour who couldn't take it any more. By that time there was nothing I could remember. I woke up the next morning with a bitter mouth and a crusty head on Ste-Bo's bedroom floor with no recollection of how I'd got there.

You've come a long way, Lizard, I thought to myself when I realised that I didn't feel totally out of place in that situation.

3.

That week marked the beginning of a series of changes to *The Almost Lizard*. The show was moving into a grittier, more adult style and I did toy with starting a new show to represent all of these changes, but I liked the idea of the press just reporting on a huge makeover to the existing format.

The first major change was to write the Proctor family out. They didn't fit in with the Lizars any more and I decided that the programme should focus on me, my mum and my dad and the characters that fell into our very separate lives. We were so disparate that it was almost like three shows in one, but the whole thing felt very manageable to me. I could keep tabs on all the main characters whilst only really thinking about my storylines.

Mum and I filmed lots of arguing scenes. She tried to ground me again when I got back from the party and I'd disobeyed her that very evening. I only went to smoke cigarettes in the park on my own, but the act of defiance was the important part. The viewer had to know that Danny just didn't give a fuck.

This happened two or three times over the next week and then the fighting stopped. Or, more accurately, Mum lost interest in the battles and stopped asking me where I was going. I'd expected the story to pan out with Danny wearing her down quite quickly but it transpired that Jacqui was a stronger character than that.

I went out of my way to orchestrate situations where she or others would get angry at me. I missed three mornings of my paper-round without calling in sick and then sauntered in on the fourth morning as if no explanation were needed. I expected a showdown with Danny turning on Mr Taylor, but he just asked me to leave and didn't speak another line. Perhaps he was annoyed at being written out and decided not to play ball for his last scene. He didn't give me the reaction I was looking for, so I stormed out, making sure I slammed the door hard enough for the whole shop front to rattle. I think I saved the scene.

I was forever seeking the conversation where someone remarked on how much I had changed for the worse, but it didn't come. There was no-one in my life who cared enough to say it. Out of school I spent most of my time with the gang doing things that people would frown upon and it felt good, but no-one took any notice of it. I missed a couple of dinners to hang out with my new friends without telling Mum that I was going to be out, so Mum responded by only making me something if I was physically there when she started cooking. When I came in late I checked the fridge, half-expecting to find that she wouldn't have me go hungry, but there was never anything prepared. The point she was making was blindingly obvious but I was in no position to make an issue out of it.

When I came home and triumphantly told her that I'd lost my paper-round, she just shrugged and said, "What are you going to do for money now?"

It was a pertinent question. Later that day Mum gave me a cheque to give in to school to pay for my lunches for the rest of the term in advance.

"Don't you trust me?" I goaded her.

"If you didn't smell like stale tobacco and breath mints I might consider answering that question," she replied emotionlessly. Her calmness irritated me and made me want to say hurtful things.

"Being a bitch suits you," I sniped.

She flinched, but held her composure. "I'll leave the cheque in the living room," she said and walked away from the scene with dignity, and the upper hand.

I hadn't expected Mum to just accept it when I pushed her away. I had counted on her relying on me now that Dad was gone. She was meant to fight for me, but instead she played a very clever part. She didn't neglect her duties as a mother; she fed me when I deigned to be at home, and she always washed my clothes and kept a tidy house. She performed the basic maternal duties and no more. Everything else I had to earn and my behaviour didn't warrant any treats. I hated her for being so calculating, which made the stealing storyline much less of a moral leap for me.

Put simply, as a result of quitting my job I needed money and Mum had made it clear to me that she wouldn't be helping me out. It was a simple story arc that meant I had to steal from her if she wouldn't willingly give me money. The viewer would have seen it coming a mile off. It was something Danny had to do on his journey to becoming Lizard.

When I filmed stealing from Mum's handbag, I made sure Danny pondered the act for a while before going through with it. It was an aesthetic gesture as the viewer needed to know that he wasn't doing this lightly, even though in reality I didn't struggle with it at all.

This should have been a flashpoint between Danny and Jacqui. It required serious action on Jacqui's part and several showdowns between the two of us. Instead, though, Mum just made a point of carrying her handbag with her everywhere she went in the house. She didn't say a word about the stealing but quietly ensured that it wouldn't happen again. I hoped that she was hurt inside and breaking down behind closed doors, weeping into her pillow over her wayward son, but I found that increasingly hard to believe.

As the weeks passed and I tried to become harder to control, Mum moved further and further into her new life. Some evenings I arrived back late hoping for a row only to find that the house was empty because she'd gone for drinks after theatre group or had been out meeting friends that I didn't know about.

She was working on a new school musical as well as the theatre group and seemed far too busy to notice that I was in freefall. She mentioned 'nights out with the girls', which confused me because I didn't think she had any girls in her life. I was so wrapped up in my own storylines that I hadn't been paying attention to how Jacqui was moving on at the same time.

It was only a matter of time before the show cast a new love interest for Jacqui, I thought resentfully. Seeing Mum busy made me question whether I had made the right choice in going with the wild child plot. Or to look at it another way, I couldn't see a feasible way of stopping it.

From the party onwards I decided that I was part of the gang. I'd earned my stripes with the back yard hand job. The others had celebrated my success loudly on the bus to school the following Monday. I ignored the part where they took the piss out of the number of times I'd vomited and focused on what I was calling (privately) my crowning glory.

When I was away from them I trained myself to be like them. I smoked cigarettes on my own, taking a small mirror to the park with me and practicing my exhalation faces. After a few weeks I was able to disguise how it made me heave sometimes.

The storyline progressed as a series of incidents where Danny did questionable things that he wouldn't have done before he became part of the gang. I shoplifted a few times – little items like chocolate bars from WH Smiths. Occasionally I teamed up with Ste-Bo to steal booze from off-licenses. We honed our little double act, with Ste-Bo walking in first and asking for some liquorice cigarette papers. I'd come in when the shop assistant turned their back, would slip a bottle under my jacket and sneak back out again. They invariably didn't sell liquorice cigarette papers and Ste-Bo would leave without arousing suspicion.

After the first couple of times I didn't even bother getting nervous. It became so normal that each theft didn't necessarily generate any scenes. There was only so much drama in undetected petty crimes.

Before I met Ste-Bo and the others I wouldn't have dreamed of skipping full weeks of school, but I did just that in the week before February half-term. When I came back after the holidays without a sick note, I told them that I'd got the weeks mixed up and accidentally taken half term early.

Mum was sent a letter, which I was sure would enrage her,

but she apologised to the school and told me not to do it again. "If I get prosecuted for your truancy you're going to end up in care," she warned me in a way that told me she didn't care what happened either way. "I could lose my job and we'd lose everything. You wouldn't have a home to come to after you've finished playing bad boy each day."

I searched her face to see how knowing that comment was, but she was getting harder and harder to read.

Most of the time, we really did very little, just heckled girls and made adults feel uncomfortable. We hung out by the canal, in parks, by fast food restaurants and outside off-licenses; anywhere we liked so long as there was a bench to gather around.

For the first few weeks this was enough to keep me entertained. I enjoyed the new scenarios and taking Danny Lizar in a completely new direction.

The party aside, it was all a bit *Grange Hill* to start with, but I couldn't change completely overnight. I had to become comfortable with each development of my new character before I was ready to become even worse. The storyline was a string of challenges, and after drinking, smoking, shoplifting and hand-sex came drugs.

I had heard the gang mention getting high but with nothing material to back it up. I wanted to ask more about it, but my undeniable inexperience was enough to deter me. If I didn't bring it up, I couldn't appear unknowledgeable. Then, one night we were hanging out in a park when L-Dog produced a block of hash that he'd stolen from his older brother's room.

Until that year, drugs had been nothing more than something I was warned about in school. They weren't something I could ever have anticipated being confronted with because I wasn't having that sort of life. My newish friends had changed that for me, and from the first smell of weed at the party I had grown to anticipate my opportunity to experiment.

Ste-Bo was given the hash and skinned up whilst we all gathered round. There was a sense of excitement surrounding the group as he prepared the joint with great expertise. It was lit and passed around to everybody, with me last in line. It was coarser than the cigarettes I had grown accustomed to inhaling and I coughed a few times. For a split second I felt like I was in *Grease*, but a grittier version of *Grease* where smoking was the least of people's moral concerns.

Danny getting stoned was a milestone moment for British soap. I couldn't think of a time when a fifteen year old had smoked real cannabis on television, and as the first waves washed over me, I thought of the outcry and publicity this storyline would get the programme. It filled me with a sense of wellbeing about how great my new life was.

"What do you expect?" I said to an interviewer that I imagined was sat before me. "His mother is acting like she doesn't care what he does and he hasn't seen his father in months. Part of him wants attention and the other part wants to self-destruct."

There had been no word from Dad but I presumed he was still a part of the show. His storyline development was unknown to me, but I think it made my part more convincing. I hoped that he was being kept away by some restaurant related gangster storyline. It was far nicer than concluding that he just didn't care.

He hadn't even come round to accuse me of smashing the restaurant window, nor had Mum passed on any messages from him. Sometimes I steered the gang to a bench near to the Lancaster branch of *ChaMal*, hoping that he might spot me. We must have loitered there at least ten times before I eventually saw him in May. He was walking from his car and I saw him eye us up cautiously, as many adults did to a bunch of youths with menacing faces and a confrontational gait. He pretended that he hadn't seen us and entered the restaurant.

I stared at the door he had just walked through wondering

whether I should go and cause a public scene. It was only then that I looked above the door and noticed the 'For Sale' sign.

4.

However much I fell into the role of Lizard, I did find it hard at times to stop being myself. Lizard was a product of Danny, who was a product of me, and some innate me-ness was retained as the personalities moved down the chain.

I went out four times a week at the very most, so when I wasn't with the gang I had no choice but to stay at home, where I surreptitiously caught up on my homework. It was one thing for me to give off the impression that I was ruining my future, but I didn't quite have the conviction to do it for real. If Mum came to check on me (which was rarely), I made out like I was playing computer games, when in reality I was working on my GCSE coursework. I think the storyline was only able to go on as long as it did because I didn't give school too much cause for concern.

This wasn't shown in the programme.

On the few occasions that Mum cried it was tough for me as well. There was one Saturday morning where I rolled in after three o'clock because I'd spent my bus fare on Smirnoff Ice and had to walk home. The two and a half hour trek had given me time to sober up, which I was relieved about when I went through the front door and heard tiny sobs emanating from the living room.

I wanted to go and see what had upset her, and part of me was curious as to whether I was the cause of her tears, but it wasn't part of my character at the time so I reluctantly went upstairs without showing any concern at all.

Seeing the 'For Sale' sign made me feel just like my old self. I had talked a good game in not caring where my dad was or that I hadn't seen him for nearly five months, but it was impossible not to be curious about this twist. Danny would have run straight in there and demanded to know the truth, but Lizard was meant to take it on the chin and not cave in to curiosity.

At that moment I knew that the Lizard construct was just a fallacy, and that no amount of acting up would kill the person I considered to be the real me. I still loved my parents and if I could have taken back everything I'd done to rewrite the previous year then I would have. At fifteen, though, you don't want to admit you're a bit of a pussy, especially when you've spent a few months trying to establish yourself as a wild child. If I'd shown emotion, I'm sure my newish friends would have kicked the shit out of me and cast me aside.

I was doing a good job of portraying myself as hard faced and in return Mum treated me as if I had no real feelings.

"Did you know Dad's selling the restaurant," I asked her when I arrived home earlier than usual.

"Oh hello Mum, how was your day? Fine thanks, Danny. How was yours? Do you have something to ask me?"

"Drop the attitude," I replied aggressively.

"Your father and Charles are selling all three restaurants," she answered my original question calmly, not following me into a confrontation. "Last I heard he was going to New York to try and establish a restaurant over there. Apparently some American really enjoyed his meal in Southport and made him an offer he couldn't refuse."

"And you don't care?" I asked incredulously, knowing that my mask was slipping a little.

"Oh, I care," she said. "I'm absolutely delighted."

Danny would have tried to make her care. Instead, Lizard feigned indifference and I went to my room to take in the shock there. I sat quietly and sadly. It was a strong message to the viewer not to give up on Danny as I sat there with my head in my hands. I didn't cry. I was bigger than that. I did, however, look visibly distressed in the direction of where I supposed the camera stood.

5.

The next day I found myself playing the Lizard character with rejuvenated enthusiasm. I could see that Danny was destroying himself without harming others and that was why people weren't noticing what was going on. What point was a cry for help when no-one was paying any attention?

I think I'd lost some of my anger in all the excitement of heading wayward, but Malcolm's proposed exit was enough to bring it all flooding back. I needed someone to shout at, and my estranged father was my one and only choice.

One evening after school I went straight over to the Lancaster restaurant, full of fire hoping my father would be there. I was alarmed when I looked in the window to see Charles. I hadn't expected him to be making a guest appearance. I reminded myself that Lizard didn't give a shit about anyone and sauntered into the restaurant without further hesitation.

"Is my dad about?" I asked without any cursory greeting. He looked startled for a second but didn't lose any composure.

"How lovely to see you, Danny," he said drolly. "No, I'm not unhappy to say that your father is elsewhere this evening."

"Will he be here tomorrow?" I continued gruffly, giving off the impression at least to myself that I was being menacing.

"Well I won't, so it's very possible that he will, yes," Charles replied brightly.

Lizard was long overdue a confrontation.

"How can you go out of your way to avoid him but forgive your slag of a wife for what she's done?"

It was too early for customers and there were only a couple of waitresses in the restaurant at the time, which was a shame because a line like that would have silenced a busy room.

"Alex said you were troubled these days," Charles said, catching me unawares.

A thousand soap opera retorts flashed through my mind

until I settled on the most unpleasant one I could think of.

"At nights, can you still smell my dad on her?" I growled and Charles stepped forward to hit me. He managed to hold himself back, so I sneered and laughed at him simultaneously. "Spineless, just like your faggot son," I said and looked him up and down disparagingly before walking back out.

That was more like it, I thought, pleased that someone else's feelings were hurt for once.

It was an exciting couple of days for slanging matches – classic episodes that I knew the viewers would love. With Mum completely passive and my friends not the sort of people you confronted, I threw myself back into a rare bit of conflict. Following the surprise cameo of Charles Proctor was the timely reappearance of Alex into the show. I could always rely on him to make good TV.

Only a few hours after my showdown with Charles, my ex-best friend came hammering on our front door unexpectedly. He was brimming with bile and making exaggerated gesticulations that were merely amusing to the toughened up version of me.

"Why did you tell my dad that I was gay?" he demanded.

"Aren't you?" I asked with one eyebrow raised.

"No, I'm bloody not! Why can't you move on with your life instead of picking fights with your past? You ruined all that, Danny, so why can't you just leave it alone?"

"I went to look for my dad. Your dad was acting like a prick so I thought I'd shut him up," I said it like it was the most natural course of action in the world.

"Then why bring me into it? Why have I had to explain to my dad that I'm not gay? You're a disease!"

"Oh get bent, Alex. You're round here mouthing off at the first opportunity and you're telling me that I'm the one who needs to move on. Don't act like you're better than any of this."

"I'm better than taking up smoking just to impress some

mindless thugs, the only people dense enough to want to go anywhere near you."

Alex fell remarkably easily when I pushed him. Even though he thought virtually nothing of me I could see that he'd just reached a new level of disappointment. He stood up and started to walk away. "Maybe you're not pretending at all. I gave you too much credit. You're just a cunt."

He had tears in his eyes and his voice was shaking, so I told myself I had walked away from that the victor, and closed the door.

6.

I didn't go and see Dad the next day, or the day after that. I decided that if he didn't have the balls to tell me personally then I shouldn't give him the satisfaction of any reaction. I had no idea that for months Mum had been telling him through letters how much I hated him and how she couldn't be sure I wouldn't kill him if he came anywhere near either of us. As far as I was concerned he simply didn't give a shit, ergo neither did I.

May turned into June and I started to think about the summer. It was time for the storyline to escalate beyond the occasional joint and needless swearing.

The gang did what they did and there were large periods of inactivity, or just the usual behaviour, which became more and more unremarkable as the weeks wore on. It meant that to keep things ticking over without just fabricating a bunch of eventualities, I had to do something myself.

As I was keeping up to date with my studies there was little for the school to be concerned about. School was also more enjoyable for me. People were curious about my new affiliations and I often sensed that everyone was talking about me. They looked at me when they were talking and stopped when someone noticed me glance over. They'd always seen me as shy and a bit weird, but my new persona intrigued them from afar. I walked around with a new found swagger and tried to intimidate some of the younger kids, but in class I retained my Dannyish fear of bollockings and detention. That had to change to keep the storyline alive.

I started being disruptive in class, piping up with cheeky comments, distracting other kids and generally looking bored. I didn't ask permission to go to the toilet and a couple of times I just left lessons ten minutes towards the end.

In my end of year geography exam I was kicked out for flicking bits of paper at the teacher. Without the show I would have been too afraid to do these things without my friends looking on, but I pretended I had cameras and directors and viewers so I didn't feel alone at all. As I had been revising sneakily in my room for weeks, I finished early and grew bored of waiting. In my head I edited things to make it look like I was flunking the exams.

I didn't do enough to make my report a cause for concern. Teachers agreed that I was bright but they'd noticed that I was more disruptive of late. "That'd be right," Mum agreed when she read it and she said nothing else. She just put the report down on the kitchen table and continued with what she was doing.

In response I got myself caught smoking in the toilets on the last day of term. I nipped out during a history lesson and had to chain smoke two and a half cigarettes before someone finally had the gumption to alert a teacher. I was immediately sent to see Mrs Owen, and Miss Lawrence was called to join us. She looked very disappointed in me. It must be harder for the teachers to see the ones they didn't expect acting up. The born fuck-ups they can expect nothing else from, but when one of the more promising ones falls by the wayside it must be more of a betrayal. I played it nonchalant. Lizard was far less scared of authority than Danny was.

I hardly disguised my disappointment when my efforts

amounted to no more than a quick bollocking and a couple of evening detentions when we returned in September. If any of the others had been caught they surely would have been in much more trouble than I was, and I wanted to be treated just like them.

The only ray of light was that they called my mother.

She didn't even come to the school. She just waited until I got home that night and told me that she was going to sell my computer. I pretended like I didn't care and another showdown was avoided, much to my consternation. I lost my PC and didn't get any particularly remarkable scenes in the process. I was frustrated at squandering my only chance to get in serious trouble. It was a sign that I just didn't have it in me to be like the others. They wouldn't have struggled in getting suspended.

I needed to be better.

The Slippery Slope Summer

1.

I was so excited about the prospect of summer with the gang that I decided *The Almost Lizard* had to take a break for six weeks and that I was going to film a late night spin-off series for the summer, entitled *Lizard*. I did toy with calling it *Lizard After Dark*, but unusually my senses got the better of me.

Earlier that year, *Hollyoaks* had done a late night episode in which a male character was raped, and that was where the idea originated. Compared to the day time episodes, suddenly everyone was undressing, swearing and being a lot more violent towards each other. It was also a guaranteed way to bring in more viewers, and I really liked the idea of pushing boundaries.

Lizard went out twice a week, always well after the watershed. With the later timeslot I was looking for a more adult themed show, complete with extra swearing and scenes of a sexual nature.

Mum's lack of reaction to my smoking in school could be apportioned to Neil. About ten minutes after she had disconnected my computer he had rung the doorbell. Mum had gone off to answer it readily, which told me she was expecting someone. I heard a male voice downstairs and my curiosity had me going to investigate within two or three minutes.

I glanced into the living room and saw him sat there.

"Hello," he said uncertainly. "I'm Neil."

"And what are you doing here?" I said in as unfriendly a manner as possible.

"Well, I'm taking your mother out for dinner," he said.

"Oh," I said and tried not to let my jaw drop.

Mum appeared behind me. "I see you've met Neil."

"You hadn't mentioned a Neil," I said.

"We've not exactly been sharing our news recently, have we?" she replied as if that were the most normal thing in the world.

"You know she's married don't you?" I asked Neil.

"I know about your father, yes," Neil said and I could tell by the way he was dealing with me that Mum had prepared him for the worst in her son. He looked about Mum's age and I wanted to ask him why he was so old and single, but he also looked like he could pack a punch and I still wasn't convinced I wanted to be properly punched in the name of my art.

"Is there anything else you'd like to add before we go?" Mum said smugly. I shrugged and walked out of the room, hoping I looked aloof. I went back upstairs and listened out for them leaving. I decided that I didn't want to go out that night. I wanted to sulk, just like Danny would have. I wanted a night off from Lizard and with the house to myself I was free to have some emotions without anyone noticing. Besides, it helped to be a little unreliable with the group, it made me seem a little less subservient.

So I raged for a while, spilled out expletives about my revitalised mother and my estranged father, and then I started to work out the best summer of my life. A clearly angry Danny was the perfect cliffhanger for the summer break, and the scenes just filmed with Jacqui and Neil led onto the spin-off series perfectly.

By then I had encountered all kinds of sex on television. Had I been a few years younger I would have been accessing an array of internet porn by the time I was twelve, but the late nineties was only the beginning of the cyber-age, so I had to educate myself in ways that the kids of today would probably see as rather primitive, like I used to think of the days of black and white televisions.

There were plenty of channels on cable television that showed risqué things – shows with plenty of sex, violence and swearing. As my family fell apart, I was given even more freedom to watch what I liked. When Mum went to bed, I'd often stay downstairs and watch a late night film or the ten minute freeview on one of the porn channels. I watched dramas solely because sex and nudity were promised in a warning at the beginning of the show, and through that I learned what adult drama was supposed to be about.

As far as I saw it, an adult show could go pretty much anywhere, and that was what I signed up for when I decided to make *Lizard*.

2.

Lizard began with me waking up, looking at the time, saying 'shit' a lot and running around the house in my boxers. Partial nudity and ample swearing was my statement of intent. It was only in the shows on later in the evening that people ran around in their underwear swearing, so it seemed like a sufficiently grown up way to start.

Scene two took it a little further – it was me in the shower. I favoured a tasteful shot where the camera panned down, showing my arse rather than the front. So many of these adult programmes pulled out all of their most outrageous moments in the first twenty minutes and then become too tame after that. I wanted each episode of *Lizard* to push a new boundary.

The next scene was me getting dressed. I checked myself in the mirror and then ran downstairs. Mum was in the kitchen and I went to see her.

"Where's Neil?" I asked her.

"It was only dinner," she replied.

"Oh, I thought – "

"Well don't think, Danny. You should have a bit more respect for me."

"It's just that you seemed to move on from Dad very quickly. I thought you might be f – "

"Don't finish that sentence!" Mum barked. She clearly wasn't so keen on my new adult direction.

"I was just saying. Fuck's sake."

"Swearing doesn't impress me, Daniel," she said, and I knew she said 'Daniel' to annoy me.

"It's Lizard," I replied triumphantly.

I imagined the opening credits kicking in at this point.

The first episode was an introduction. I ran to the bus stop, carrying on the idea that I was late for something. I smoked whilst waiting for the bus, and looked moodily out of the window on my way into town. I then swaggered my way through town to the bench outside McDonald's where Ste-Bo had said they were going to be.

I imagined viewers complaining about the amount of swearing in the scene where the gang were introduced. I think it went something like this:

"Alright, Lizard. Where the fuck were you last night?"

"Ah, couldn't be fucked. Got a bit pissed at home and couldn't be fucked coming out."

"Fucking pussy."

"Fuck off!"

"So what the fuck are we going to do today?"

"Fucked if I know."

"I wanna get pissed."

"Pissed on what, dickhead? We ain't got no fucking money."

"Then let's make some fucking money, dickhead."

"How? Get a shitty little part-time job for a couple of hours?"

"We don't usually have to pay to get booze."

"Whose turn is it?"

"Knucks, I reckon it's you."

"Fuck off. I fucking did it last time."

"Like fuck you did. You haven't robbed a fucking thing in weeks."

"Fuck off you cunt. I fucking brought some fucking cider two weeks ago."

"From your mum's fucking fridge, you pussy."

"It fucking counts!"

"It fucking doesn't."

"Do it, prick."

"Fuck off. I get you all cigs all the time."

"Cigs isn't fucking alcohol."

"You're all fucking gays."

"Good boy."

"Fuck off, pricks."

No wonder people looked on disapprovingly. I ended the scene by meeting the eye of a scowling passerby and saying with conveyed menace, "What the fuck are you looking at?"

Knucks came back with supermarket whisky and we all took the piss a bit more, saying he could have stolen a better brand, and then the day descended into a drunken haze. We went up to the Ashton Memorial, where people were playing Frisbee, walking dogs and lying on towels in the sun.

We were rowdy and obnoxious, scuffling and play-fighting with each other, rolling into the sunbathers and generally making a nuisance of ourselves. Ste-Bo flicked a cigarette butt and it hit one male sunbather in the head. He stood up, looking irate and ridiculous. He had overdone the lotion and was still burning a little, so he looked oily, red and angry and there was no way we could have taken that seriously.

"Watch where you're flicking those," he shouted over to us.

"Fucking make me!" Ste-Bo shouted back and we all jeered.

The man thought about it, and weighed up the odds of him being able to take on all of us.

"Just be careful," he said more timidly and sat down.

That should have been the end of it, but I was upping the ante.

"Fucking prick," I said to Ste-Bo. "Look at him, all fucking oiled up like some fucking poof."

I was a little drunk and feeling very brave as a result. I was getting better at being drunk but my reactions were still often extreme. I didn't consider whether I should be trying to start on someone who was a good few years older than me, and I didn't consider whether it was fair to pick on someone who had done absolutely nothing wrong. I just saw the scene and improvised.

I marched over to where the man had laid back down. I stood near him and his girlfriend looked up just as I spat on his chest.

"You owe my friend an apology," I said before either of them could react.

"You just spat on him!" the girlfriend shrieked and I saw the bloke try to silence her with a look.

"What's he going to do about it?" I asked.

"He should take you out!" she said boldly.

"Fucking do it then!" I hollered at the man, who had sat up. "Come on! Fucking stand up you prick!"

This wasn't me and I knew it, but it felt awesome to not be me. The adrenaline was coursing through me and I wanted to get hit. I wanted the violence.

"There's no need," the bloke said.

I cuffed him with the back of my hand. The lads were metres away, laughing at what I was doing. "I said stand up!"

When the bloke stood up reluctantly, I was surprised to see that he was much taller than me. He looked a lot stronger than me as well, but I had four people stood to my rear willing to back up any of my threats.

"Listen, I'm sorry," the bloke said to Ste-Bo. His girlfriend gasped in the background.

"Your bird has got a big fucking mouth," I said to him. "I'd tell her to fuck off before she gets you in real trouble. Prick."

I looked him up and down once before turning away dismissively and returning to my friends. I snatched the bottle from L-Dog and took a massive swig, walking tall; being Lizard.

Our fun was over by seven o'clock when we all started sobering up and feeling a bit hung over. We lost our energy and Ste-Bo said he was bored and was going home. It would have been weird for us to stay out once Ste-Bo had gone. He was our leader, so we all went our separate ways.

I started to feel quite rough on my way home and threw up all over the back of the bus. Some people looked over and moved away as the smell started to creep towards the front, but when anyone caught my gaze, I gave them the same threatening look I'd used on the sunbather earlier on and it seemed to deter any sort of intervention. Puking on a bus and not giving a damn felt pretty hardcore.

There wasn't quite enough footage for the first episode, so I took a wander through the village and into the park where I used to sit and read all the updates on *Jubilee Line*. I pulled some fish and chip wrapper from a nearby bin and lit it, chucking it underneath the bench. The ensuing brief fire caused no more than superficial damage, but it looked reckless and definitely showed the viewer the sort of person that Lizard was.

With nothing else to do, I went home. Mum was watching television and didn't call out when I got in. I was sad that Neil wasn't there. Neil was an important part of the story. He was the new reason that Lizard was as horrible as he was. I threw together a basic sandwich in the kitchen and went to up to my room, stealing a bottle of Mum's wine as I went.

The final scenes of the episode were Lizard drinking in his room, again down to his boxers. Night fell and a sexy film started on Channel 5. There had been no scenes of a sexual nature to that point, so episode one ended with Lizard masturbating over barely porn and passing out, naked on top of his duvet. When you're fifteen, sex scenes involving a fifteen year old don't seem so inappropriate.

All in all, it had been the high impact opening episode I was going for.

3.

Although I very much doubt that each and every member of the gang was undertaking the same weird fantasy-reality game that I was playing, they did seem to want to up the ante for the summer as well. *Lizard* was on the cusp of being reality television, because almost nothing was imagined, aside from the fact that it was being filmed in the first place.

Ste-Bo was great for generating plots. He seemed to turn up with the most ideas and his were the only ones that were accepted without exception. It was Ste-Bo who pointed out that there were shitloads of girls at the seaside and initiated an outing to Blackpool a few days into the holidays. We still had the problem of having no money between us, but Ste-Bo told us to dress smart and not to worry.

Getting to Blackpool for free was easy. We separated on the train and hid out in the two toilets for the duration. Occasionally people banged on and they were promptly told to fuck off. We legged it out of the station and were greeted by absolutely no-one checking tickets. It seems harder to do that these days, but at the time free-riding was not really a challenge. It was a transgression I didn't think twice about.

We spent the day wandering around Blackpool instead of wandering around Lancaster. We were in direct contrast to the familial atmosphere of the seafront. We were a pack of youths, strutting about like we meant business and could take on the world, shouting and swearing and making people go to great lengths to avoid us.

It was a hot day and there were lots of women hanging out on the beach wearing very little. Boner and L-Dog were in their element, describing an array of things that they'd like to do to each of the women, and I found myself chipping in.

"Fuck off Lizard, you're still a virgin," L-Dog laughed at me at one point. "Or did you think that wank you got at the party counted?"

They all laughed at this and I joined in, quietly seething.

"I've not exactly seen you banging a queue of women," I retorted and everyone jeered.

"Doesn't mean I haven't."

"Doesn't mean you have either. I've known you for a while and I've never seen you get into anyone," Ste-Bo joined in. I liked it when he backed me, it made me feel like I was fitting in.

"Fuck off, of course I have," protested L-Dog and Boner made the wanker sign behind his back.

Boner had lost his virginity when he was twelve. This was well known, and it was also known that he had been sleeping with the girls no-one else would touch ever since. He claimed it was fifteen, but Ste-Bo could only be sure of five. There had been a couple of women over thirty in this number, friends of his mum with little self-esteem and no qualms about sleeping with a minor. Knucks had been with a couple of his sister's friends when they'd been drunk at his house.

There was no question of Ste-Bo's virginity being intact. As group leader it was unquestioned that he'd got the most pussy. He was seeing some girl called Tanya who lived with him for a while, and there had been plenty of days where he'd decided not to go out in order to get some action.

"Maybe you and Lizard should help each other out," joked Boner and L-Dog punched him in the face. Ste-Bo held back L-Dog and Boner was restrained by Knucks. I just stood and watched. I had never seen a gang member turn on another and it had taken me by surprise.

"Quit it ladies," Ste-Bo said as he grappled with L-Dog, "or you don't get a pill."

I wasn't sure that I'd heard him right, but it was confirmed that Ste-Bo had promised to let his mum have the house to herself that night for the princely sum of thirty quid. He had used a tenner to buy five pills and the rest of the money was to be saved for having a bit of fun at the Pleasure Beach. My stomach knotted immediately. I hadn't been expecting this development so soon, but this was a late night show and this was the sort thing I had to be doing.

They'd all done it before – they'd told me about pills and the things they had done, how they'd stayed awake all weekend once at Ste-Bo's when his mum was abroad. It had been the best weekend ever, apparently, but that didn't dampen my apprehension.

A bottle of water was passed around as we all took our dose. I couldn't not do it, and in spite of my nerves I washed it down and waited to die.

It hit me hard and quickly. One minute I was chatting away normally, wondering what I'd let myself into, and then the rush hit me. It was an internal thing at first, just the nerves and that, and then it got to my brain and my vision, and suddenly I was super-chatty and happy and I kind of wanted to hug my friends. I kept saying stupid things and apologising as we went round Blackpool Pleasure Beach. I stopped to stare at the lights on a fish and chip stall, then realised what I was doing.

"Shit, sorry. How lame am I?" I asked with a massive smile.

"Nah, man, it's beautiful," Boner said and put his arm around me. I smiled and we walked on.

I don't really recall what we did for all those hours, wandering around. We realised we couldn't afford any rides at all and instead spent some of Ste-Bo's money in the arcades, where we had all been drawn by the noises, lights and colourful games. I remember dancing to the music coming from a racing game at one point.

Other than that, we walked and walked, inspecting things up close and just having a nice time. We must have been completely unthreatening compared to our usual state, because we didn't have it in us to have a go.

"Nah, fucking leave 'em to enjoy their holidays," Ste-Bo said. "People work hard to have a nice time. Don't need fuckheads like us ruining it for 'em."

"Not today anyway," Knucks added and we all laughed.

Ecstasy wasn't what I had expected. There was no fear of dying or being out of control, just mates being nice and sometimes saying nice things to each other. This experience made a mockery of all those tutorials where Miss Lawrence warned us about the perils of drugs and how horrible they were. Being daring had never felt so good.

We smoked lots of cigarettes, passing them around almost continually. I liked it. We were a gang. I was part of a gang and in joining them in the experience I felt like they had accepted me. I found it incredibly difficult to conceal the inner Danny, the Danny who wanted to gush emotionally about the amazing things he was experiencing.

I was still high on the train and spent much of the journey staring out of the window and thinking about how great things were for me now. Lights flashed by, each sparking off a new thought – how a year ago I had been a bullied geek with a closed mind, who couldn't have seen the wonderful people buried within these supposed thugs.

I presume no-one came to inspect tickets because we didn't hide in the toilets and we certainly didn't get thrown off. I was too busy staring out of the window to notice.

When we got back to Lancaster, we parted with elaborate, ghetto-derivative handshakes and man hugs and I set off for home. I decided to walk back from town, which took considerably less time than when I was drunk. It was a nice night and I was in no rush to get to bed. I was more coherent than I had been back in Blackpool, but these little rushes kept passing through me and filling me with an absolute sense of wellbeing.

I got home shortly after one and lay awake until it got light, just thinking about the world and trying to get to sleep. Mum was already in bed and thus spared the knowledge of what I had done.

Another episode ended with Lizard in his room, this time wide-awake. I got out of bed once in a while and looked out of my window, trying to see it in a different light.

A few times I thought to myself, 'It's strange what you do, you know. You pretend life is a TV show. You imagine your days as scenes and episodes and everyone you know is a character. It's weird.' That thought sent a jolt through me, like I was skirting a little too near to a very important truth.

And then I thought, 'I couldn't imagine it any other way.' I backed away from the realisation and started to think about other things – like losing my virginity, and what would be happening in the remaining episodes of the series. I'd always imagined the storyline coming to an abrupt end at the point when I was done with the gang, but I was starting to think that I didn't want that day to come.

I drifted off before the real self-doubt kicked in.

4.

After a night of unity and experience, the world seemed drab in the cold light of day. I hadn't been informed of comedowns and it just seemed to me that my eyes had been opened to some real happiness and in comparison, everything I had known before didn't add up. Those hours had been carefree and full of optimism, but when things wore off the gloom was unavoidable.

I slept until four. Mum was at her summer school, so I took

the opportunity to get dressed and get out before she came home. I was looking quite unwell and didn't want her to see me and ask questions. It was hard to know whether what I'd done was written all over my face, and if she'd found out then it might've seriously scuppered the rest of the spin-off series. I was getting used to the freedoms her indifference afforded me, and I certainly wasn't ready to bring things to an emotional head just yet, not with so many episodes left in the series.

There were two things that sent a pang of despondency through my central nervous system. First was the stigma attached to my virginity. It showed me up for my inexperience, and when I thought about it, I felt a little sad. It was important that I lose my virginity, but when I tried to think of girls who I could possibly sleep with, I drew a blank. I didn't really keep the company of girls – especially the ones at school, who avoided me more than ever now that I was hanging out with the undesirables.

The second nagging thought was money, and in this part of my comedown the main motivation for the rest of the series presented itself. I had been raised with money and I couldn't help but think that we'd have a lot more fun if we had some cash between us.

I was opening up a new episode, really, where money was the problem and the storyline would follow from there. Lizard needed money, and he didn't know how to get it. I took to my bed that night in the throes of a chemical depression, thinking the situation useless, my cloud only lifting when Dad cropped up as a solution.

5.

Dad looked visibly shaken when he saw me enter the restaurant, but still saw to three tables before coming over.

"Danny," he said.

"So you remember my name," I replied sternly.

Dad looked around at his customers. “I can’t talk right now, but can you stick around?”

I shrugged, meaning yes, and Dad went back to what he was doing. Every time he looked over at me I was looking right back.

Customers left and the waitresses cleaned up. The kitchen staff filtered out one by one, followed by others until it was just Dad and I left.

“How have you been?” he asked me.

“Like you fucking care,” I snapped back.

“You wouldn’t speak to me,” he said in return and I curled my lip in response. “Your mother told me categorically that you wanted nothing to do with me.”

“Bullshit.”

“I see you’ve picked up some choice language recently,” he said sadly.

“You’re in no position to make statements about me,” I barked back. I had lost my cool far too soon, having discovered my feelings on the matter unexpectedly. He’d challenged my assertion that he’d just abandoned me, and that left me less than sure of myself. “What did Mum say to you?”

As far as I was aware Dad hadn’t called since the day he came round after Christmas.

“Not much. Just to leave you both alone. Oh, and that you hated me and wished I was dead.” At the peak of my angry fits that probably wasn’t too far from the truth, but it wasn’t anything that I’d expressed to Mum.

Dad continued: “She told me how mad you were and how she thought if you saw me you’d be capable of anything. The way you’ve been looking at me all evening I can see her point.”

“Bollocks! You didn’t call. You just didn’t give a shit.”

“I called,” he insisted. “She said you have a baseball bat in your room. Danny, it’s not hard to believe, after what you did at Christmas – ”

“Don’t try and blame me for this,” I retorted inappropriately.

"Christmas wouldn't have happened if you hadn't been out screwing – "

"I think we've been over this."

"No dad, we haven't. We've never been over this. You've never given me the benefit of a little chat since all of this happened."

"I was willing to talk a long time ago. I don't particularly like my son hating me enough to do what you did. It was wrong, Danny, but you had your reasons and I didn't want this to go on forever."

"So you stay away and then make plans to move to America?"

"I did tell your mother and she said you were both delighted."

They were the same words Mum had used with me.

The scene wasn't playing out how I'd expected. I was uneasy because everything he said was plausible.

"I offered to send money and she said you didn't need it," Dad continued.

I scrambled around looking for another advantage. "You could have tried to find me. You know where I go to school for a start."

"Your mother threatened legal action and all sorts. She's threatened to sue me for everything I have if I didn't just walk away."

She is a fucking bitch, I agreed silently.

"That's why I'm going, Danny. There's nothing here for me without you and your mother."

"You're going because you're a wimp and you've given up immediately. Mum's told me how you let yourself get pushed around, just let people make decisions for you and that's what you're doing again. Someone tells you to run away and off you go. Just like you walked out on your own family."

There was a silence and I wondered if the scene had run out of steam. I was concerned about my performance; there was too much Danny. I used the silence to try and think like Lizard.

"I'm not running away, Danny," Dad said. "If I thought there was anything to stay for."

"You'll not get Mum back. I presume you've heard about Neil?"

"I've heard nothing," Dad said. "I don't know anything about either of you."

For a split second I was disappointed that my ongoing derailment hadn't made it back to Dad, but then I realised what an advantage that was.

"Whatever I think of you I don't think he's any better," I replied. "He has an effect on her. He tells her what to do and how to look after me."

I gave him a moment or two to look stunned.

"She won't give me any pocket money any more so I just have to live on nothing. She cooks things for him and just saves me the scraps."

I'd seen plenty of abusive stepfather storylines in my time.

"I stopped my paper-round to focus on schoolwork and so he told her not to support me any more. I don't get to see any of my friends because I never have any money. It's shit, Dad, and it's all your fault!"

I looked a little bereft and turned away from him.

"Danny, I had no idea," he said to me. He went to touch my shoulder but thought better of it. "Has he hit you?"

I thought about it, then realised the repercussions. Who would feel sorry for me if I was making up lies like that? Characters who made up lies like that could expect to be written out within weeks when the moral justice system of soapland kicked in. Upon swift consideration I shook my head. I was after money, not sympathy.

"It's not like that. I'd hit him back. But he is making Mum different with me. She's moved on from the both of us."

"I'm sorry to hear that, mate."

"Don't call me mate." I looked at him resentfully before turning on the emotional blackmail. "I don't know how I'm meant to get by. I just want to move out. Can I live with you?"

This could have backfired quite easily.

"I'm leaving in three weeks," Dad said simply. "It's too late to change anything."

I bowed my head. He had decided to go to New York and there was little that could change that course now it had happened. Just like Mum had thrown him out, none of this was of his own volition because he was weak.

Dad didn't know what to say. He was meant to offer me money and I wasn't prepared to ask.

"If I'd known you still wanted to see me," he offered up after several moments thinking.

I looked up at him with all the hatred I could muster. He'd run out of words but I could tell that he was troubled. When there was nothing else to say, decisive action was needed. I was angry with him for abandoning me in spite of all the lies I had just told him. I walked over to the cash till. Dad watched on quietly as I pulled up a fistful of notes and stuffed them into my pocket.

"I can't be left with nothing, can I?" I asked him. He didn't move to stop me, or to try and make me see sense. I glared at him one last time and made my exit.

Lizard had added blackmail to his credentials. From that week on Dad put fifty pounds in my account each week. As it turned out, having an estranged father was the easiest part-time job on the planet.

6.

Whilst money was no longer a problem, my virginity was still very much on my mind. My hopes lay in a party that Ste-Bo was having over the weekend, where he'd promised me 'all the gash I could chuck a cock at'. His words.

Before the gang I'd had a rather romantic notion of sex that fell much more towards making love than fucking, but I was a changed man (I thought of myself as a man at that age, boy sounds derogatory any moment after primary school), and I wanted to get some action.

I didn't like to tell the others that I was receiving a healthy allowance from my father, but I wanted to bring some money to the group. I told them that I'd taken to sitting next to women on the bus and stealing from their purses when they weren't looking. I played upon my relative respectability and pointed out that these women never expected it from someone as angelic as me. They liked my style and appreciated having some extra money for booze.

The off-licenses in town were getting a little wary of us. You could only really pull the same scam once per shop, and we were running low on obvious options. The thrill of stealing had gone for me by then, so I was happy to be buying alcohol underage in a legitimate fashion.

Ste-Bo's girlfriend, Tanya, had invited a load of her mates to the party, which made us all happy. I joined the lads in chatting up various girls over the course of the night. I interacted at that party, which was an improvement on the last and found that I was playing a very convincing part.

At some point a girl called Natasha started talking to me about how Ste-Bo was saying I was a virgin. Initially I was fuming, but I laughed it off and stood there feeling like I was shrinking before her.

"Are you?" she asked.

"What's it to you?" I answered defensively.

"I like virgins," she smiled at me naughtily and I thought I was going to shit myself on the spot. I had been building up to trying on some serious moves later in the evening. I'd never thought of my virginity as appealing before.

We snuck into Ste-Bo's Mum's room and I was deflowered shortly thereafter. It was a quick and fumbly affair that I spent mainly wondering whether I was doing it right. There was little in the way of foreplay – I stroked her breasts and she gave me a love-bite. I was grateful to her for providing a condom and then guiding me in because I wasn't so sure on how it was all meant to happen, but she was clearly experienced and took control of the operation.

It was drunken, novice sex. I concentrated on moving about a bit and she didn't look all that satisfied when our ten minutes were over. As we did it on a bed of coats, I thought of the outcry over a couple of actors really having sex whilst filming a television drama. I pictured close ups of body parts and little beads of sweat as Danny Lizar lost his virginity in a spectacular fashion. I was no stranger to a bit of nudity, but this was my raunchiest scene ever.

There were no cuddles. Natasha pulled her clothes back on and left me in the dark. I dressed quickly, grinning from ear to ear. It was the thrill of having it over and done with.

Nothing else mattered about that party. I'd had sex. What else was there to report?

Natasha wasn't discreet. She'd won a bet, in fact, in screwing me and had told pretty much the whole party before the night was over. I didn't realise that she was known to the group, but I was informed later that both Ste-Bo and Knuckles had been with Natasha in the past. Were I a woman I might have felt cheap and used, but a whole bunch of people knew that I was sexually experienced and it changed my standing within the group.

L-Dog became the sole virgin among us, and I stepped above him in the pecking order. This meant I was passed joints before L-Dog, received booze before L-Dog and was the butt of the jokes less often than L-Dog.

Over the remaining weeks of the summer there was always at least one mother away on holiday within the gang. I spent most of my nights at Ste-Bo's, but when his mum returned I shifted over to Boner's place. It was easier than trekking to and from my house all of the time, and I could smoke in the living rooms of my friends' houses.

This caused a bit of tension when I deigned to return home, as Mum would start acting concerned, asking where I was.

"Don't pretend you care now," I typically shouted back.

"I have a right to know where you're staying."

"I'm staying at Steve's. Happy?"

And that would be that.

This left me free to stay up late, smoke joints and drink beer in my friends' homes. Often we'd all stay at the same house but there were some nights when I was the only one kipping over. It became commonplace to wake up and have a joint or a beer, at the very least a cigarette. We watched porn into the early hours of the morning and sometimes Tanya and her mates came round and something sexual would happen with one of them. There was brief talk of an orgy one night, but Tanya's friends thought that would make them slags and the idea was dismissed.

I did have sex with one girl whilst Ste-Bo had sex with Tanya in the same room, but there was no looking and no touching, so I don't think that counts as an orgy. It made for a very graphic episode, though.

I could only imagine the shock of the nation as Danny spun further and further off the rails. When I went home for a day or two at a time I'd look around my room and find myself completely disconnected to the person I used to be. My concerns had changed and my priorities were different. I was all about getting wrecked and not succeeding in life. I couldn't imagine how I would adjust when it was time to go back to school.

During this time Dad left and I only realised a week after his departure date.

I looked into getting a tattoo but there was no-one willing to break the law for me, even when I said please. I wanted to do something unprompted to show that I was real and not just the middle class pretender that I knew myself to be. I wanted to prove to myself that I was Lizard, because I nearly was. I also wanted the scenes to get more shocking. Things had to continue in a direction and I was concerned that just falling into this life wasn't going to be enough for the viewer, who had grown used to ground-breaking drama with every episode.

The next best thing I could think of was a knife. I didn't see how things could unravel from there.

7.

A knife was much easier to obtain than a tattoo. There was a tobacconist in town who didn't check IDs so I just went and bought something simple to tuck in my waistband. I was itching for the chance to show the others what I had, but at the same time I wanted to go for maximum impact.

There was little fun to be had in just showing them that I had a blade. I was a little worried that one of them might decide to stab me for fun, or that I would just have to give Ste-Bo the knife.

These measures were all about status. I wanted to be second in command. If a mere shag had put me above L-Dog, a grand gesture like carrying a weapon could topple even the likes of Knuckles. They were meant to be dangerous, I thought, but not one of them was armed.

Occasionally we got a bit of grief from other people like us. These exchanges didn't usually step beyond the trash talk, but there had been one or two occasions where threats had been made. I decided that the next one of these confrontations was the time to show my pretend true colours.

Unsurprisingly the action occurred whilst congregated around a park bench. It was late in the evening, but not quite dark yet, and some older kids were passing by. There was a certain level of respect for those at least two years older than you, but those from the year above were considered to be fair game. These guys were border-line, but we'd been drinking as well and I was feeling brave. More than anything I was desperate to get the knife out.

There were three of them, two of them fat and the other short and rodent-like. We clearly outnumbered them, which gave me extra confidence. As they passed an eyeballing contest took place between us and them.

"What you staring at, pricks?" I heckled unexpectedly, and I noticed that my friends were a little startled. They didn't flinch, though. As they said, they were always ready.

"Who you calling a prick?" one of them asked.

"You, you fat cunt," I answered and they all started approaching. We automatically stood up.

Then the knife was out. Everyone took a step back. "Keep fucking moving," I growled at them and they conferred with each other wordlessly. They made it look like they couldn't be bothered with us, muttering about 'fucking kids' as they walked off, but the victory was ours.

"Fucking hell, Lizard," they each said over the course of the next minute, and I couldn't tell whether they were pleased with me or not.

8.

I expected Lizard's status within the group to have been elevated in the wake of the knife incident. It should have earned him respect from his friends, who were no strangers themselves to going too far. It proved that he gave less of a fuck than most of them, and that's where I imagined the reverence would have stemmed from.

Instead I left them unsettled. L-Dog had been wary of me since I lost my virginity ahead of him, but he kept his feelings to himself because he didn't want to turn the group against him. The knife, though, was a cause of concern for them all.

I thought nothing of it when Boner said I couldn't stay at his a few nights later.

"I'm getting lucky tonight," he told me.

"That's never stopped you before," I laughed back.

"Yeah, well," Boner stumbled, "Some birds are funny about that."

I didn't question him further, but I have to assume that the plotting began that night.

In hindsight I tried to work out what went wrong, and imagined an episode that I didn't appear in. In it, L-Dog gathered Knuckles and Boner to tell them he was suspicious about Lizard.

"What the fuck was all that about?" he asked them. "He's trying to prove something."

"That's what I thought," Boner agreed straight away. "That's why I didn't want him in my house."

"Who the fuck is he, anyway? We were giving him a hard time a year ago," Knuckles chimed in.

"We've never been to his house – he just says he lives out of town."

"Doesn't throw parties or invite us round."

"Is anything he says true?"

And so it was decided that Lizard was trouble.

The trio set about finding out more about their friend. It was too soon to tell Ste-Bo, who'd introduced Lizard to them, so they just excused themselves for a couple of days to make enquiries.

They saw Alex in town and remembered that he was a friend of Lizard's and followed him back to Galgate, where they gathered round and threatened him until he told them where Lizard lived. Alex, still vengeful, gave up the information immediately. The three of them were shocked to see Lizard's nice detached cottage style abode. They saw Neil's BMW on the drive which made things look even worse.

That night they went over to see Ste-Bo to tell him everything. Ste-Bo was stunned and agreed that Lizard had to pay. "I'll keep him busy tomorrow," the leader told them.

The first I knew of any plan was when I came home to find that the house had been burgled. I had been in town with Ste-Bo until he'd taken a call on his mobile phone and said he had to go. The house was a state, with everything needlessly thrown about and quite a few valuables stolen in the process, like the DVD player, a stack of my CDs and the television that Mum had bought for the kitchen when Dad moved out. Later we found out that Mum had lost jewellery as well.

Mum had been instantly suspicious about the burglary. She thought it was me and didn't try to disguise it. "If I find out that you've had something to do with this, Daniel, I'll hand you over to the police myself."

"It wasn't me!" I raged.

"I'm sure you'll understand why I'm not so sure," she replied and left it at that. I spent the night fuming in my room at the injustice.

It was unusual for crime to happen near us, but it was only the next day that I started to get suspicious. The burglary was the talk of the village, and it didn't take long to get back to the Proctors.

It was lunch time and I was just getting out of the shower when the doorbell rang. I heard Mum gasp and then Robyn spoke.

"I know you don't want to see me, Jacqui, but Alex has told me he thinks he knows who burgled your house."

I froze in the bathroom as Robyn mentioned three of my friends, and even though I knew it was true, I also knew I had to defend them blindly.

I legged it down the stairs with just a towel around my waist. "You liar!" I shouted at her. "They wouldn't rob me. They're my mates."

"They followed Alex back to the village and threatened to stab him if he didn't tell them where you lived," she replied smugly.

"It's not true," I shook my head. "You're full of shit!" I ran up the stairs in a flounce only achievable by a livid teenager. Robyn was gone by the time I stormed out five minutes later.

Infuriatingly, *Lizard* was robbed of a real climactic finale. I called Ste-Bo from home before leaving and he'd told me where they were going to hang out. I went to the bench, but there was no-one to be seen. I found the nearest phone box and called him up, feeling increasingly uneasy.

To my surprise he answered.

"Where are you?"

"We went."

"Where?"

"Nowhere."

"What do you mean?"

"I mean fuck off."

"People are saying you guys robbed my house."

"Who's saying that? The butler or the chauffer?"

I could hear them all laughing. The camera panned in on Danny in the phone box as the realisation took hold. They all started singing the chorus of 'Common People' by Pulp and then hung up.

The storyline was over and all I had to show for it was the knife in my hand. It had fallen apart so quickly and unexpectedly that I was still reeling from all of the punches. I knelt down in the phone box and tried to work out what the hell I would do next.

The camera panned away as the credits rolled over the finishing tableau. *Lizard* was over in every possible sense.

A New Old Leaf

1.

The Almost Lizard returned from its summer hiatus to find Danny at an all time low. In between series, Malcolm had been written out and Jacqui had found her new romance with Neil. There was no-one else there for him, so it was hard to know where to take things next.

The only thing I had left was my pretend television show.

The problem with turning a character evil is that you usually need to kill them off when their wrongdoing is over. People don't trust the bad boys, even when they reform. Underneath there always lurks that possibility that they'll go back to their old ways.

Danny had done pretty rotten things during his Lizard phase, and for that the viewer wouldn't be sympathetic. I wondered if they felt sorry for him as he covered up for his old friends through either a misplaced loyalty or fear of retribution.

Mum didn't believe me when I told her that my friends had ditched me because I accused them of the burglary, but that was the story I stuck to.

In the days after I was ditched I felt very sorry for myself. I had to endure the return to school, where the gang pretended I was invisible on the bus, as if it had all been some elaborate dream. I didn't try to let on to them. At least I was astute enough to tell that there was no point in that.

Alex and his new friends also looked at me with scorn, and I detected a great pleasure in them as they realised that I was on my own again. I had been so cocky at the end of the previous year, and it was obvious to all that the tide had turned.

I also had to serve my detention from the previous term. I remember a time when a new school year was like a fresh start, but this one stank of carryover. My disruptive behaviour had changed many teachers' attitude towards me and they regarded me with suspicion. Miss Lawrence didn't smile at me when I walked into tutorial on the first day back, and she remained frosty in the subsequent weeks.

I hadn't done any of the coursework I was supposed to do during the holidays which left me way behind many of my classmates. The one benefit of having no friends was that it gave me plenty of time to study in the evenings whilst Mum and Neil sat downstairs watching television.

So the first episode back focussed on Danny's new found loneliness. I decided that he shouldn't utter a line in the entire episode, which wasn't a tough task. My days were largely wordless. I had no-one to talk to and with my PC sold I didn't even have the internet for company.

I couldn't carry on with the Lizard character. There was no motivation and alone I would have cut a pathetic figure. I couldn't roll a joint and more often than not I had been sent packing when I tried to buy booze. Now I didn't have the gang, none of the girls would be interested and if I tried to set foot on their estate again I'm sure I would have been battered.

I kept up with the smoking, but aside from that I dropped all of my Lizard traits the moment I'd put the phone down at the end of the series.

I took solace in television. I watched the soaps avidly, seeking inspiration. They were brilliant at contriving ways of making characters look sympathetic again. There was a difference between bad guys and good guys who screwed up, and I considered myself to be the latter. Danny and I were both backed into a corner and I had to think of a way to try and win some people over.

After much thinking of previous plots that I had seen, and a couple of apt moments in that week's viewing, I came up with a list of three:

Make people feel sorry for you
Make a grand gesture
Go missing

I didn't know which was the best, so I decided to try all three, starting from the top.

2.

I figured that if I could win one person over then others would follow naturally. I didn't care who it was, as long as someone showed an interest in me. As a fifteen year old boy there were many ways in which I could become a cause for concern, but I decided on bulimia.

To me, it was something that people did when bad things happened. More importantly, it made everyone feel sorry for them.

I didn't know too much about bulimia, only what the teen soaps had taught me. It usually happened to girls, it involved looking at my reflection in the mirror a lot, brushing my teeth at every opportunity, and I had to spend as much time as possible hiding sweet wrappers in places that people could find them. It was a classic cry for help. I even bought all of my sweets and chocolates from Mr Taylor, just in case he might raise the alarm.

Bulimia is tough when you don't mean it. Locked in my room, I started to flag on the fourth chocolate bar and moved over to some fruity sweets. There was only so much sugar I could take and I had to purge after a pathetic amount.

If Mum heard me vomiting then she didn't feel the need to come and ask if I was alright.

Over the next few nights I built up more of a tolerance to chocolate. I could put away seven or eight bars easily, with a few packs of fruity sweets to go with them. Each night I threw up at home, getting louder and louder on each occasion.

"Are you unwell Danny?" Neil asked me unpleasantly one evening as I was leaving the bathroom. He wasn't there every night, but he did seem to be around an awful lot. I guess he was there for Mum when both the men in her life walked away.

"I'm fine thanks, Neil," I said knowing full well that my blotchy eyes were more than a little suspicious. Unfortunately, I'd done nothing to earn Neil's concern for my welfare in the time I'd known him. Even if he was aware that I was making myself sick on a nightly basis, he was hardly likely to rush in and pull me back from the brink with some fatherly words and a reassuring hug.

The strange thing was it made me feel better. Not better in that it made me feel thinner – I've never needed to diet – but it kept me busy. It was a meaty storyline and it kept me occupied. Sneaking around trying to get people to notice my new problem stopped me thinking about the friends I'd lost and the lifestyle I'd been forced to walk away from. No part of me felt like Lizard any more, but at least Lizard hadn't been lonely.

After Neil ignored my warning sign I decided to be a little more obvious.

The next day we were in tutorial, and I purposely unzipped my bag so that when I stood up to leave at the end of the lesson, the contents spilled out, including a small pile of about thirty chocolate bar wrappers.

If it had been a girl who'd done that she would have been surrounded by a circle of concerned teachers and friends thrilled to be involved in a bit of drama. All I got in response from Miss Lawrence was: "You should empty your bag out more often, Danny. Make sure you pick all of those up."

Even if no-one else was picking up on the hints, I thought that the viewers would be showing concern.

I saved my vomiting for later in the evening so that it was almost impossible not to hear me. Mum didn't come to the rescue and I think I realised how much damage I had done. I had systematically prevented her from caring about me.

The day after that, I went and locked myself in the toilets half way through tutorial. By the smell of me it was obvious that I still smoked and I knew that I wouldn't be away for long before Miss Lawrence assumed that I was puffing away.

I waited until I heard someone coming and forced two fingers down my throat, which as always caused me to make a horrible hurling sound. I struggled to force up my breakfast, but I found that if I put my fingers a little bit further down than I felt comfortable with, I was always able to produce something.

Whoever it was that came in ran away. I waited it out, hoping that they had gone to raise the alarm.

A few minutes later I heard Miss Lawrence call through the door. "Danny, are you alright in there?"

I remained quiet, daring her to step into no-woman's land. I spat into the toilet bowl and sniffed a little.

"Danny you didn't seem unwell a moment ago," she said.

"Go away!" I yelled back at her with phlegm in my throat. I clearly sounded like I'd just vomited.

"I'm coming in," she said. I loved it when a scene went to plan.

After a moment or two I stepped out of the cubicle wiping a little bit of sick off my chin. "I'm sorry," I said pathetically and started to sob. The tears had been a surprise even to me.

Miss Lawrence hugged me and I hugged her back for a moment. We pulled apart and I went to kiss her. So many soap kisses happen at a low point, and they always emanate from hugging. She was being kind to me, and I was grateful. And what a scandalous storyline! It was completely unplanned and for a split second I thought I was really in with a chance.

"Danny, no!" she said sternly. She was clearly flustered, as any teacher would when a vomit-breathed weeping schoolboy tried to kiss you. "That was very wrong of you. Now clean yourself up and either come back to class or go home."

"But Miss Lawrence – " I pleaded. She darted back out into the corridor. I slid down a wall and wept on the toilet floor. It was a bleak end to an episode where Danny had come so close to making amends.

Miss Lawrence didn't seem to hate me any more, though. She feared me, maybe, but she definitely didn't hate me.

I gave up on bulimia after that. Nobody was taking notice and it was a lot of hard work to act out. I filmed a quick scene where Danny realised how stupid it all was and laughed at his reflection in the mirror. Had this been real I think the show would have been annihilated for the simplistic end to the storyline, but as it was all in my head I could be as inaccurate and dangerous with my issue-led plots as I wished.

The point was that I was no better off in trying to get into anyone's good books.

3.

My attempts at a grand gesture were equally as futile as the bulimia plot. I don't understand how people were easier to manipulate when I was younger and therefore less devious, but it did seem in the earlier days they were much more prone to playing along with the storylines.

With the money coming in thick and fast from Dad, I was able to buy Mum an ostentatious bunch of flowers, which were delivered to her at her school. I thought she would have been thrilled, but she only asked where I got the money from. She asked me outright if I was selling drugs, and I lost my rag with her.

"I was trying to be nice!" I yelled at her. "I'm trying to make amends and say I'm sorry."

"It's going to take a lot more than a bunch of flowers," she warned. "Now where did you get the money?"

I stormed out, fearing that she would put a stop to the cash I was amassing. I was saving up to buy my own PC because I was missing the online world quite a lot.

I offered to go fishing with Neil, but he politely declined. "Who's to know you wouldn't drown me?" he joked meaningfully.

I made Alex a photo album of pictures collected from our years growing up together and delivered it to his house. During my Lizard months I had hoped that he would take more notice than he had. He could at least have been there to tell me what my friends were really like instead of sending Robyn in his place.

Just because you only have yourself to blame doesn't make it any easier.

By the next morning, the photo album was on my doorstep, with various coarse comments scribbled next to each snapshot of our lives.

I had no choice but to go missing.

4.

Part of me wondered whether the world would call my bluff once more and not even notice that I'd vanished. I packed a minimal amount of stuff and headed out one Saturday afternoon in November. I didn't say where I was going, nor was I asked.

I didn't have to be too sneaky in order to get away because I was essentially invisible at that time. I didn't leave a note. It just didn't seem appropriate.

I kept looking behind me all the way to the train station, nervously expecting someone to come after me and convince me not to go at the last minute.

On TV, running away changes everything. Someone goes missing and they fall into the realm of the nearly dead, where everything that went before it is forgotten just as long as they are alive. The search for the missing brings enemies together and unites a community. It inspires human goodwill and charity. For me, it would erase the immediate past, which I had been trying to do for some time.

I wanted to keep the viewers guessing, so the moment I stepped on the train was the last they saw of me for a while. I was going to film a special week of episodes that would be shown as a retrospective of my adventures once I was found. The doors shut and I looked back thoughtfully. Exit Danny Lizar.

It excited me to think of how huge this storyline was. I imagined faked press releases being sent out to the newspapers, announcing my intention to leave the programme to focus on my studies. I wanted my return to be a surprise for everyone, so the television magazines were told that the train scene marked the end of my time with *The Almost Lizard*.

I imagined people on set were dispatched to hint to journalists that they had just been working on the scenes where Danny's body was recovered. I imagined sentences like, "In the most heartbreaking scenes in the show's history, the search for outcast Danny Lizar reaches a devastating climax."

Being involved in a major storyline gave me a purpose at a time when there was nothing else. This little dementia of mine wasn't completely destructive, not always.

Mum worked out that I wasn't there that night, to her credit. I'd obviously been around home more in recent weeks, doing what she thought was my sulky teenager act. She didn't like me still, but she had grown used to me being at home again. When I missed dinner, she initially thought I was going back to my old ways and only began to worry when I didn't come home all night.

The next morning she became genuinely concerned. Not knowing who else to ask, she reluctantly made her way over to the Proctors house, where she was told categorically by Robyn that I was unwelcome over there. It was also suggested that Mum try harder to rein me in a bit. Mum did well not to punch her by all accounts.

She knew nothing of my other friends, not that there were any. There was no-one else she could think to contact. Mum enlisted Neil to help with the search and they did a drive around the Lancaster area, and asked at the railway and bus stations. After that she started to think of all the possibilities. Neil assured her that this wasn't unlike me, and that she shouldn't worry. It was Neil who told her not to call the police.

Another night passed and Mum phoned the school. Teachers were alerted and questions were asked. Nobody knew anything, and my isolation was exposed for all to see. Each member of the gang faced a lengthy grilling about my whereabouts, but they all protested their innocence. They were innocent, of course, but they were the sort of people who looked terminally guilty. The school advised calling the police.

Neil still insisted that I was just attention-seeking and Mum told him to leave. He told her that she was a sucker for her sicko son and she praised him on the alliteration. That was the last time she saw him. He was hardly off the drive before Mum phoned the police. They asked her if there were any family members I could be staying with and her gut reaction was to say no. Her second thought was to call Dad in New York, even though she knew I didn't have my own passport.

Dad offered to catch the next plane home and Mum told him to wait it out a little bit. She apologised for losing his son and he was calm, comforting and helpful.

I was surprised to see Mum turn up at the Pleasant Rise Guest

House so soon. She'd called up soon after Dad had asked her if she'd tried his family.

My big runaway turned out to be a long weekend in Blackpool, where I had got to know my Auntie Jennifer and Uncle Alfred a little better. I'd turned up on their doorstep and they hadn't really recognised me. I lied and said Mum knew where I was, then I shocked them by telling them that Dad had emigrated. They'd had no idea. "We don't really see much of Malcolm," Jennifer said as if it were news.

"I missed him," I lied, "So I thought I'd come and see you."

They loved having me about. It felt like the first time in a while that people had encouraged my company. We exchanged stories – them about guests at the hotel and me about school and friends and other such fallacies. We talked mainly about what it was like for them growing up and more details of my family history came to light.

There was something sad about the two of them as they reflected on their teen years, which had clearly been the highlight of both their lives. They had dedicated everything to their parents' earlier dream and all they had to show for it was a bunch of tales about guests.

I thought about a future at the seaside, living and working at the B&B. It could have been a whole new way of life for my character. I had no idea how long I was going to stay with them, or how long I could hide out there at the very least, but I started to see more potential in the storyline than I'd previously expected. It was a future, a fresh start.

I had hoped to make the papers before anyone found me. I liked the idea of being part of the news, my face plastered on front pages all over the country.

I was in my room up on the third floor when Mum arrived, but I'd seen her car when I looked out of the window. I made my way downstairs into the guest lounge, where Mum was sat with Alfred and Jennifer making awkward small-talk. It had been years since they had seen each other and so much had happened. They were talking about Dad moving to New York, and they spoke of him with such reverence for being the one who escaped into the big wide world.

"New York, hey?" Alfred was saying. He chuckled as if it were the craziest thing in the world. "Although of course it's very sad about your marriage," he added.

"It was a good marriage for a long time," Mum assured them, then noticed that I was stood in the doorway.

She didn't get up to hug me, but her face had softened in the days I'd been away.

"I think we need to have a bit of a chat, don't you?" she said.

It was decided that we should stay another night. Mum called the school and told them that I was fine. Alfred and Jennifer gave us a room and we had a long and frank chat. There was no doubt it was enough for a two-handed episode, one that I suspected would win the show more accolades.

From her: "You destroyed my life last Christmas and it wasn't something I could forgive easily. Everything that happened was a shock. You must have hated me so much to do what you did. You were the face of it all at a time when really I needed you more than ever."

From me: "I wanted to make things right but you kept pushing me away. We were both busy with our own stuff but I had no-one left in my life. Then those guys wanted to know me. I did try to get your attention."

We talked for hours and concluded that she had pushed me away, but it was my fault that she had been driven to do that. We shook on it and agreed to move on. It was a relief to know that things could still pan out the way I plotted them.

5.

Neil's departure was an unexpected bonus for me and I'm sure it was instrumental in the success of Mum and I reconstructing our relationship. We settled down and willingly watched television again. It felt like the old days in a way, with Dad just out at work instead of thousands of miles away.

I enjoyed the return to family life and relished the break from a punishing series of storylines. I knew I had to take a break as an actor and filmed nothing for three months. I pretended that Danny remained missing and the scenes we filmed in Blackpool were saved for my return. I knuckled down and worked hard on my mock GCSEs. Although I wasn't acting, I was pretending to be a soap actor on a break for a show, so it wasn't like I just normalised for a few months.

Christmas was quiet and poignant, and the New Year brought promising exam results. I grew comfortable with things being back on track, and like anyone who is comfortable, I again started looking for something more.

Having Mum back was great, but I missed Alex more than anything. So when Danny returned to *The Almost Lizard* his first storyline was to get his best friend back.

I filmed some returning home scenes walking around the village and pretending that I was the centre of attention at school. In his time away Danny had turned over a new leaf and was looking forward to returning to his old life. At the end of his first episode back he followed Alex home from the bus. I hid behind a tree near his front door and whispered, "I want you back, mate." Poignant, hey?

Initially I tried to talk to him at the bus stop, but he blanked me and went to talk to someone else. I sighed without resentment, knowing that the reformed Danny didn't blame Alex for anything.

I tried to sit next to him in classes but he would either move or ask me to do so. I'd find another seat and look distressed at the camera.

I made attempts to get to know some of his new friends but they were all reluctant to make contact with me. They had obviously heard plenty of reasons to avoid Danny Lizar.

Against all my instincts I didn't try and make Alex's friends turn against him or create a situation where he needed saving by me. I waited until the time was right. I occupied my time with little plotlines that were largely imagined, just like the good old days when no-one got hurt. But I always kept an eye out for an opportunity to make him like me again.

I can honestly say that the rumours didn't come from me.

I was in my usual spot in the library one lunch time studying at a table that overlooked the playground, when I saw Alex walking along near the picnic benches. As he walked by, some people were whispering to each other and pointing. It was hard to tell whether Alex was aware of this and ignoring people, or just completely oblivious to what was going on.

When he usually walked across the playground he would stop and talk to one or two people before meeting with his group of friends. They weren't in their regular spot when he got there and I observed him glancing around with a bewildered expression on his face. Something unusual had obviously happened and he sat down on his own looking perplexed. No-one came to talk to him over the course of lunch time and he cut a sad figure eating his sandwiches on his own. It was a way of eating that I had become accustomed to during my fifth year, but I still felt sorry to see it happen to someone else.

To avoid any accusations of opportunism I left him there on his own, instead looking thoughtfully into the camera. I understood that the plot I was seeking had transpired.

That afternoon things became more apparent. Alex entered our science class to sniggers and muttering that he couldn't ignore. He was dignified enough not to respond, but on the numerous times I glanced over he looked troubled. A note was passed around at some point but it wasn't passed to me. I didn't get included in things like that. It was intercepted by Mr Balshaw, our science teacher of the stereotypical schoolmaster breed. He had bushy eyebrows, a bald pate and a look of permanent rage that I assume became a fixture when corporal punishment was abolished. He glanced at the note, then at Alex, and demanded to know which individual he had to send to the headmaster. Colin Brown was ratted out and skulked away.

Colin Brown had been one of Alex's replacement friends. I'd seen him in Galgate numerous times heading over to Alex's house.

Something was going on with Alex, and Danny was particularly keen to find out what. This was a quick-moving plot, and on the bus home my old gang revealed the source of the mystery whilst Alex sat rigidly a few seats in front.

"Proctor, Proctor!" L-Dog shouted, "I think I've got a cock in my hand!"

The gang fell about in hysterics. Alex's face reddened but he didn't flinch.

"Man goes to a Proctors," Steve joined in, "says, Proctor, Proctor, I've got a pain in my arse. That's not a pain, the Proctor replies, it's my cock." They laughed even louder.

Once in town, most people dispersed but the gang decided to loiter around. The four of them circled Alex, puckering up and grabbing at their crotches. "Does this turn you on, gayboy?" L-Dog barked. "Can I have a kiss?"

"Leave me alone," Alex tried to assert himself, but he was shaking and looked on the verge of tears.

"What's wrong, don't you fancy him?" Boner mocked.

I understood what was being implied, but I didn't understand why.

"What's wrong with L-Dog?" Ste-Bo asked menacingly.

"Well he calls himself L-Dog for a start," Alex replied unexpectedly. "It's very sweet that he likes to pretend to be a black rapper, but we can all see that he's clearly white, however baggy his tracksuit is."

Knuckles was straight in there, lunging for Alex. Opportunism was no longer a consideration. "Oi!" I bellowed and all five of them turned around.

"Fuck off Lizard," Ste-Bo sneered.

"Just one minute whilst I try and remember where my friends were on the day my house was burgled," I replied. I hadn't tried to be hard for a long time, but I spoke with such ferocity that we all seemed to believe me.

"We're not your fucking friends," Boner spat.

"No, you're not," I countered, "Which makes me wonder why I keep my silence."

"Because you know we'll knock your rich fucking brains out," Ste-Bo answered.

"Yeah, when you get out."

They moved away from Alex, four pairs of eyeballs resting firmly on me.

"They're probably both queer together," L-Dog concluded as they walked away.

Alex waited until they left the bus station before he spoke to me.

"If you'd told me this morning I'd be grateful to you I probably would have spat in your face," he said with an ironic smile. "You didn't have to do that."

"I couldn't see them do that to you," I replied. "I'll catch you later."

I walked over to the spot where I usually stood on my own at the bus station, not looking over at Alex. I made it look like I didn't expect anything, like intervening was just an intrinsic part of my good nature. I waited for him to get on the bus and then sat apart from him, looking out of the window.

We walked on opposite sides of the street through the village and I thought of leaving it for the day, but that wasn't in my nature.

"If you do want to talk," I called out to him. "I know I'm not your favourite person but just in case."

Alex stopped and thought about this for a second. "Thanks," he replied with a look of mild gratitude. We continued on other sides of the road in silence until I broke off to go to my house.

I had sensed the thaw but I really hadn't expected Alex to turn up at my house that night.

"I think I do want to talk," he said.

"Come in," I said gravely. Mum was at theatre group so the whole house was our set.

He sat nervously in the kitchen whilst I boiled the kettle, unsure how to open the scene. I had to play my part carefully, not overly keen but not unfriendly either. More than anything, I had to ensure that my concern looked genuine. It was genuine, but my fear of appearing false could easily have become a self-fulfilling prophecy.

"Do you want to talk about the past or the present?" I eventually asked. Part of him must have been tempted to up and walk out, but instead he started from the beginning.

He'd been having quite a lot of fun in the time since we'd been friends, making new acquaintances and developing a bit of a social life for himself. He'd been out with a couple of girls for short periods of time but nothing exciting had happened in the process – no lost virginity or even a cursory hand-job. As the time had worn on, he'd found himself particularly close to a lad called Ewan who I knew from several of our classes. It was Ewan I'd seen him hanging around with the most.

The closer they'd got, the more Alex was concerned that there was something more to their friendship than he'd initially thought. He had detected some flirtation in Ewan's behaviour, just little things like Ewan would get changed in front of him, or he'd touch his arm more than most. He was very strong on eye contact as well and didn't mind sharing a bed if Alex wanted to crash over. This had left Alex wondering on several occasions whether Ewan had romantic intentions towards him, and Alex hadn't known what to do about that. His first thoughts had been to try and let him down gently but he couldn't find the opportunity to do it.

The weekend before, Alex stayed at Ewan's house for a film night whilst Ewan's parents were away. They'd watched the *Scream* trilogy and his parents had left out a few beers for them.

"He tried it on?" I interjected, trying not to sound too sensationalist in my approach.

"Not quite," Alex replied.

They'd drunk their beers and were onto *Scream 3* when Alex broached the subject. "Are you a virgin?" he'd asked Ewan.

"Indeed," Ewan replied. "Not that I'm not keen."

To be fair it was an ambiguous sentence and Alex – drunk through his inexperience with alcohol – had gone with his first interpretation.

"I kissed him," he confessed, looking crestfallen.

Immediately '*Almost Lizard* in gay kiss shocker!' headlines flashed through my mind.

"Did he kiss you back?" I asked.

Alex shook his head. "Only for a second before he realised what had happened. He backed right off, told me I should probably go back to my house. He let me sleep on the couch eventually but the night ended there."

"Shit," I said, resting an arm on his shoulder sympathetically.

6.

Alex hadn't shown that much interest in women during our years of sexual awakening, but there had been no indication that he swung the other way either. We talked for a long time that night as he explained the fleeting thoughts he'd had, that perhaps Ewan didn't fancy him and it might be the other way around. He explained funny feelings that he'd had when Ewan was changing, feelings that sounded similar to the ones I'd had when I'd been seeking sex.

I rewrote history and imagined that Alex had remained a full-time cast member throughout and this storyline had been building up for ages. This was an episode that the viewers had been waiting a long time for, Alex finally acknowledging his potential homosexuality. More than anything else, homosexuality on television outraged the general public. In my lifetime, soaps have caused huge furores by screening brief kisses between men. It was an amazing turn of events for the show.

"I don't know if I am gay," he said, "but I definitely wanted to see what happened next."

"Was it him in particular?" I asked. Alex nodded and I was a little relieved. I didn't think I was ready for a scene like that. I was more than happy for Alex to have this storyline.

"It's not like I want to fuck him or anything, I just wanted to kiss him. I guess so anyway. I'm just confused. Part of me thinks he's in denial and another thinks that I only thought he was gay because I wanted him to be."

"That is confusing," I said uselessly.

"But now he won't talk to me anyway."

It was a tough situation and I felt for Alex, but at the same time it felt great to be filming with him again.

"If that's his attitude then you don't want to be his friend," I pointed out. This didn't seem to help him either. He looked miserable and I was scared he'd walk out if I didn't help.

"I do want to be his friend," he insisted. "I might want to be more than that."

I know it's perfectly natural and absolutely not an issue, but it took a little adjusting to hear Alex talking about lads in that kind of way. It's the way of the world to assume that a person is straight until proven otherwise, it's just we're not allowed to say that. I'd have seen him differently if he'd suddenly decided he liked football or dressed like a goth.

"Then you have to pretend it was nothing," I said cryptically. I imagined the ending of the episode. I went through the plan with Alex off-camera. He had to give himself time to find out how he really felt and fight off these rumours. It was the only idea I had that seemed to give him a little bit of hope.

The next day at school, the giggling and talking continued, but I stood up to fend it off. "Alex isn't gay," I said to anyone who would and wouldn't listen, "I've seen him get off with loads of girls."

That didn't seem to be enough for the salacious rumour mill, and my day of Alex promotion did nothing more than provide me with a busy filming schedule for the first time in months.

It was my idea to fight fire with fire and started to spread word that it was the other way round and Ewan had tried to kiss Alex. I commenced my campaign one morning on the bus.

"So he invites you round to watch scary movies and drink beer with him when his parents were out," I said in a stage whisper. "And you were surprised when he came onto you?"

I hadn't warned Alex that I was going to do this, but he ran with it anyway. "I didn't think he was gay," Alex replied.

"Bollocks," I laughed. "Have you seen the way he runs?"

We both laughed at this. Ewan's Mum had consistently sent him to school in trousers that were a little too tight for him and it did make him run in a funny way.

The seed was planted.

I snuck into our maths classroom during lunch time and scribbled 'EWAN IS A FAGGOT' on the blackboard. Our teacher pulled it down a few minutes into the lesson and everyone started to laugh.

The upshot was that no-one could really know who hit on who and so everyone just thought they both were gay, but as there were two of them they didn't really point and stare so much. The Easter holidays came and went and everyone was too busy thinking about GCSEs to worry about who may or may not be gay.

The exams themselves were a big part of the show for several months. I had college and A-levels in mind and the potential to be treated like a grown-up for once. The school and all of the associated characters were going to be written out, with all the damage done written off. I was returning to education in Lancaster and could leave the high school years behind. I didn't need to see the gang, or the teacher I hit on, or the people who had labelled me an outcast as I had developed as a person. I was on my way to having a best friend back, and I had my mum. Admittedly my dad was on the other side of the Atlantic, but by the time school was over I was feeling very much like Danny again.

I don't really remember much about the exams, but they passed, and I passed. I made a meal out of results day, building up the tension in a real time episode. My grades were good and Mum was proud of me.

And with the exams so faded Alex's moment of sexual confusion. He and Ewan became friends again, which was lucky because Ewan was one of the few from school going to the same college as Alex and me. I saw a new phase for *The Almost Lizard* and I was delighted to have turned my character around just in time. It could have been my chance to be a good person.

DANNY, AGAIN

Revamp

1.

For my new start, I wanted a new approach. For his college years, I wanted Danny to be popular.

It took a lot of consideration for me to work out what made someone likeable. I'd not seen myself as a bad person on the whole (recent years aside) but I had never been well liked either. I wanted the new Danny to be well liked, which required much planning.

I turned once more to the soaps and thought about which characters were the most popular. The people that stuck around for years and found places in the hearts of the nation were the boys next door and the genuinely good people. I wanted to be both.

It helped to be cool. I didn't want people to like Danny in the pitying way. I had no desire to be some hapless loser. The people who had been respected at school had been good at sports or into their music. I had no hope with the sports, so I opted to get into guitars. I picked up copies of NME to learn which bands I should like and if I saw something that received a good review, I'd go into town and buy it on a Saturday. I got into some really interesting stuff very quickly. I looked at music websites on the internet and band forums. By the time

I started college I had a fair bit of knowledge.

This helped me fashion my image and I started wearing skinny jeans and stripy tops like they did in the magazines. I got my hair cut to look purposefully messy and I changed cigarette brands to Marlboro Lights. I bought a mobile phone so that I could look busy sending text messages, giving off the impression of popularity even when I was on my own.

Liking music gave me something to talk to people about, a potential common interest. However much I would have liked to introduce myself by saying that I had my own television programme but only in my head, it obviously wouldn't have endeared me to people.

I worked on being funnier. I watched comedy and satirical panel shows on television and thought about what it was that made people laugh. I practiced being nice to people in the mirror, working on an inviting smile and an aloof demeanour.

Likeable people were also busy. I didn't have a ready-made social life so I enquired for work in a pub just outside of the village. The Fox and Whistle needed a kitchen porter, so I took that as work for three nights a week. It gave the appearance of looking like I had stuff to do and it brought me into the epicentre of any soap. I had a pub to go to. There were three of us in the kitchen – me, the head chef who laughably made us call him 'Chef,' even as he was microwaving up a Sunday roast, and Ed, who was a few years older than me. He had a heart of gold but a fine line in bullshit.

The pub was a rustic, small affair run by an affable middle aged couple. They had a full-time bar maid and three extras to do weekend shifts. They had a waitress from Thursday to Sunday as well. I started two weeks before college started and I immediately saw places for these people when the show re-launched.

I practiced being good natured on my new colleagues and I was delighted to find that they liked me. I answered back when I could think of something funny to say and otherwise I was courteous and hard working. I gave Ed loads of cigarettes so he always invited me out for a smoke break, where we'd talk about music, computer games and women. He told me about women he'd supposedly slept with at the end of raucous nights out that I couldn't be sure had happened.

At the end of most shifts I was allowed a drink in the bar despite being underage. It wasn't the sort of pub the police would do a raid on, and it was generally full of locals who saw nothing wrong with a beer at the end of my shift. It was certainly a lot less harmful than the sessions I'd had in my Lizard days. The customers joked with me about how young I looked and I laughed with them. I found that they liked me as well. It was all so simple – talk to people and be nice and genuine and most of the time they will like you. I'd spent so much of my time being insular and satisfied with my small world that these obvious truths had eluded me.

A couple of weeks into the job and I felt that it was time to introduce the new Danny Lizar to the viewers.

2.

The Almost Lizard returned to the screens with a special ninety minute episode. The opening scenes were of Danny working in the kitchen, having a laugh with Chef and Ed. Then there was a scene in the bar where I talked with Annie the barmaid about my new college and how much I was looking forward to starting. "It feels like a fresh start," I said. That was where the new credits rolled.

The episode covered all of the first week at college, with the enrolment and ice-breaking games in our tutorials. I imagined Ewan filming scenes at home. Likewise, I imagined Alex getting ready for the big day as well.

I was doing four AS levels in my first year, and I'd made them wildly different so that I could interact with more people who would potentially like me. My choices, sociology, performing arts, maths and geography (which I dropped in my second year), also stemmed from the fact that I had no idea what I wanted to be when I grew up. In spite of everything I was doing I had no desire to be an actor, but I'd chosen performing arts to make sure of it.

In classes I made new acquaintances and spoke self-effacingly when we had to do introductions. I found it easy to talk to people and tell them which school I was from and how I'd done in my GCSEs. We could call the teachers by their first names and they all treated us differently. We were in charge of buying our own books and providing paper and stationery for lessons. We were given a lot more homework and from the first week we were preparing for exams that folklore told us would be the hardest thing we ever did in our lives. It was very exciting.

By smoking and always having lots of cigarettes on me I found I made new friends to talk to almost every time I popped off for a fag. Alex and Ewan didn't like smoking, apparently, so I had to do that bit on my own, which gave me the opportunity to meet new people.

"Oh my God!" someone cried out as we walked into our first performing arts class, and for a second I wondered if I was secretly famous.

"No way!" Alex grinned and ran across the room to hug Lauren Bell, who neither of us had seen since primary school. The years had changed her – she had long hair and some impressive bumps where nothing used to be. Puberty had been kind to Lauren that was for sure. Likeable as I now was, I followed Alex over to her and gave her a bigger hug than the one she'd just received.

"I thought we'd seen the last of you," I said from my side of the embrace. "This is amazing."

I immediately decided she was hot and so did Danny.

Though it's beyond me, many people crave love and happiness in their soaps more than violence and tragedy, which was something my character had gone through in spades over the years.

People the world over know who Ross and Rachel are, such is the power of a popular television romance. People speak of soap weddings as if they happened in the family. It's that whole Romeo and Juliet thing, really. We're told that for centuries the world has been gripped by tales of other people's romance. We're also bred to believe that romance completes a person and makes them happy. I wanted to be the most special person in someone's world; someone who wasn't my mother. I realised all of this the moment I saw Lauren Bell for the first time in over five years and decided that she was Danny's immediate future.

We all went for a coffee after the lesson, trying to fit five years into one conversation.

"Are you still writing grim stories?" she said and laughed. I could quite easily see how we could fall in love. I talked a little about the music I liked and she said we'd have to go to a gig together. She left us and went back to her other friends, promising to see us for performing arts later in the week.

In that episode it was all happiness and newness in Danny Lizar's world. I knew that the audience demanded drama, so I imagined a storyline where Annie the barmaid was raped walking home from work. Well it couldn't be all fun, after all.

3.

We became a soap with two pubs on the first Friday of college when I joined Alex and Ewan in what was apparently Lancaster Academy tradition. It just so happened that my lessons finished at half past eleven on a Friday, and about half a mile away from college there was a pub that willingly served those under age. I could see that Alex and Ewan were quite excited at the prospect of going over there, but I'd had my share of thrills from purchasing alcohol in the past so I got to act blasé about the whole experience.

"This is a little different than drinking round a park bench," Alex joked.

The pub was filled with sixteen and seventeen year olds chain smoking and getting drunk on weak lager. The landlady told us that the police did a spot check on the place once a year on a date that she agreed with them first. On that day all the students had to stay away, but for the rest of the year they freely drank in there.

I was chuffed to see Lauren turn up after us, just as I was beating Alex at pool. If she'd arrived a little sooner she would have seen the pathetic display of two novices struggling to complete a game in under forty minutes, but as it was she saw me pot the black and light a cigarette to celebrate, before heading over to the jukebox and putting on the most obscure tracks that I'd heard of.

I commandeered Lauren for much of the afternoon, playing games of 'remember when' and asking questions about our missing years. I made her laugh numerous times, I bought her drinks and I cut her off to say hello to people I recognised from my classes. Alongside Lauren were several other faces from my primary school days, many of who remained wary of me after all these years.

It was a busy afternoon of drinking and socialising. This felt like growing up. I had given my character an overhaul at the same time as everyone else and thrown him out into a receptive crowd.

Alex commented on the change in me. "I'm glad you're my best friend again," he slurred.

"Me too," I grinned back. "I never did tell you how sorry I was."

"It's history," he said and we hugged tipsily.

People started to drift away and I was surprised to see that it was nearly five o'clock. I'd been well behaved for months and I was concerned that my drinking might scare Mum into hating me. I called her at home and slurred that I would be back in a while. She asked who I was out with and sounded comforted when I said Alex. Mum had welcomed him back into my life with open arms, holding no resentment over what had happened. It was better than Robyn. She told Alex he could be friends with who he liked, but she'd throw him out if she ever found out I'd set foot in the house.

Experience had taught me the benefits of a sobering four mile walk home and I suggested it to Alex. We reflected on our first week at college for the first two miles, talking about new friends and new people. I mentioned Lauren repeatedly until Alex picked up on the theme.

"You don't have a crush there do you?" he asked and I smiled knowingly. "Ha! I knew it!"

"Don't you dare tell her," I warned jovially. "I do really like her."

"She's gorgeous," he said. "It'd be so cool if you got together. Proper childhood sweetheart stuff."

"So you're not interested yourself?"

"No," he scoffed. "There is someone I like though."

"Who? Is it Jodie?" I asked, referring to a girl from our general studies class.

"You're way off," he said, then staggered a little.

"Who then?"

"Ewan," he admitted with a look of thinly disguised shame.

I was genuinely gobsmacked. I'd thought that storyline had been put to bed and forgotten about months ago. If anything, it had only been a hook for reuniting the show's favourite double act.

"Are you gay then?" I asked without an ounce of tact.

"I guess so."

"Wow."

Then we both laughed. Danny Lizar was cool with homosexuality.

Going Global

1.

To my knowledge, no other soap out there did an episode dedicated to the events of September 11th 2001, but then fake soaps don't have to worry too much about logistics.

2.

The Almost Lizard was filling up nicely with storylines to compel the viewers. There was Danny falling for Lauren, and the anguish of Alex as he came to terms with his sexuality and his attraction to Ewan, plus the imagined rape of Annie.

I was so immersed in helping Alex and trying to woo Lauren that I really didn't have the time for any more twists.

Very few people in the world could have anticipated what happened next. I was in the common room with Ewan watching *Neighbours* and talking about our favourite women on there. I was trying to see how enthusiastically he responded to the questions. In the episode Danny was trying to work out whether Ewan was gay or, at the very least, bi. I complained that there were too many half naked blokes on the screen to see whether he agreed. He didn't give anything away and by the end of the episode I had to conclude that he was most probably straight. I planned a sad scene where Danny let Alex down gently, and thought of a new plot of trying to find Alex someone else.

The soap turned into news as reports of a plane hitting the Twin Towers was broken by a newsreader facing the biggest day of their career. It was a plane crash in New York, quite an unexpected one, but it wasn't as if Madonna had died or anything. We talked about other things for a little while and someone went to change the channel just as footage of the second plane hitting the towers appeared.

"That's a coincidence," I said stupidly. I didn't understand why people I didn't really know looked at me incredulously. The news spoke of terrorism and I suddenly got the message. The original footage was supplemented by scenes of terror and pandemonium on the streets of New York. It took me a good fifteen minutes before I thought about Dad.

3.

At the time, Dad meant £50 a week to me and the occasional phone call, but I had been so preoccupied with reinventing myself that I hadn't found time to give him much thought until 9/11.

I called Mum at her school and insisted that she be fetched out of class. At that point the news wasn't big enough to stop classes or afternoons at work. It was hours, if not days, before the international ramifications really became clear. I waited for nearly ten minutes before she answered the phone suspiciously, presumably anticipating some misdeed on my part. I told her about the World Trade Centre and then asked her if she knew where Dad had his restaurant.

We agreed to meet at home and I made my exit. "My dad lives in New York," I informed Ewan gravely. "He could have been in there."

It went without saying that a one plot episode was happening. I didn't need to act. I'd learned by this point that sometimes my life made good television. It didn't detract from how real anything I felt was – just like the affair, meeting Auntie Anne and my time with the gang. It was no less real just because I thought in terms of a television programme. It's just how I processed things. I don't think I'm emphasising that enough, I look back and think I just appear calculated.

But you have to ask yourself why I did this. There was no obvious gain for me. I knew even then that it was something unusual and quite probably very unfortunate as well. I took no pleasure in worrying that my father had been involved in a terrorist attack, but I did act up for the situation. I dashed out of college, pelting down the corridors and shouting for people to move out of my way.

"Danny!" I heard Alex call out.

"I can't stop. My dad!" I hollered back and disappeared around a corner. I ran out of the building and down the hill towards the bus stop, imagining close ups on my panic stricken face. I just missed a bus and swore loudly as it disappeared from view. I paced around the bus stop muttering to myself and tapping my hands together in an agitated fashion. A couple of people stared at me and I couldn't resist a, "What are you staring at?" When your father was trapped in a city under siege you were allowed to say something like that without it implying that you were a rude person. I eventually hailed a taxi and told the driver to step on it.

Mum was already at home. We shared a hug and I knew that I wasn't over-reacting. The television was on and I flicked through the channels. It was blanket coverage of the same footage – terrified New Yorkers fleeing dust clouds, covering their mouths and rescuing strangers.

"Do you have his number?"

"I can't get through."

"How many times have you tried?"

"About forty."

We mainly sat in silence as we took turns calling Dad's mobile. We stared at the television waiting for some more news, scanning the images for the familiar face that we never saw. Once in a while the emotion got too much for one of us.

I felt the need to confess about my last meeting with Dad, and the money he'd been giving me. I apologised again for being so vile back then. "The last memory he has of me is that one. His own son stealing from him and just walking out like he didn't give a shit. How can that be the last thing?"

"It won't be," she assured me. "As soon as all this has settled down we'll get you out there to see him."

It pacified me for a while and we returned to absorbing the news in between futile repeat dialling. In the silence, Mum started thinking and it wasn't long before she started crumbling as well.

"He won't even know that we're worried about him," she said and started to sob. "He hurt me so much."

I hugged her, feeling hypocritical. I had no right to comfort her about that.

Intermittently, either Alex or Ewan phoned up to hear if there was any news. Each time I told them that I'd let them know, but they persisted in showing their support. They told me they'd gone to the pub and that I should join them if I felt up to it. I said I was staying home but thanked them for the offer. I would have been well within my rights to snap that it wasn't a time for drinking, but I didn't think that was something my latest incarnation would have done.

No soap had come close to anything like this. I imagined the next instalment showing the day from Malcolm's perspective, but I had no idea whether it was an episode that ended in his death or not.

The Western world was shutting down; flights were cancelled and people were stranded in far flung places, potential bombers were identified and eyewitnesses wailed about explosions and confusion. The news started getting itself together once the attacks seemed to stop, and speculation and analysis took over. There was plenty of new news, but it wasn't the news we were waiting for.

I sent out emails once in a while telling Dad to contact us if he could, just to let us know that he was alive. Friends of Mum's started to call the house and one or two from the theatre group even came to the door. They didn't stay long – I think they just wanted to look, to have a personal slant on this international disaster, to feel involved. I didn't resent them, had it been someone I knew I would have been round trying to be involved as well.

We stayed up late, which gave us plenty of time for heart to hearts. I talked at length at my regret at splitting the family up, and we raked over history with a candidness that had previously eluded us.

"Everything changed when the plan worked," I explained. "I realised how wrong it had been the moment I saw your face when you found out."

"You and Malcolm were my world. My family was the thing I was most proud of. I had nothing left."

I knew all this. She knew I knew all this, but I think we were both keen to learn a lesson from this disaster.

A hotline was set up for concerned relatives, and when we eventually got through they had no news on Dad. Political leaders spoke out in condemnation of the attacks and warnings were issued that we would not bow down to terrorism. Not one newsreader spoke of where my father was.

"We didn't do so well last year, did we?" Mum said.

"Not at all, but you did deserve to hate me."

"I still loved you at the same time. I thought you were going to get killed the way you were going, but I didn't have the energy to fight with you, and I just couldn't forgive your father."

"But you still loved him as well, didn't you?"

Mum didn't reply.

"Neil was never going to replace him."

"Neil made me smile at a time when I needed it."

I gave her a funny look.

"Not like that," she slapped my shoulder playfully. "Honestly, Danny!" We both chuckled for a second, then remembered ourselves and returned to staring at the news.

4.

At some point into the early hours we gave up and went to our bedrooms. I couldn't sleep because of all the question marks. I kept checking online for updates to the news but nothing important emerged. I bored very quickly of pacing around my room.

It shocked me how little I'd thought of Dad since he left. I'd been busy trying to piece my life back together and his absenteeism seemed to be the least of my woes. I'd spoken to him a little on the phone but shown no real interest in how things were working out for him, which if pushed by a psychologist would say I was merely in denial. I'm sure I resented him for giving up on me and Mum so easily, so in return I chose to know nothing of his restaurant, apartment or friends.

His potential death filled me with regret over my ambivalence towards him. I imagined the story arc his life had taken when he moved away. I decided there would be a special week of episodes that detailed Malcolm's life after he left Lancaster. I pictured triumph over initial struggles as he adjusted to life in America and opened up his restaurant. He came into contact with several potential love interests, but a picture of his wife and son in his apartment was always enough to deter him.

The restaurant headed towards success, in spite of a thieving restaurant manager and a volatile head chef. He made friends with his neighbours. At numerous points Malcolm would reflect on how any amount of success didn't make up for what he had left behind.

The story had him planning a return to the UK in the run up

to September 11th. The week ended with news footage of the second plane hitting the tower before fading to black.

My storylining saw me through until it got light and I made my way downstairs for day two of our vigil. Alex dropped by on his way to college looking quite weary and hungover. Inwardly I resented him for having a good time whilst I was suffering, but new Danny didn't get irked by things like thoughtlessness. He asked if he could help and I told him there was nothing he could do. He sloped off after that.

Mum joined me on the couch not long after and we watched as nothing really happened. We grew jaded with the calls from concerned well-wishers, so when the phone rang at lunch time neither of us were really expecting it to be Dad.

"Danny?" he said when I picked up the phone. I had nothing to say. I gasped a little and choked back real tears.

Mum was behind me in a flash.

"Danny, who is it?" she asked fearfully.

"Dad?" I asked down the phone.

An award winning moment. I later imagined saying in an acceptance speech that it had all stemmed from the emotion of 9/11 that I'd channelled into my work. I dedicated it to all those who died in the attacks, which saw several fellow actors welling up.

"Danny, how are you? I've not been able to get through to you," Dad said casually. "It's been crazy here. Have you seen?"

I nodded, which was a useless thing to do when you're on the phone. I couldn't think of a line so I passed the phone to Mum.

In soaps it takes a big dramatic event to make someone realise that they love someone after all, but it isn't beyond the realms of possibility for that to happen in real life as well.

"Come home, Malcolm," she wept. It was the first thing she said to him, delivered with the rawest of emotion.

Who would have thought it would take a terrorist attack to bring my parents back together? They talked for hours on the phone that day. I found myself with very little to do, so I got on my mobile and let everyone know that he was alright. The afternoon passed and they finally said goodbye to each other. Dad was coming home when flights resumed.

The drama was all about human responses. Dad had been nowhere near danger, but had suffered from the network outages. It hadn't even crossed his mind that his family might want to hear if he was alright, and from this, our family had been reconciled. I silently praised life for outdoing my wildest imaginations.

5.

I was back on the phone to Dad when the doorbell rang. Mum answered it and soon let two people through the door and into the living room. I finished the call with Dad, telling him I loved him, and then went to find Mum, who had gone to make hot drinks in the kitchen.

"*Lancaster Gazette*," she told me.

On a local level, we were news.

I followed Mum back into the living room where she introduced me to a male reporter and a female photographer.

Their story was simple: 'Family terror at father missing on 9/11'. We told them how worried we were and how happy we were that Dad was coming home to be reunited with us, and then they left. Just after they left, a local TV news crew replaced them at the door asking if they could have a word.

They got us to leaf through a family photo album with looks of glee on our faces. They then sat us by our fireplace and asked us about how we'd felt when we thought that Dad was dead. Mum was considerate enough to add how sorry we felt for all those who hadn't been as lucky as us and we both nodded solemnly.

I was on TV for real!

In the most unusual television crossover of all time, Danny

and Jacqui Lizar from *The Almost Lizard* appeared on *North West Tonight*. The segment was shown in full on my show only a week later.

Watching myself on the news was a bit of a shock. I hoped I didn't come across like that on television all the time. I appeared a little nervous and I wasn't pulling the right faces. It made me question whether I was a good actor at all, albeit briefly, as I had to remind myself that it really didn't matter. Humanity was the unstaged, arse-scratching, awkward version of television, where people tripped over their words and didn't play things out to their full potential. I saw the performance as me acting as Danny acting as a normal person would on the screen.

All the scenes I filmed that week were far more than I ever expected to enjoy in my life. Whilst this little fantasy world may have developed from a dull childhood, it wasn't tempered by my more turbulent adolescence. Things like appearing on television for real almost validated what I was doing. My life was big enough for the news, so it was definitely big enough for a soap.

At college I experienced a modicum of fame. Through the news and local gossip, word had got out about my proximity to the overseas disaster. People felt involved just by talking to me about it. They talked to their friends and family about me, because it was news that had happened to someone.

Lauren gave me a huge hug when she saw me. "Mental, mate," she said in a comforting way. "We're getting rat-arsed on Friday for this one. You've earned it."

I made the most of the hug but managed to fend off a tell-tale erection. "I'm so glad you're back in my life," I whispered in her ear, knowing full well that I was milking the situation.

In The Fox and Whistle, I held the room as I recounted what happened over those surreal days. They'd all been very worried about "young Danny's old man," and I imagined them gathered there on the night of September 11th, just like people did in the soaps. After that I became part of the furniture there; everybody knew my name.

A week on and we were completely forgotten about, though it had done me the world of good. People knew who I was at college and I found myself making all sorts of new acquaintances. Is it vulgar to comment on how much I benefitted from 9/11? It brought me closer to Lauren, it brought my dad home to us and it made me popular at college. Those things can't be denied.

Dad returned to Lancaster undetected just over a fortnight after the terrorist attacks. People had moved on with their lives once the initial hysteria died down, and we were able to adjust to his return without anyone paying attention. We helped him with his stuff and spent several days feeling very weird about this apparent return to normality. We all knew that it wasn't the same, but we were all keen to give it a go. We slipped into this new norm almost effortlessly, though, and at times it felt much more like a relaxed house-share than a family home.

Being involved in this real drama made me feel so much better about my fake one. The way almost everyone had feasted on a bit of terror and sadness, especially because it had been linked to an international crisis. People validate their existence with these moments all of the time. I just did it with much more dedication than most.

6.

Some of my favourite soap moments have come from ratings boosting special weeks of episodes where a series of monumental things happen at the same time. These can be crashes, explosions, expositions or murders, anything like that. This was our week. At the centre of things were the Lizars, but in the background to this chaos Alex was working on his own plot developments, as he informed me once things had settled down.

His night in the pub with Ewan on September 11th had taken a surprise turn somewhere after the sixth pint. They were getting philosophical about the day (which, as with most people, mainly involved saying how much it was like the movies) and started talking about what they would want to say to people if they knew that it was going to be the last time they saw them. Alex said he'd tell his dad how proud he was of him for the way he dealt with Robyn's affair.

"I think I'd tell my mum that she deserved more than me as a son," Ewan had said.

"What do you mean?" asked Alex.

"Well, I've never been grateful for anything," he said. "It's just stuff like this, like Danny's going through, it makes you think doesn't it?"

"It does. I'd apologise for turning that gay rumour on you," Alex replied.

Ewan had smiled at him and looked away. "It's in the past, isn't it?"

"Yeah," Alex said.

"I regret not kissing you back," Ewan added and Alex's mouth dropped open.

"I thought I was going to shit myself," he told me over a coffee in one of the college canteens. "But I just looked at him and smiled and looked away. I thought I was misreading things again."

"And were you?" I asked. I admit feeling a little bit jealous when Alex spoke like this. I think I was worried that Ewan was now his best friend.

"Well that's the thing," he continued. "I finished my pint and decided to leave, saying that all this talk of losing my parents made me want to go home. But he asked me to stay. He grabbed my hand."

The excitement in the way he said that told me once and for all that he was gay, if there was an ounce of doubt left at that point. He continued to tell me how Ewan had suggested that they go for a walk through town. They went out to the park and into a small wood where no-one was around. Some time after that Alex had his first sexual experience. I didn't ask for the details but I got the impression he didn't go all the way.

"So are you an item?" I asked him, feeling a little pensive.

"Not at all," he shook his head. "He's not spoken to me for nearly a week."

I'd been so caught up with my micro-celebrity and returning father storylines that I hadn't noticed that particular rift taking place. Combined with everything else it ensured us the highest ratings in the show's history. The critics loved the revamp and I wrote out a series of glowing reviews for us. In many ways I thought less about the show as all this was going on, but upon reflection I put it all into the context of episodes.

Parallels

1.

As a soap teenager it was my duty to get involved in long and complex romantic situations. I'd been ready for quieter times long before September 11th, and once everything calmed down I jumped at the chance to take the character in a less turbulent direction. I relished the idea of more human interest stories with less horrible repercussions. When Alex told me that things were happening with Ewan, I knew that I had to step up the storyline with Lauren.

I saw her in performing arts on Mondays and Wednesdays and then down the pub on Fridays. This was enough to keep me present in her life, and I was pleased when she started to hang out with us during free periods on the other days. If I'd been a little bolder I would have asked her out there and then, but convention taught me that if it was going to be worth it, there had to be a protracted period of getting together.

Lauren helped me with this by getting a boyfriend a month into our first term at college. His name was Dave and he liked philosophy, apparently. The announcement came like a swift blow to the gut as the storyline I'd mapped out fell apart. It was nothing a swift rewrite wouldn't fix, but the other problem was that I really did like Lauren.

It prolonged the storyline at the very least. She hung around with us less and I filmed many a scene of faraway longing.

When she was around I had to act like I was becoming one of her best friends, which in many ways I was. She felt comfortable going to gigs alone with me because she knew that it couldn't possibly be a date. She often confided in me about Dave's faults, and I listened intently, patiently biding my time.

The trouble with the life I've led is that I don't know how much of what I've done involved active manipulation, or whether people have just responded to me unintentionally. I can't pretend that I've ever been able to command women to do what I want romantically, I've had to let those storylines happen to me. But at the same time I went about making myself more appealing to Lauren as time went on, but then isn't that the dating game?

We all try and get others to do what we want. We do it through persuasion and lies and sometimes we play upon people's weaknesses to steer a situation towards our favour. It's just most of you don't pretend that it's for television. That's almost the only difference.

2.

It was big news for a week when Alex and Ewan came out together. They didn't do it in any grand style, they just let it be known that they were a couple. They had spent weeks alternating between symbiosis and avoidance, and things reached a head when Alex told him that he couldn't take the ambiguity anymore. They went to a coffee shop in town to argue about things. Alex had told me all about it later.

"I don't want to be gay," Ewan protested. "I fancy women."

"And you don't fancy me?" Alex asked.

"No," Ewan had said but failed to catch his eye. Alex had taken his hand and Ewan had tried to punch him.

"And what was the other week then?"

Ewan had flinched and looked revolted in return. "Yeah,

and both times I was pissed," he snapped back. "You just wait for your chance don't you?"

"Next time you want to experiment, find some other mug," Alex spat with tears in his eyes and stormed out of the coffee shop. It had taken Ewan a good minute or two before he decided to follow him. He found Alex at the bus station, where the argument had continued for some time. I was jealous not to have been involved in such emotive scenes. Ewan talked Alex down and they went for a walk near the river.

"I'm not gay," Ewan repeated.

"You've already said that. I've got the message Ewan. You tried it, you didn't like it, I feel like a tit – "

"But I might be bisexual," he interrupted. Shortly after that they'd decided to give their relationship a go.

There was no grand kiss in a public place, or some announcement in class, they just mentioned to Lauren that they were a couple and let the rumour mill do the rest. Although it was far from the most unusual thing in the world, they were certainly the first 'out' couple in our year and that generated a lot of attention. I imagined special episodes filmed just at college as the news filtered out and the word spread rapidly from class to class. Through no effort of my own the world fitted in with the show perfectly and I was afforded extras left, right and centre. People pointed them out to their friends and others asked awkward questions. A few people made jibes and I was forced to angrily defend them when I overheard them being referred to as benders.

"Have they asked you to join in?" one asked me whilst I was smoking.

"Pardon?"

"You know, your queer mates. Do you think they like threesomes?"

"Only with your dad," I retorted and his friends all started laughing at him.

On the whole, coming out wasn't a popular move in the

college. It only worked for the performing arts class, where everyone seemed to be bi-curious at the very least. They received theatrical kudos for being so open with their feelings and their sexuality, but in the wider college environment, people were suspicious. Alex told me that people got stage-fright if he was stood next to them at urinals, and others asked them both outright about AIDS.

My character existed during that time vicariously through Alex and Ewan. I was a supporting role at best, helping Alex as he prepared to tell his parents. He came over and talked to me a lot during the time and I gave him the generic advice that a good friend would. I did a week or so of filming Danny being jealous of their relationship and being left behind. Lauren was with Dave a lot of the time and Alex and Ewan naturally wanted to spend time just the two of them, so I felt a little out of sorts within this new group that I had created at the beginning of term.

I started to focus on work storylines for a while. I had a bit to do with Dad's resettlement storylines, as he sought buyers for his restaurants with Charles, which they had been unable to sell in his absence.

Robyn took Alex's news well, but Charles apparently laughed in his son's face. "Bloody typical," he muttered before retiring to his study. There were many scenes with Alex in floods of tears when his dad didn't talk to him. I wonder if the reality worked as well on screen as I imagined it at the time. I took it upon myself to stop Charles in the village one day and demand to know why he was shunning his son.

"Of all the people I need advice from in this world, Danny," he said calmly, "the musings of a demented, hormonal brat like you are fairly low on the list, wouldn't you say?"

"You're scared of your own son's sexuality and you think I'm the one who's demented?" I said and walked away.

Sure enough, Alex and Charles had a heart to heart later that day.

People got used to the idea of Ewan and Alex after a while. Even then people didn't stop commenting entirely, but as a storyline the acceptance thing came to an end just before Christmas. I imagined that the show was praised for its sensitive dealing of the issue, and would be further lauded for incorporating a normal gay relationship as a regular part of the programme. All in all, I think I dealt with it very well.

3.

As a new year started, the cracks began to show in Lauren's relationship with Philosophy Dave. She came to The Fox and Whistle with me, Alex and Ewan after Dave told her he was going to spend the night reinterpreting the non-ending of Kafka's *The Castle*. Each year the pub threw on a free buffet and disco for anyone who wanted to go, and all the staff and locals were there, as well as me and my friends. I'd warned Alex and Ewan not to be too gay that night, telling them that it wasn't that kind of place. Sadly, they understood.

I built my hopes up at midnight and managed to kiss Lauren on the lips, but she pulled away after the briefest of pecks and I knew that it wasn't to be that night.

"Bad luck mate," Ed said afterwards. I had been confiding in him more than anyone about Lauren. "I remember one year I managed to get three girls back to my place for a private party. I was raw the next morning." Ed still lived with his mother so I highly doubted that, but nodded along anyway.

"I don't know how I'll get her to like me," I said as I watched her dancing along to The Proclaimers on the tiny makeshift dance floor.

"I started to get lots of pussy when I got a car," Ed informed me. Bingo.

I took driving lessons at the rate of three per week, which of course provided plenty of comedy scenes. All the time I was doing this, Lauren and Philosophy Dave continued to have problems and she confided in me more and more. A lot of her school friends had dispersed into college life and made new friends and she told me after Christmas that she liked hanging out with us more than anyone.

Philosophy Dave kept trying to educate her, and what had once seemed cool and enigmatic now felt boring and controlling. I didn't advise her to split up with him, covering my tracks by saying that she should give him another go and then inviting her to go and see a local band with me. I was positioning myself to be right in front of her very eyes, hopefully driving a car, the moment that her relationship with Dave imploded.

That night turned out to be 14th February, when Dave set his books aside and decided to take his girlfriend out for a nice meal. Lauren had been thrilled about it, and I'd filmed some scenes over the course of the day where I deliberated over giving her the Valentine's card I'd written. I decided against it, realising that the torment made better television. Dave did all the hard work for me when he bought her a copy of the *Kama Sutra* as a gift and handed it over during dinner. Lauren had stormed out of the restaurant, spilling a glass of wine over his lap in the process. She'd gone home and called me immediately to tell me what a bastard he was.

I spent the latter part of Valentine's night in a bar in town with Lauren crying over what she believed to be the best relationship she was ever going to have. I told her how beautiful she was, how much fun and how cool she was. She smiled and appreciated it and told me what a good friend I was, and once again managed to trample all over my expectations completely unwittingly.

"It's never going to happen," I whispered into the mirror in the pub toilets when I was sure I was alone. "Give up."

We'd had boy meets girl, boy falls for girl, then girl falls for someone else. It was a fairly well built up romance that the viewers would be rooting for. But these things simply had to go on longer than is almost tolerable, and so I introduced another stumbling block.

Lauren stayed away from Philosophy Dave, who took the rest of the term off with depression, and to 'find himself'. When he eventually returned, his thoughtful air had vanished completely and he'd turned into the most average person in the world. His attempt to find a personality had failed spectacularly and had left him a shell of a human being. In the process of breaking up with him, she reiterated to us all several times that she'd sworn off men for the foreseeable future.

I was getting bored of being the thwarted admirer, so I took it upon myself to get a girlfriend. Michelle was in my sociology class. She had a whole string of opinions and a budding feminist streak that made her fun but scary at the same time. We'd entered a heated debate about postmodernism in which I had detected some flirting, so I didn't wait around in inviting her for a drink at the weekend. She'd agreed, but insisted that she would be paying for half of everything. She was trying to make a point, but it sounded perfect to me. God bless the twenty-first century.

Our drink went well. We went to watch a local band that she really got into and at the end of the night we parted with a kiss. We went on two more dates during the week. She gave me a hand-job in the cinema and I decided that we were a couple. After that she started to hang out with the four of us, and I sensed in Lauren the same feelings I'd had only the term before. Five was a crowd when there were couples involved.

Throughout my time with Michelle I always knew that it was for the storyline more than my feelings. I fancied Michelle, but I fancied Lauren more. Philosophy Dave and Michelle were merely part of the prelude to the great romance that I hoped would happen. I suggested double dating to

Alex and Ewan solely because it would provoke something from Lauren and move the storyline in the direction I'd been hoping for all along.

We were in the pub one Friday afternoon before Easter and we got up to leave.

"Where are you off to?" Lauren asked as we all started fiddling around with our bags and coats.

"Bowling," Ewan replied.

"Cool. Can I come?"

There was an awkward silence.

"It's kind of a date," I said guiltily. Lauren blinked as her eyes welled up a little. "Sorry, I should have said."

"Not at all," she smiled. "Have fun." She picked up her drink and went to talk to a table of lads she knew. All of them bar none immediately started flirting with her. She caught my eye on the way out and we shared a meaningful glance. Just like they do on TV.

As I hoped, Lauren was distant with me after that. We parted for the Easter holidays barely speaking, but I did see her climb into a car with a bloke from the year above at the end of the day. The sex I had with Michelle that night was extra passionate.

I caught Lauren on instant messenger one day and asked why she was being funny with me. She said she just felt a bit left out and I asked her whether she was jealous. She went offline.

I passed my driving test that afternoon and my dad had bought me a car just as I suspected he might. Things were different at home by then, more grown up. We shared details of our lives and they allowed Michelle to sleep over. I talked at length about Alex and Ewan and their troubles, and they often gave me advice on how to help out. Mum and Dad weren't head over heels in love but they were happy to be together. The honesty made us all relax a little. The Dad I knew from before would never have bought me a car, but by the time I passed my test I almost expected the treat.

It was perfect. I took the car for a test drive straight over to Lauren's house. She was getting ready for a date and didn't look pleased to see me. I looked more stricken than I felt and demanded to know if she was jealous of my relationship with Michelle. I was glad that her dad wasn't in. He hadn't seen me since I'd brought shame on the primary school, and this little row wouldn't have been the greatest reintroduction.

"I'm with someone now, Danny," she said flatly.

"So am I."

"Then we're all happy."

"Are we?"

I figured it was high time this came to a head either way, which gave me the impetus just to kiss her there and then. I was as shocked as the viewer when she started to kiss me back. We filmed some nude scenes over the next hour and then I drove off to finish with my interim girlfriend, the viewers cheering at the resolution.

4.

The foursome I'd hoped for was finally in place for the summer term. I fumbled my way through the trials and tribulations of a fledgling relationship: the acts of thoughtlessness, meeting the parents (again, in the case of Lauren's father), and sneaking around to be alone at every opportunity. I had lots of storylines at The Fox and Whistle as it changed hands and the staff underwent a mutiny, but much of my filming centred around the two couples. We went on trips to Blackpool and camping in the Lake District. We attended gigs in Manchester, and just going out and having fun made for good television. There were broken down car incidents, and Ewan got hit on by a girl in Blackpool. Alex got hammered and fell into a ditch when we were camping and Lauren and I nearly got thrown out of Alton Towers for getting frisky in a secluded area. We got the results of our AS-levels and started to look towards bright futures.

The second year started and everyone was talking about UCAS forms, first and second choices, and courses taught in far-flung parts of the country. I'd silently expected us all to make applications to Lancaster University and have done with it, but it soon transpired that the others had very different ambitions. We were having a night out in town when the conversation cropped up.

Lauren wanted to be a teacher and had heard of a good English Literature course being taught at Leicester. Ewan planned to study Law at Durham and I was surprised to hear that Alex was keen to study in Brighton, citing the thriving gay scene as his main motivation. I'd spent so long appreciating the present that I hadn't foreseen any natural end to it.

"I'm reviewing my options," I lied. "As far away from here as possible," I added, just so they knew that I was in no way being left behind.

I didn't instantly stop caring for my friends and girlfriend the moment I found out we would be going our separate ways, but I did regard them less for it. I had worked hard to bring together this small but lively band of teens. The revamp had been hugely successful, and in no small part due to the engaging but down to earth storylines that this group had been involved in. It seemed like we'd only been together for a few months before we were talking of disbanding, and it unsettled me greatly.

In a state of panic I applied for as many prospectuses as possible and went on a hurried tour of universities on the quiet. I made it sound like I had a plan but I was keeping it under wraps in case it was jinxed, which bought me the time to think up my contingency plan. My relatively new love of music and an impressive enough open day took me in the direction of Manchester. I had the predicted grades that they were looking for to study sociology, so I pinned all of my hopes on that particular future.

I didn't instantly realise that I was sowing the seeds of a long-term storyline. Eventually, though, it dawned on me that I was leaving Galgate, leaving Lancaster, and effectively leaving the show. *The Almost Lizard* could travel with me into a whole new phase, or I could leave it all behind.

I went through the motions that I thought an actor did when they started to think about their career. I imagined interviews where I explained that I had been in the show for several years, and that it was just time to move on. I told the press that I didn't want to become typecast and that I was ready for new challenges. I laughed when the interviewer asked me if I was planning to launch a music career. "God no," I chuckled in my head. "I want to further my career, not become some hopeless cliché."

I imagined weeks of tabloid rumours and denials in the run up to the announcement that I was going to move on to new projects once my contract ended the next summer. I imagined speculation about fights on set between me and other cast members that had been the real reason behind my departure. I spoke out about the tabloid lies, explaining that I loved my co-stars dearly and was just ready to move on. I promised them that Danny Lizar would not be leaving quietly, and I imagined the press leaking potential exit storylines. It was a whirlwind sort of time.

5.

Danny's last storyline with *The Almost Lizard* really began during the conversation where he realised that the group would be disbanding in just over a year. There was a sudden change in his behaviour, one that the viewers may have recognised from when he discovered that his father was having an affair. It was that sudden detachment from people he'd felt close to, it made him do things that were a little less than morally sound.

I told myself that Lauren was a dishonest person. She had gone and planned a future without consulting me, which made a mockery of what I had thought to be a solid relationship. It was tantamount to cheating in my book. I held my tongue until I had my plan sorted, but when I was in a position of power I didn't hesitate in trying to aggravate her. I constantly brought up our uncertain future and eventually suggested that we just split up immediately.

"Don't be a dick!" she snorted. "We're going to stick together. I love you." We'd exchanged 'I love you's' on a road trip to Chester during the summer. She said it first and I hadn't hesitating in reciprocating tenderly. It had been a long time coming and it was nice to see Danny in love.

"You mean it?" I asked her. She hugged me and I looked towards the camera, bleeding insecurity.

The problem with relationships in soaps is that once the prolonged chase is dispatched with and the getting to know you part has been wrung dry, you have few options. Relationships progress at rocket speed to keep the viewer interested, but I was not quite eighteen and didn't want to destroy my life by moving in with Lauren, or getting her pregnant and having a shotgun wedding. After that, there are very few things for characters to do as a couple, aside from hurt each other and split up. I didn't see the point in co-habitation, marriage or kids, so I skipped that stage and aimed straight for the hurt.

My new life became something of a private obsession of mine and it tainted the way that I viewed everything. I walked around Lancaster thinking how insignificant it was compared to what I had to look forward to. I lost any affection for my surroundings from the moment I realised that I would be moving on.

One negative thought led to another and soon I hated

everything about the Lancaster life, with its three half decent pubs and derelict music scene. Danny had been worn down by his turbulent years and the sad memories that haunted his every footstep. His reunited parents suddenly appeared to him a pathetic sham, and his friends were only biding their time before running away at the first opportunity. Every person in The Fox and Whistle was stagnating, stuck in a time warp where each new day was indistinguishable from the last.

When he was alone, Danny skulked around looking like he could take it no more. I stood on bridges over the river staring out contemplatively and on one occasion I filmed a cliffhanger where Danny considered jumping off.

He could have just gone quietly, but the resentment had built up to something much more. However much new Danny had suited me, my instinctive response was to be vengeful.

Writing myself out of the show gave me the freedom to be as destructive as I liked with this last storyline. I considered many, many eventualities, but my thinking led me to the same conclusion on many occasions. I did initially think of acts of sabotage to try and keep us all in Lancaster. We were working on performing arts coursework together but I investigated and discovered that the system didn't allow for collective responsibility when it came to exam grades, so there was nothing I could do there.

The only real way I could properly hurt people was cheating. If I cheated on Lauren I was pretty sure that I would incur the wrath of Alex and Ewan, even though I had known them both for longer. I planned to find myself an affair around Christmas time (another classic soap thing to do) with a view to bringing things to a head in the late summer, preferably with plate smashing and street rows.

My only issue was that Lauren would be the sole victim in the storyline, and Alex and Ewan might have forgiven me after their initial disgust had waned. I want to ruin things for them just as much, I thought, and at that very same moment it came to me exactly how I would achieve that. It was one hell of a storyline, and it formed perfectly in my head within seconds.

6.

It's remarkable that I hadn't exploited Alex's homosexuality before I did, really. It would have been just like me to have muscled in on the biggest storyline of his life for my own entertainment, but until I started to map out my exit plot it had remained something that I wasn't prepared to do. I much preferred the idea of heterosexual storylines. With Alex, my over-riding attitude had been 'rather him than me,' especially when I thought about the nitty-gritty of what they did. Not in a homophobic way, it just sounded a little sore, that's all.

I'd already seen in my life the effects of close to home cheating on families and friends, so I looked to my past for inspiration when working this out. As two couples, our lives were interconnected in the way my parents had been with Charles and Robyn, so I knew exactly how to make everyone miserable. If things had been different I would have tried to seduce Alex's girlfriend, but instead I reduced his sexuality to a delicious little twist. Our lives had been intertwined from the beginning of *The Almost Lizard* and before, so it was the ideal way to end my tenure on the show.

I reinterpreted the past and thought of how Alex had shunned me when I was low, and we only became friends again because no-one else would talk to him. Ewan's friendship became false, and I decided that he only tolerated me because Alex told him to. Lauren just didn't want a future together and was using me until she could go and shag a hundred boys in her first week at uni. Combined, these were the reasons I used in interviews as to why Danny had started doing terrible things again.

It started simply enough with a few surreptitious glances when Ewan and Alex were joking around together. I filmed some scenes of me looking on gay websites, with a close-up on the screen when I tapped in 'bisexual' on Google. I acted distracted around Lauren, and pushed her away a couple of times when she made sexual advances. She would retreat into herself and wonder whether she was getting fat or boring, whilst I looked blankly into the camera. It planted the seed with the viewer that something wasn't quite right with Danny.

Alex came to see me at work after my shift one night and I took the opportunity to start talking about the future. I realised then how infrequently I saw him without Ewan and it served as a timely reminder as to why I shouldn't care about what I was doing.

"I don't think me and Lauren will stay together," I admitted as we drank. "No relationship survives uni."

"I don't think that's true," Alex said back.

I scoffed. "Have you discussed the future with Ewan?"

"We're going to stay together, if that's what you mean. It's not something I'm worried about."

"You're lucky, then. I don't think we'll even be together when we go away." He didn't agree with me, but he looked pensive for the remainder of the evening. It played over and over in his head until he eventually raised the subject with Ewan two days later. Ewan made things worse without any intervention from me. The storyline was always there, lying dormant, but it had been my musings that had unlocked its potential.

"Who knows what might happen?" Ewan said to him. "You might meet some nice girl."

"I'm gay!" Alex had snapped back. "You of all people should know that." He realised for sure that Ewan still saw himself as essentially straight, and their evening ended sourly, but without the argument that was brewing. They saved that for the two weeks that followed, with Alex coming to me to complain about everything that his boyfriend said to him.

I then spoke to Lauren in order to film an argument with her. We had started by discussing their fall-out sympathetically, but I soon ensured that we were taking sides.

"It's Ewan's sexuality and only he can decide that," she said.

"But it makes Alex feel uncomfortable, like they're different."

"They are different. Everyone's different! If he's faithful, it doesn't matter how he labels himself."

"It's deceitful."

"Bollocks! Danny, you're so naïve sometimes."

"Don't patronise me, like you're so worldly-fucking-wise," I snapped. "You think you know all the answers, but you're just reciting stuff from those stupid magazines you read."

I was sent home without sex that evening and we avoided each other at college the next day. Things were going as I hoped and it was largely an organic process. I spent time with Alex whilst Lauren gravitated towards Ewan. It showed who was on whose side when things got rocky and the divide was set, even when the arguments faded and things seemed harmonious. By then, we all had quite a few doubts.

7.

When trying to negotiate some weird fiction using real life, you have to be ready to respond to the unexpected. My exit storyline was momentarily thrown into chaos when Lauren dumped me on the last day of term before Christmas. In a surprise scene, we were in my car in the college parking area when she told me that I had become inattentive with her, which was right because that was exactly how I'd been playing it. I'd thought that the change had been subtle and that her tolerance of my shift would have held out for a good while longer, so I was floored by the news.

"Your heart's just not in it, Danny," she informed me. I

took the words silently and refused to look directly at her. She kissed me on the cheek and climbed out of the car. I stared into the distance, my eyes slightly wet with the shock, but I just couldn't quite find the tears to make the scene truly heartbreaking.

On the way home I thought about how angry it made me that she had ruined my big storyline. By the time I got home I'd changed my tune and was thinking about how this change could improve the way things went from here. It was an extra hurdle in a long running story, and not one without drama either. I knew that I had to call on Alex for support, and I was pretty sure I knew how it would end up.

We met in a bar in town without Ewan, who had rather predictably gone to see Lauren. Surrounded by the shrieks of office parties and festive nights out, I cut a miserable figure nursing a blue WKD and looking like my world had ended.

To take the scenes where I wanted them, I drank heavily and encouraged Alex to do the same. I played it sad, then angry, then philosophical. Alex sat through each phase and offered up words of wisdom where appropriate. We left at last orders and I suggested walking home. The lengthy stagger back gave me enough chance to pluck up the courage to take the episode to the conclusion I was seeking.

"You've got the right idea," I said out of nothing, at a point where I could contain myself no longer. "Women are a nightmare."

Alex laughed.

"No, seriously," I continued. "I thought it was a cool thing to do when you came out."

"I didn't do it to be cool," he corrected me, smiling. He enjoyed the compliment.

"No, but it was brave. I wish I could be brave like that."

That stopped Alex dead in his tracks. He looked at me to try and see if I was saying what he thought I was saying. I knew I was drunk enough to go through with the scene at that point, and in a second I could see how every frame would play out. I looked straight at him and darted in for an awkward kiss on the lips.

"Shit," I said, backing away from him. "Mate, I'm so sorry." That was the first line of the next episode, which picked up the story straight from the kiss. If something big happened the British soaps continued from the previous episode, rather than starting the next morning. It was a way of telling if that particular instalment was intended to be monumental. I apologised again and dashed off down the street ahead of him. He called out my name twice, then let me go. I ran all the way back to the village and slowed down for the walk back to my house.

He had kissed me back. However briefly it may have been, he definitely kissed me back.

8.

I avoided Alex in the wake of the kiss, which was the right thing to do for the storyline. There was still a clear nine months before my exit, which gave me time for a considerable period of denial. I replied to his texts but always made out that I was busy when he suggested meeting up. I took on extra shifts at The Fox and Whistle and filmed lots of scenes there with Danny being grumpy and getting annoyed at the slightest of provocations. Ed rose to the bait and took me outside for a smoke and a confession.

I told him that I had been dumped and he suggested that – like all women – she was just looking for a token of my commitment. Instantly I knew this had to lead to a Christmas Day proposal. It was exactly what someone in denial would do to cover their tracks.

"You're a genius," I informed Ed, who I think already believed that to be true.

With Dad's return, his generous payments into my bank

account stopped, so I searched for the nicest ring you could expect to find on the wage of a part-time kitchen porter. That was how I ended up browsing the Argos catalogue. I knew when I bought it that there wasn't the slightest possibility of a wedding. It was merely an attempt on my part to get my girlfriend back so that I could break her heart and exit the show in a blaze of glory.

I think it was a blinding episode as well – the most exciting Christmas Day since the one where I destroyed my family. In the morning I called Alex and asked him to go for a drink with me. It was the first time we'd seen each other since our kiss. I could only assume that he hadn't told Ewan about what had happened. Indiscretion from Alex was the only way for the story to unravel prematurely.

"I'm really sorry," I said after I'd bought him a pint and wished him a merry Christmas. "I don't know why I did it."

"Rebound?" Alex suggested. "It took me by surprise that's for sure."

"You must have been mortified," I offered up meekly, implying that Alex should take the lead on this conversation.

"I'm not too outraged by homosexuality," he said with a grin. "I can see you're pretty gutted about the whole thing. Don't worry, I'm not going to say anything. Bi or otherwise, I don't think Ewan would be too happy if he found out."

I smiled gratefully. "Thanks." After a pause I added, "I'm not ashamed though."

"But you do regret it?"

I looked right into his eyes, so deeply that it made us both shift a little in our seats. "I didn't say that."

I took a swig of lager and looked away. I changed the subject. "So, what did you get for Christmas then?"

After Christmas dinner I left the awkwardness of home, where the day held far too many unpleasant memories for us to enjoy it properly, and drove over to Lauren's house to drop in unannounced. Lauren didn't seem unhappy to see me and invited me in for a little while.

"Can we go somewhere private?" I asked.

"No funny business!" her dad called from the living room. I think even if I'd turned out to be the model boyfriend he would never have liked me. My naughty story aged eleven ear-marked me as a rapist for life.

"Chance would be a fine thing," I responded and instantly regretted it. We went up to her room and left the door ajar.

"I bought this before we split up," I said, producing the ring box from my pocket as I went down on one knee. "I'd like you to have it anyway."

Lauren gasped.

Then she laughed.

"Aw, Dan, you're very sweet," she giggled, then accidentally snorted, which made me laugh as well. "You don't go from splitting up to getting married just like that."

"Can we go from splitting up to not splitting up?" I asked. She pulled me up from my one legged kneel and kissed me urgently. "Best Christmas ever," I said and hugged her. I looked pensively beyond the embrace, staring directly at the viewer to show them how wrong everything most certainly was.

9.

Lauren was keen to spare my blushes and kept my little proposal a secret, which went against everything I was trying to do. I brought it up in front of Alex and Ewan at the first possible opportunity, as we gathered for drinks one evening after Christmas.

"Bit extreme, that, Danny," Alex said pointedly and remained noticeably sullen for the remainder of the evening. I knew to expect a call later on. Sure enough, an hour after we'd parted I received a text asking if I was still awake. I replied that I was and my phone rang almost immediately.

"Well that was unexpected," he said.

"What was?"

"Your little proposal." I remember everyone referring to it as my 'little' proposal, such a dismissive sentiment.

"It felt like the right thing to do."

"And only a short time after you kissed a man," Alex slurred.

"It had nothing to do with that," I protested semi-convincingly.

"It stinks of insecurity. You're clearly confused."

"Alex, drop it!" I snapped. "I thought we'd cleared all of this up. I'm sorry that I kissed you, but it was a mistake and you need to get over it. If you want to talk about this more when you're sober, just let me know." I hung up and the matter was dropped.

The conversation scared me. I had been so adamant in my denials to him that I wasn't sure that I could rely on his doubts to keep things moving along.

I spent the beginning of the year sending signals out to Alex that he wasn't wrong to be suspicious. I made a big deal of being touchy-feely with Lauren in public, to the point where she privately asked me not to stroke her breasts when we were at college. On a couple of occasions when I knew Alex was coming over, I stripped down to my boxers when I heard Mum let him in and looked surprised when he entered, before slowly putting some clothes on. When I thought he might use my computer I filled up the address history on my internet browser with gay sites. When we were drunk and out and about, I tried to catch his gaze, and even winked at him once or twice.

To the viewer and to me it was obvious was what happening. To the other three, it was all pretty much a surprise. I think by the time Valentine's Day arrived, Alex had all but forgotten about my alleged sexual confusion.

I had earmarked the date as an important one for the

storyline, but it was Ewan who filled in the blanks. He was sat with me and Lauren in a college smoking area when I asked him what he and Alex had planned for Valentine's Day. I was keen to know so I could think of how I could make it go wrong.

"Nothing," he told me. "It's more of a boy-girl thing, isn't it?"

Perfect, I thought. Ewan's reluctance to label himself as gay was the thread that I believed would have unravelled Ewan and Alex eventually, had I not intervened. He was completely against public displays of affection and only reluctantly told people that he was in a same-sex relationship when he was pushed for details.

"Have you asked Alex?" I replied.

"No. He's not said anything. Has he said anything to you?"

"No, not at all. It's just best to clear these things up, don't you think?"

It raised the subject anyway. I knew that Alex had been a little disappointed that they hadn't marked the occasion the previous year, and I struggled to contain my excitement as my immediate plot needs were catered for. In response I arranged to take Lauren out for dinner on that night, and promised not to propose to her.

Alex and Ewan did a lot of the work after that. Ewan told Alex he didn't want to do anything, Alex got angry and didn't talk to him for a couple of days. I listened attentively as Alex complained about Ewan's insecurities.

"I'd just like to know what it's like to be with someone on that day," he explained. "Mum and Dad are going to be out somewhere and I'm going to be sat at home on my own like I'm single. I wouldn't mind but I've been in a supposedly loving relationship for the best part of two years."

I touched his leg sympathetically a few times during these chats, but didn't draw attention to the fact. It was for the benefit of close up camera shots and not for Alex to respond to.

"He might not be gay," I said. I'd said this before. Had I not got so much invested in it, the cyclical nature of the ups and downs of their relationship would have bored me rigid.

"The problem is that he's ashamed to be with me," Alex moaned. "He doesn't mind sleeping with me, but to acknowledge our relationship in public is something else. He's ashamed of it. He's ashamed of me."

"I think it's more that other people make him feel ashamed," I reasoned. "It's not like we live in a place where people can walk around comfortably gay. We've not reached a point where people don't point and stare."

"I had noticed," Alex said. He got uppity when you tried to tell him something about how gay people felt, like teachers do when their pupils correct them in class.

"So he might not want to spend the night in a restaurant being stared at by curious couples."

"Then maybe I should find someone who does," Alex concluded. A look passed between us that was so tangible I could have vomited. We were sat inches apart, so I stood up and went to put a CD on, purposely killing the moment. It was too soon.

I thought it was a brilliant idea to invite Alex to join me and Lauren for our Valentine's Day dinner. He didn't accept immediately, but I told him we would be happy to have him there and it would stop him being alone. It was a win-win situation for the show. If Lauren hadn't gone ballistic, that is. As it was, I had to tell him he couldn't join us after all and left him alone and miserable on the most romantic night of the year.

I made sure that Lauren and I didn't have a good time. I checked my phone every few minutes and went to the toilet frequently. When we spoke I turned it into a hushed argument, and by the time our main courses had arrived we were barely speaking to each other. I brought up the subject of Alex and we descended into another of our familiar rows. Neither of us ordered dessert. I drove her home before half past eight and didn't even attempt to follow her inside. She departed with a brief kiss on the cheek and I drove home. For the cameras I paced around my room a little and then sent Alex a text message: Valentine's sucks, doesn't it?

Five messages later and I was on my way over to his house with a bottle of vodka. He got us some glasses from the kitchen whilst I complained about the meal, telling Alex that she had been in a funny mood from the outset, how it would have been a lot more fun if she'd let him come.

"Honestly, at least there would have been some conversation."

"I doubt it. I would only have complained about not being there with Ewan."

"Fuck 'em," I laughed and raised my glass, draining the contents and trying to look like I enjoyed it.

"Fuck 'em!" Alex joined in the toast and we laughed.

"Do you think I'm wasting my time with Ewan?" he asked me a couple of drinks later.

"I think he seems to cause you a lot of trouble," I replied. "And I think you deserve someone who isn't embarrassed about what you are."

I couldn't look directly at him.

"Me too," he agreed. "Would you be ashamed of me?"

Whilst not trying to absolve myself of blame in this situation, I have to note here that it was Alex that was making all of the suggestive comments. I had done so little to get him into this situation that I started to see it as being completely real. I was feeling nervous around him in a way that I hadn't before.

I just shook my head and looked at him directly. He leaned in and I nearly backed away. I was thrown by how the scene was going, with Alex making all of the moves, but I knew it somehow made the storyline better. We kissed, then pulled away from each other. We both thought of something to say, but I nipped that in the bud and kissed him again. We carried on until Alex asked me, "Are you sure?"

I nodded gravely.

His hand was just toying with my belt buckle when the door opened and Robyn and Charles strolled through the door. I made it through the patio door before they saw me, leaving Alex to explain away the two drinks. I left through their side gate and walked on home, stopping under a street lamp to consider what had happened. I was visibly shaken, having not expected to uncover any emotional involvement from me in the storyline. I'd been enjoying myself, though, which was the biggest shock of all.

10.

With a sober head the next morning, I felt less inclined to progress the storyline and decided once again to avoid Alex in the wake of kissing him. After a few days, my courage returned, but by then Alex was avoiding me.

Naturally, I didn't let this thwart me. There was good material for a couple of weeks in us completely avoiding each other, and me making things up to Lauren. Alex had run off to tell Ewan that it didn't matter whether he was completely gay or not, just so long as they loved each other.

We eventually converged when Ewan insisted on us all going out for dinner one Saturday night. It was TV gold as Alex and I sat uncomfortably across the table from each other, trying to make as little verbal contact as possible. It was a trying evening, not that Lauren and Ewan seemed to notice. They thought that we should do it more often. I hoped the viewers squirmed with us.

I texted Alex that night and told him that we had to act normally to avoid suspicion. He texted me back and said that he agreed. I texted him again, suggesting that he come over. He didn't reply; he just turned up.

We talked about nothing and then I told him that I missed him when he got mad at me. He smiled flirtatiously, and I looked away. "I kind of miss you too," he said. "I'm never short of a head-fuck or two when you're around."

He thought about the sentence for a second.

"I didn't mean it like that," he blustered and I let out a stilted laugh. As we sat in the awkwardness, I inwardly breathed a sigh of relief to know that the storyline was back on.

To be fair, it was Lauren who suggested the holiday. I was just the one who thought it was a fucking brilliant idea.

After we'd made up, she'd started ruminating on how sad it was that this would be our last proper summer together, the four of us. "We need to mark it," she said.

"Like going camping again?" I asked, thinking of the possibilities.

"Like going abroad. A proper blowout after A-levels."

I liked it. It would bring things back full circle seeing as *The Almost Lizard* had started at a holiday resort. We suggested it to Ewan and Alex at college the next day and they needed little persuading. I think they were all in a flurry of trying to convince themselves that our relationships were strong when we all signed up for a week in Majorca together. I, on the other hand, was planning a monumental week of episodes.

11.

Our final exams were the perfect backdrop for the next phase of the storyline, which was all about keeping the viewer guessing. For a while, I was the dutiful boyfriend to the point that fans probably began to think that the plot had fizzled out. Her father was involved in a car accident and I was by her side for some dramatic nights at the hospital. Danny was her rock throughout, and numerous episodes found her crying on his shoulder.

Conveniently enough, Alex had been informed by our sociology tutor that he stood a good chance of failing the course if he didn't do well in the exams. When he was going through the initial shock I was busy with Lauren's family crisis, but her dad started to recover and I was able to offer my services as a tutor for him. It fitted in with the story arc perfectly. From the end of March right through to the exams in June, Alex and I spent three evenings together revising obsessively. Whatever else he thinks of me these days, I did get him through his sociology A-level.

Along with the job at the pub, this new commitment kept me very busy in the evenings and I found that I was spending less time with Lauren. I was also keeping Alex away from Ewan for three nights. In response Ewan joined a pub football team, so I made sure that our study nights didn't clash with those.

When Lauren complained about us hardly seeing each other, I suggested she come to see me at the pub. She did once or twice, but on the whole she didn't really want to make the effort when pushed. That hurt and encouraged me at the same time.

It was just studying that we were doing as well. I was a good and patient tutor and at no point did I orchestrate some potentially compromising situation. I was relaxed and hassle-free, which I hoped was the opposite of Ewan.

He was having trouble with his football team. His relationship with Alex had been discovered and the matter wasn't being treated sensitively. He told Alex not to come to any of the games and made sure that he didn't invite his boyfriend out on team socials. When Alex complained about this to me, I gave impartial advice, and most often took Ewan's side.

"You must know what football teams are like," I often said. "They'll be making him feel dirty."

"But I think he understands where they're coming from."

"I think we all do. It's just something to take the piss out of him for."

"It makes him think less of me."

"If that were true, he would have just dumped you," I reassured him.

Alex asked me once if these conversations made me feel uncomfortable.

"Not at all," I answered without hesitation. "I'm glad you feel you can still talk to me about this stuff."

When the recriminations were eventually dished out, I didn't want to be entirely to blame. Ewan and Alex weren't talking to each other about their problems. They just had brief spats and then plastered over the cracks until the next flare-up.

Alex and I finished our exams on the same day, with the long awaited sociology exam. Alex walked out grinning, knowing that he had done well, and was insistent on buying me some thank you pints. Lauren and Ewan had exams for two more days, so we were left on our own. That had been something I'd discovered months before so I had set that as the date for things to progress.

I'd planned for this being a big episode. I imagined ambiguous trailers on television and screen shots appearing in the press. Soap was so archaic with homosexuality, that it wouldn't take much to top anything that had been seen before. It was an episode with just Danny and Alex.

We had a few beers in town, sat in a beer garden by the canal celebrating the beginning of a long and glorious summer. After the third pint, I suggested doing something bigger than Lancaster. Within the hour we were on a train to Manchester (drinking cans to stave off sobriety or a premature hangover). It seemed spontaneous to Alex, but the suggestion had been in my head for weeks.

Our respective partners called over the course of the evening and bollocked us for going off without saying anything. It made us appreciate being away from them even more. We drank more to spite them. The night was dominated by snide remarks about Lauren and Ewan, and what little fun they really were. I suggested that Alex should make the most of Canal Street whilst we were there.

"Cheat?" he asked, beaming from ear to ear. He was drunk enough to think that it was a hilarious idea.

"Yeah, what happens in Manchester stays in Manchester."

"I will if you will," he answered.

"I don't think you meet many women on Canal Street."

"Then we'll go somewhere with women afterwards," he replied and started laughing hysterically.

"You're on."

It must have been quite late. It was dark and we had no chance of catching a last train back. With our fate sealed we resolved to get even more drunk upon arrival in the gay village. We threw back shots and joked around. I pointed out potential men for Alex, going from serious suggestions to singling out old queens in no time.

"Just go for it," I said when I spied someone who was just his type.

"I can't. His eyes are too close together," he shouted over loud trance music.

"Bollocks. You're just scared."

"You fucking pull him then!" Alex answered back.

"Alright," I grinned at him with drunken bravado. I hadn't planned for this, but it was right for the episode. Alex watched on with both shock and amusement as I confidently chatted up his potential suitor. It's strange, but I found it so much easier to flirt with a man. I've never been one to snog a woman in a bar within a minute of meeting her, but that's exactly what happened with this guy, who I'm not sure ever had a name.

I made my excuses and returned to Alex proudly. He mock applauded me and insisted on buying me a drink.

"Are you sure you're not gay?" he asked me as we stood

at the bar. It was a light-hearted question, but it was the ideal cue for me.

"Not normally. Not for him," I pointed over in the vague direction of where the bloke had been. I leaned in and kissed Alex. He pushed me away angrily and a couple of people stared.

"Not this game again, Danny," he snarled.

I shook my head emphatically. "Not a game. I think I'm in love with you."

I'd been waiting to throw that line out all day – it was the climax of the episode. I knew that things had to be different after this, and not just further confusion. Danny had to tell Alex he was in love with him or Alex would have just stormed off. I'd been working with his character all my life so I'd more or less known what to expect.

He raised his hands to his mouth as if he were trying to have a surreptitious pray. He surveyed me with caution, waiting for me to start laughing again. I didn't flinch. I played it like I meant it.

He leaned into me and whispered, "Perhaps we stay in a hotel tonight?"

It was the most risqué thing I had ever filmed.

12.

So this was the summer of my gay affair. I tried a lot of new things that night in Manchester and returned to Lancaster in the middle of my most outrageous storyline to date. I imagined doing some interviews for television, sat on my bedroom set talking about what a bold plot it was. These interviews helped me rationalise what I was doing. It made me a little different to the person who had slept with his best friend the night before. When I was playing Danny, I was in love with Alex. But when I was Danny, me, I talked about myself as if it were all a script.

We agreed at the train station to not see each other for a couple of days. I worked more nights to save up some money for the holiday, but we got to meeting up with each other during the day time. Sometimes we went and had coffee and held hands on the steps up at the university, where no-one we knew would see us. Other days he just came round to mine and we did things to each other. I'll spare you the details. Sitting here writing about sex that I've had doesn't feel appropriate, unless it's relevant, like my virginity was. You don't want to hear about pulses and thrusts, you just need to know that I was filming some edgy stuff that caused a record number of complaints at whatever TV station I'd decided was broadcasting *The Almost Lizard* at that point.

But some stuff you have to know, and you probably need to know that Mum walked in on Alex giving me a blowjob once. It was a few days before our big holiday and I'd genuinely forgotten that her summer school was over. She'd gone out to the shops when I thought she'd gone to work, and I hadn't heard her come back over the music that I put on. The first I knew of it was a shriek that made me open my eyes in time to see Mum rushing out of the room.

Alex was out of the house within five minutes and I was left facing a difficult dialogue with Mum.

"I didn't know you were into that, Danny," she said. I didn't think of Mum as a prude, but the older she got, the more she seemed to disapprove of anything sexual. I think if it had happened before Dad's affair then she might have seen the funny side.

"It was just an experiment," I said. Me-as-Danny was completely mortified.

"And what about Lauren?"

"I'm not going to tell her."

"You shouldn't lie to her, Danny."

"She wouldn't understand."

"And nor should she!"

"I didn't enjoy it," I said, lacking anything else to say. A grin briefly spread across Mum's face. "Alex said he wanted to improve his technique."

"You should watch that Alex," she said less severely. "That sounds like a line to me."

"Well I won't be doing it again," I replied.

"I bet that's what your father said," she said. Occasionally she liked to let it be known that the affair wasn't completely forgotten. It was a well-timed line, though. It highlighted the parallels between the two storylines.

That incident was one of several that kept things interesting in the build up to the holiday. Couples having affairs can only really be involved in two types of storylines – nearly getting caught and feelings of guilt. There were scenes when we were together and either Lauren or Ewan called up. There was the night that Alex accidentally fell asleep at mine and we had to sneak him out at five in the morning. Dad asked me what the noise was the next day and I made up some stupid lie about a cat coming in. Mum hadn't caught us by then, otherwise she would have dealt me a knowing look.

There were also moments when we both said something we shouldn't in front of Lauren and Ewan. I referred to a trip to Manchester that had happened on a night when I was supposed to be working and Alex was supposed to be out for a meal with his parents.

"I meant last month, not last week," I flushed and the moment passed, I'm not sure how awkwardly.

Alex made a joke about Annie from my work, who had stormed out the night before following a row with one of the locals about her breasts. Alex had come to meet me at work and we'd taken a slow walk home together.

"How did you know about that?" Lauren asked.

"I told him about it before," I jumped in.

"You just made it sound like you were there," she continued

to speak to Alex, who looked in danger of crumbling. I had enough faith in myself to cover things up efficiently, but Alex was less accustomed to deception.

"You'd have wished you'd been there, it was hilarious," I interjected again.

"I really do," Alex agreed and again the moment passed.

We both made attempts to call it off during that summer. We had attacks of conscience, or a bad reaction to nearly getting busted, and one of us would tell the other that it could go nowhere.

The flipside to this feeling was wanting to end our other relationships. Alex led the way on this one, discussing it with me in bed one evening not long after we'd got together. "I think I enjoy being with you more than Ewan."

"And me so new to this?" I joked.

"I don't mean that," he said quite seriously. "I like the time we spend together, it's more fun."

I made him realise that we didn't want to hurt people.

Another month passed before I made the same declaration, when we were on one of our nights out in Manchester. "I wish it could be like this all the time," I said as we drank outside one of the bars on Canal Street. "I hate all the secrecy. I think we should tell them."

I went through the motions of getting my phone out and bringing up Lauren's number, but Alex intervened.

"You can't tell her over the phone."

"I might as well. Our relationship died the moment I fell in love with you."

"That's not true."

"It is," I insisted. "I find her less attractive every day I spend with you."

"But they're both good people," he assured me. "They don't deserve to be hurt, especially if we head off to uni and things don't work out." I resented that a little. I wanted him to expect things to work out. I let him talk me round, though.

It was an amazing plot to be involved in. I thrived on the deception, it was a challenge to me as an actor and the real nature of the scenes made the near misses quite exhilarating. The whole storyline could have unravelled with one of those risks, but that was part of the fun. I lived for those moments of drama.

There was a novelty in doing the things with a bloke that I usually did with women, and also in exploring what a gay relationship was like. In Manchester I thrived on being openly homosexual on dance-floors, but we often got funny looks in local pubs if we sat too close together. It was interesting to experience that alienation, safe in the knowledge that it wasn't a precursor to the rest of my life.

There was something a little deviant about having sex with my girlfriend in the afternoon and doing the same – but different – with my male best friend in the evening. I think I might have used the word decadent in interviews.

So I think I enjoyed being temporarily gay, knowing full well that the straight future with a wife and kids was secured. The shroud of teenage experimentation was a safe way for me to approach that storyline. I was excited by Danny Lizar again.

This was coupled with the uncertainty of exam grades and potential futures, which gripped us during the middle of August. Those nerves were as real as any from a pre-fabricated situation.

Results day brought some unexpected drama when Ewan walked out with a clutch of B grades, short of the marks he needed to study law at Durham. All of a sudden his 'what next?' was up in the air and Alex was tucked away in a corner with him trying to work out what the hell he was going to do. I was sympathetic, but couldn't help but wonder what this meant for the show.

Whilst Ewan sorted out his life, Alex and I kept our affair to text messages only, meeting up only once between results day and going on holiday. We discussed the trip with apprehension.

"It's all bit close to home, isn't it?"

"We just have to behave ourselves," I informed him. "We only need to get through this holiday and we're clear. When we all go to uni, we can visit each other and they won't have a clue."

"I don't want to behave myself," Alex answered seductively. I always found the seductive looks a bit of a challenge. It exposed my lack of real feeling. It was too staged for me and I was sure my sexy responses sounded forced.

"Well we can't ruin their holiday," was my answer. "We should enjoy the torture, and perhaps reward ourselves if the chance arises."

That appeased him. We both relaxed and watched television together. The evening was marked by several interruptions from Mum, asking us if we wanted cups of tea or cakes, or whether we wanted to watch television downstairs. It was pretty funny, she was trying her best not to look ruffled, but her routine visits gave her away.

"I'm really worried something's going to go wrong," he said later. "I think I'm going to get drunk and grope you in front of everyone, or just not be able to resist any longer and do something really blatant."

"Nothing can go wrong," I replied. "It's going to be a great holiday. And afterwards we can start to think about the rest of our lives." Soaps needed these proclamations. Doom had to be foretold with a naïve prediction of future happiness.

Our arrival at Manchester Airport marked the beginning of a special week of episodes filmed entirely on location. I made sure I looked uncomfortable with Lauren as much as possible and exchanged looks with Alex at every covert opportunity. As we were collecting our luggage at Palma de Mallorca Airport, I whispered to Alex not to get drunk that night. He didn't ask me why.

We made a deal that when we were buying rounds that night, we'd get ourselves just coke whilst Lauren and Ewan received at least double shots with their mixers. We were out until the early hours, our partners getting more hammered whilst we barely wandered past tipsy. The only alcohol we had was on the rounds that the others were buying.

It meant that the next day, Lauren and Ewan had stinking hangovers. Alex and I were up, about and off to the beach whilst they rolled around their beds in agony. We wandered out of the main village to a beach where few tourists seemed to venture, and spent the afternoon in the sun, away from our supposed loved ones. We kissed in the sea and talked about going somewhere secluded.

"Not today," I said, looking like it was the most immense sacrifice I'd ever made. "But we can get them drunk again."

Getting away together became the theme of the holiday. When we were with them we were planning how to get them out of the way, and getting them drunk seemed to be the way forward. On our fourth night there they were both sound asleep by half past eight after an early session, so we went out and hit the resort until the early hours, both 'accidentally' leaving our phones in our apartments.

That was the night that Alex decided it all had to end.

"This holiday has proven to me who I want to be with, if I didn't know it before," Alex slurred at me as we staggered back as it started to get light. "It's like they're intruding on our time away. My favourite bits of this trip have been our day at the beach, and tonight."

I felt that. I understood where he was coming from.

"It's like I'm now with someone who's known me all of my life, my best friend. It's the best thing about being gay, I get to be in love with my best friend." I ensured that he wasn't going to do anything drastic when we got back – it wasn't time. I'd already decided that the climax should happen at the end of the week.

"Why did you go and get hammered when you knew we were going out?" Lauren barked the next morning when she realised I was too ruined to go on a booze cruise. "It's really selfish, Danny."

"Unlike passing out before sunset," I replied weakly through the layers of a muggy headache.

"I'm up and ready to go now."

"Only because you were a lightweight yesterday."

"Fuck you, Danny," she shrieked, making me flinch.

"Well don't let me stop you. You three go."

She stormed out to tell Alex and Ewan what a disgrace I was, not then realising that Alex was suffering just as much as me. When he heard that I wasn't going, he ran to the toilet to be sick. They were both angry enough to leave us behind for the day.

It was really a couple of days early, but I was concerned that the opportunity wouldn't arise again. Lauren returned to our apartment and informed me that Alex was equally pathetic and that we were both trying to ruin the holiday.

"You're a fucking hypocrite," I snapped at her. It hurt my head to do so, but she was being pretty annoying.

I had a point, so she stormed out without another word. I waited for half an hour before I sent Alex a text from across the hallway. He knocked on my apartment door two minutes later, wrapped in a duvet and looking sheepish.

We sunbathed on the balcony, sweating out the booze as the day grew hotter. Sometime mid-afternoon we started to feel better and I dispatched Alex to buy a bottle of vodka from the supermarket. We sat out in the sun getting drunk again and complaining about our judgemental partners.

"What time does this booze cruise finish?" I eventually asked, knowing full well that we could expect them back for eight o'clock. Alex said he wasn't sure. I said that I was willing to take a risk.

Lauren and Ewan had initially been mad with us, but over

the course of the booze cruise had talked themselves into not only forgiving us, but admitting that there were double standards at play. They were ready for an apology and a good night out.

Scenes of them walking back to the apartment block were spliced with close-ups of me and Alex in bed together, taking the tension to fever pitch. They went back to Ewan and Alex's apartment first and found it empty. They headed to my apartment and Lauren let them in. The duvet from Alex's apartment had been left on the floor of the reception room, but this didn't concern them. Presumably they expected to find us on the balcony, or a note to say that we'd gone for dinner. They were probably quite amused by the near litre of vodka that was missing from the bottle bought that afternoon.

I let out what I can only describe as a sexy moan from the bedroom.

"What was that?" Lauren said and we froze in our compromising position, not daring to breathe as the sound of two sets of footsteps approached the bedroom. I hadn't shut the door, so the moment they turned the corner they saw Alex and me in bed together, with no room for misinterpretation.

13.

The success of these scenes relied not on my planning, but on how my co-stars improvised their way through it. It was a showdown matched in magnitude only by 'that' Christmas Day. I decided that the next episode was a ninety minute special, shot in real-time, starting from the moment that I threw the duvet over me and my best friend in a futile attempt to cover up what they had walked in on.

Lauren said little but "Oh my God" repeatedly for the first few minutes. I was unsure as to whether I should be making attempts to get dressed. Alex and I weren't making contact any more, just lying next to each other not knowing where to look. Eventually they both left the room and we hurriedly put each other's underwear on by mistake. I pulled some more clothes out of my suitcase, which was when Alex realised that he had nothing but my boxers and the duvet he'd abandoned in the living room. When we emerged from the room with him wearing my clothes, it only served to make things worse.

Over time I've had to accept that humans aren't as dramatic as television characters. They stumble over their words at times of high tension, and say stupid things that often make little sense. The arguments go round and round in circles until someone gets bored, or there's nothing else to say. But this, this was pure soap.

Ewan had gone back to his apartment, where he was kicking furniture around and shouting wildly. Alex and I stood next to each other facing Lauren, who couldn't return our gazes.

"Interesting time to experiment, Danny," she said.

"I wasn't experimenting," I replied. At this point I was close to throwing in a twist and deciding to make a go of things with Alex. I admit it, I enjoyed the relationship to a certain degree.

"And what does that mean?" The booze made her more confrontational. Neither of us looked at her and the penny dropped. "Oh, I see. This isn't the first time. Nice."

"I need to go and see Ewan," Alex said and made for the door, just about ducking the flip-flop that Lauren had pulled off her foot and launched at him. That left just the two of us.

I went for disaffected honesty. She asked me questions and I answered them coldly.

"It just happened," I said. "We didn't plan it."

"No, I can't imagine you did. How long have you known you were gay for?"

"I'm not gay."

"You were sticking parts of yourself into parts of another man and you think you're not gay," she laughed viciously. "You're going to tell me you're not confused next."

"I am confused."

"I know!" she bellowed. "What wasn't I giving you? Was it my arse? I always said I'd never do that, but I thought you'd respect that."

"You make it sound so dirty."

"It is fucking dirty!" She nearly slapped me at that point, but I dodged it.

I stepped onto the balcony and stared out at the resort below. The evening was in full swing and it seemed that everyone was having a nice time apart from us. Inside, Lauren guessed that this all began shortly before I proposed to her, and she came out after me to have that confirmed. My silence was sufficient.

"But nothing else happened for months," I added. "Not until Valentine's Day." It was a revelation that I'd been saving up.

"We were out together on Valentine's. I remember, you wanted Alex to… Oh my God."

Ewan barged in. "This is so fucked up!" he shouted at the room. "If this was a girlfriend, I'd hit the bloke she'd been shagging. But now I have two blokes I want to hit and it's possible that they might just twat me instead."

There was a knock at the door. There had been complaints from other guests. I apologised and promised that the shouting had finished, that it was just a misunderstanding. The arguments calmed down to make room for questions. Alex returned.

"You've always been funny with me," Ewan said. "I thought it was just jealousy because I'd become Alex's best friend."

"You're my boyfriend," Alex corrected him. "Danny is my best friend."

For Ewan, that was possibly the most hurtful thing.

"Danny's not ashamed of me," he added.

"So that's what this is? I don't want to run around Lancaster screaming that I suck cock and you go and fuck your best mate. One of my best mates, supposedly."

"You've only ever tolerated me," I piped up.

"I didn't ask you to speak," he hissed at me. It was the

campest I'd ever seen him.

"I just don't think you should make stuff up."

"There's a whole load of things I don't think you should have done, but that doesn't seem to have stopped you."

"Oh shut up, Ewan," Lauren said unexpectedly. "Don't act like you're any better than they are."

This I hadn't predicted. She told us that Ewan had occasionally succumbed to his heterosexual tendencies and had slept with a girl called Claire, who had been in his psychology class. This news seemed to cheer Alex.

So we learned of Ewan's infidelity, and I had the gall to ask Lauren why she'd never told me about this. She threw a glass at me and scurried from the room. The door to the other apartment slammed, so we knew where she had gone.

"I'm going to see if she's alright," Ewan told us. "Try to keep your hands off each other."

"At least we don't have to worry how to tell them now," Alex said as soon as his boyfriend had exited.

"It's over," I said into my hands. "She's never going to forgive me for this."

Alex's mood altered immediately. This was what the episode had been building up to.

"But it means we can be together," he said, quite desperately.

I looked at him and shook my head. "I'm not gay," I told him for the first time in months.

"I can name some pretty gay things you've done recently," he responded indignantly.

"But I'm not gay forever. I can't see myself growing old with a man, sitting in a bungalow with another man. I like women. I like fucking women. I like women whispering in my ear, or waking me up with wandering hands. It's different with you."

"How?" his voice was wobbling. He'd been so confident in the hour or so since we'd been caught, but that evaporated instantaneously.

I couldn't think of a line that spoke more strongly than silence. He touched my face and I looked away.

"Danny, no. You're just getting cold feet because of what's happened. It's all just raw."

I returned to the balcony.

"I don't have anywhere to go," Alex called to me from inside.

"You can stay there on the couch," I replied without turning around. I knew that across the hallway, Lauren and Ewan were getting their revenge with each other. I'd seen it the moment Ewan had left. That particular episode had ended with Lauren and Ewan falling into some desperate fuck to try and redress the balance. I hadn't anticipated it until then, but when I realised it, it seemed absolutely right. I didn't feel jealous, I appreciated the twist.

I went to bed on my own and lay awake, listening to the noises from the street; screaming Brits and Europop anthems, the occasional broken glass and the sound of a street cleaner shortly before it started getting light. The deviant within me got the better of me and I went to get a glass of water, knowing that Alex was not going to be sleeping.

"Are you alright?" I asked him as I looked in the wrong cupboards for a glass. I could see that his eyes were open in the semi-light.

"Was this all just a game?" he asked. He'd been crying. I abandoned my search and sat down next to him, aware that I was still wearing his boxer shorts.

"No," I put my hand on his shoulder. I hugged him, skin on skin. I'd struggled to get used to that contact with him initially, but by then it was second nature. In spite of everything he still decided to follow me back into my room.

Afterwards I sent him back to the couch. I sounded cold when I told him that I didn't want us to be found again, but the optimist within him said that it was just to stop things being more awkward.

"That didn't feel right, did it?" I said as he was heading

out. He was naked and I found that I could barely look at him. I reminded myself of how wronged I'd felt when they all decided to move far away.

"It was awesome," he answered.

"It was the last time," I answered back. "I don't love you," I added before he had a chance to respond. Quietly he gathered up the clothes of mine that he had borrowed and went back to the couch. I fell asleep to the sound of him crying from the next room.

We lived as four separate entities for the final two days of the holiday. Ewan and Lauren found themselves disgusted with each other in the wake of their revenge shag, whilst I avoided any sort of discussion with Alex, who stayed in my apartment looking distraught at all times. That was why I'd wanted things to happen on the last night, to avoid these painful, awkward and quite frankly drama-free encounters.

On the last night I went out alone and brought a girl back with me. Alex was on the balcony staring at the floor, much in the position that I'd left him before going out. At some point before orgasm, I heard the apartment door slam shut and I knew that he'd got the message.

We travelled back together via coach, plane, and train. From there we each took separate taxis.

14.

As far as the show was concerned, my parents disowned me and I was forced to flee Galgate with only as much as I could carry in a large rucksack. In reality, they drove me to Manchester and made sure that I was set up in halls. Dad gave me some extra money for food and told me to come and visit soon.

I imagined that I burned my bridges at The Fox and Whistle just to complete the effect. Chef asked me to decarbonise a grill-plate and I told him to go fuck himself. I picked up dirty plates and started launching them at the walls. I stormed out of the kitchen. Ed followed me, so I told him to go off and tell some bullshit stories to someone who was actually gullible enough to believe him, then I yelled at the customers for being small-minded no marks who wasted their lives in the same pub every day until they finally expired, to be missed by no-one. With that, I left for good.

It was a success, the whole thing. I unravelled Danny Lizar's complex little life and he left the show alone and vilified. I filled up a rucksack and caught a bus into town to film my final scenes, without an ounce of sadness. I'd hoped in a way that this would be an end to the dramas, but I was only deluding myself. Already, I had a new show in mind. A new character, a new start.

DAN

Ensemble

1.

It's safe to say that my disorder was diluted a little after I left *The Almost Lizard*. I wanted to follow the route of other actors and move on from soap into drama with clear distinct series.

I left *The Almost Lizard* to star in a new sixteen part drama about an eighteen year old leaving home for the first time and starting out life at university. To represent my new start as an adult actor, I arrived in Manchester without my 'ny'. From that day on I was known as Dan Lizar.

I was part of the influx of reckless teenagers being let loose on the world for the first time with a healthy disposable income and the time to get paralytic at least six nights a week. The opening scenes of my new show were a series of quick-fire moments of drinking in clubs, waking up late and having irresponsible sex with girls I hoped never to see again. The moment I arrived I forgot about everything that had gone before. It had taken only a short car journey for me to become someone else entirely.

It's not like I was the only person reinventing myself for the university experience. Everyone was telling everyone else everything about themselves as rapidly as possible, whoring out their personalities to the nearest friendly face. It's amazing that amid this chaos any life-affirming bonds can be made, but

I found making friends very easy. I didn't plan who I was going to be, I was kind of playing myself.

I was in a position to select who I wanted to hang around with, and it was important to have the right co-stars. Every new acquaintance effectively had a screen test, where I decided whether or not they were suitable. There were many who I initially took a liking to who actually turned out to be mind-blowingly dull, or just a little too disaffected to take seriously. Then there were the try-hards who asked for your number within a minute of meeting you, or the ones who started talking about capitalists before they'd even got your name. I met a lot of Philosophy Dave types, and learned to steer clear of them very quickly.

There was one girl I slept with on Freshers' Week who thought that our drunken, quite difficult encounter meant that we were in some loving relationship. I made the mistake of giving her my phone number and had to fend off all sorts of calls and texts before she got the message. These encounters emboldened me in the early weeks of my new life. It's not often over the course of our existence that we are gifted the opportunity to completely reinvent ourselves. We pick up baggage and make bonds, and we settle somewhere and become part of something. We collect. Moving to Manchester was just that clean break for me. There was no-one there who knew me and anything that had gone before was completely irrelevant. There had been no gay affair or destroyed ex-girlfriend. Lauren phoned me up a few times after I moved away to tell me what a shit I was, and how she was coming to Manchester to tell everyone that I was gay. I stopped answering her calls, safe in the knowledge that Manchester was a big place and she was unlikely to track me down.

Suddenly I was having one night stands and receiving real attention, which naturally gave me confidence. I was cooking my own meals and smoking in bed when I woke up. In the space of a few weeks I made myself a great collection of friends. Even better, I met an awesome girl.

David lived two doors further down the corridor from me in halls and he became one of my favourite people almost immediately. He was clutching a Manchester Academy gig guide when I first encountered him in the kitchen, and the first thing he asked was whether I wanted to go and see Interpol. I asked the standard questions:

"Where are you from?"

"Cardiff. Outside Cardiff, actually, but you'll never be able to pronounce it."

I detected a friendly arrogance immediately, which I liked and returned. I felt my character forming during that first meeting. A lucky break, considering he was the first person I met. We dispensed with our A-level results and then things nearly soured when I asked him what he was studying.

"Philosophy," he told me.

"Why?" I snorted.

"Because I can get away with smoking weed for the next three years and still walk away with a degree to show my parents. Speaking of which." He led me to his room, where he had a spliff on his desk and a bong already unpacked. It didn't take much for me to decide that Dan was into smoking. I told myself it was different than during my Lizard days. Taking drugs with intelligent people was about experiencing, it was less mindless. That's how I rationalised it.

I missed the very first night of Freshers' Week because I was too paranoid to leave David's room. In doing so, I found my first co-star with the most minimal effort.

It took me a few more days to find my next friend. The other six people in my area of halls were okay, but they were also generally average. David made some disparaging remarks about them to me and from that I decided that they would only play a small role in things. David quite liked to keep things as an 'us-versus-them' situation, and as I was keen to have him in my life I went along with it.

Chris was one guy who I actually got along with well. He was the opposite of David; he didn't drink or smoke, and he seemed to be at university to get an education. He was studying economics and had a career plan, but he had a wicked sense of humour and was forever lending me comedy DVDs. He also couldn't stand David, and he didn't disguise the fact.

Chris was great for those nights when I didn't want to go out, or couldn't quite bring myself to get stoned yet again. We'd sit in his room and watch TV, and talk to each other in a way that I didn't with any of my other new friends. The rest of us were so irreverent that half the time we didn't finish a sentence because at least one of us would break into some comedy routine and shout over the speaker until the point was lost.

I liked it that way, but Chris was a nice respite from all that. He was a nice, normal person; an essential straight-man to complement all the other personalities I met.

I met Ellie in my first sociology seminar. She was a full on metal geek, walking in wearing an Iron Maiden t-shirt, with about seventy badges pinned to her bag. She was completely sexless, of course. She made no effort to make herself attractive and really didn't care. She was always good for a debate in our seminars, and I always tried to get into group work with her. We only really socialised after lectures, when we'd go and grab a coffee and bitch about each other's music tastes. I spent my first weeks of knowing her hoping that she wouldn't get a crush on me because, lovely as she was, I wouldn't have hesitated in rejecting her.

We angered others in our seminars by deliberately taking opposite stances and stealing the hour with our often two-handed arguments. A couple of tutors got together to ask us privately to give the other students a chance. It seemed that they were disengaging with the sessions because of our dominance. Being young and hot-headed, we identified their apathy as the problem.

"They sit back there and feel all detached without doing anything," Ellie raged when we went for coffee afterwards.

I kept Ellie at a distance from everyone else I knew because she was a bit of a safety net for me if I messed things up with the main group.

I found two more co-stars as I was queuing up to buy gig tickets in the union. It was one of my things to loudly ask for whoever I was going to see, using the band in question as a badge of honour that displayed my effortless coolness to anyone who was brave enough to comment on it. Jack was just that. I was booking up for an American rock'n'soul act called The Bellrays, who I hadn't really imagined anyone in the lunch time queue behind me would have known.

"The Bellrays are playing?" I heard a voice say. I turned around and saw a lad dressed directly from the pages of the NME, complete with expensive, messy-effect hair and restrictively skinny jeans. We were both showing off, and I liked him for it. He also dressed the way I felt I should be dressing. As with David, I felt I could learn a lot from him.

He insisted that I wait whilst he and his girlfriend got their tickets and then we went for a beer in the union bar. She was called Katie and they had been together since the first night and were enjoying their third week of blissful togetherness.

Jack was from Leeds and had spent most of his college years going to gigs and honing his personality, so that when he arrived at university he had ten times the confidence of most of the blank pages that we had encountered. He didn't say this, but it was what I read into his story. If I mentioned bands, he'd seen them three times already, and at every other opportunity he referred to some experience or another that he'd had at Glastonbury. It was important to him that he'd been to the smallest gigs of the biggest bands, and that people knew how much he loved music. It was exactly how I wanted to be.

Katie was almost exclusively sarcastic and Jack seemed to enjoy having the piss taken out of him, so it was a good match. She was from the suburbs of Bristol and spoke with a twinge of West Country, which took the spite out of her mickey taking.

We talked music, mainly, and a little about ourselves. The fluid exchanges worked well for the programme, with plenty of witty banter. Later in the day, one of Katie's new friends joined us. Imogen. She's the girl I've been waiting to tell you about.

I was bowled over by her in a way that Lauren could never have achieved. She was just suddenly stood there looking the epitome of anti-cool, dressed in vintage clothing, more beautiful than a million high street clones. She introduced herself with a warm smile and a giggle that made me want to kiss her there and then. I'd never felt that instant attraction, or felt anything that real before.

"You must be studying fashion," I said, quite stupidly.

"Aw, I love him already," she said and introduced herself. The four pints I'd consumed didn't spare my blushes and I excused myself to go to the toilet. In the mirror, I told myself to be cool, and then heard a flush from one of the cubicles behind me. The person who emerged was trying not to smirk. He left before me and I buried my head in my hands with relished embarrassment.

A little later that same person walked past and said, "Are you being cool?" He had a spiteful air about him, that of someone who doesn't realise how detested they are, in spite of a shallow popularity.

"I dunno," I replied. "Have you been back to the toilets yet? You forgot to wash your hands on the way out."

Jack, Katie and Imogen laughed and pulled disgusted faces at the guy, who stalked on silently.

"What did he mean?" Katie asked.

I probably wouldn't have admitted it sober, but I told them about the incident in the toilets.

"Be cool?" Katie shrieked. "Be cool! Nice work, Dan. You were being cool up until that moment." They all laughed, but it wasn't malicious. I liked laughing about what a dick I was. "You don't have to be cool to hang around with us."

"I know that," I retorted with a wink. "God, when I met you I decided to tone down my coolness so as not to phase you." They all laughed. "I was doing fine until Imogen turned up."

She reddened a little and giggled, then looked away shyly.

"That was a little full on, wasn't it?" I added in a jolt of realisation.

"No Dan, that was smooth," Jack replied with a broad grin.

"Sorry, I just don't fart around with what I say," I answered, quite seriously. So from then on I didn't fart around with what I said.

Imogen talked to me lots that night. I learned that she was from Leicester, which made me think of Lauren and the possibility that they could one day accidentally meet. She was a history student with an unashamed interest in the textile industry, which made her geeky and even prettier to me.

Nothing happened between us for a while. Imogen had left the love of her life at home and needed a little time to get over it.

That was how this show was different. It was character-led and required almost no fabrication. My life was interesting enough for me not to fake things. It didn't require the high impact storylines like *The Almost Lizard*. It felt different. It felt better. Less dangerous.

2.

So it became a programme about immoral living without consequence. It was like *Lizard* but over the age of consent and with a more sympathetic cast. My character wasn't defined by a series of plots geared up to dramatic climaxes, it was just about life. The show was supported by a wealth of sets and places to hang out: refectories, coffee shops, bars, gig venues and libraries, as well as lecture theatres and all of our student village bedrooms. I got a sense of grandeur when I walked through Piccadilly Gardens, imagining the beginning of an episode with a cool indie track playing, the long-range camera homed in on me as I walked towards the record shops of the Northern Quarter.

Loads happened in the first series, but at the same time it felt like not much happened. There weren't many slanging matches or shocking revelations. Instead there were many concurrent threads for all of the main characters. In other words, it was more like life.

Dan had his love story for a start. I couldn't believe how much I'd fallen for Imogen in real life. I didn't often believe in my feelings, but with her it was uncontrollable. When I heard that she'd had a one night stand a few nights after we met, I was devastated. David and I had gone out and got leathered in response and I'd ended up bringing home some girl who I literally remember nothing about. She wasn't there when I woke up the next day, and to my knowledge I didn't see her again.

I made excuses to see Imogen, and often if I saw her I'd follow to where she was going just so I could bump into her by surprise. I talked to Ellie about her at great length in glowing platitudes that emphasised how much she was the best thing that might happen to me. I wanted the viewers to know that it was genuine.

"If she appears from nowhere it totally throws me," I went on during one such speech. "I jibber on like I've never spoken to a girl before and by the time I've composed myself she's already half way to wherever she was going in the first place. She makes me retarded."

"Just fuck her or shut up, please," Ellie said. "I think I liked you better when you didn't have a brain full of vagina."

We had our moments of coming tantalisingly close to getting it together. There was one evening where Jack, Katie, Imogen and David had gathered in my room for a smoke. It was David's birthday, as I remember. After everyone had stumbled back to their various rooms, Imogen had stayed a bit longer.

"Aw, I'm really fucked," she said a few times.

"Are you okay?" I asked with concern, suddenly worrying that she was ill.

"I'm fine. I just can't move my legs," she answered and started giggling. She was lying on my bed with her head against the plasterboard wall. I lay down next to her and we discussed possible ways of getting her to move.

"How about if I punched them?"

"My arms work fine," she replied. "I'd knock you out if you did."

"How about if I pulled you off the bed, you'd have to get up then?"

"The same applies. You don't want me to knock you out, do you Dan?"

"How about," I started slowly and paused for effect before tickling her feet. She started to squeal and convulse with laughter, then lurched forward and banged her head on my desk. The shock of it took the fun out of the moment, and even though she laughed it off – we both laughed a lot – there was no scope for me to make a move.

Things eventually came to a head in the eighth week of term, which was Chris' birthday. Even though he wasn't a drinker, everyone else in the corridor insisted on throwing a party. It was during the lull between Halloween and Christmas when we found there were less obvious reasons to get drunk. Poor Chris sat in the kitchen for the duration, smiling tolerantly as everyone else got hammered around him. He told me afterwards that he had a terrible time, but it was quite amusing how cautious people were around him the next morning.

Over the evening David welcomed many visitors to his room, often people who were quite amazed to find drugs at the party. It was a nice place to be, but sitting in a room full of stoners when there was a party going on somehow seemed like a waste. I kept my intake to a minimum and managed to get Imogen on board with me.

I purposely spent the night going from group to group, talking to semi-familiar faces about anything ranging from how my course was going to whether you should spend your last two pounds on beer or Pot Noodles. I kept up the group tradition of screaming 'random' at the top of my voice whenever I heard someone use the word inappropriately. It was something David had brought to my attention on the first week, how everyone seemed to think that everything was either random, or totally random. I'd told the others about it and we all looked out for it, and if we heard the word being used inappropriately, we would scream it at the top of our voices.

My new friends had made me very full of myself. Our opinions seemed so right, which is why I inflicted them on others with such confidence, especially after the best part of a bottle of whisky.

"Who the fuck are you?" a sporty looking dullard called Tim shouted at me.

"You're in my kitchen and I'm just trying to point out that you sound like a moron."

"I didn't come here to be lectured by some skinny-jeans wanker about how to speak."

"No, you came here to be random," I smirked.

"Dan, leave it," Imogen chipped in. "The guy's clearly an idiot."

"Fuck you," the guy shouted at her. Imogen spat her drink in his face. I saw Chris sat on the chest freezer trying to make himself invisible. One of my flatmates – Archie – walked over and diffused the situation. It was his friend that I was berating, and he took him away to dry the spirit and mixer from his face. In sobriety I knew that I was in the wrong, but it worked out in my favour, so the evidence suggested that I wasn't.

Imogen was angry, so I took her to my room to calm down as she was aggravating some of the southern guy's friends with her loud bitching.

"It just makes me so mad," she fumed as I shut my door. "I thought after school and college all the meatheads would fuck off and leave me alone, but they're everywhere."

"He's gone and you never have to see him again." I assured her. "There are always going to be idiots."

She kissed me unexpectedly, so beginning the great love of affair of my life.

Our relationship was usually uneventful. I had my little doses of jealousy when blokes off her course sniffed around, and one drunken outburst on the matter, which involved me storming out of the union and having a row with her at a bus stop.

"The history boys don't see many women," she said. "You could send a pig in a dress into one our seminars and they'd all come in their pants." And that was that.

I didn't fancy another cheating storyline. Any trials were things that they faced together, like when Imogen's gran died and Dan went back to Leicester with her to go to the funeral. That was when I met her family, a picture of normality that Imogen was violently rebelling against with her untold drug taking and wild abandonment. The trip humanised her a little to me. I revered her less but loved her more when I saw where she came from, and how little she had to rally against. I wondered what she would make of my family and resolved that they should never meet.

That was another short thread in our lives, where she asked to meet the parents and I refused over and over again. It never got to the argument stage, but she did ask me if I was ashamed of her. I said I was ashamed of them, and made up a story about them being swingers. It was one of the few fabrications I came up with in Manchester, but it kept the story light-hearted. Although they probably would have found my story decadent, I wasn't particularly proud of everything that had gone before. I also didn't want Imogen to think that I was sexually confused in any way.

We weren't a boring couple, I know that much. We had good times with our friends and we experimented with our minds. It didn't all end in slanging matches and two-handers, it didn't have to. I wasn't in a soap any more.

3.

As I got caught up in my new life there seemed to be longer gaps between filming sessions. Sometimes two or three days would pass and I wouldn't consider *Open Books* at all. I'd chosen the name a few weeks into term, thinking it clever for depicting both the characters and the setting of the show. Often it was only at night that I put things into the perspective of the show, taking out the best moments of what had happened during the day.

I wanted to be part of an ensemble cast. I wasn't the main character in every episode and sometimes only found myself doing two or three scenes a week. If I'd accepted that I had a problem at all, I might have thought that I was starting to get better.

From the word go, though, a recurring plot on *Open Books* was the complete and utter contempt Chris and David showed for each other. They'd met when David had offered Chris a bong upon arrival, in front of his parents. Chris had refused, not just for the sake of his parents, but he did have to deal with phone calls every night for a month because his mother was convinced that she was going to catch him out stoned. David disliked Chris in return because he didn't drink and he didn't get high, and he just didn't know how to deal with that person, a person with no vices.

"I bet he's a chronic masturbator," David said to me one day. "No drink, no drugs, but he beats one out on the hour every hour." I laughed along, but never joined in. I liked Chris. When I was on a comedown he'd happily bring me brews to my room, and when I needed someone to tell me that I had to do coursework, he'd offer the disapproving eye I needed. He was also an amazing pool player and I wasted many an afternoon commandeering a table in the union bar whilst he taught me how to play better.

David felt that Chris had chosen to dislike him with little just cause, and I think this hurt him. He showed this through routinely stealing his milk, despite being told specifically not to. He started buying Weetabix just because of the sheer amount of milk they absorbed, which tipped Chris over the edge just before Christmas. Upon findings the dregs of his previously full milk carton replaced in his fridge, Chris decided to throw out all of David's food. Half an hour later he'd padlocked his cupboard and locked himself away.

David saved his revenge for the next term, when Chris was once again being dropped off by his parents. He waited for them to walk into the corridor before marching out of his room, completely naked bar a trilby hat that his grandmother had bought him for Christmas, and brushing past them on his way to the kitchen. I was hiding in my room at the time, laughing hysterically.

Chris was losing patience and showed good humour himself by wiping his cock on David's door handle. I didn't have the heart to tell David, but Chris brought it up at the first opportunity. David laughed, but you could tell he was annoyed.

When David came in drunk, he'd purposely stand outside Chris' door and shout loudly. Chris used to come out and get angry, but soon learned how futile that was, so instead shouted profanities into his pillow. In retaliation, he started hiding alarm clocks inside David's room that went off at obscenely early times of day.

I felt terrible when Chris asked me if I wanted to live with him in the second year. He said that he wasn't sure he was suited to living with many people, but he knew I was alright. "You could smoke weed in the living room and everything," he offered.

I'd assumed from an early stage that I'd be living with David, and Jack and I had talked about getting a house between the three of us. It was a contingency plan for avoiding potentially dangerous conversations about moving in with our girlfriends.

I didn't do the grown up thing and give Chris an immediate answer, I told him that I'd let him know. I dramatised the moment a little. I pondered over it, and actually weighed up the two potential second years I could have. Eventually I let him down gently. He moved in with two Chinese exchange students in Rusholme in the end, and without that proximity I found that I only saw him if I bumped into him on campus. We always had a quick chat, but neither of us would have bothered to notify the other if we'd changed our mobile numbers. I liked drugs and excitement more than comedy DVDs and cocoa.

David and Chris shook hands at the end of the year, and sort of smiled over their arguments. This cordiality was clearly on the basis that they never intended to cross paths again.

Ellie took the lead role in a few episodes around the middle of the series when she told me over coffee that she was a lesbian. I was pretty shocked, but then it all made sense.

"I should have guessed," I replied when she told me. I imagined for her a whole run of scenes where the viewers found out before me, and then more episodes afterwards where she went and got her first girlfriend. I had little involvement with the storyline, but I know the show was praised for the way it dealt with it.

Katie had a dramatic few weeks when she was mugged walking home from uni. It had been a nice evening and she'd decided to save the bus fare and walk through Rusholme down to Fallowfield. She was mugged in broad daylight, on a fairly busy street by a teenager who held a knife to her side and walked with her until she handed over her handbag before running off.

Katie was scared to go out for a few weeks and we all went round and visited her. We had a lost weekend in her honour with magic mushrooms, but she freaked out and we were all sent away, Jack included. After that she headed back to Bristol for a couple of weeks. When she returned, she dumped Jack.

They stayed apart for the rest of the term, and there was an episode dedicated to the fall-out of this seismic event. We'd only known each other for six months, but it felt like much longer and this split stunned us all. Imogen was there to support Katie, and our lads' house was born as a result.

Jack insisted on drinking away his anguish, and fell into the habit of taking home a different woman from each club night he went to.

Then Imogen told me that Katie didn't really want to break up with him, it was just the shock of the mugging that made her lash out. I had to pass this on to Jack, who was in the middle of a pregnancy scare with a one night stand who had come back to haunt him. It was negative in the end, but it was a mad couple of weeks and the last thing Jack could think of was getting back together with Katie.

They reunited in the summer term without fanfare. We'd all gone out on pills one night and they'd found themselves back in bed during the early hours. After that it was like the break up had never happened.

My life and all the things that happened in it fascinated me. That was the show.

4.

There were two things that concerned me in my first year at university: my past and money. They were kind of intertwined as well. Dan was very secretive about his past and didn't give much away to his new friends at all. I visited them in their hometowns over the holidays, but never suggested that anyone come to Lancaster.

Despite the shame I'd brought to the family with my bisexual love square, Mum and Dad were still funding me through university. They paid the rent and the tuition fees whilst I was free to squander my student loan as I saw fit. In return, I went home infrequently and deliberately missed their calls.

I didn't want any crossovers between the shows, which is why I kept my parents at bay. I was so chuffed with my new life that I didn't want anything from the past leaking in.

I made a token visit at Christmas, and then conveniently got a job in Manchester that involved me staying there for the holidays. I worked on Tuesdays and Wednesdays in a bar in Fallowfield, which helped me a bit with money. We never had enough cash between us, mainly because our lost weekends were expensive and we spent without consideration. I picked up my car when I went home at Christmas, and by the reading week of that term I'd sold it to keep my cash flow looking healthy. On my brief visits home after that I said it was much easier for me to get the train back and no questions were asked.

I liked my life too much to let something like family get in the way. It meant that I hadn't noticed how separately they were living their lives. Before I went away, Dad bought a country pub with the proceeds from the sale of the ChaMal chain. He had been waiting for the right investment and purchased the pub in a location completely unsuitable for Mum and her work. She herself had been promoted to deputy headteacher and was unwilling to move away from Galgate, so Dad spent at least half the week away from home. He had been around for most of my Christmas visit so this detail had eluded me.

I should add here that Dad's need to be guided in life was once again crucial in making this decision. He had broken down near to the pub on his way to view another place, and the retiring owner had helped him out. They got to talking and Dad made an offer there and then. It was an unconventional, almost gutless way to live your life, but it had served Dad very well when it came to business and career decisions.

I'd enjoyed my home comforts and most of my childhood had been picture perfect, but I was so excited at being out in the world and discovering people and places that I didn't have the chance to look back and miss it at all. I'd burned my bridges so effectively that I couldn't possibly even want to return.

Everything else aside, I told myself that I was too busy having a life to go home. I just didn't associate with Danny Lizar any more and I certainly didn't want to have anything to do with him.

5.

By the end of the first year, most of my savings from the car had been spent on good times and a minimum of four nights out a week. I took Imogen for nice meals and we played at being grown-ups before returning to our halls of residence. We ate out a lot, often going a full fortnight with neither of us making a single meal, including breakfast.

Out of character with the rest of the show, series one ended in a high drama completely made up by me. I imagined a fire in our kitchen and me trapped in my first floor room. I was able to film this on my own with absolutely no-one detecting me. It was a return to the old days, really, but I was adamant that the series needed a cliffhanger. I had, of course, commissioned a second series to start for the next term, and as I was moving out of halls it made sense to destroy that particular set. I could only picture the explosion that marked the end of the series, with the credits rolling over the burning embers and an ominous silence marking some tragedy. Viewers were left guessing who survived, as I had pretended that all of my friends were trapped in my room with me.

I knew already that I'd be killing off a couple of the people I was living with in halls and would never plausibly see again.

I think I'd expected to grow out of it by the time I went to university, and I never stopped to rationalise these weird behaviours when they happened. I didn't stop and reproach myself for imagining credits as I walked down Market Street, or the time I pretended that I'd been pick-pocketed and just ran through the Arndale Centre chasing after an invisible assailant. I always found it more convenient not to dwell on it.

I'd been dreading filming the last episode of the series as the prospect of returning home for three months and keeping my head down loomed large. In a moment of panic I signed up with some recruitment agency and found myself temping in an office in town. I imagined that I was filming a guest stint in an already established drama, which prevented me from returning to *The Almost Lizard*. I arranged to move straight into my second year house at the end of the term and called home to say that I wouldn't be coming back after all.

In the form of guest characters on a show, I decided to play mine with a slightly evil edge. I was doing bank admin work, which involved constant data entry and occasional bits of banter. I decided that I was a hacker with a drug problem, who was breaking into the systems to earn drug money. I smoked spliffs and once or twice snorted coke when I was at home in the evenings in order to represent this. Snorting coke alone was quite an unpleasant experience and I found myself acting out a series of monologues in the house.

It was just a stopgap between series, and something that

kept me occupied whilst everyone else was away. It meant lots of acting alone, which I was beginning to see as quite unhealthy. I suppose with the summer to myself, I spent a bit of quality time with my madness.

The end of my job meant the beginning of series two of *Open Books*, which immediately filled me with enthusiasm. I imagined a cryptic five minutes where a death was being talked about within the group. First Imogen was shown to be alive, then Katie and Jack, followed by David. After fifteen minutes, I appeared unexpectedly, just when the viewers were starting to think that I was the unfortunate one. It turned out that we all escaped through my bedroom window, jumping to a safe landing whilst those who I used to live with perished. I'm sorry to say that I imagined that Chris had been one of the victims, knowing in advance that I wouldn't be keeping in touch with him so much.

Again I decided to let the plots form themselves. I wasn't prepared to mess around with these people. My friends and girlfriend felt like they were for keeps, and I didn't intend to go destroying any more lives.

6.

The second year, in my opinion, marked the beginning of the end for me. Jack and David turned up two weeks before term started, just as I was ending my guest stint in the office drama. Imogen returned a week later and Katie a couple of days after that. It was Katie's return that marked the beginning of series two of *Open Books*, and I spent a few agitated days wondering where the storylines would come from. At first I thought it might have started with a summer drift between me and Imogen. We'd seen each other most weekends over the break, but things were a little awkward on her first few days back and I started to worry about our future. We were soon back to normal though, and the thread lasted no more than a few scenes. It's exactly what nineteen year olds are like in relationships, I thought, and praised the realism of the show.

Our lives hadn't changed enormously, but our living in houses made us feel older. We were in Manchester with none of the uncertainty of the first year, established and well-liked within our group. We could use the term 'fresher' in a derogatory sense and we knew which buses to catch to avoid all of the other students. We had our hang-outs; a favourite café in the precinct near uni, and bars with dark basements where various club nights were held. We knew where to go for fashion that no-one else had and we just felt more clued up.

Jack and Katie had become inseparable, which caused a certain amount of consternation amongst the rest of us, particularly with David who was too lazy to go and find himself a woman. His cannabis dependency was shaping up to be an interesting storyline.

Away from us, Ellie was experiencing cohabiting with her girlfriend, and most of our coffee sessions were outlets for her frustrations over dirty knickers and congealed cereal rotting away in bowls. Personality-wise, it turned out they weren't much suited either, so their idyllic flat-sharing near the gay village had turned out to be less than perfect. I liked that *Open Books* was dealing with a lesbian relationship in a non-sensational way.

"It's the characters and the relationship that's the storyline there," I said in a rare pretend interview. With no lock on my door, and Imogen around a lot of the time, I didn't have much chance to do interviews in my room.

The focus at the start of the series was on a forthcoming lost weekend. Jack had returned with a line on some acid, which none of us had taken before and were therefore interested in doing. We'd heard so many good things from the enlightened that we all took this to be great news. Jack was dispatched to Leeds to pick it up and we all set aside a weekend to lock ourselves in the girls' house and go a bit loopy.

The anxious excitement of taking a new drug is something I remember fondly, that slight risk that something might go awry and you'll never be the same again. We agreed to hold down anyone who thought they could fly and promised to support those who went seriously under. We looked after each other like that.

Acid was all about time for me. It was stepping out of the real world, away from linear progression and exploring the mind with no sense of whether minutes or hours had passed. It was a collective madness that reduced us to countless bursts of laughter and made us interested in everything from the pattern on the kitchen lino to the hairs on our arms. After that, I understood psychedelia and the need to expand the mind. I loved acid, aside from one thing. I saw myself that night.

In a moment of unexpected lucidity, I thought about me and my television programmes, and these scenes that I acted out. I thought about how I packaged my current life into episodes and threads and at first I thought it was alright. I pictured moments when I'd answer a pretend interviewer's question, in direct imitation of celebrities, having a real conversation with someone I absolutely knew wasn't there. Images appeared of scenes I'd done back home, wrecking lives of people who cared about me in order to make the best show I could. The fact that I knew none of it was real, but it was real in my head. As in, I knew that this was something I did, and it was something unreal, but it was something I did nonetheless.

The more I thought about it, the stranger I realised it was. This was the reflection I had been circumventing for years. I nearly spoke out about it to the others, but it's not like I'd totally lost my head, I knew that some things had to be kept secret. The mind was stripped, it was simple, but it was still me, and it was me as I hadn't looked at myself before.

"It really is fucking weird," I said aloud at one point when we were all stood in the back yard looking at the sky change colour.

"Yeah," Imogen said with a demented grin on her face, but I wasn't talking about the sky.

As clarity started filtering back in and we resisted the urge to take more acid, I found myself exploring this new insight into my behaviour. I shuddered a little at the things I did, and I laughed about them to myself. "How ridiculous," I said a few times. No-one challenged me. We were all a little ridiculous that evening.

It needs to stop, I told myself that night, and the sentiment carried over into the next day.

7.

It was like a small awakening, that acid trip. It gave me the opportunity to really think about something I hadn't given much consideration before. I exposed it for the ridiculous dementia that it really was. I thought about confessing and writing letters to everyone who had been affected by the contents of my programmes; the Proctor family, my family, Lauren, Ewan, the gang, my old teachers. I felt like I wanted to explain myself, that I was normal here at uni. I wasn't trouble, or damaged, but people wouldn't understand.

I stopped production immediately. When I felt a scene coming on, I told myself that it wasn't and acted as normally as possible, which was an act in itself. I insisted that life was happening, it wasn't a show and it didn't need that way of thinking any more.

When Jack announced that he was starting a band, I thought what a good character development it was, then told myself it was nothing of the sort.

When David was nearly thrown out for not paying his tuition fees, I saw the ending of an episode, but there were no episodes to end. I knew that.

When Ellie knocked on my door with a gash across her head, I had to persuade myself away from a twenty minute two handed scene where I heard how her relationship had got violent.

When Katie and Imogen got burgled, I comforted them and wondered how long the aftermath would last. But not in episodes for *Open Books*. I was starting to get better.

I thought about the show less, and when I did, I reminded myself that it was over. It was a whole new kind of performance, like I'd gone from being Dan (or Daniel or Danny) to Dan who had this problem, to Dan who had this problem but was acting it away. We studied post-modernism in classes, and I couldn't help but apply it to myself. I got on with things, and I did improve.

Then I relapsed, and it was over the stupidest thing. It was Jack's first gig and they were playing at The Roadhouse, and it was just the perfect start to series two, better than the one that had gone before. It showed progression between series, and we were all gathered to watch. So much had happened that I imagined the first (feature length) episode contained a lot of flashback scenes that recounted all of the things that had already taken place. I felt warm, stood there being Dan Lizar again. I felt complete.

8.

Like characters in a show, we were all picking up baggage and emotional scars from our life in Manchester. David was engaging less and less with his studies, so his dropping out just after Christmas was inevitable. He found office work easily enough and enjoyed bringing in a wage. He was much happier, somehow too cynical to be a student.

The girls were feeling the effects of the burglary. Imogen would only stay at their house if I was with her, or Jack was staying over at the very least. We didn't notice at first but David was beginning to drift away from us, with his early starts and new friends.

Ellie returned to her girlfriend and became subdued. The vitriolic seminar rants ceased almost completely and when we went for coffee she seemed too drained to tell me what an idiot I was. I asked questions but she was always vague and dismissive, occasionally aggressive. I knew it was one of our more dramatic storylines, but respected her right not to tell me about it.

Jack had lots of band storylines, singers leaving and gigs going wrong. Katie started to feel a little neglected and Jack told me he wanted to end things. Girls were responding favourably to him at gigs and he sniffed the potential for a taste of the rock and roll lifestyle.

And me, well I'd just gone off on my own tangent. In bringing the show back, I somehow wanted to reflect my heightened awareness about what it was that I was doing. I decided that Dan would have what I had. It had never been done before in television history. It was a mental illness storyline with a twist. So Dan started to act like he was acting out a television show in his head. It was the only part of me that I had kept away from the show, and I sensed that I'd be pushing boundaries by running with this storyline. By playing this character I hoped to understand him more. I expected this to somehow bring things to a conclusion.

It was how the new first episode of the second series ended, and it was chilling. Imogen had just phoned up to get me to come over to hers before she went to bed, and I pretended that David had walked into the room.

"I'm heading over to Imogen's place now," I said to the empty space. I imagined the camera was in a corner looking down on me, showing the viewers that there was nobody there.

"What do you mean I'm under the thumb? I think you're just bitter because you can't get a girlfriend."

I thought out David's lines in my head. I imagined him storming out and me lying on the bed. Then I sat up and said "good scene", again to the empty room. That's how the landmark episode ended, and how Dan Lizar became the most intriguing character on British television.

It was a slow burning storyline with only one incident per episode at first, but upon finding myself home alone for the first week of the Christmas holidays, I was able to film an entire episode with just me in it, acting out moments of high drama in my living room. The viewer had to see how mad it could all get. I stripped naked and filmed a pretend sex scene, before filming a pretend break up scene in the kitchen just wearing my boxers. Then I struck upon the idea of filming the episode for real.

Having started on this storyline I was finally intrigued as to how I looked when I did these things. It had never been something I'd wanted to see. I think I was scared that I'd see how crap I was at what I spent most of my life doing, but if this was an experiment conducted by Dan the character, then it wasn't essentially me. It's fair to say those were days of confusion.

I headed home for three days over Christmas and had a pleasant time with my parents as an adult. It was a happy Christmas where I didn't leave the house. Mum picked me up and drove me back to the station, so I didn't set foot in Galgate really; I was just shipped in and out. I returned the day after Boxing Day with Dad's video camera and set about filming the episode.

I still have the recording. I began in the morning by starting the camera and then jumping back into bed and simulating waking up all over again. "Morning," I said to the space next to me, smiling. It was a shock. I was acting like there was nobody there. Suddenly every imagined scene that I had filmed didn't seem authentic to me.

I continued with the fake sex scene, keeping my boxers on this time to spare my blushes in watching it back. I wasn't *that* inquisitive. Then I set the camera up in the kitchen for the fake argument scene, followed by a smoking session scene in the living room. During the playback I saw how unlike television all of this was, how it was just the ramblings of a person going through some psychotic episode. There was no humour in this. It destroyed everything.

I filmed Dan watching back the episode, and realising that he needed help. We both did.

9.

I could see the end of the show then. I wasn't sure whether it would be during the second or third series, but at the end, Dan would be cured and the show would end immediately. It was an ending that I imagined would stun people, and the show would become a hit posthumously. Of course, when it ended I wasn't allowed to have thoughts like that, so I anticipated the future whilst I had the chance.

I let my guard down, really. The storyline excited me, and I felt like I was pushing this thing as far as it could go, like I'd stumbled across the cure for this illness that had been with me at least since my early teens, probably earlier. We thought together, Dan and I. We sought moments to take one of our friends into our confidence and tell them what was going on. I needed someone to know what I did and help me understand it.

I decided to wait until our next lost weekend, when I planned to pick out someone who seemed like they might be receptive to quite a lot of unusual information.

The term was rattling on towards Easter, and we were lost in a flurry of coursework. Imogen and I found that we could study together, and I'd discuss my work with her to try and get a different perspective. We were a team like that.

I can't describe how well the relationship was going. There was little turbulence and none of the contempt I'd shown for Lauren. I loved that she got excited about how excited I was when a much anticipated new album came out. I loved that

I could go and buy two gig tickets and know she'd take the other one without thinking about it. I loved that she answered back when the lads tried to take the piss out of her, and that she played practical jokes on me when she got bored. It was going so well that I couldn't imagine that she'd be the one I'd tell.

So it was strange that it was. Our lost weekend was a strictly in the house affair, where we locked the doors and closed the curtains before holing ourselves inside until we were fit for human consumption again. It was an MDMA night, hours of listening to loud music, trying to roll joints and going to the kitchen for glasses of water. At other points we watched countless episodes of television comedies, or attempted some sort of board game. There were moments when we were all talking crap or someone saw something and we all went a bit mad. It was a classic lost weekend.

I laughed when a call came through from Mum. She was not someone I was capable of speaking to at that point. I could only deal with the people in the same room and the same state as me.

Sometime on Sunday morning, me and Imogen left my place and took a stroll back to hers. It was a cloudy day, but we both wore sunglasses regardless. I allowed myself to imagine a paparazzi picture appearing in the newspaper the next morning, perhaps speculating at the real life romance between the two of us. I realised as we were walking back that I hadn't spoken to anyone like I'd planned. For most of the night it had completely slipped my mind, and when I did remember it didn't seem right. It was only as I walked along with Imogen that I realised it had to be her. I thought of all the things she meant to me and how she was the love of my life, the one to save me from it. I could sense the cameras following us on our walk, our departure from the house marking the beginning of a new episode.

It must have been about half six. There was no-one around at that time, which was a blessing because we were both unfit for human interaction. Our faces had gone pale with a hint of yellow, and Imogen's eyebrows poked out over her sunglasses so she looked permanently surprised. In Fallowfield the streets were heaving at four in the morning, but everyone was out cold at the time when joggers and old people emerged to take their daily outing to the newsagents.

Imogen let us in, we rolled a spliff together and sat under a duvet on her couch. "This is one of the best bits, you know," she said. "I love it when you're still half fucked but the spliffs start taking effect as well. You can just sit and think, and appreciate stuff, you know?"

"Yeah," I smiled and kissed her on the head. I wondered if that was the moment.

"What are you thinking about now?" she asked me and I found it charming. From Imogen it didn't sound clichéd.

"I'm thinking about myself," I answered and she giggled playfully.

"Typical." I knew she was going to say that exact word. I loved that I knew that.

"I'm a strange person," I added, with a hint of a smile on my face. I feared bringing the mood down, but I was so in love with her at that moment that I knew it would be alright.

"I know," she giggled again. "That's why I love you." She swiped the joint from my hand and smiled mischievously.

"I have my own television show in my head," I continued, as if she weren't even speaking. "We're on series two now. It's about all of us, and Ellie as well. It's a well-respected drama that's full of gritty dialogue and character-led plotlines. People like it for being so natural. We all play ourselves and almost everything that happens is real."

Another giggle. "I don't understand. Are you being cryptic?"

"No, I'm being as literal as I can. I pretend that we're a television drama. A cult one."

"Do you mean you film us?"

"No, not at all. I filmed myself once, but only once. It's all in my head. When things happen that I think fit, it's a scene in a show."

"You're funny," she said and I stopped speaking. I couldn't find the words to describe it. I thought about going right back to the day that Diana died and telling her the lot, but I didn't think it would help. I lost my nerve.

We said meaningless things to each other and watched a box set of an HBO drama until we both passed out on the couch. She fell asleep first. The moment was lost and I imagined the camera panning away from my distressed face.

I woke up before Imogen and exited from the flat, passing Katie as I left. On the way home I thought about how Imogen would remember that conversation, and lying in bed alone that night I confirmed my worst fears, that she knew but would never understand. She would confide in Katie, who would confide in Jack. Everyone would know and it would become an issue. They'd think I was mental and try and have me sectioned, or at least remove me from their lives.

She phoned at one point and I tried to work out if she sounded strange. She asked what I was up to.

"Sleeping, mainly," I said. "Shall I see you tomorrow?"

I was too afraid to see her that night. I didn't think I could ever see her again. My high crashed into a low, dominated by paranoia.

I ignored another call from Mum. I was too scared to talk to her. I thought maybe Imogen might have phoned and asked about what I had told her.

Upon blurting out his secret, Dan Lizar feared everyone knowing and becoming the talk of Manchester. He would be outed as a nutter and his life would be ruined forever. He had to leave.

Exit storylines sometimes came about suddenly. Events had turned and I had to start again. I could go to a new city in September and do a new course with new people. There'd be no television show. I was done with Manchester. These friendships are shallow, I told myself. Fused by hedonism but with little substance. I could walk away tomorrow and it wouldn't make a difference.

Home. My family. The past. Only for a few weeks. I'd get a job and move to a different place, meet people who really cared about me and not just my money. I had the freedom to just go.

I didn't sleep. Just before daybreak I was packing some clothes and as many CDs as I could carry in a rucksack. I looked out of the window, taking in the view for the last time. I heard David getting up for work and decided to make my dash when he was in the shower. My phone rang and it was Mum again. I was ready to talk to her, mainly to ask her to pick me up from the station.

"Daniel, your father's dead," she said in response to my greeting.

Shock Exit!

1.

I have to speed things up here because I'm running out of time. It's my 21st today, you see.

2.

I didn't even need to pack. I just picked up my things and walked on out of *Open Books* as planned. I was numb as I took in the strangeness of the news. I mouthed it to myself a few times, "My father is dead." It crossed my mind that this would at least make returning to Galgate a little easier. I had lots of thoughts in the hours it took me to go home, in the epicentre of my lost weekend comedown and having to deal with the sudden death of my father. In and amongst the socially correct grief thoughts, were flashes of self-serving considerations, tiny moments where I thought something I shouldn't: if I'd get any inheritance, and if I'd get to see the body.

I did the guilt thing as well. Between Horwich Parkway and Chorley I spent the time counting on my fingers the number of times I'd seen my father since I left home. It was six. I only just about justified using the second hand in counting. I tried to remember the last thing he'd said to me at Christmas, but it slipped my mind. I thought of the horrible way I destroyed our family, then shunned him, and how crazy it was that he could still love me in spite of that.

Somewhere between Leyland and Preston I realised that I was returning to *The Almost Lizard*. I hated it in soaps when characters died and their own family didn't turn up because the actor had moved on to bigger and better things. It was unrealistic and I knew that *The Almost Lizard* was better than that. I saw an episode beginning with cryptic close-ups of me on the train, a montage scene with Mum being comforted by friends, the Proctors hearing the news and a village in mourning. The show had moved to focus more on Galgate after our brat pack moved on. I decided all of this on the train, in between waves of shock, and remembering, and thinking that I understood the magnitude of what had happened. I didn't realise that I hadn't even begun to feel at that point.

Mum picked me up at the station and we shared a genuine hug.

"Am I allowed to ask questions?" I said as she started to drive. I'd wondered on the train whether Mum would ask why I didn't drive straight home. I would have told her that I'd been unable to afford the insurance, had that happened.

"I can certainly tell you what I know."

Mum had phoned Dad and insisted that he come home for a meal. He had been at the pub for the whole week after his assistant manager had walked out. Mum had demanded his presence because she'd had a terrible few days at work and no-one to come home to inflict it on. The drama department had received some negative comments in an otherwise glowing Ofsted report and she'd endured a massive bollocking as a result.

"We're meant to be in a marriage, Malcolm," she had said. "I need my husband."

He died in a car crash on the way home from his pub. Some speeding lorry on a country lane jack-knifed and took out my father. This was how it was reported and it's how everyone will remember Dad. That poor man, at best.

"That doesn't make it your fault," I told her, feeling full of wisdom from my time in the city. The viewers would see that Danny had matured. He returned as Dan, I wasn't prepared to go that far back.

"I know it doesn't," she shrieked, putting an end to the question and answers sessions. She apologised a minute later.

"I don't think we have to apologise for anything we do for a while," I answered, quietly satisfied that I was grown up enough to comfort my grieving mother.

I put on a performance that day, there's no way of denying it. I walked around my house like I was rediscovering it, and I looked out of the window with trepidation. I stared at things in my room like they were distant memories of a far away time. I cried for my father and took calls from well-wishers. I answered the door to bunches of flowers, each time digging the card out, expecting it to be from a familiar name. My unplanned shock return was a good episode.

I wondered how my sudden exit was being received over on *Open Books*. My phone was switched off and I ignored my emails. Two days later Mum picked up a call on the home telephone, telling me there was a Jack who wanted to speak to me. He must have done some hunting to find that, because it wasn't a number I'd divulged to any of them. I took the phone off Mum and waited for her to go back into the kitchen before replacing the handset without saying a word. I was back in my old show and that was that.

With no other adult in her family, Mum confided in me frequently during the week leading up to the funeral. It was like 9/11 all over again. Her grief was filled with guilt about how the marriage hadn't really worked after he came back.

"I never really trusted him. That's why I wanted him home. I thought he was seeing someone. I even thought he could be seeing Robyn again."

She spoke at length about the inner torment she felt every time he worked late, and how she had tried to protect herself by making herself busier.

"If I'd known he was going to die, I would have taken more time out to acknowledge the man I loved. He was still there, deep down, the man that completely changed my life all those years ago."

He wasn't a dynamic man, my father. He didn't possess a rapier wit or a wide circle of friends. He just did well for himself and his family, quietly providing. He was a closed book; a man so destroyed by his past that he couldn't really tell someone that he loved them. He made mistakes, but he forgave mistakes as well. He didn't give up on me. He gave me my freedom to roam. That was my guilt – that I'd wilfully ruined my life in Lancaster and cast aside my family in the process. Most people are fortunate enough to know their parents after the rebelling finishes, but I guess that wasn't something Dad and I were allowed.

"I've done terrible things," I told Mum.

"We've all had our wild times, Dan," she assured me. "You're not the first generation to live, you know."

"It's more how much I hurt people and didn't really dwell on it. I made his life much harder than it was."

To summarise, if we'd known he was only going to live to be forty-six, we would have been a bit more forgiving and a bit more loving. We used him for stability, financial for me and emotional for Mum. We took him for granted and he died. It's a fable, really. It showed up how stupid my games were, how life could always top me at any moment it wanted to. I planned a big exit from a programme and my father died. I wasn't in charge of all the scripts. I was struggling with the storyline because it had thrown me much more than mere improvisation could rectify. It became my most dramatic moment, and all the time I was wishing that I could stop thinking of the bloody programme, about the hour-long specials that were accompanying this tragedy, and the documentary on the life of Malcolm Lizar. These were the things I didn't share with Mum.

3.

I hoped for a peaceful funeral, so when I noticed Robyn Proctor sitting at the back of the crematorium I thought hard about how to play it. She looked younger than the last time I saw her. My gut instinct was that she was looking for trouble, but for once I didn't want to cause a scene, even with my eulogy presenting the perfect opportunity.

I wanted to say something about those that brought pain into his life, and shoot a horrible look in her direction. I wanted to stand up and demand to know what the hell she was doing there. I wanted to forgive her in front of all of these people.

But this was Malcolm's final hoorah and I wanted him to leave the show respectfully, so I eulogised through very real tears about what I'd remember my dad for. I listed some of the things he taught me to do, and how he could never be replaced because of that. I made a lot of people cry. It was a touching performance, which was the way it should have been.

When someone young dies it's a surprise when you see all of the lives that they have touched gathered in one room. Friends from London and colleagues from years of running businesses surfaced to pay their respects. If you'd have asked me to name any of Dad's friends or acquaintances before that day I would have struggled.

I wasn't so far gone that I would ruin my dad's funeral for the show. I wonder if at fifteen I would have been so restrained.

Mum tensed when she saw Robyn arrive and I grabbed her hand. She shook me away, clearly remembering my role in that particular incident. No further glances were exchanged. We sat through an appropriate humanitarian service charged with emotion, but without friction. I'd secretly hoped that Alex would turn up, but he was nowhere to be seen.

The staff at Dad's pub had insisted on having the post-funeral gathering there. I'd promised Dad on numerous occasions that I'd go and look at it, but this was my first visit. Another stupid little poignant thing that sticks in a throat clogged up with all the things you should have done. Another knock when you think, nine months later, that you're starting to get over it, then the pain comes back even harder. That you can, yourself, be resigning yourself to death the moment you finish writing your life story, yet still grieve for the father who passed on only nine months ahead of you.

I wish I'd believed in religion. I wish that could have been my mental illness.

People approached me individually at the wake and told me kind things about my dad. I learned a different side to him, the boss who everyone cared about. A boss who made them laugh.

"It makes sense," Uncle Alfred said. "That's what he was brought up to care about."

And so I listened for an hour about his childhood and heard the stories I knew but from a different angle. The more I heard the more I wanted him back, just for a while, just to show some appreciation. The death of your father makes you sentimental like that.

During my afternoon of enlightenment, I was always conscious that Robyn had made the journey to the wake. I'd considered telling her to leave, but we didn't want a scene. We knew that she had cared about Dad, and for that she was at least semi-welcome. But as she mingled with other guests, both Mum and I would glance up to see whether she was telling them about her years as Dad's mistress. She didn't seem to be causing any offence and she even acknowledged me in a humane way. It was only when she fell off a bar stool drunk that we realised she might be an issue.

Mum looked at me for support and it struck me that I was the man of the family now. I stepped in and picked Robyn up. "I think we should get you home, don't you?"

"No offence, Danny," she slurred at me from the floor, "but I don't really need to hear your opinion."

"I'll drive her home," I said to Mum. She looked at me quizzically. She wasn't keen on being left behind because she really didn't know that many of the people in the room beyond Alfred and Jennifer.

"Can't we just get her a taxi?" she asked.

"Do you want her staying here for another half hour?"

Mum nodded her assent and told Robyn to pass me her car keys. Robyn tried to protest, but could see the eyes of the room willing her to leave. She pushed them into my hand and I guided her out of the bar, keeping her calm so as to avoid any dramatic outburst. I believed that she had come to pay her respects and had drunk more than she realised. The fact that she had driven there was testament to that.

I was happy to take the journey in silence, the fractious tension making for a short scene in the already packed funeral episode. I wanted to ask about Alex. I guess my old viewers would have liked an update as well. I thought then about how I needed to get away before everyone returned for the summer. Would I be able to leave Mum? It was something I had considered several times, and I was ashamed to conclude that I didn't want to be held back by my widowed mother. I was deep in this contemplation when Robyn spoke.

"Charles left me," she said abruptly.

"Oh," I replied. I wasn't sorry to hear it and I refused to say so.

"The night that we found out Malcolm was dead," she added and I couldn't help but be interested.

I think she was starting to sober up because she told me quite lucidly how upon hearing the news of Dad's death, Charles sat in quiet contemplation for a few minutes. "That's that, then," he said eventually and went upstairs to start packing a suitcase. Robyn, already in shock, ran after him.

"I couldn't stand the thought of you being with him," Charles informed her. "I didn't want him to have you, so I did. There's no competition now, Robyn. I won."

He was out within the hour. Two days later he returned with a van and took everything that he wanted and moved into a house he had been privately saving up for.

"He was a good actor," she continued. I don't think anyone had heard this story before. "He could still fuck me. I guess it was all part of the revenge, having the thing your father couldn't. I was just his possession."

I had no real sympathy for her, but I was feeling fragile myself that day and her tears got to me.

"You're better off in a way. At least the lie is over."

"It doesn't feel better. He waited until the best years of my life were over."

"You're not even fifty, Robyn. People reinvent themselves all of the time."

"You must be pleased to hear this."

"We've both done things that have hurt people," I said. "We can't take them back, but that doesn't mean we can't regret them and hope for a happy life."

How this progressed to Robyn's bed is anyone's guess. It sounds unbelievable, but my father had died prematurely and my new life had been categorically destroyed, so I'd kind of hit a plateau with how odd the world could be. It felt like we'd seen eye to eye at last, and in a way we both thought that we were as bad as each other. We both needed comfort and I think I knew what she was implying when she asked me to help her to the door.

'FUNERAL SHOCKER!' the TV guides bellowed.

She made a coffee and I asked if I could call a taxi to get back to Dad's celebration. She cried and told me what a wonderful man my father was, and how now I'd grown up a bit she could see some of him in me. It struck a chord with both of us and we kissed. We saw the moment and we took it.

It was a tragic, functional shag that we both managed not to cry through. I dressed afterwards and she passed out. It was best that I was gone when she woke up. I called a taxi from my house and returned to the dwindling wake. The buffet had gone and only the real drunks and Mum remained. Mum thanked me for getting rid of Robyn and we hugged again. "We'll get through this," I told her.

I thought about the sex that night and realised how dark and awful it had been. The pathetic expectation in her eyes, looking at a young man and hoping to feel young again. The lack of mood, the insulting slapping noises, the sense of defeat in ejaculating. By morning I was horrified.

It hadn't been a scene, or a plot twist. It had happened without me thinking about it. Someone had taken my scripts and run with them. It felt out of control again. The morning after that, the police turned up at the door with questions about a rape.

4.

In the months that have followed I have had plenty of time to weigh up which way this court case will go. I've made my way through the justice system and they don't think I'm a threat anyway – they've imposed strict bail conditions on me, but they don't think I'm going to rape another woman.

They were hesitant about charging me. After I confirmed that I had slept with Robyn (I can't begin to describe Mum's face when I admitted to it in front of her), they double-checked with her that she did not believe it was consensual. They came back and arrested me. They questioned me with a duty solicitor, who advised me to say nothing, but I wasn't prepared to do that. I answered their questions and they said that they were charging me with rape.

Robyn told them I orchestrated the whole thing, that I got her drunk at the funeral and insisted on taking her home. She says she doesn't remember getting in the house. She just remembers waking up naked feeling like she had been violated. I insisted that we had kissed and had sex. I explained that my father had recently died and my mother was on her own. My solicitor explained this in court the next day, and pointed out my otherwise unblemished criminal record. The magistrates took pity and committed me to the Crown Court, free but not without conditions.

Robyn's so ashamed of sleeping with a father and a son, formerly her own son's best friend and lover, that she'd rather send me to jail than admit what happened. The viewers, they know, but this is where doing fake TV shows proves useless.

My solicitor is going to play up my grief, and Robyn's sadness at the death of her former lover and her marriage. She's going to overstate how fragile we both were, and how we sought brief comfort in each other. She's going to paint a picture of Robyn as an unhinged and bitter lady. Twelve people will be told how she destroyed my family once and is looking to do it again. A judge will be made to understand that this vindictive hag preyed upon me and my mother at our weakest moment. We have a very strong case. We have the truth on our side.

But she has a convincing offence as well. She has Alex as a witness, ready to open up about my disregard for people when it comes to sex, how I seduced him just to cause trouble and pretended to be gay for no legitimate reason. Lauren has been called to talk about her sex life with me. We had our rough times, she will tell them. We did, but it was always consensual. Robyn can weep and appeal to the jury, show them just how this assault has stolen her confidence and kept her away from work. She can plead shame and flashbacks, which is a much more persuasive argument than confusion and living in the moment. She can go back a decade and reveal how I was obsessed with writing about rape in the stories I penned in primary school.

I'm not surprised that Alex and Lauren have agreed to speak out against me. Really, it's my comeuppance. I trivialised their lives for the programme, and now they're getting the revenge they probably didn't think they'd have the chance to enjoy. Alex should believe his mother over me. She hasn't done as much as me to lose his trust. I'm sure he doesn't doubt it for a second.

And I know Lauren wanted an opportunity to stick the knife in. She'll be there with a new boyfriend holding her hand and supporting her through it, as she too sheds a tear and explains what I'm capable of, that I have form.

I have my mother to discredit Robyn, to give the history of what has happened between them. I also have Charles, to my surprise. It seems Charles feels about his wife what his wife feels about me. He called Mum and offered himself up. He's willing to talk about times when his ex-wife went a bit mad, and how she often wanted to spice up their marriage by bringing in other people. He was happy to mention that she seemed to have an attraction to younger men, and to the Lizar men as well. That's not to say he likes me, he just hates her more.

I have the mourners from my father's funeral who can pick holes in her lies and explain that I had nothing to do with her until she fell off her bar stool. We can ask why she started drinking at a party that she had driven to. We can produce vaginal swabs and point to nothing but consent. We can accuse her of making a mockery of rape to meet her own needs.

It will get ugly.

Were the trial to go ahead, two endings would have to be prepared. It's close, even my solicitor told me that. She believes me, and she believes that having a woman defending me might just tip the balance in my favour. She's turning me into a victim to save my skin. It's due to start early in the new year, and should last no more than a week, were it going ahead.

In the meantime I've been stuck indoors. I can't get a job or look at uni courses. My summer was spent in the back garden reading books and trying to soak up as much freedom as has been permitted. Mum went back to work and I spend the days on my own now. I film scenes like I used to, with the house to myself. I have mini-plotlines where people come round to attack me and accuse me of rape. I even filmed a scene where Robyn came over and rubbed my nose in it, reminding the viewers that she is an evil liar.

For a couple of weeks I took to wearing a dressing gown and sitting in the dark. I filmed monologues where I protested my innocence to my father, just so he knows. I looked at razor blades meaningfully, just to add some drama to my life. I've woken from prison dreams, and dreams about me raping Robyn Proctor. I've seen how it would have happened, but only in sleeping imagination.

Much of my drama takes place online now. I go on internet forums, and post contentious blogs to get strangers annoyed. I think of things to write that will get me more blog hits, and these little things keep me going on an episode-by-episode basis.

5.

About two weeks after I was falsely charged with raping Alex's Mum, I finally switched my phone back on. I was home alone and a little bored when I remembered about it even being there. I know we can't live without them these days but once you get out of the habit of being contacted, you hardly notice it at all. I sat and waited for it to catch up with nearly a month's worth of messages before starting from the beginning. There were lots of 'whr r u?' and 'switch ur phn on' messages to begin with. Then there were some 'hp ur ok' ones to follow. Imogen and Jack were the two making the most effort there. Jack texted me after I had hung up on him asking me what was going on. He'd followed this up with a 'Fuck U thn' message, and a final one to say they'd rented out my room and chucked my stuff out.

Ellie's first text told me that she really needed a friend. Then there was another more aggressive one accusing me of abandoning her completely. Katie chucked in a couple about how they'd misjudged me. David said that he'd spoken to Imogen and I should come back to talk.

Imogen, though, she kept texting, hoping that she got through to me. Sometimes she was nice and told me not to worry about the things that I'd said, then she accused me of being a childish shit who'd never loved her. 'U've ruined me,' she accused me in one text.

The last one she sent was to inform me that she'd just had an abortion. 'Good riddance,' it concluded. I'd been a father in waiting and not had the chance to do anything about it. I'm the opposite of my father – I like to make my own decisions.

I thought about calling her and discussing it, but there was nothing to say. I accepted that she hated me, and that everyone knew about my problem. They might even want to step up and hammer home to the jury what a terrible person I am.

I could have been looking forward to being a father. Here, in this house, it seems like the world to me. Had I been there with her, we would have approached it as an unmitigated disaster, and I would have told her that I'd support her either way, whilst quietly ushering her to the abortion clinic. But I didn't have my say, and I have no chance of getting back there to do anything about it. I'd have to ask permission if I wanted to go to Manchester. There's a tag around my leg that would land me behind bars if I did otherwise.

That's why I can't go over to Robyn's to do a witness intimidation routine. Or try and wangle Alex round to my way of thinking. He's back here full-time as well now, his mother so shell-shocked that she can't do without him. Some days I think about going to apologise to him, but somehow common sense prevails.

My old friends know I'm mentally unhinged, but I haven't had the chance to explain it to them properly. I won't get that chance. They'll read about me in the papers and they'll think about it, and they'll conclude that it's not implausible. Not with me involved.

I have no opportunity to start again. A 'not guilty' verdict and I could go and see them and make amends, explain everything. I can use Dad's death to make them feel sorry for me. I loved those guys so much. They were bigger than any show. They're among the first ten people that I want to read this.

Mum believes me but she has learned not to rely on anyone. She's seeing someone now. It was only three months after Dad died that she brought him to meet me. Christian's a teacher from her school, from the maths department, so they have a lot of debate over science versus art. He's not even forty yet, so she's done well for herself. He's a funny, dynamic man, is Christian, and he's not afraid to share it with Mum. She felt like she missed out on that side of Dad, so Christian is somehow redressing the balance. He's even joined her theatre group.

The worst thing is I like him. I'd love for him to have been another annoyance like Neil, but Christian is someone I can imagine being my friend. He doesn't know me, but he knows Mum well enough to know that I'm not a rapist. He's moving in here after Christmas, although I figure that Mum might want to find somewhere else to live after I've finished writing this book.

She was worried about what I'd think. Bless her, worrying about the opinion of an accused rapist who has done nothing but bring misery into her life. She wants me to like Christian, and I am pleased to say that's the least I can do.

I understand that she'd already moved on from the marriage.

I don't suspect that she stopped loving Dad, but somewhere pragmatism kicked in and she knew that they would have ended up living separately eventually. People probably talk about how she hasn't wasted any time, but their judgement is unfounded, that's all I can say.

Christian makes this a bit easier as well. When I started writing this book, my biggest fear was that I might end up leaving Mum alone. Now I'm convinced that my death will leave her better off. No more rape charges, or family affairs, or blockbusting storylines to contend with. Just love and appreciation. I think in the long run, my mum is set for a happy ending. Just give her six or twelve months.

6.

It was in the third month of my pre-trial purgatory that this all came together. I had time and little else, so I thought of writing my life story. I thought of trying to put into words the strange life I'd lived inside my head, in the hope that the next time someone wanted to know what was wrong with me, there would be an extensive response.

Dad died – not my storyline.

Imogen had an abortion – not my storyline.

Robyn accused me of rape – not my storyline.

I'm not writing my own scripts anymore. I don't know where the next plot development is going to come from. I'm not in control.

Those were the thoughts that drove me to write this in the first place. My summer and autumn evenings have been spent committing to paper my side of the story. I knew that I had to kill myself once it was over. There really was no other ending, and to conclude things on my 21st birthday feels both poignant and appropriate.

The only way to dictate my end is to write Dan out once and for all. No new programmes or new life. This is the only way.

It's not a depressed suicide. I don't feel sad about what I'm going to do. I just don't want to be typecast as a mentally ill human. I don't even know whether this whole thing has been a disease or a particularly aggressive quirk. I'll never know. This is a pragmatic suicide.

A definite not guilty verdict and things might be different, but probably not. I'm trapped in my old show and my contract isn't up for renewal any time soon. I have a chance of a lengthy stint in a prison show full of arse rape and battery, but I don't want to be that gritty character.

I have no idea what the future had in store for Dan Lizar, but even if the jury saw the truth, there's not much left for him. I want to know Robyn's motives. I can't help it. Did she set me up or did she just regret what we did? Was I lured in to participate in one of her plots? I know soap. She'll get her comeuppance at some point. This battle, though, I have to concede.

This has been the big storyline for me recently, writing my memoirs and reflecting on the things that have gone before. I've placed this in a ninety minute special filled with flashbacks and explanations, one last ditch attempt to explain to the viewer that Dan's not, deep down, an evil person. There have been lots of scenes with me typing, drifting into the events I'm writing about. The viewers aren't sure whether he'll go through with it.

Only I know how it will definitely end. Those last ten minutes of footage where Dan writes his final sentence, goes to the garage to get the rope he found a few weeks ago. He silently goes back to his room and fashions a noose, which he hammers to the ceiling. As he's going he's thinking of those he cares about one last time. He dwells on Imogen, and then his mother. Two people he wants with him in thought during his final moments.

He goes back to his computer and scrolls to the top of the document he has been penning for five months. He gives it a title – *The Almost Lizard* – and then puts in a page break. On the centre of page two he types 'For Alex. Sorry.'

There are close ups of his feet as he steps away from the computer and onto the chair, and then face shots as he pulls the noose over his head. Back to the feet as he kicks the chair away, a clatter, then more silence. The scene fades to black. Credits. No music.

Cover Design

The cover design for *The Almost Lizard* is by Lupen Crook.

Lupen Crook is a visual artist and singer-songwriter whose distinctive and prolific output has perplexed and delighted audiences over a period of eight years. Working in oil paints and mixed media, the 'magpie' aesthetic of his rich and layered artworks incorporates jigsaw puzzle pieces, discarded newspapers, cigarette butts and bad pennies, amongst other everyday treasures.

His songs are noted for their intense and often viscerally honest lyrical content, coupled with a musical virtuosity that marries intricate detail with melodic simplicity. Characterised by a strong DIY ethos, his relentless urge for self-expression has also manifested itself via other outlets, including a series of strikingly inventive videos, a range of jewellery charms drawing on his personal iconography, and the written word.

Lupen's musical activities are documented at:
www.lupencrook.com

A catalogue of his visual work can be found at:
www.brokenarts.co.uk